The Princess of Park Lane

Jacqueline Navin

B

BERKLEY SENSATION, NEW YORK

This is a work of fiction. Names, characters, places, and incidents either are
the product of the author's imagination or are used fictitiously,
and any resemblance to actual persons, living or dead, business
establishments, events, or locales is entirely coincidental.

THE PRINCESS OF PARK LANE

A Berkley Sensation Book / published by arrangement with

Berkley Sensation edition / December 2003

Copyright © 2003 by Jacqueline Navin
Excerpt from *The Heiress of Hyde Park*
copyright © 2003 by Jacqueline Navin
Cover art by Tim Barrall
Cover design by George Long
Book design by Julie Rogers

ISBN: 0-425-19326-8

A BERKLEY SENSATION™ BOOK
Berkley Sensation Books are published by The Berkley Publishing Group,
a division of Penguin Group (USA) Inc.,
375 Hudson Street, New York, New York 10014.
BERKLEY SENSATION and the "B" design
are trademarks belonging to Penguin Group (USA) Inc.

PRINTED IN THE UNITED STATES OF AMERICA

10 9 8 7 6 5 4 3 2 1

Prologue

LONDON, 1811

In her boudoir, Lady May Hayworth handed her companion a
book.

"What is it?" the handsome man asked. May was distracted for a moment by the sight of his hands against the
aged leather binding, strong, capable hands darkened by the
sun and roughened by hard work.

Thinking about how those hands felt on her skin gave her
a little shiver, and she smiled in anticipation of the night
ahead. She was looking forward to a wonderful evening of
erotic pleasures. But first, she had something she wished to
discuss with him. "It is Woolrich's journal."

"A journal?" He turned it over, examining it with interest.

Robert Carsons might be a laborer, but he spoke in cultured tones with a voice that was deep and sonorous. And he
was completely at home among her delicately appointed furnishings and softly colored draperies here in her private
rooms. From the first moment he had stepped foot in her

Park Lane town house, he hadn't experienced a moment's awkwardness. For an owner of a carriage house near Regents Park, he had all the earmarkings of a man whose background had provided education and a certain level of privilege.

He was a man with a secret, a past as mysterious as his fathomless eyes.

"Your brother led an interesting life." He shrugged. "It should prove excellent reading."

"Indeed, it is what I wish to discuss with you," she told him. "This book was held by his solicitor. When poor Wooly was taken from us so unexpectedly, it arrived just as he directed."

"Unexpected?" Robert replied, casting her a look askance. "I don't think losing a duel completely unexpected when the man was being called out regularly."

"Well, it was beastly of Hanover to kill him. You simply don't do such a thing in a civilized society."

"May," Robert said patiently, "it was a duel. It was tragic for you to lose your brother, I realize, but these things happen when men play with firearms."

"Well, they don't happen to a Woolrich. They never did before. Wooly did this dozens of times before. He was famous for it."

"I do not wish to overset you, my love, but you cannot fault Hanover for the accident. Woolrich's gun misfired, and he lost too much blood from the wound before the surgeon could be called in. It was foolish of him not to have one on hand, but I suppose he never anticipated needing one, since he never had before. Poor lamb, I know you want to blame someone, but it was an accident, that is all. It is one of those misfortunes that comes of reckless living, pet."

She couldn't stay angry with him, not when he cooed endearments to her in that rough voice of his. She almost forgot what she was talking about.

Sniffing away the impulse, she said, "Wooly is dead, and I miss him terribly. You know how fond we were of one another. It is true my brother was a rake and a scoundrel, but everyone knew there was no harm in him."

Robert issued a long-suffering sigh. "It is true enough he

didn't have a malicious bone in his body, but for God's sake, May, he seduced women as blithely as you and I might indulge in a bit of spirits. And he never allowed such a little thing as the object of his desire being married to another man ever stand in the way of his pleasures. I do not wish to seem insensitive, darling, but it was bound to catch up to him sooner or later."

She smoothed her blond hair and gave him her most practiced coquette's smile. "He was wicked, it's true. But one couldn't help but love him."

He touched her cheek. "You most of all."

"He was my brother, but more than that, as you know. He was my best friend. And my hero. I adored him."

"Come here." He wrapped strong arms around her. Close like this, May felt the hardness of his lean, muscular body against her slender, feminine curves. She loved the way he made her feel so small, so protected. This dalliance was becoming serious, she knew. The thought was alarming.

"You are making me forget my head," she said, pulling away.

He released her with a sexy smile that indicated he knew he had had an effect on her. Oh, yes, she was far into an infatuation with Robert. She had taken him as her lover over six months ago. Or he had taken her. She wasn't quite sure of how it all transpired. She'd met him when she'd gone to purchase a curricle, and the rest was a blur.

A deliciously sensual blur.

May had never experienced anything quite like this relationship before. She, like her brother, had a very practical attitude toward the sexual appetites men and women shared. Robert was by far not her first lover, but he was as different from any man she had known before as it was possible to be. And while he delighted her in bed, he had also become important in other areas of her life. Very soon after their torrid affair began, her only sibling had been fatally wounded in a duel of honor at Wimbledon Commons. Robert had quickly become a confidant.

A widow for thirteen years, May enjoyed her unique status to live life on her terms. She'd maintained her elite standing in the ton by being discreet and following the rules. In fact, among *haute société,* she was a force to be reckoned with. She was known to be fiercely independent and strong-willed, admired for her regal beauty, which had not been diminished by the advancing of years. Now, at forty-three, she was comfortable and liked being in control of her own destiny.

But when she was with Robert, she didn't have to be strong, and she found, to her amazement and delight, that she liked that. It felt good to lean on his shoulder sometimes. He asked nothing of her, and yet she gave. How wonderful it was to have this haven in his arms. She was coming to depend on him.

She valued his opinion. Having waited anxiously to let Robert in on her little scheme, she was now nearly giddy with excitement. "Open the book," she said. "Go ahead."

The brittle spine crackled as he lifted the leather cover. "It is nothing but names. Women's names, with dates written . . ." He squinted. "These are his lovers. Good God, he kept an accounting?"

"Don't sound so horrified. There were simply too many for him to store in his brain."

"I can see." There was disbelief and admiration in Robert's voice. "The devil kept busy. What are these names here?"

"Children," May said and gave her lover a level look. "Robert . . . those are the names of his children."

"What? Good Lord, look at this. Some of these are from his youth. Why did he keep them secret all of these years?"

"Well, part of Wooly's charm was his discretion. Unless a woman wanted it to be known that they were trysting, it simply wasn't known, not by anyone. The reason he had all those damned duels was because the silly creatures blabbed. It was considered quite the thing to have Woolrich in one's bed, you know. But even I didn't realize half of the women he dallied with. Look, my governess, for goodness' sake, when he was just sixteen. And the vicar's wife a year later. And . . . Lord almighty, he and stuffy old Mrs. Standish! Oh, Wooly, you were a naughty one!"

She laughed, delighted at the idea of her brother's unlikely conquest.

Robert's eyes were warm as he regarded her. He said softly, "You are a very beautiful woman, May. But you know that, don't you? A woman of your charms does not reach maturity without knowing exactly what her effect is on a man."

Many men had spoken of her beauty, but never before had the words affected her like this. God help her, she was going to fall in love with him if she didn't watch herself.

He held up the book. "What are you going to do with this?"

"I am going to find them," she said with satisfaction. "Wooly spoke to one of his seconds in the last moments of his life, directing me to use the book to find these children, to make reparation for his never having acknowledged them. And that is exactly what I am going to do."

"A sort of posthumous reckoning. Bloody irresponsible of him to leave it to you."

"Not at all, Robert, darling. Don't you see? This is his legacy, to me. When I lost Woolrich, I lost my only blood. But now, oh, Robert, I have gained so much. All these nieces and nephews, and all of them Wooly's. I will have a part of him with me through them. Will some have his wild gypsy hair, or his green eyes? Will they have his charm, his recklessness? It is going to be so much fun!"

"You are mad." His eyes danced. She knew he liked her outrageousness. In fact, he liked her best when she was at her most outrageous.

"Why? I have always believed family is the most important thing in the world."

He changed immediately, scowling and turning away. She pursed her lips. She knew he had a tender spot there, the key to his mysterious past. Mention of family never failed to make him cross.

"These are my brother's blood, *my* blood. Don't you see? I intend to track down each and every one and tell them of their heritage. Wooly was rich as Croeseus, and they are entitled to their share. They should have what is rightfully theirs. That should please them."

"Some of them might not wish you to find them," he said darkly, as if he knew something of what might drive a person to extreme privacy.

"Then they can tell me so, and I will go away. But this is so wonderful! I want you to be happy for me. It really has given me a renewed vigor since Wooly died. Come, now, Robert."

He smiled slowly, as if reluctant to indulge her but unable to stop himself. "You are very excited about this. If it will make you happy, then you should do what you wish. Lord help anyone who would think to stop you, in any event."

His mood shifted, and she knew he was tiring of conversation. The air around him seemed to thicken. Strolling to the dressing table, he stretched his long body. Then he removed his shirt.

Even after all these months with him, the sight of his body robbed her of breath. May felt the quickening in the pit of her stomach, the tendrils of spiraling desire already beginning to build.

He leaned over the bottles lined up on the table and selected one. "What is this?"

"Oil," she said rather creakily. "For after my bath."

"It will serve." With a sly smile, he brought it with him to bed.

✒ *Chapter 1*

Michaela Standish believed in love. The curl-your-toes, steal-your-breath, make-you-want-to-swoon sort of love. And to her mother's great embarrassment and frustration, she was waiting for great love in her life.

This was why, at the advanced age of two-and-twenty—not quite "on the shelf" but near enough to it—she had not yet married. She'd not even been engaged, although she'd had an offer or two over the years. The problem wasn't the men—as her mother observed with tight lips. It was Michaela. She was waiting to fall in love.

It was a mystery where she got such ideas. Certainly not from her mother. Dorothy Standish was a practical woman who dealt with life with a complete dearth of imagination, as far as Michaela could tell. And her papa, from what she could remember of him, as he'd passed away when she was still in the nursery, was a busy, absentminded fellow consumed with books cataloguing his various interests. He used to read to her, she recalled, and he'd smelled of tobacco. She missed her papa sometimes, for these thin memories were precious. And she imagined things would be easier for her for his buffering presence. She and Mother had a tendency to clash, and Papa could soothe things, she remembered.

But Papa hadn't been a romantic, either. He was a scholar, and so she would not have confided any of her thoughts of love to him. These she kept in the quiet privacy of her dreams, where she wished for things she would have blushed to confide even to her journal. Not that anyone would suspect that side of her, for she busied herself with practical matters for the most part. The majority of her time was spent working for various societies here in London to better the plight of unfortunates and advance certain reformist ideals for their benefit. It was upon this matter that Michaela had been summoned to face her mother's displeasure this afternoon.

The ripe September chill could not be mitigated by the fire that crackled with a cheeriness at odds with the tension in the room. There was a history here, of long-standing failure to come to an understanding over matters of disagreement.

"I but wrote a letter to the newspapers, Mother." She spoke on a sigh of resignation. There would be an argument.

"Such ideas! What will people think? Isn't it enough that you work?"

"I teach. I do not get paid, so it is not like I am in service. It is the charity work you yourself schooled me to."

Mother ignored the clarification. "And besides, it is not your place to voice political views. You should be thinking about more feminine pursuits. Do I need to remind you that while you fill your day with all of your pet projects, you have found yourself at this advanced age without the slightest prospect of a marriage proposal?"

If Mother was going to go on about her feminine failures, she was surely going to get an earful about the most shameful—this was Mother's estimation—condition of finding herself unattached. The unmarried state of her three daughters consumed her.

In an effort to avoid this, she indicated the letter. "I merely voiced my opinion that Miss Hannah More's success in Cheddar with her Sunday school should encourage more parishes to undertake the task of educating the poor. It is a worthy cause."

A twitter of giggles came from her left, and she glanced over at her twin sisters, Delinda and Delilah, who were enjoying every moment. They were two years older than herself, unmarried the both of them, though not for want of trying. After Howard Standish's death, the family fortunes were stretched to an alarming degree, and there were no funds for a season. Despite their mother's fervent efforts, the painfully brash Delinda and equally painfully shy Delilah had attracted no offers from their circle of friends and acquaintances.

The two were devoted to the rather distressing pastime of making Michaela's life as trying as possible. Delinda, bedecked as usual in a ridiculous costume full of affectations and flounces, was the ringleader. Delilah, whose plainer face and plumper form made her the slightly less attractive of the nearly identical set, followed suit.

"Did you think of what would happen to peasants if they are educated, Michaela?" Mother snapped, her entire body quivering. "It is never a good thing. Look what happened in France. A blood-soaked revolution, that's what."

What do you care? Your head will not roll since you are no longer of the noble class. Ah, but Mother had never given up her sense of belonging to the aristocracy, not even when she married Papa, who was considered less than a stellar match and whose fortunes, modest to start with, had dwindled to a household of seven, the four women, their housekeeper, Mrs. Hansen, their maid, Nora, who took care of the inside work, and Albert, who served as butler, footman, and gardener.

"Maybe Michaela is becoming a religious radical like Miss More and the Methodists," Delinda said, the tiniest squeal of delight detectable in her tone. "After all, she has the Bible in her room again."

Michaela whirled. "What were you doing in my room, Delinda?"

Delinda smirked back.

Mother heaved a weary sigh and demanded, "You deliberately disobey me? I have told you before to leave that Bible alone. It is old, and the binding is cracked. Why are you so fascinated by that moldering relic, anyway?"

Michaela shrugged. "There is no fascination." It was easy to lie to Mother, so much easier on her than the truth.

"I can only think you do this over and over out of spite. If you wish to read the scriptures, then read the Bible you were given on your eighth birthday."

Oh, but it wasn't tales of Noah, or Jonah and the whale, or naughty King David that interested Michaela. It was the story of *herself* she craved. For as far back as she could remember, she wondered how it could be that she was part of this family where her every thought, every act seemed to be at odds with all the others.

In looks alone, she was a cuckoo in a sparrow's nest: tall and dark-haired, with almond-shaped eyes of glittering green among small-boned, fair-skinned Standishes with their dark eyes and blond lashes. Her mother was tall, like her—the only point of similarity with anyone she'd been able to identify. Dorothy was attractive, though never a beauty. She had, however, the sort of strong bone structure and fine bearing that aged well.

As for her sisters, the pair were fair, with fine, thin hair, which they adored twisting into ringlets that bobbed when they moved. Her mane was thick, lustrous, curling wildly on its own. It refused to tame into a decorous style.

She was as different from their soft fairness as a Hun among Swedes. Her dim memories of her deceased father, rotund with hair the color of sand as thin as a spider's web swept over a freckled scalp, gave no hint of belonging.

So she searched the history documented in the brittle-spined family Bible for some name hinting at the origins of her rather unique physical and metaphysical differences in the legions of ancestors, someone from an exotic land with odd ideas and rampant passions, who would account for her presence.

When she had been only seven years old or so, she had asked why she looked so different, why everyone seemed content with each other but completely at odds to understand her. Dorothy Standish had turned stark white. Without warning, she had slapped Michaela soundly across her cheek. Michaela had never spoken of it again. But she hadn't forgotten.

She had no idea that she was about to learn the answer this very day. For at that moment, as Michaela exited the parlor to retrieve the Bible from her room, a caller was announced.

The Bible was still under the mattress where she had left it. No doubt Beelzebub and Satan—which was how she privately thought of Delilah and Delinda—had left it there to be revealed in case their mother had required proof of her transgression.

Tucking the volume under her arm, she immediately returned downstairs. She paused at the commotion coming from the drawing room, and she recalled the visitor. She heard her mother bark an order, and her sisters emerged, hurrying past her, their faces flushed and eyes snapping with excitement. They stared at her, as if she looked shocking all of a sudden, and rushed by with harsh whispers barely muffled behind their hands.

Going to the pocket doors left slightly open, she peered inside. A woman stood with Mother, dressed in the most lavish costume Michaela had ever seen. She looked so out of place standing there in the center of the middling decor of their small house in the respectable but hardly fashionable St. Alban's Crescent; as exotic as a peacock in a henhouse.

She was blond and very beautiful. Petite in stature, fine-boned, with strong features. In fact, she was not young, but her years gave her poise that youthful beauty could not approach. She had on a well-cut pink dress with a matching hat festooned with an abundance of feathers. It was the most stylish, certainly the most costly, array of finery Michaela had ever beheld.

"Come here, Michaela," Dorothy said, spying her standing at the threshold. Her voice was so different than usual. Stiff, choked perhaps.

Doing as she was bid, Michaela approached the two, she noticing something about the other woman.

She had almond-shaped eyes. Green, almond-shaped eyes. Like hers.

Then, in a tight, strangled tone, her mother said, "This is Lady May Hayworth. She is your aunt."

The beautiful lady glided forward. Her smile deepened, and there were tears in her eyes.

This was her aunt? How . . . ?

"My dear, there is no easy way for me to tell you. My brother, Dudley Ellinsworth, the fifth Earl of Woolrich, was . . ." She cast a delicate glance to Dorothy. "Well, dear. He was your father."

And with those words, everything in Michaela Standish's life changed.

 *Chapter 2*

In the days after that startling announcement, Michaela was told that she was to be given a season, and that in preparation for this she would go on an extended visit to live in Lady May's Park Lane home.

Park Lane! The most prestigious address in the city. The dream of every girl began one overcast day when she drew up to the neat Georgian facade. She alighted, filled with awe. Beside her, her sisters and mother gawked as a well-dressed woman passed, sniffed, and proceeded without another glance.

Michaela was suddenly all too aware of the inferior stylishness of her clothing. Though clean and functional and certainly nothing to be ashamed of, she had nothing like the smartly tailored garments the women from these parts wore. She could never afford the delicately sprigged muslins with matching spencers and bonnets with frills and geegaws abounding. Her hair tied into a simple knot was unlike the lovely coifs of those with talented ladies' maids to see to their toilette every day.

But Michaela learned quickly she could afford it now. She could afford a great deal. The money from her father's estate meant an entirely new life, a new world. This world.

Lady May graciously supplemented the income left to the family by Howard Standish, which was officially overseen by his brother, Edgar. He had no contact with the women other than to execute Mother's requests. But there was no need for the Standishes to go into the family coffers too deeply, for Lady May was generous.

Dorothy insisted on fairness to all the girls, and Lady May readily agreed. It was clear she was eager to take Michaela under her wing and would do this kindness for her sisters in order to avoid Dorothy interfering with her plans. Thus the twins were included in learning the finer manners necessary for a large dinner party, dancing lessons for the waltz, which May particularly loved, and quizzed mercilessly on the names of all of those they were likely to come in contact with, famous and infamous, but all of the highest pedigree.

In the evenings when the girls returned home, and on the days the twins didn't come to the West End, Michaela had her aunt all to herself. May delighted in two things: shopping and telling Michaela about her father. The two women spent long hours at both.

Michaela was taken to Lady May's modiste, a woman so in demand she refused to accept any new customers. But when Lady May waved aside Madam Bonvant's assistant and swept into the salon with Michaela in tow, the woman had taken one look at Michaela, tall and straight with a regal tilt to her chin and her exotic coloring, and declared that Madam would make an exception, her eager eye taking in the figure as her mind worked on color and cut. Michaela glanced nervously at her aunt under this scrutiny, but May only beamed. The modiste and her aunt conferred, barely consulting her as they began Michaela's transformation.

Everything about her was critiqued with a stern eye. Aunt May expected absolute perfection in everything from her posture ("You must think as if there is a board strapped to your back. Do not under any circumstances touch the back of the chair. Think of it as if it's burning hot.") to her walk

("Glide, Michaela, *glide*.") to her speech ("Roll your *r*, please. And open your mouth *wider* on your vowels.").

A fussy man came to the Park Lane house and cut her hair to release the winsome curls. May treated the man like a Prussian prince and explained later that he was as temperamental as a cranky adolescent, but his skill with scissors was unmatched, and so she gave him his due. Afterwards, they shared a laugh at his eccentricities and admired his work.

The dresses ordered by Madam Bonvant began to arrive. They were beyond exquisite. Michaela didn't recognize herself the first time she looked in the mirror, in yards and yards of expensive silks, her hair dressed in coils by Ilsa, Lady May's personal maid.

And yet, she did. There she was—Woolrich's daughter, standing tall and proud, gazing back at her with a new self-assurance she'd never seen in herself. She knew who she was at last, and why she was different from the rest of her family. The resemblance to her father, her real father, Lord Woolrich, infused her with pride and confidence.

He was like her in so many ways from what Lady May told her. His portraits showed him at various ages, always wickedly handsome with thick dark curls, green eyes, and a glint of perpetual mischief, even in his old age, and in those paintings she found peace and a sense of herself she'd been searching for.

There was a bitter side to the sweetness of finding her family. It was odd to think of Papa not being her real father, but it didn't pain her overmuch. She would still love his memory always, more so for the knowledge that he'd known she wasn't his and yet was so kind to her. This was increased when she learned about how the man had wed her mother to save her from disgrace. Her mother had reluctantly explained the circumstances in the sketchiest of manners. "I had the affair with Woolrich after being widowed. I was bereft after my first husband died of fever. I was not thinking clearly, and I mistook myself."

She couldn't imagine her mother ever getting carried away with a man, of all things. But to hear Lady May tell it,

Woolrich could charm a woman witless on a whim, and so she supposed it was possible her mother was seduced.

"I succumbed to the charms of an infamous rake," Dorothy said, as if scolding herself. Perhaps she had done this many times throughout the years. "Upon finding myself with child, I married Mr. Standish. He was good enough to offer for me when he learned of the situation."

Michaela's love for Howard Standish swelled, knowing he had done such a valiant thing. But because he was rich only in heart, Dorothy's family had spurned her, cutting her completely from their lives.

"So this is why we do not speak to your relatives."

Dorothy sniffed. "They looked down on the Standishes. But as things have turned to our favor, they may regret the rift." The thought pleased her, and it pleased Michaela as well.

It did salve her guilt for how her mother had suffered because of her to know that perhaps she would be restored because of the connection to Lady May, who was as prominent a patroness as anyone coming into society would wish. She knew everyone and everything, and even if Dorothy were a tad jealous of the graceful lady as Michaela suspected she was, she obviously savored the thought that despite her stumble from grace, all would be restored.

And so it was five months later, just as March blew out the worst of winter's cold, that Michaela and Lady May sat in the earl's carriage on Park Lane, ready for her to attend her first ball. Behind them, in the Standish carriage, were her mother and sisters. She had made her toilette at Lady May's house, and her family had joined them to attend the ball together. Michaela hadn't seen them yet and was eager to. She'd been already waiting in the carriage when they had arrived at the town house, and May had insisted they leave immediately to avoid being stuck in the queue.

Despite the frigid weather, the interior was cozy. Ermine-trimmed rugs were drawn up over them, draped loosely so as not to crush the expertly stitched gowns of silk and tulle.

Coal foot warmers toasted their toes through the thin kid of their expensive shoes.

Michaela gazed at the house alight with an untold amount of candles and teeming with the crush of polite society as the guests entered the ball of the Marquess and Marchioness of Islington. "It's so beautiful."

May smiled, well-pleased with her protégée. "Your delight always charms me. It is so refreshing a perspective after years of boredom with all of this nonsense."

Touching her hair, Michaela chewed on her bottom lip. "It is nearly time. I am suddenly unaccountably nervous. The footmen are coming over!"

"Relax, Michaela. You are well prepared. You have studied hard, prepared for this. You know everything you need to know."

"I've been terribly dense. I don't think I'll remember anything! I was not bred for this. What if I make a mistake? I would die rather than embarrass you." She sighed, staring broodingly at the mansion. "I wonder if Cinderella was as nervous as this the night of her first ball."

"I am sure she was," May replied with a smile. She patted Michaela's hand.

"I wonder if she tripped or greeted some dignitary by the wrong title or made the wrong comment to the wrong person and raised everyone's eyebrows."

"But of course she did." May laughed. "It was part of her charm. Oh, assuredly you will make a mistake, Michaela, so there is no bother to be worried about it. It is guaranteed. None of us do a thing perfectly the first time out, do we? Not even Cinderella. However, I have every faith that not only shall you pass muster, you will dazzle everyone and charm them as completely as you have me. After all, how can you miss? You are Woolrich's daughter. Your blood will show true, so don't worry. I know you will make me very proud."

"Yes. About that." Her gloved hands twisted her ivory and silk fan. "People are bound to notice my resemblance to him. Everyone will know that I am his child."

"I know it seems in your world to be a great disgrace to have an *affaire de coeur,* but in the world of the ton, such things are accepted, dear." Her laughter was like music. "Why, the Lady Harley has so many children from different men, they are referred to as 'the Harleian Miscellany.' And Lady Caroline Lamb carried out the most outrageous affair with Byron right under the noses of everyone, although no one would dare slight her with a snub, not with Lady Bessborough, her mother, presiding over the polite world like an empress."

She shrugged kindly, seeing Michaela was still worried. "Yes, I suppose there will be whispers, winks, a few smirks, but they will quiet soon enough, for I am not without my influence as well. No one would dare say anything, at least not openly. And, after all, a decades-old scandal is not all that enticing."

"Mother will be mortified," she said. And she was surprised by feeling badly on this account.

"Your mother," Lady May said with the first sign of annoyance this evening, "understands that her daughters' prospects are greatly advanced, thanks to your connection to our family. You have done them a service. Besides, the official story of an old friendship between Dorothy and myself to explain my sponsoring her three daughters is a sound one. There is a constant influx of distant relations and renewed friends, even business partners—as long as they are not in trade, of course—into the beau monde. Now relax. Now is not the time to worry."

With a lift of her arched brow and a smile for Michaela, she descended gracefully out of the carriage.

Steeling herself, Michaela checked her reticule, her gloves, her daring neckline—so daring she didn't know how she was to keep from blushing all night. Then the servant appeared for her, and she stepped out of the carriage, emerging resplendent onto the courtyard and bracing herself for this night, this tremendously fantastic night. Her very first ball.

Everything she had dreamed such an event would be was before her as she entered the mansion. Lords and ladies promenaded in full regalia. The hall was aglitter with gilt and glass and the music so lovely it was impossible not to sway to the lilting strains.

"Smile," May prompted gently.

Michaela did so.

"Now. Try to enjoy it, my dear. It is, after all, the entire object of this endeavor." May took her hand and tucked it in her arm. She felt her mother's presence behind her, but there was no time to turn and speak to her. They were in the receiving line, meeting their hosts.

Michaela passed a pier glass in the center hall as they queued up for the receiving line. She started at the reflection.

May placed her hands on Michaela's shoulders and peered with her into the glass. "You look like a princess. Your father would be so proud."

Michaela felt a well of calmness with this. She had been done up like a duchess for tonight, and the sight of her reflection bolstered her confidence. Her gown, a lime silk sewn with clear beads to set it sparkling, was the latest style, the color and cut perfectly complementing the paleness of her skin and the long lines of her elegant figure. Her hair was worked into a bevy of twists, and the cascade of curls was daring. She felt beautiful and invincible. Once they were through the pleasantries of introductions, she turned anxiously for her mother's approval.

What struck her first was Delinda draped in deep cobalt silks that drew the eye, and not favorably. She stood festooned with rushing and feathers as was her habit. Beside her, Delilah wore a shapeless dress of ivory that washed out her already pale complexion. Mother was dressed simply, but she appeared handsome tonight with a blush of excitement on her cheeks and her eyes glittering as they darted over the crowd. It must be something of a homecoming for her.

Both twins' mouths dropped open when they saw Michaela, and Dorothy's jaw opened into a soft "o". She stepped forward, her sharp gaze taking in the gown, the hair—everything from head to foot. Her expression was sour, disturbed, and Michaela panicked, thinking something was terribly wrong. Had she split a seam?

"My God," Dorothy murmured, and her eyes blurred. Michaela knew then that she was seeing Woolrich, for she

had never played up the resemblance as much as she had
done tonight, under Lady May's guidance.

It didn't seem her mother cared for the likeness.

Michaela felt her pleasure and pride deflate. She had
thought her mother would be delighted. She knew she looked
lovely. What fault could she find?

"Your dress is wrinkled. Smooth it, like so," Mother said
at last.

After so many years, so many slights, it was curious why
this one would cut. Michaela trembled with disappointment.
She looked neither left at Delinda's snide smile nor right to
Lady May's pitying eyes.

Lady May stepped forward, placing her small frame between Dorothy and Michaela. "Fine silk does have a tendency to crush. It is unavoidable."

She really did love her aunt, but nothing could take away
the sting of her mother's coldness.

"Mother!" Delinda hissed, her hand coming up in an arc,
finger pointing across the room. "Look there. You were right;
he *is* here."

With a quick motion, Dorothy slapped Delinda's hand
down. No one took much notice of either the rudeness or the
swift admonition. Their attention was riveted on the man to
whom she had pointed.

"Is that him?" Delilah squeaked.

Lady May peered in the direction they were looking.
"Who?"

In a reverential tone, Delilah said, "Major Adrian Khoury,
that is who."

May shook her head. "It cannot be. Major Khoury? In
London? I thought he was a recluse."

"He is a famous war hero. Why should he not go anywhere he pleases?" Delinda was petulant.

Michaela stared at the man whose legend was as familiar
since the Battle of Waterloo as Wellington himself, as he
made his way across the room with the aid of his cane. She'd
imagined him as Byronic, romantic and slender, dark, mysterious, with fathomless eyes and a haunted air from all his
many brushes with death.

In contrast to her fantasies, Major Khoury was light-haired, worn longer than was strictly the fashion. It was tied into a queue in the back, the front brushed back off a high, wide brow that denoted intelligence. His face was square, his features blunt but pleasant. His mouth was cut into a straight line, a serious mouth with not a twitch of whimsy to it. A businesslike square jaw brooked no nonsense, and his body was solid, thick with muscle, with shoulders that strained the cloth of his tailcoat. His limp was not so pronounced to impede his progress, being only slightly noticeable, and the easy way he swung his cane in rhythm to his stride was actually quite dashing.

But it was his eyes most of all that defined the man. They were direct, combative almost, as he caught them all looking his way. He stared back at them, seeming to wonder if he knew them. When he realized he did not, he raised one tawny brow.

He appeared not at all fazed at finding five women ogling him, and it was this coolness more than anything else about him that struck Michaela as extraordinary.

"It is said he fought with his leg hanging in tatters beneath him," Delinda breathed in awe, "one hand holding an injured infantryman as he fought with the other. He dragged the man to safety through musket fire and sword attack. Then when they sewed his leg, he made no sound and would have no tinctures to ease the pain."

Soft-spoken Delilah added, "The French ran in fear of him. They say he fights like a Red Indian, with war cries to strike terror in the hearts of his enemies and vicious ruthlessness." She shivered delicately.

"Bosh," Lady May said, but she said it softly, with a hint of speculation in her voice. "These tales get inflated beyond recognition of the original."

He continued to stare, his strange eyes homing in on Michaela. She felt a sudden and visceral reaction reach like a fist across the room and squeeze her in its grip.

"Oh, goodness," Delinda squeaked, whirling away. "I fear I am going to get an attack of the vapors. I cannot wait to meet him. I am half besotted already. Did you see him look at me? Oh, I feel faint."

"Did you know he would be here?" Michaela asked, surprised that these three would not have mentioned this to her before tonight.

She had spoken to her mother, but it was Delinda who replied. "Of course. The gossips have it he is looking for a wife. They say he's thinking of running in the new election for the Surrey seat in the House of Commons." She threw a triumphant glance at Lady May and added, "We have planned for me to be introduced to him. Oh, and Delilah, of course."

Michaela couldn't hide how offended she was to be excluded. To her mother, she said, "Are you thinking of Major Khoury for Delinda? Isn't that a bit ambitious?"

"Why not?" Dorothy snapped back, her eyes glittering with excitement. "Delinda and Delilah are charming. Why wouldn't they catch the eye of a discriminating man? Delinda and Delilah are my chief concern. Not only are they without Lady May to keep their interests paramount, which you have, but they are older. I must think of the best marriage for them and quickly."

Michaela felt a curious heat and realized it was a mingling of hurt and anger. Dorothy sensed this and grew defensive. "I assumed Lady May had your coming out well in hand, so I did not think you would be interested with a major, a mere younger son of a marquess. Surely, she has her eye on an earl at least for you, Michaela."

Understanding dawned. Lady May's mentoring of Michaela seemed to have struck up a competition in her mother's mind. And Major Khoury was to be the first challenge.

"Mother, let us go now! I am impatient to meet him!" Delinda said.

Michaela felt an immediate and devilish impulse rise within her. She didn't think, she never did, not when she felt this particular sensation of exclusion. One would imagine she'd have grown immune to her mother's favoritism, but it stung, and as always, the sting made her angrier than a wet cat. "He is quite a catch, isn't he?" she murmured, looking over the man again.

He was. Her stomach fisted, and she told herself it was merely aggravation that did it.

Dorothy put a staying hand on the twin's arm. "Now, calm yourself, and I will call on my friend to present you." She clasped her hands together. "Who knows, girls, this could be your destiny."

The three women shifted, huddling together in a quick conference, effectively shutting Michaela out of their circle.

Michaela stood, at her first ball, bedecked like a princess, and stared miserably at them. She stewed, thinking that this moment symbolized her whole life of feeling the outsider.

Mother hadn't even noticed she was beautiful.

Lady May placed a hand on her arm. She meant it to be comforting, but it only embarrassed her.

"Excuse me," she murmured. She needed to find the ladies' retiring room so as to take a few moments to collect herself. She left the four of them behind, making her way through the crowd to the door.

A large figure stepped in front of her. He glanced over just as he passed, his eyes a very pale hazel, and she had a sudden, sharp reaction as she recognized Major Khoury. He was not more than an arm's length from her.

His gaze burned into her for a moment. His mouth quirked, as if acknowledging her.

A shot of something liquid-hot poured through her veins. She felt altogether aware of the blush of her flesh above her décolletage. She was suddenly awkward, forgetting the right thing to do when a man stared at a young woman so forwardly like this. So she simply stared back.

He was close enough that if she reached out, she could touch him. As they had not been introduced, they did not speak. Instead, her body throbbed with acute awareness.

She was not petite, and all of her life, next to her tiny-boned sisters, she'd felt like something of an Amazon, but the major was a very large man. He seemed hewn of rock rather than flesh and blood, and she was suddenly slender and willowy, almost insubstantial as she was caught in the sights of those extraordinary eyes.

He walked away, the slightest hitch in his stride in deference to his injury. She felt quite breathless and not like herself in the wake of this close encounter. Her body tingled, and her mind worked feverishly.

He was the man her mother wanted for her eldest: the great war hero, the most desirable man in the entire room, perhaps in all of London. The thought of him bowing to either one of the twins suddenly came to her, and a keen draining feeling that was decidedly unpleasant washed all through her body.

"Delinda and Delilah are my priority."

It wasn't fair. She would not stand for it.

She'd get her mother to notice her, all right, she thought suddenly and changed direction, setting off with a determined stride after the great Major Khoury.

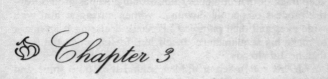

Chapter 3

Major Adrian Khoury noticed the tall woman. She was very lovely, with neat features, a pert nose, and large green eyes. Her mouth was full, her hair lush and dark. But most of all, he noted the trim figure encased in an expertly cut gown. Very fashionable, he supposed, and made perfectly to draw a man's eye.

His blood seemed to grow thick at the open way she stared at him. He was cornered, forced to chat while picking at the hors d'oeuvres in the refreshment room.

Others were vying for his attentions. His presence tonight, the first time he'd made an appearance in society since he retired several years ago, had created something of a furor. He had expected it, knowing how these people had mutated his "legend" in the years since the war with Napoleon, but the foreknowledge didn't grant him any more patience to deal with this most annoying effect of his war reputation.

The stories of his exploits as a commander of a Horse Guard regiment had not, as he had initially hoped, died down in his absence from the public eye. In effect, they had grown to proportions approaching the ridiculous. He understood, of course, that the country clamored for heroes in the wake of Napoleon's glorious defeat, and he, Major Khoury—the legend, not the man—furnished a prime piece of lore.

It was damnably bothersome, however. Firstly, he hated to attract all of this notice, especially when he was trying to keep track of that brunette. And secondly, he despised the entire process of people fawning: women gazing at him with wide eyes and men pumping his hand, declaring it an honor to make his acquaintance. It left him feeling more the fraud than he did already.

Ah, his rotten secret hidden behind the polite smile and cold eyes with which he met his admirers. All anyone knew, all they cared about, were tales of his exploits. What little they knew of the flesh-and-blood man.

His eyes once again clashed with delicately tilted ones, green ones, pale as jade and as mysterious. Who *was* that woman? She was an outrageous flirt, whoever she was, staring at him so boldly. She looked like a gypsy, slightly untamed.

A thought occurred to him, warming his blood as he studied the exquisite creature. He'd heard high-priced courtesans and aristocratic mistresses looking for a new benefactor infiltrated these sorts of affairs. As a rule, he never went in much for bought women, but this one might prove the exception. He knew quality when he saw it.

Yes. The idea grew to certainty. The ton dictated every faction of social life, each moved prescribed and inspected. No well-bred miss would dare act as did this gypsy.

God, no deb who'd been schooled in the mincing steps and demure posture walked like this. She moved with the graceful swing of the long-limbed, erect without being stiff.

He liked his women tall and slender as this one was. He liked her hair as well. He wanted to know how those thick tresses would look uncoiled, what the texture would feel like in his hand. He eyed her figure. It was full in the bust, narrow everywhere else.

Yes, he liked what he saw.

She was coming over to him. By God, he had to be the luckiest of fools if she indeed meant to speak to him. Her boldness, that purposeful way she approached, could only mean she was what he suspected, and his heartbeat picked up with delicious expectation. If she were indeed a courtesan—a very elite one—then he was going to have a very pleasant evening indeed.

The woman did not stop as he had hoped, and he cursed himself for a ridiculous thought. Disappointment heated his chest in a slow burn as she glanced at him in that deliciously flirtatious way she had and continued on. She spoke to a woman, a strikingly lovely blond several years her elder, and they exited the room. He racked his brain, thinking of who the woman could be and how in the world he could wangle an introduction.

He was obviously wrong, he decided. But how to explain her unconventional behavior? No, he could not have mistaken those glances. Could he?

It was not until a half hour later that he spied the particular lady again. He paused to watch her as she spoke with a gentleman, his eyes narrowed. If she was a courtesan, then was this the man she would entertain for the night? The thought made his stomach tighten uncomfortably.

She didn't retire with him. Instead, she snapped open her fan, and damn if her eyes didn't meet Adrian's over the fluttering ivory. She excused herself and, looking about, she located a door and headed for it. His heart jerked with a delirious thrill. She'd all but crooked her finger at him!

He threw back the last of the fine champagne he'd been nursing as he'd brooded. He was not about to let such an opportunity as this pass him by. He followed without delay.

It was not as dark as he would have liked on the flagstone terrace, and not as deserted. Couples strolled, and knots of people took in the cool air. But the long figure in pale green was easy to spot. She stood by the balustrade, the white kid of her gloves nearly glowing against the stone, gazing out over the gardens.

He went up to her, his gait maddeningly slow. His limp

never bothered him much, but any impediment that caused delay ignited impatience in him.

"It's much more pleasant out here," he said softly.

She started. What eyes she possessed, wide and iridescent green. They gazed at him with expectation for a heartbeat too long before she remembered to lower her lashes. They fell like a fringed curtain over an emerald.

"I could arrange an introduction," he began, smiling slightly.

She snuck a look up at him, unable to keep up the demure pose.

"But it would be a bother."

"I . . ."

Oh, that was very pretty indeed. She actually looked bewildered.

He shrugged, lifting one heavy shoulder. "But no one is here to see that we've done it right, so it hardly seems worth the trouble. Those people over there might think we've already been introduced. And those inside might think we enlisted some helpful Samaritan out here to do the honors. Either way, there is no one the wiser, and by the time we seek someone out, we've wasted time. So, if I may present myself, I am Major Adrian Khoury."

It was a temptation tossed to her to gauge her reaction. He found himself holding his breath to see what she would do.

"I know."

Now she was smiling, showing no simple maid's tricks or artifice. His blood thrust harder in his veins.

"Hello," she said.

He raked his eyes down her. She didn't flinch. "Hello," he replied.

"You are, of course, Major Khoury. Everyone knows who you are, you see." Her smile deepened, bringing out little indentations in the sides of her cheeks.

He inclined his head slightly. "I am your servant. But you have me at a disadvantage. I still do not know your name."

"I am Michaela Standish, sir. I know this is completely unorthodox, as you yourself said, and you must not think ill of me, but I confess I was anxious to meet you. I do have good reason for flaunting manners, or rather agreeing to, as it was your idea. You see, I am afraid if you went off to find a suitable friend to present us, I would lose you to the admiring crowd. And it does seem a lot of stuff and nonsense to ask someone to do what we can perfectly well do ourselves, don't you think? But then, I am a forward-thinking person, and although I've been taught my manners, I'm not used to the exacting standards of the ton." She winced most prettily. "Oh, I shouldn't have said that, should I? I think I might be prattling. I don't usually. I suppose I'm nervous."

His pulse kicked higher, his heart squeezing hard in his chest. She was more delightful than he could have imagined. His visceral reaction surprised him. He hadn't had this sort of reaction to a woman, to anything, since . . . no, not even with Frances.

"Do you forgive me?"

Yes, he thought. He did see quite clearly what she was about. A courtesan's tricks, but charming nonetheless.

"You are not only forgiven, Miss Standish," he said, taking a step closer, enticed by that scent. Rosewater. French milled soap, perhaps, and something unique and feminine, "I am entirely convinced as to the justifiable nature of your reasons."

She looked nervous and took a step back, her hand falling away.

Bold at first, now coy. How interesting. She tilted her head at him and smiled, as if in apology, or . . . or an invitation. To a game of sorts. A flirtation right here in public, a parry of the forbidden cloaked under the guise of the conventional.

He didn't mind. Hell, he was already half rabid for this ravishing creature, and the lark intrigued him.

He kept his distance, resisting the urge to touch her.

"I suppose you've been very busy tonight. You are much in demand."

Her eyes slid sideways, as if she were on alert for that very thing at the moment. It was a very flattering look—seductive while not seeming so. "No fears, Miss Standish," he replied. "I am not going anywhere. I am content to take in the night air with you right here."

"Well," she said, looking over his shoulder. She seemed uncertain. Was she supposed to meet someone out here?

Suddenly, it became imperative for him to get her away from the terrace. He would not have her stolen from him, not when he was about to plunge into the most exciting evening he'd had in a while.

"If you'd like, we could take some refreshment. I was just going that way. Are you hungry?"

"A lady never admits to needing food." Her lips curled.

"But if they are faint with such need, they had better see to it."

She accepted, and they went inside. He scanned jealously for her phantom assignation, determined not to give way without a good stand should any other man approach.

She peered at the offerings on the linen-draped tables. "They look interesting, do they not?"

Ah. He was forgetting the game. "We must take a look if anything you see tempts you."

"Indeed, I think I am a bit hungry."

He smiled a predator's smile.

He attended her, fetching her a china dish. He found he could hardly concentrate on so simple a task as placing her selections on the platter, what with how closely she hovered next to his arm.

"Good Lord, what is that?" she said, pointing to a green substance in a silver chafing dish. She laughed at his grimace as he peered at it and pronounced, "It doesn't seem to be food."

"Then what can it be?" She tilted her head back and laughed up at him. "As the brave and intrepid soldier, I think you should try it."

He gave a shake of his head. "Not I, Miss Standish."

"But you have a reputation for unmatched courage. Pray do not disappoint me," she pleaded playfully.

"Miss Standish, I seriously doubt any man would venture a single bite of this mystery dish were the only nourishment for miles."

A man cut in beside them, reaching in and heaping several spoonfuls onto his plate. He glanced apologetically at them and said, "Spinach and turnip soufflé. I do love it," and moved happily on.

He met her incredulous gaze. "I seem to be in error," he admitted dryly. She erupted in giggles. Staring after the man, he mused with incredulity in his voice, "Spinach and turnips?"

Her eyes gleamed in the most beguiling manner, clearly delighted at his humor. He had forgotten he could be charming. It had been a long time since he'd tried.

"Ah, so you are a man who can admit his mistakes," she teased.

Shrugging, he proceeded down the line. "As infrequently as that occasion happens, it does not tax me."

She laughed again, then pretended to look over the food. Placing a finger in the corner of her mouth, she posed for him as she thought about her selections.

She was very, very good at her job. He was enjoying this interesting form of foreplay. The best Cyprians understood that sex was more than a function of the body. This one had a keen instinct for pulling the tension to just the right pitch. It was a delicious contrast, posing in this setting of the polite world, all the while knowing what would come later between them. The anticipation was to be savored.

And yet nothing about her could be construed as proper, in terms of what polite society considered proper, that is. In a world of mincing tones and twitters, this one's forwardness, her wide, open smiles, her quick wit and teasing took her out of the ordinary and solidly into a far more desirable class.

A woman he would sleep with tonight, he thought, fighting the surge of delicious sensation that trickled down his spine.

"I think that is enough," she pronounced. "Unless you would like to go back for the soufflé?"

"I am quite content," he said, "for now."

They sat at a small table in the corner. He fetched her punch, marveling at himself acting like some besotted beau. But it was worth it. He observed her as she ate delicately, trying not to think of carnal associations as her plump moist lips glistened with each tiny nibble of food. "Tell me of yourself, Major."

He frowned. "I dislike speaking of myself. It is not necessary. I suppose most men enjoy it, but I do not."

"Major, you shock me," she said, unperturbed.

"And I would rather you not use my military title."

"Why ever not? Such an elevated rank is a fine accomplishment."

"In battle, not in society."

"Everywhere. Your achievements recommend your character."

He scowled. "Are you always so opinionated? I would think a woman such as yourself would be inclined to accommodate me."

She smiled. "Why should I? You are not my husband or my father. And yes, I am always opinionated. Now I do not understand your aversion to your rank. Everyone refers to you this way, so to pretend you are what you are not is just silly. That is like an earl deciding he doesn't wish to be addressed as 'my lord.' It simply isn't done."

"Why, Miss Standish, I believe you are scolding me. I must warn you *that* simply isn't done."

Those green eyes twinkled. "Spoken like a major used to giving commands and brooking no insubordination. I've heard much of you, sir."

He leaned back. "Such as?"

"Ah, so you do enjoy talking of yourself!"

"It seems I have no choice. You are quite determined, aren't you?"

"Well, one hears the most intriguing things. For example, I know you sometimes have problems with your superiors and do not always follow orders. If it weren't for it working out so brilliantly when you break rank and strike out on your own, you might have been court-martialed. Is this true?"

"Nominally." He grinned. "Go on."

"When a captain demanded you explain yourself after executing your own maneuver on the battlefield, you told him you never explain yourself to anyone."

"I admit, that was rude of me," he said as if penitent. "However, it was a lieutenant colonel, and he was a jackass, but he was my superior officer. I was soundly reprimanded for that."

"Which meant some colonel took you into his office and gave you a wink and a cigar and shared some port with you."

He raised his brows.

"I guessed rightly, did I?" she asked with a show of false innocence that made his stomach catch fire. "I heard someone say that was the worst that ever happened to you because you were Wellington's man. You had caught the eye of the great man himself, and none dared contend with you." She glanced down, suddenly shy. "They say it made you a bit arrogant."

He leaned forward, propping his chin on his fist as he eyed her provocatively. "Do you find me so?"

"I find you perfectly enjoyable company. But then, I am not a lieutenant colonel."

He laughed, taken off guard. "How extraordinary you are. You chastise me yet again. However, you do so in such a completely charming way I can hardly mind it."

She feigned a blush and said, "You embarrass me."

"I think it rather pleases you."

She was startled, then shrugged. "Very well, yes it does. My aunt told me I must never allow that I have been pleased by flattery, but I suppose I need more practice in fooling people about my feelings."

"Ah, so now we have turned the tables, much more to my liking. Let us talk of you, then, Miss Standish. That is the second time you've made reference that this"—he waved his hand at the scene around them—"is not your normal life. You seem to be rather as new to the polite world as I am."

He was curious about her. Where had she come from? How had she ended up in this life? He could hardly ask her. Perhaps later . . . afterward. He might enjoy getting to know her.

"I should not have spoken so openly of my inexperience. I fear it gives me away. Aunt May warned me." She looked worried all of a sudden. "Oh. Let me explain about Aunt

May, that is, why I call her Aunt May. She isn't my aunt, of course." She laughed nervously. "I call her aunt as a courtesy—my sisters and I do—since she is such a good friend and has sponsored us this season, being a good friend of the family. I . . . I should quit talking."

Why did she keep mentioning her aunt? Her madam, perhaps. Was she intimating a *ménage à trois*? Not that he didn't find the idea appealing, but perhaps some future date. Right now, he wanted this woman all to himself, no distractions. And as soon as possible. However, she seemed bent on toying with him, and, for once, he was content to surrender the lead.

She cocked her head and listened to the music, abandoning half her plate uneaten. "It is so beautiful. My feet simply cannot keep still. Do you dance?" she asked, then stopped, looking shocked. "Oh. I shouldn't have asked that."

He was sensitive about the injury; he never mentioned the damned thing and never answered questions by curiosity seekers. It was a flaw, an imperfection, and as such, a symbol of the incomplete man who had returned home from war. Somehow, however, the words, "I don't mind," came out of his mouth.

"Were you injured in battle?"

"Yes. It does not render me the most graceful of men."

Why the devil had he said that? It made him seem as if he were making excuses. He didn't dance. Period.

And he never explained himself to anyone.

"Oh, goodness." Her distress was obvious. "I think you do mind and are being polite. I am used to being outspoken. It is my worst fault, believe me. I can't seem to help myself."

"Very pretty. Your coloring actually deepens as if you really are embarrassed. It flatters you. It must be why you are going on so about such an inconsequential thing as a dance. In any event, I cannot help but sense that my answer disappoints you. Do you like to dance, Miss Standish?"

"I do, yes," she replied. "Though I've never done so at a ball. I should very much like to, however."

"What an enticing prospect, being your first." He smiled, telling her he knew the lure of what she had given him. Not her virginity, that would be too unbelievable, but one small distinction to heighten his interest.

For a man who had long ago styled himself a cynic, he was surprisingly interested. "I am toying with the improbable idea of trying out my legs on a measured quadrille. I might be able to manage it, if you would help me. I am rather more of a plodder than a glider, as these things go, but we can give it a try."

He didn't know why he wished to dance with her except that the pleasant fiction they were enacting was going to his head. And, as she was very good at what she did, he could almost believe she and he were two very different people. Normal people, like those around them. Whole people.

Just for a while, what a soothing diversion.

She appeared so delighted at the prospect, he was glad he had done it and didn't second-guess his strange impulses any longer. He supposed courtesans never got much of an opportunity to actually take in any of the entertainments at these affairs. Odd that it mattered if he pleased her. She was a stranger and . . . well, it hardly mattered if she were happy in the circumstances. Her job was to make *him* happy.

But, oh, how clever she was to make it all seem so different. With her guileless act, she provided a safe transport for his darkness, and he was unencumbered. It felt good, this pretty play. It was the first time he'd been without a care in another person's presence since coming home.

He cupped his hand under her elbow, pulling her tight up against him as they negotiated the crush to get upstairs. She didn't pull away. Her hair held the perfume of roses he had smelled before. The soap was expensive and subtle, artfully chosen to tempt a man's reason. It was quite effective.

Miss Standish—what a prudish name. She must have chosen it especially to go along with the playacting she was doing of the proper young lady at her first ball. It was a fetching illusion. She was probably coached by this "Aunt May," no doubt an expert procurer of quality women for discriminating gentlemen. She and her "sisters" would make quite a splash with the men.

He felt a weird surge of possessiveness. He shook it off;

that was absurd. He hardly knew her, hadn't even had her yet.

As luck would have it, there was a waltz being played as they settled themselves on the dance floor. She gave him an appealing look and declared, "Oh, no. I've only just learned. I am afraid I am not any good!"

He moved her carefully, relaxing a little at her laughter, the way her face lit from within as they puzzled out the steps together in a stately if stilted waltz. They made a merry time of it until the last strains of the violins faded away.

They froze in place, staring at one another as the next piece of music picked up. She left her hand in his, her face flushed and beaming. No lady of breeding would do such a thing. It was the essence of her game, looking like an ingenue while making her overtures as brazen as a wanton in a crimson pleasure parlor.

He turned with her and led her off the floor, easing her closer under the pretext of making their way through the crowd. He was not surprised when she didn't balk when he rode his hand on the small of her back, just above the gentle swell of her very nicely rounded derriere.

She seemed to be looking about, perhaps trying to find someone. He wasn't interested in anyone joining their party. She murmured, "I wonder where Aunt May is."

His patience was gone. It was time.

There were intrigues, and then there were annoyances. "Come with me," he said.

"Oh? Where are we going?"

"It is too crowded in here," he said, bending low to speak into her ear. She titled her head into his, her hair brushing up against his nose. He closed his eyes, riding a wave of pure pleasure at her scent, the feel of her so close.

"Come."

He led her to the stairs, then down to the first floor. The mansion had a massive pair of front doors, and although both of them were flung open, the press of the late arrivals glutted it.

She paused. "I cannot leave."

His brows forked down in confusion. Did she wish to stay here, find some place within the mansion?

He thought of the possibility that she hoped to circulate again after they were through, ensnaring another man to earn a double fee this night. The idea repelled him. He recoiled, thinking for the first time that this sort of . . . thing was not to his taste.

Then she looked at him with a wide, catlike blink of complete innocence and said, "Where are you taking me?" and any scruples he might have laid claim to evaporated under the scorching heat of desire.

"In here," he said hoarsely, pushing her in front of him down a short, dimly lit hallway leading toward the back of the house. They entered a small parlor, probably utilized for the housekeeper to make out the weekly menu and oversee the staff. It was dark. He closed the door quietly behind them.

He found the flint box and lit a candle.

"What is it?" she asked, her voice holding an edge as if she expected some excitement.

She stood in the middle of the room, unmoving, as he advanced on her.

"What is your real name?" he murmured, brushing up close. She skittered away.

He'd had enough of the play. His body was throbbing, his groin heavy with need. He advanced, his brows drawn down in a determined cast.

He slipped his hand around her waist from behind and pulled her back, lowering his head to touch the curve of her neck and pressing his lips to it. The flesh was like silk.

She made a small sound of pleasure, not resisting. "What are you doing?" she whispered.

He turned her, staring down at her face. Her expression was wide-eyed, shocked but not displeased. He lowered his lips to hers without preamble.

Her mouth had been slightly open, from surprise, and his lips settled pleasantly over hers. Making a soft sound, she placed her hands on his shoulders, squeezing tightly. It was a marvelous response, and he opened her mouth, invading her with his tongue.

He felt hungrier than he ever remembered being for a woman. He was not gentle, as a result, taking everything he'd been promised, vowing he'd do it all again more gently when he had the time.

He broke off, staring down at her. Her lips were red and full, moist from their kiss. Her body rested softly in his arms. He touched her neck, his fingertips brushing the tendrils curling lazily at her hairline. His breathing was jagged, making his voice a harsh rasp. "Not here."

"Hmmm?" she replied. She acted drugged, as if kissing him had filled her with lassitude. He found that very exciting, even more when he thought that perhaps she wasn't pretending. But that was the trouble with professionals. One never knew.

He indulged once again in a long, slow kiss. She swayed forward, and he caught her body up against his, feeling the supple, yielding flesh that was undeniably feminine along every inch of his own male hardness. What the hell did it matter if her reaction was real or not, he told himself harshly. *This* was real. It would be all the reality he needed when he sheathed himself in her and took his pleasure.

Although the conditions were not what he would consider ideal, they were alone. Later, he would take his time, undress her, and study this long, graceful body by candlelight. But now . . .

A long divan near the empty fireplace would serve, he decided quickly. He kissed her again. She clung to him in the most intoxicating way. He maneuvered them to the divan and eased her back, then down. She was limp in his arms, pliant and obedient, as if her will was his now.

She roused, looking about her in surprise as if wondering how she came to be here. He sealed his mouth over hers to stem any protests. Her lips were like satin, and very soft. He almost lost his head as he feasted on their plumpness, feeling a swirling light-headedness he attributed to blood loss to the north of him since it was all, quite obviously, pumping vigorously to his south.

Putting a knee on the other side of her, he braced a hand on the curved back of the divan and bent down to kiss her as his free hand reached under the hem of her skirt and pulled it up. His palm grazed the fine silk of her stockings. Slowly, he slid his hand along the curve of her leg, her calf first, and then the tender softness behind her knee. He touched her thigh, felt the garter, and made contact with bare skin just above it.

Her hands came up to him, reaching for him, he thought. He deepened the kiss, and his hand slid unerringly to the vee between her thighs. His fingertips brushed aside the cut in her pantaloons and found the curls secreted there. There waited the most tantalizing hint of hot moistness, and then the pressure of her hands on his shoulder increased.

He was groggy with desire, blood starved in his brain, but even in such a state it registered that she was pushing him away.

She *was* pushing him away. And she was twisting, not squirming in delight. He ceased, lifting his head to peer down at her.

"My God, get off of me this instant!" she cried, and there was a touch of real panic that brought him instantly aware that something was wrong. He removed his hand.

She bit her lip, turning her head away. "What are you doing? This is . . . this . . . Let me up at once!"

She fought him, seeking to free herself. He sobered from his lust-induced haze like a drunk doused in the Thames. Springing back from her as if electric current had repelled him, he was on his feet in an instant.

She tossed her skirts back into place and scrambled to her feet, dashing to a safe distance before whirling to face him. And, damn it, she was crying.

"My God, what is this? You were going to . . . you tried to lay with me."

Years in battle had taught him the value of assessing a situation quickly, summoning options, evaluating them, and choosing the best approach all within a matter of seconds. He did so now as she collected herself, his mind clicking over the facts, revising them, and coming to the obvious conclusion that he had been desperately misled.

"I don't suppose I was correct in assuming you were a courtesan, then," he drawled, finding the right tone of self-derision and anger to catch her off guard.

She looked up at him, her expression one of pure shock as if this had affronted her more than all the liberties he had taken. "Of course I am not. How dare you say such a thing."

"You sure as hell acted like one."

His body, which was in an acute state of discomfort at present, was proving reluctant to accept that Miss Standish was not what she had appeared to be. And he was not going to get laid tonight.

She was bristling, finding it difficult to choke out the words, "I most certainly did not!"

"You allowed me to speak to you without an introduction."

"But you said—agh!"

"Why did you?" he pressed.

"I but wanted to make your acquaintance before—" She stopped short, biting her bottom lip.

"You made a joke of flaunting convention. You touched my arm, you did that thing . . ." He waved an expressive hand in the air. "That thing with your eyes where you look straight through a person. You flirted outrageously, saying all the right things to flatter, paying me compliments."

"I was being nice," she cried defensively.

He paused. "Not that nice," he drawled with a caustic glance at the abandoned divan. "So, are you really here with your aunt? I mean, not your . . . I mean a real aunt?"

"Yes. Well, a real friend of the family. And my mother and sisters."

"Real sisters?" He gave a rough laugh. "God help me, real sisters. And a mother. For the love of God, why didn't you mention a mother?"

"Don't blame me. You are the one who made a mistake. It was a dreadful, awful mistake, and I had nothing to do with it. I thought I was going to get my first kiss, and you made it all sordid."

"Oh, no you don't, Miss Standish . . . what the devil is your first name again?"

"How dreadful—you don't even know it? It's Michaela." Fresh tears spilled onto her cheeks.

"Dry your eyes. No good will come of crying. Dear Lord, did you say a moment ago that this was your first kiss? How the devil could a woman who looks like you reach your age and never be kissed? Have you never had a suitor?"

"Of course I have." She jerked up her chin.

"But no kisses."

"Of course not. There was always Mother there, and besides, I wouldn't have allowed it. I didn't . . . feel that way."

"So you refused them? Lucky fellows."

"I didn't love them."

"Love? Oh, good God. This is beyond absurd. You had to have known what was happening tonight. You didn't even balk when I brought you in here."

"It is not absurd." She bit her lips to steady her quivering chin. "I never found anyone to interest me . . . that way. I wanted . . ." She lost her voice, casting her eyes downward in sudden helplessness. "It was all just a lark at first, because of Delinda. I wanted to show them, and then you were so charming, and I thought it was magical. I wanted to dance, and then you kissed me. It was what I'd waited for until—" She broke off, her eyes shut as she indicated the divan. "You did that . . . that . . ."

"No need to look so disgusted by the act. I only tried to make love to you."

She gasped in a quick breath and jerked her face away.

"A damned shame," he muttered. "It was all going so nicely until then."

Her eyes flew open, and she stared angrily at him. "You thought I was a whore!"

"Not a common doxy," he said with conciliation in his voice. "A courtesan. Very different, Miss Standish."

She donned a cool look, throwing off her distress with an agility that told him she'd done it before. She wasn't so sheltered as all that, and she could think on her feet. What an odd bird she was: gorgeous virgin who had never even been kissed. Good Lord.

"That was a ridiculous presumption, no matter how much provocation you try to invent on my part. I think it is you, Major Khoury, who has the explaining to do. After all, you were the one who lured me in here and chose to interpret my very understandable and *innocent* mistakes—and, yes, I admit I made mistakes—very vilely."

"You came quite willingly when I led you in here. What did you think would happen once we were alone, may I ask?"

Her face paled. "I told you, I was merely intrigued. I wanted you to kiss me."

"You wanted more than that. I have lived long enough to know when a woman desires me, and it is no conceit in that statement, but fact."

"A kiss merely. You are a bounder to have taken such advantage!"

"I beg your pardon, but you know you are lying. I am generally known as brash to a fault and honest to an uncomfortable degree. It is something I take pride in, as a matter of fact, for it is an asset in the military."

"Do you also take pride in mauling innocents in public places?"

"I take pride," he said, stepping toward her, "in giving enticing young ladies who throw themselves at me exactly what they are after."

He had a moment of regret at her disturbed, shattered look. "I did not mean to . . . I did nothing but flirt a bit."

"A bit? I'd hate to see what you are capable of, then, if you mean it."

"It was completely your fault. I still find it horrifying to contemplate you believed I was a . . ."

"A courtesan," he supplied. "Not a whore." Why was it important she understood the distinction? Wasn't it all just sex in the end?

If it wasn't, he wanted her to know. "Let me teach you something, Michaela Standish," he said. "I mean no insult when I said what I thought you were. Courtesans don't saunter into polite affairs with painted lips, their bodices dampened to show off rouged nipples. They don't sashay up to men and announce their price. Strumpets of that sort would never be allowed to mingle in polite society."

Her mouth had fallen open, forming a delicious O. He continued, enjoying the shocking effect of his words. "The art of enticing, the subtle innuendo, the look, the touch, all combine to convey what they are about while they admit nothing, give away nothing. Everything about them is mystery. They are skilled at enticing a man's interest, of making him do things his better judgment tells him not to. They are sirens, masters at their craft of using sensuality and sexuality to their advantage. They seduce a man so that he never even questions what he is doing as he hands them exorbitant amounts of money for the privilege of touching their body."

He cut off abruptly, realizing he had said far too much. She could misconstrue it. He had only meant to convey that he had never intended an insult when he had thought her a sophisticated Cyprian, but she might guess how potent her effect had been, and Adrian was not used to allowing anyone that kind of insight.

She was bemused. "I've never flirted with a man. I don't even know how. I'd never even met anyone I'd wanted to flirt with. But with you, it just seemed to happen, if it were natural. I didn't imagine you would think me to be . . ." She flushed, making an odd, endearingly sweet squeak and waving her hands in a gesture of supplication, as if begging him to understand. "I only wished to get you to notice me before my sisters."

"Ah. Some sort of competition." Their conversation had not done much to diminish the dull throb centered squarely in his groin, but he didn't wish to berate her. "For what it is worth . . . I noticed."

"I made a fool of myself—worse. I disgraced myself."

"Well, it isn't entirely your fault. Didn't your aunt teach you anything before setting you loose, looking like that, on poor defenseless males? It sounds as if you've led a very sheltered life. It takes time for a woman to grow into the effect she has on men."

"She did tell me. I just . . . I forgot it. I was having such a wonderful time. Oh, I should have known this wouldn't work. I may be born to this, but I wasn't raised to it. It takes a lifetime to have the right instincts, and mine are all wrong. I'm not a princess at all. I'm just an ordinary girl in a green silk dress."

She lapsed into an expression that was so despondent, he actually had a moment of sympathy. An insane thought that didn't bear consideration.

He folded his arms over his chest and took her measure. "So tell me, why were you trying to beat your sisters to the game? I take it I was some sort of prize in some test of feminine wiles."

"It was Delinda, really. And Mother." Her voice had changed, grating slightly as if there were emotion caught in her throat. "I wanted her to see."

"See?"

Her gaze connected to his, and a soft punch landed on his heart. "Yes. See me."

It didn't make any sense to him, but he sensed her vulnerability. "There is no harm done," he said at last, donning a brusque air to dispel her melancholy. "In the end no one knows of it besides the two of us, and neither one of us is likely to reveal a thing. Why do we not simply take our leave of one another and spare ourselves these pointless recriminations?"

"All right. I . . . I suppose I should thank you." She frowned. "Although I cannot precisely manage to feel grateful after all that has transpired."

"As you will. I am leaving. It was . . ." He let his eyes take in the whole of her, savoring this last look, then finished quite honestly, and with a touch of mischief he couldn't have resisted for the world, "almost a pleasure."

Her temper gathered over her features like thunderheads claiming the sky, but he left before the storm exploded.

ᥲ Chapter 4

The topic of Major Khoury dancing with the youngest Stan-dish girl made the rounds with the morning calls the follow-ing day. When the news reached the small house in St. Alban's Crescent, Dorothy Standish listened white-lipped as her friend, Mrs. Hancock, related the details of what every-one was saying.

"Why, Dorothy, the man never dances; he simply doesn't." Mrs. Hancock turned her chubby face, reddened with excite-ment, expectantly toward Michaela. "Is it true?"

"Yes, we danced," she admitted. Delinda looked explo-sive, and not feeling up to one of her tantrums, she rushed to add, "but only a bit, and we weren't very good. In fact, we were awful. It was the waltz—"

Delinda exploded. "The waltz? Mother!"

"Quiet, Delinda. Go on, Michaela."

Mother's calm tone didn't deceive Michaela. She had not said a word to her mother or to anyone of her dreadful encounter with the major the night before. Therefore, Dorothy, who had been too preoccupied during the party to notice what she had been up to, was hearing it for the first time.

And none too pleased, by the look of her.

"Well, then, tell us, darling," Mrs. Hancock prodded, "what was he like?"

"He was rude, actually," Michaela said with a shrug.

"But you spent time with him," Mrs. Hancock protested, "so there must be something charming about the man."

"No. It really was of no moment, Mrs. Hancock. There is no juicy tidbit in the tale, just a lackluster meeting between two people who didn't suit."

Michaela went to the desk in the corner and sat with her back to the others. It was a miracle that she had not given herself away when speaking of the major. Her heart was beating rapidly. She wasn't used to lying.

Now that the gossip about herself and Major Khoury was concluded, the conversation would move on to other topics. She was free to concentrate on her work.

She was laboring on an essay to be included in a pamphlet that the Society for the Promotion of Aid to the Poor was preparing to try to establish one of Miss Hannah More's Sunday schools here in the city, at the local church. She could no longer write to the newspapers because it had upset her mother. However, she was still dedicated to teaching poor children, and ultimately their illiterate parents, to read.

Therefore, she and the other members of the society had come up with this tactic where she could write her persuasion for the schools anonymously.

Her heart wasn't in her usual pursuits, however. She kept hearing a voice—his voice, his very *distinctive* voice as it was last night in the aftermath of her spurning him, with a rasp of emotion edging its deep, sonorous tones. She could recollect it exactly enough to raise fine bumps along her arms.

He had thought her a courtesan. This was preposterous! The man must have taken too many blows to the head in combat. Yet, even as she tried to work up a righteous rage, she heard that voice echo, telling her that she had been seductive, alluring, making men do things their better sense told them not to.

As if she could do something like that. Never in her life had she had that kind of talent.

Then again, she had been kept away from the young gentlemen considered immoral "blades." There had never been a man like Major Khoury. Never.

He had thought she was a Cyprian, a high-priced whore, no matter how you dressed it up with poetry and praise. The sobering thoughts dashed her dreamy reflections like fine china against rock. He had kissed her like a woman of ill repute; hard and demanding, holding none of his passion back.

"What did you say, Michaela?" Mother called.

Michaela started. To her horror, Michaela realized she had emitted a throaty groan.

"No, nothing. I . . . I just yawned." She stretched her fists over her head and stretched, issuing an illustrative yawn as demonstration.

Mother frowned and went back to her friend.

With determination, Michaela picked up her quill and hunched over her essay. She managed a few lines. There was no telling how long this harrowing exercise took, but when she sensed a presence beside her, she looked up to find Dorothy there.

Everyone else had gone. She was holding a card sealed with familiar pink wax that denoted all Lady May's correspondence.

"Lady May has sent word that a last-minute invitation for a dinner party arrived for tomorrow evening." Dorothy laid the message on the desk next to Michaela's essay. She asks for you to go there today, however, to enjoy a quiet afternoon and evening with her tonight. I . . . I had plans this afternoon with a friend for tea, but you may go instead with her if you prefer."

"Thank you."

"She is very kind to you. You must enjoy the attention. I don't suppose having to share my attention with your two sisters was to your liking."

"I find her pleasant company," Michaela replied neutrally.

When her mother didn't move away, Michaela turned in her seat. "Was there something else?"

"Yes. I am quite put out with you, Michaela. What you did last night was reprehensible."

Against reason, her heart stopped. Of course Mother didn't know about her shameful behavior, but the reference caused a shot of alarm to race through her, nonetheless. "What do you mean?"

"You deliberately set your cap for Major Khoury to spite me. You knew I wanted to present Delinda and Delilah to him. You monopolized him the entire evening for the sole purpose of thwarting me."

Michaela stood. On her feet, her height gave her the advantage, at least mentally. "And why is it Major Khoury was so important, Mother?" she inquired dispassionately. "Wasn't it you who wished to spite me? Snare the most eligible bachelor at the ball for one of your precious twins and show me what quality could really do over an odd little bird like myself."

Mother's eyes flared, and it was only when she saw the shocked expression on her face that Michaela realized she had finally given voice to her secret thoughts. She hadn't meant to say it, but the words had flown from her lips unchecked.

Now they were out and could not be taken back. She regretted them instantly.

Mother's hand came up to her throat. "What would make you say such a thing?"

"I . . ." She was disconcerted. She had never been exactly a tractable child, but she had never been hateful.

Coldness came over Dorothy's features, obliterating the glimpse of vulnerability. "What is it to you? You have Lady May to worry over you. I should think that is quite enough to satisfy. You don't need me anymore."

That was when Michaela made an astonishing discovery. It struck her dumb, so that when her mother stalked out of the room, she didn't utter a word in reply. Instead, she spoke moments later into an empty space.

"You feel disfavored. I think I've hurt you," she said softly.

Michaela dressed that night in a lovely shimmering silk of lavender trimmed with ecru lace and ribbons of deep purple velvet crossing over her breasts to draw the eye. The color brought out the richness in her hair and made her eyes shine like emeralds as she checked her face in the mirror just as she left the house with Lady May.

"My apologies for our lateness," May said casually as they entered the well-appointed home in Grosvenor Square, fluffing the pink rushing at her neck. May always wore at least one pink thing, usually a flounce, feather, or fluff. She made it look fabulous, and it added to her delicate air, a contrast to her strong personality and enduring beauty. "It is quite a matter getting two of us ready in the evenings. I suppose I shall have to hire more staff."

Michaela stopped short, emitting a short, high gasp as she stared at the man seated in the far corner. Major Khoury reclined as easily as if he were taking his ease in his own home. His left ankle rested casually on his right knee, his hands steepled in front of his chin, and his eyes, grayish green right at this moment, were focused directly on her.

His eyebrows lifted, softening his craggy, hard features, and one corner of his mouth thinned in a tiny curve as if in silent welcome.

Lady May's eyes darted in the same direction. Without seeming to move, she delivered a swift kick that hit Michaela squarely in the shin. The pain snapped her out of raw reaction, and she struck on the idea to rifle through her reticule to cover her gaffe.

Lady May twisted her body so that a seemingly impulsive touch on Lady Wisterling's arm blocked Michaela from view, giving her time to collect herself. "I simply adore your hair, Martha. Do you have a new maid doing it for you?"

"No, but I asked for something new this evening." She brushed aside the compliment and smiled, leaning around May to peer at Michaela. "I was delighted to know that your young protégée was to come tonight. You know she is always welcome. What a delightful girl she is. But it threw me off numbers, you see. An odd number at the dinner table is very bad luck."

"Oh, Martha, you are very silly to be superstitious."

"Perhaps I may be, but it unnerved me. Major Khoury was good enough to come upon a last-minute invitation, with the enticement of Mr. Hanvers, the Tory leader, being in attendance." Her narrow face grew narrower as she added slyly, "And no doubt you, Miss Standish. You know the major, I believe. Did not you two meet recently?"

"Yes, indeed we did," Michaela answered calmly, retrieving a handkerchief and making a production folding it. Lady Wisterling watched her with rabid eyes, greedy for some sign of her reaction.

"You even enticed the man to dance."

"One dance. It was rather unimportant, just a turn about the floor, that is all. It didn't signify, I assure you."

Lady Wisterling blinked, then smiled as if she saw something Michaela would have desperately wished to keep hidden. "Just so," she murmured.

Lady May intervened, leading Michaela to safety as she declared, "Oh, darling, look, it is my good friend Lord Carver. Come and let me present you to him."

With her back to Major Khoury, Michaela concentrated on the introductions. She felt him, however. As if she'd developed an allergic reaction to the touch of his gaze, tiny sensations traced a ghostly touch over her exposed flesh.

With her aunt's help, she was able to avoid him for the duration of the before-dinner gathering. She began to calculate that with any luck of the seating arrangement, she might be able to ignore him at dinner as well. If so, she could beg off immediately afterward and escape his nerve-rattling presence.

But her hostess had other plans. When dinner was announced, the pairings for the procession down to the first-floor dining room put her next to Major Khoury.

He regarded her with amusement as he extended his arm. "Miss Standish. I am delighted to see you again."

She had no choice but to take his arm. It felt like warm steel under the smooth wool of his tailcoat. She remembered how his hard, muscled body had felt pressed up against hers and a wash of scalding heat rose up and through her.

His eyes were rather intense, burning out of a stoic, blunt-featured face as he regarded her. "I hope it isn't my presence that has you undone."

She jerked her head around and glared at him. "Most certainly not. You do not disconcert me, I assure you, Major." As an afterthought, she asserted. "And I am not undone."

He leaned forward on his cane. "Not even when you think of the other night?"

"I assure you I do not think of the other night."

"But it was your first kiss, if you are to be believed. Surely that would be of some moment to a young lady."

She regarded him coolly, feeling very happy that he had so obligingly handed her an opportunity to cut him. "Oddly, however, it was not," she lied, and didn't even blanch.

He chuckled, as if he were pleased with her tart reply. It was then she realized that he had been baiting her.

They proceeded in line with others. Major Khoury's importance was denoted by their position near the front of the line. Elderly couples in front and behind were otherwise occupied, and for all of Lady Wisterling's interest in the possibility of a budding romance between them, no one else seemed to be paying them any mind.

"You are still angry with me," he said. "I wouldn't think you were the kind to hold a grudge. I must confess, it is surprisingly wounding to get the cut from you. Come, tell me. Weren't you pleased, even in the least part, to see me?"

"I was not. Moreover, we were invited here together tonight on Lady Wisterling's whim to gather gossip. I fear we have been duped in order to provide the evening's entertainment."

"I regret if you have been misled. I, however, was delighted to accept tonight's invitation to serve as your dinner partner."

She was astonished. "You knew I would be here?"

"Of course. Why else would I come? I am hardly the social sort, in case you haven't heard."

The look she sent him was pure disdain. "You didn't come tonight for me. You came for the Tory whip of the House of Commons. It is out that you have ambitions toward that end."

"Perhaps I do. I haven't made up my mind yet on that matter. As to Hanvers, he and I speak frequently enough. But his presence here did make for a convenient excuse to make an appearance without giving away my true motivation."

"Please, do not play me for a fool."

"Why will you not believe that I wanted to see you again?"

"Because it was a ridiculous and most likely inconsequential encounter, not to mention humiliating for the both of us. I would have thought you'd forgotten all about it by now, or done your best to try."

"Don't be modest." The graze of his eyes was close to insulting. It was hot, stripped of all civility. "You are not that easy to forget."

The words, the look made her skin warm. Eddies of excitement stirred slowly, as if time were speeding backwards and it was that moment when he had kissed her and she'd lost her will to him.

She was seated at his right, with Aunt May all the way down at the other end. She meant to give him the cut in no uncertain terms, so she sat staring straight ahead as the first course was brought out.

"May I inquire as to your headache?" he said as the soup was set before them by liveried servants.

"I have no headache. At least not yet." She cast him a most meaningful look. "I may develop one this evening, however."

"Not because of me, although I daresay it is what you meant." He held back a smile as he addressed his soup.

Unable to resist, she snapped, "Why did you think I had a headache?"

He lifted one large shoulder. "Today, at a tea at Lady Hannaberry's, I had the pleasure of making the acquaintance of your mother. She explained you were unable to attend because of being indisposed. A migraine, she told one and all."

"But I . . ." She stopped, checked his crafty eyes, and snapped her mouth shut.

Mother had mentioned the tea party. She had probably pled Michaela having a headache so as not to offend Lady Hannaberry's feelings when Michaela chose to visit Lady May instead of attending the party with her family.

"Are you a friend of Lady Hannaberry's?" she inquired.

"She was a good friend of my mother, and always invites me to her social gatherings."

Ah. Mother must have caught wind of the connection. Had she been happy to have Michaela not go to advance Delinda and Delilah's prospects with the major?

He shrugged. "I hardly ever accept, although I force myself to do so at least once each time I am in town. She has a very forgiving nature, however, and refuses to be slighted by all my other refusals."

"Why is it you never go?"

"The usual crowd possesses an average age of ninety," he replied, reaching for the tureen as the soup was served. "And all they ever wish is to speak of my heroic exploits, which is their term, not mine."

She wrestled with the realization that he had met her family.

"Miss Standish?"

"Hmmm?"

"You look disturbed," he said, picking up his wine. "Do you wish me to fetch you a vinaigrette?"

"No," she said, "I am fine. The soup . . . it is too hot."

He nodded sagely. His heavily hooded eyes missed nothing. She had the feeling he was privy to her very thoughts, or was that just the way of him, with that grating stare of his that seemed to slice through all artifice?

"Then," she said casually, "you had a chance to meet my sisters today."

There was a fraction of hesitation as he set his glass down again. "Yes. They are identical twins, and so everyone made a supreme fuss over them. But I am sure they are used to a great deal of attention."

"Everyone thinks they are adorable. And yet their personalities are quite different. Delilah is the quiet one, Delinda much more outgoing."

She was amazed with how glib she sounded, as if she weren't jealous and burning with curiosity. Did Major Khoury find the twins appealing? More appealing than she?

"Which one of them is possessed of wearing all of that . . ." He trailed off, his large, square hand making an expressive gesture around the shoulders. She took that to denote the trademark gaudiness of dress for which Delinda was known.

She informed him which twin he meant; then she asked, with a composed air of indifference, "They've been so anxious to meet you. It would be quite exciting for them if you had gotten the opportunity to speak with them for any length of time."

"We conversed briefly." His lips twitched. "We absolutely analyzed every aspect of the weather to the most minute detail. It was an utterly fascinating exercise."

She laughed despite herself.

"And their names . . . er, they are very . . . interesting," he continued. "You don't find many Delindas or Delilahs these days, let alone one of each."

"Twins are so fascinating; everyone says so. It comes from them being so alike. I could have guessed you were charmed."

"Oh, I would not say that." He hiked one brow and gave her what was perilously close to a conspiratorial look. "There was the one with all of that . . ." Again the hand movement.

"Delinda," she supplied.

"Ah. Just so. She talks a great deal."

"What did she talk about?"

"My war record. And you well know my lack of enthusiasm for that topic. So I ventured into a different topic, one far more to my interest. I asked about you."

She started, nearly dropping her spoon. "Why?"

He leaned closer. "Because that is a topic in which I am

interested. As a matter of fact, I made it my business to find out about you. But De . . . Delilah?"

"Delinda," she corrected miserably.

"Ah, Delinda . . . was more than happy to supply me with all kinds of information."

"No doubt. I don't suppose any of it recommended me favorably. I know fully well my family thinks me odd."

"Well, she did suggest you had odd ideas," he said, leaning back as the soup was cleared. He took his napkin from his lap and passed it over his chin, although there was no need. His hands, she noticed, were large and capable, with blunt-tipped fingers and trimmed nails. She thought of those hands holding a weapon, and the jarring thought of him wielding that weapon and ending someone's life occurred to her. They had done so, she knew.

His voice snapped her out of her strange musing. "But I didn't find liking books so strange, in fact."

"My sisters think it is peculiar that I read so much. And that I teach, although I don't have to earn an income."

"Yes, she mentioned your teaching post." He leaned forward on his elbows, folding his arms together. "What a curious thing, that. Most ladies would find it desirable to take their leisure if they are able, and advance their social standing."

"I find leisure, at least too much of it, makes me restless and bored. And I daresay Delinda also told you that I am of the radical notion to advance Miss More's efforts to educate the poor."

"Tell me why."

She wondered if he were baiting her again. In the end, however, she found she couldn't resist. "Because if the poor can read, they can avail themselves of the Bible. That was what Miss More was concerned with, but it is more useful than that. The education of the lower classes helps to elevate their thinking out of the traditions of foolish lore and superstition. These sorts of things keep them from seeking legal or medical aid. It will also help dispel the mistrust of their landlords. Do you know how many are duped into bad contracts because they don't know their letters?"

His eyes danced. "Their 'betters' will say that the status must be preserved for the public good, and those in the underclass are better left in ignorance, 'knowing their place,' as it were." She wasn't certain if he was mocking her, but he seemed very interested in the debate. And that, of course, was nearly as intoxicating as his kisses.

"Public good," she replied indignantly. "How is it in the *public* good? The good of those in power, more likely. It serves only the rich and titled to keep the poor ignorant. And it is exactly those kinds of fright tactics that impede progress. What I cannot understand is why they are so willing to allow themselves to be oppressed, even fight themselves against advances to bring about change. Some of the most stiff-necked resistance has come from the very people one is trying to help."

"Tradition," he said solemnly. "It is a powerful thing. Never underestimate the need for people to preserve their way of life. Change is to be feared for many, even if it promises improvement." He shifted, moving imperceptibly closer. "They are of a mentality that cannot comprehend true advancement in their situation, and they fear retribution that will land them worse off in the end."

"The devil you know is better than the devil you don't, you mean."

"Now," he drawled, "how did we get on the subject of devils?"

"I suppose," she countered just as dryly, "it is unavoidable when you are concerned."

He grinned. "I confess," he said softly, "to an occasional wicked thought or two where you are concerned. But that hardly makes me a devil. Rather, I plead the same affliction as would befall any sighted man in your presence."

"Strangely enough, many men have found it within their powers to resist me."

"What extraordinary men they must be. Unless . . ." He squinted, as if assessing her. "You frightened them off."

"Why thank you," she said with a sniff.

He laughed. A footman paused between them and offered a tray. He made selections for her.

When the servant had moved away, he said, "Now, are you going to tell me why you and your sisters are in this odd little battle that seems to involve me?"

She swallowed, and a piece of pheasant got caught in her throat. As she reached for her wine, he watched her dispassionately.

"Stalling will not help you."

"I am choking," she whispered, drinking.

"Shall I pound on your back?"

Her throat cleared. She blinked away the tears that had formed on her eyelashes and shook her head. "Thank you for your touching concern, but I am fine now."

"Good. Now. Tell me about this competition you have with your family. It was why you accosted me the other night, isn't it?"

"It is nothing you would understand. I don't wish to discuss it. And if you were any kind of gentleman, you would cease bringing up that most unpleasant subject."

He pursed his lips. "But I am no gentleman, not of any kind."

"Major," a man across the table said. "There are rumors you will run for the House of Commons in the next general election."

Khoury dragged his gaze from his dinner companion. "I may."

Once the table conversation was focused on Major Khoury, she was relieved to lapse into silence and observe.

She felt as if she were seeing him for the first time, and more strangely, that if she looked at him for a year, she would see every day a different, new facet of his complex nature. He was intense, but he was gentle. He was sensitive, and yet he was completely uncompromising in his honesty.

He caught her staring at him, and she looked away quickly.

He was like a damned bloodhound, watching, noting, filing it all away. She thought of the stories about him on the battlefield, tales of his shrewdness, and could believe them full well.

As soon as they rose from the table, Lady May came to

her side as the women moved off to the room where they had
gathered before dinner to await the men.

"Have a care to watch every reaction, every expression,"
May warned. "You are quite the center of attention."

It wasn't until after the musical portion of the evening that
Michaela found herself alone with Major Khoury again when
he cornered her in the parlor.

"I hope you have enjoyed the evening, Miss Standish."
His words were polite, but his gaze was as intent as a predator's. "I know I was not disappointed. It was quite worth all
of the trouble I arranged to have you invited."

"What?"

He was too proud of himself, shrugging casually and donning an insufferable smirk. "Why do you think you and your
aunt were given last-minute invitations?"

"Because there was an odd number . . ." She blinked, her
mind grasping the inanity of her own statement.

"You don't invite two when there is an odd number. It results in another odd number—"

"You don't have to explain it. I have a good enough grasp
of mathematics to understand. It is just that I didn't think
about it before. I . . ." Throwing up her hands, she looked at
him, amazed. "Why did you do such a thing?"

His answer was a throaty chuckle. "Because I knew if I
called on you that you wouldn't receive me. As you know, I
am a friend of Lady and Lord Wisterling's, and I asked her to
add a few names to her guest list as a favor to me. She was
happy to oblige."

"Why in the world would you wish to see me after that
terrible night?"

His brows rose together, and she caught a glimpse of a
vague disconcert in his expression. "Would you believe me if
I said I don't rightly know?"

She laughed harshly. "Hardly. You impress me as a man
who always knows precisely what he is about."

"Ah," he said, "it would seem so, would it not?"

He paused, inching much too close. "So tell me, did your
ruse work to make your mother jealous?"

"I didn't . . . that was wrong of me to speak of private

matters. I was confused that night, after everything that happened, I—"

"Answer the question, Michaela." He was impatient. "Unless you lack the courage to be honest with me."

She glared. "Very well. I acted impulsively on a hurt that was, I am sure, not meant to be the way I took it. It is unkind of you, Major, to bring it up."

"My soldiers call me Major. I would prefer you do not. My name is Adrian."

"That would be untoward."

He laughed, as if he'd predicted she'd say this. "Yes, it absolutely would be. Do it anyway."

"That is preposterous. I don't know why you bother so much with me, pressing our unfortunate acquaintance, when it is obvious that we do not suit," she said, glancing around to see who was watching.

"Because I still want you," he said bluntly.

She gaped at him, struck into speechlessness for a moment. When she recovered, she was vehement. "How dare you. You disrespect me gravely. Did I wrong you so greatly that you need to take such a revenge? People are watching, and if you don't already know it, we are already the object of a good amount of curiosity."

"Does it bother you so much what people think? You do not seem the type to trouble yourself on such a trivial sort of thing."

"I am certainly concerned about my reputation. Would you ruin it to amuse yourself, Major?"

"I said I wish you to call me—"

"All right," she hissed. "Adrian."

Saying his name did something powerful to the inner regions of her chest. He, too, was affected. His eyes flashed, and she sensed he was deeply satisfied.

"There," she said tightly, "you've won another battle."

"Then I shall be a graceful victor and take my spoils and leave. One more thing. Regarding your reputation, I would guard it with my life. If I've given you any other impression, then you must forgive me. I don't suppose the years among rough-mannered soldiers have done me much good for polite company. So, good evening to you."

He gave a short bow, his eyes locked with hers so that his gentle words seemed at war with the challenge of his gaze. She never knew how to take the man, she thought as he left her.

Michaela darted a look to her aunt, who didn't disguise her relief to see Major Khoury gone. Michaela assured herself she felt the same way.

Chapter 5

Samantha Khoury touched Adrian's face, tracing the wide, powerful jaw with a small finger. Brushing her hand away, Adrian smiled. "You are tickling me."

The little girl giggled and tried again. It became a game quickly enough, drawing the attention of the tall man by the window. He frowned in disapproval and said, "Set her down if she's bothering you."

"I didn't say she was bothering me," Adrian replied, capturing the child's hands and kissing her noisily on the cheek. Samantha shrieked in delight.

"Samantha, behave," her father said, turning away from the window and placing his hands on the back of the chair behind a large mahogany desk. "Go on, and find your mother. Tell her we will be ready for tea shortly."

The seven-year-old pouted. Crossing her arms, she tossed her brown ringlets and stuck out her bottom lip. "I do not wish to go. I wish Uncle Adrian to read to me."

"Not now, Samantha," Adrian said firmly, but his touch

was gentle as he smoothed her hair back from her face. "I have to speak to your father. Run along."

"I want to stay with you."

"See what happens when you indulge her?" Richard warned. He was taller than Adrian, his features more aristocratic, as if even when he was being formed in the womb, nature fixed him with a slender elegance befitting the heir of Granville. He was the marquess since their father's passing three years ago.

"I missed him horribly when he was in London," Samantha told her father petulantly, then turned her perfect miniature beauty, so like her mother's, on her uncle. "Don't go there again, Uncle Adrian. I know you have to find a wife, but I want you to marry me. I love you."

Adrian raised his brows. "That is quite an honor. But you shall not be ready to be married for many years."

She pressed closer, using instinctive charm to disarm him. "You can wait for me, can't you?"

"But by the time you are grown, I shall be old and feeble, and you won't want me."

She frowned, stubbornly sticking out her bottom lip again. "If I can't have you, I don't want to marry."

"Neither do I," Adrian said dryly, shifting his gaze to his elder brother.

Richard came around the desk, shooing his daughter. "Go now. You will marry a prince when your time comes, and your uncle will be glad if you remember to throw him a kiss on your wedding day. Now go to your mother, or I will tell her you were being naughty."

As the little girl hopped down off of her uncle's lap and finally obeyed, albeit with a toss of her head that would make any Khoury proud, Richard said, "She needs a firmer hand, but she is so pretty a thing, I fear I am powerless against her. Now the boys, I could be stern with. Many is the time I turned Oliver or Richard over my knee and applied the switch. Can't say I enjoyed it, but I knew it had to be done. But her—she is a terror and getting worse every day, and I only moon at her like some milksop."

Adrian chose his words very carefully. "Her charm is

her mother's, but her stubbornness can only come from you."

Richard didn't notice the subtle tension in Adrian's voice at the mention of his wife; he never did. He didn't know, of course, of the history that lay there between Frances and Adrian. They had made certain he didn't.

"You make it worse. You encourage her dreadfully."

"It is an uncle's right to spoil his niece."

"So you claim," Richard replied. "Now, don't keep me in suspense. Did you get a chance to speak to Glenarvon while in London?"

"I met with an undersecretary, Christopher Bishop. Do you know him?"

"No. But if the Chancellor of the Exchequer recommended him, I trust he is good. Well, do not keep me in suspense. What did he say?"

"He said they would back me. And he was full of advice."

"You've made up your mind, then? You are going to run in the general election. Adrian, I am pleased! Reform is the future. You know you wish to be a part of that."

Did he? He couldn't muster the same enthusiasm he had once felt. The realities of a political career had proven much different than the ideals with which he'd begun.

"I don't know if political life is right for me." He held up a hand at Richard's protests. "For you, it is natural. You were bred to it, arguably even born to it. It is in your nature. But I can't pander to the power brokers. You know that sort of thing is against my nature. And I find the posturing for public consumption unbearable. I hate the attention."

"I am relegated to the House of Lords, and you know that is not where the power is. It is hardly even relevant any longer. You, in the House of Commons, will have a chance to affect the country's course more than I. And I know your desire to effect change is a cause you feel deeply."

That much was true. Obligation tore at him, and he sighed. Perhaps he should resign himself to a life of politics. It certainly seemed an obvious action.

Richard cocked his head. "And as for your war record, you cannot argue that your good reputation serves you in this. My God, the campaign isn't even begun, and already your name is praised." His eyes glazed over, as they often did as he mused about the possibilities for the future. "I tell you, Adrian, it is as near a sure thing as I've known. And think of it. We two brothers, each in Parliament, a representative in both Lords and Commons. Now, at this very vital juncture in history, when the country is poised to bring about an era of reform, the Khourys shall be a major force in government. Father would be most pleased."

Far removed from Richard's ambition, Adrian shrugged casually. "Father never had much use for me, so I doubt he would be impressed by anything I've done. Not that it matters. I never thought much of him, either."

Richard shook his head. "Father was a political animal, not a family man. That was his gift and his fault. Surely it isn't for contempt of him that you hesitate to make a firm commitment to the election."

Adrian rose, walking to the window. The gardens that formed the formal park framing the drive and circular carriage-way in front of the house were well-tended and greening with the onset of spring. The warm weather was already making an appearance, a day here and a day there.

As a boy, those mild days, the first to break the long, confining days of winter, had been like holidays. He and his brothers had run on those lawns and played hide-and-seek in the hedges, and ridden their ponies like convicts let loose from prison.

And beyond the lawn were the woods, where he had fallen in love. He turned away, giving his back to the crisp breeze blowing in. It brought a fine rise of gooseflesh along the back of his neck.

"I don't like what is required of me to enter public service."

Richard nodded sagely. "Ah. If you are going to accomplish anything in government, you must be connected to the right men, the ones who have a hold on power, and you never did care for being told what to do. I thought it the supreme irony that you joined the military." He folded his arms and considered his broader, more muscular brother. "You were a brilliant tactician, Adrian. It brought you favor, even saved your hide on an occasion or two. But there is no Wellington to intervene for you now."

Scowling, Adrian replied heatedly. "It is not insubordination to point out the incompetence of your superiors. I merely advocated for good men who were being used as pawns by a few bad officers whose family influence and money had bought them authority over better men. I fought that inane process, yes, and if it got my grand 'legend' tarnished, then so be it."

"Well, if Glenarvon isn't worried about it, then let's not belabor the matter. He thinks it actually enhances the mystique, and he knows the game politic better than anyone. I don't know why we are arguing about it in the first place. Whenever your military years are mentioned, you become so—"

"Don't say it," Adrian growled.

Richard grinned. "Of course. You are not sensitive at all. You are a man devoid of emotion in the extreme. There, does that please you?" He waved away the argument and began to pace. "Tell me more of your meeting with this Mr. Bishop. There are issues besides the auspice of reform that will figure prominently in the election. Did Glenarvon's man suggest any that we might begin to put forth to generate debate?"

"What do you think of the idea of education for the poor?" Adrian asked suddenly. "I was recently introduced to a most persuasive argument on the topic. The idea is that the more educated the poor are, the better able they will be to help themselves. I thought it an intriguing concept."

Richard was startled. "Good God, Adrian, you cannot be serious. You would never get the endorsement of the party. Reform is one thing—and that is difficult enough—but this kind of radical thinking would put you out of it for good."

"If people are afraid of change, how will we make any progress?" Adrian countered.

"You always were the one to rush in when measured steps are better. I hope this isn't some rising sentiment in town, because I can tell you that out here in the counties, such a preposterous vision will seal your political demise."

"It is not a popular political view." He brushed his two fingers over his top lip, hiding a slight smile that wouldn't be dispelled. "An acquaintance of mine is attempting to establish a Sunday school. She spoke most persuasively."

The recollection of Michaela Standish's face flushed with emotion as she heatedly proposed her progressive ideas brought his temperature up. He crooked his forefinger in his cravat and worked the knot loose to ease the heat.

"Ah. A woman's heart is a soft thing." Richard gave a dismissive grunt, as if the matter were settled on that fact alone. "Sentimental females who've grown fat and bored like to have things like helping the poor to make them feel important. It is all well and good. It all serves a purpose, I suppose, but such platitudes have their limits. Let her bake scones and collect money, but a Sunday school . . . it will never happen."

"You don't know this particular lady," Adrian murmured.

"What did you say? I didn't hear you."

"Nothing. I meant to tell you that Bishop said he thought Harris would be my opposition."

"Good God, the man is a bull. He will be ruthless." Richard paced, clearly set back by the news. "It will be a fight, indeed. But the course of change never did run smooth."

"Richard, a philistine like yourself should never attempt to quote Shakespeare. You've botched it." Adrian went to the fire and stoked the coals. "The correct saying is that the course of true love never did run smooth."

"True love?" Richard frowned. "Are you certain? What rubbish. It has nothing to do with what we are about."

Adrian stared musingly into the fire.

Richard came up behind him, and stood for a moment before broaching the subject Adrian had most been dreading.

"Have you given any thought to a wife?"

Adrian bolted upright. "Devil take it, not this again."

"Didn't Bishop bring it up? Glenarvon believes it impossible for a man to get elected without a family."

Adrian made an impatient sound.

"Every man marries, Adrian. But the man who is headed toward national leadership must marry *rightly*."

"I have no wish to marry. You hounded me about this before, and I promised to go to London and look at the debs, which I did, and I found them unacceptable."

Richard hesitated. "I wasn't going to mention this. . . . I know you are bullish about your privacy, but a friend mentioned in a letter I received just yesterday that you had danced recently with a young lady. It caused something of a stir."

"Miss Standish? Don't be ridiculous."

"Why do you look cross? Am I misinformed?"

"No," Adrian replied. "You are not. But it was of no import."

"I am glad to hear it. I have been made aware of speculation that she is Woolrich's by-blow. That would be a disastrous association for you."

"That she is Woolrich's daughter is glaringly evident in her appearance. She is the image of the man. But the polite society has accepted her. Lady May Hayworth, her aunt, is well-established ton, and not many would stand in contention with her."

Richard sighed. "You should have nabbed the Widow Pearson when you had the chance. I tried to persuade you, but you would have none of her. It would have been ideal, a ready-made family. Then we wouldn't have any worries now."

"Richard, the woman was fairly a dwarf."

"She was petite."

But Adrian liked his women tall and dark, with thick, lustrous hair and eyes that met his with a lively twinkle. He groused, "As for the ready-made-family aspect, your Samantha would never have forgiven me if I brought more boys into the Khoury fold."

Richard gave a grudging nod to accede the logic of Adrian's argument. "You have to admit she was convenient, though."

"She had the intellect of a flea." Adrian held up his hand, signaling an end to the conversation. "We are not going to discuss this any further. I get the message quite clearly. Glenarvon, the master in this realm, has deemed I must marry."

Clearly not liking the tone, Richard scowled. "Do not let your repulsion to authority defeat you here. You have to admit the wisdom in the argument for marriage. He knows the electorate well, and he has made and broken powerful men before."

Adrian paused, then said, "I do. He is right. I am only reluctant because . . ."

Because once he'd thought to marry for love. And then he'd thought he'd die for love. Now he was to live and marry without it.

Ah, hell, he'd been a foolish boy, after all, so what did it matter now? He didn't know why he rebelled so strongly against the idea of taking a wife. He hoped he wasn't entertaining any ridiculous notions after all of these years. One would think the same man couldn't be so foolish to dream the impossible twice.

Giving Richard an arch look, he replied, "I know what is at stake, and I know what is required of me. I will find a wife, a suitable, biddable wife to credit me in my political life." He more fell backwards into a chair than sat and added, "But in my own time. And I don't have to like it."

Richard spread his hands. "I am only trying to help."

Adrian glared at his brother, then caught himself and checked the undercurrent of tension coursing through him. Why was he so agitated?

Richard was only speaking the truth. However, his relationship with his eldest brother was a complex one.

There was love there, a strong and enduring family bond forged in shared childhood. It had to be strong to withstand the other, darker emotions that had strained the relationship since Richard had married the woman Adrian loved. He had hated Richard once for that, another guilt for which he suffered, until he'd accepted that his brother had not been the one to blame.

Richard spoke gently. "I want what you want, Adrian. The world has to change. You feel a duty to progress, as do I. We can be on the forefront of a great era. You more than I, for the House of Commons is coming into its own as the arm of the people."

Adrian gave a huff of a laugh. He slid his fingers into his hair. "Yes, I am sure I can see to making the world just as it should be."

Richard took a step forward, placing a hand on his brother's shoulder. Although he was the elder by only three years, he had always deferred to his stronger-willed, physically more imposing younger brother.

"You mock, but you do yourself a disservice. You are a

hero, as great a man as I've known, and I have great faith in you."

"The stories about me are exaggerated."

Richard looked at him for a long time. "You forget I know you best. I don't know what happened to you at Quatre Bras, for you will not speak of it, but I know it eats at you. And it drives you. If I pester you on account of the less glorious aspects of politics, it is because I respect what you are doing, and I want you to succeed."

The words did not soothe as they intended. They came perilously close to water best left becalmed. "Careful," Adrian said calmly. "Do not push me."

Richard paused, weighing the wisdom of continuing the conversation or tactical retreat. He walked back to his desk and sat. "When do you return to your home?"

"I will ride back after tea. I promised Samantha."

"Let us hope that appeases her. She will be quite put out with you for not staying the night. Not to mention I had hoped to continue talking with you. Frances said she wished to see you."

It was out of the question that he would spend the night under this roof, but Adrian could hardly say so. "I must be home, then back to London, probably by the weekend."

"You just arrived from town. What calls you back there?"

Adrian hardly knew how to answer him.

In the garden of the Standish house, Michaela walked out into the sun. Albert heard her and sat back on his heels with a hearty smile. He performed many duties for the Standish household, but gardening was his passion.

"There's Miss Michaela," he said, his eyes checking quickly to make certain they were alone. He didn't speak to her, especially so familiarly, when anyone else was about. "I've got plants that need tending, and you know I look for you when it comes time for the garden."

She laughed at their old joke. As a child, Michaela had felt a supreme sense of importance at being his "helper."

She said, "Thinning the perennials?"

"It's a never-ending chore's what it is."

"The hostas again?"

"They ain't even the half of it, what with the columbine growing like some wild weed."

"It's pretty, though." She rose and began pinching off the dead blossoms from the annuals blooming amid the greenery. "They look like they need water."

"And some food, too, if I ever get to it today. I swear, your mum has me running like I'm Cinderella's footman, I swear it. Going to this shop to pick up one thing, then to the other shop for another, an' all the while me beauties is wasting away."

"I know how you love the garden." She sighed, leaning back on her hands. Never had she had to bother with conventions with Albert. Here in this garden, her private retreat—Delinda and Delilah would never be caught dead out of doors where the sun might mar their pasty complexions—she could count on being alone among the well-tended shrubs and flowering plants and the comfortable companionship of Albert.

"Aye, 'tis true. In Cornwall, we had lovely gardens, all of us. Didn't matter how small it was, it was always a source of pride."

"Oh, no, not another treatise on the superiority on life below the Tamar."

He grinned. "Laugh at me, missy, go right ahead, and it'll be me laughing last when you realize that I'm in the right of it. One day, you'll go down toward Land's End, and you'll see for yourself the beauty and majesty of the Cornish coast."

She loved the music of the man's accent, the hard *r*s, the rough cadence that was symbolic of simplicity and hominess and affection to Michaela's mind. He'd been with the Standishes since as far back as she could remember.

He had never returned to Cornwall for a visit in all of that time, yet he'd spoken warmly of his home and always with such longing that she had asked him once why he didn't go back if he loved it so much. He had gotten misty-eyed and shrugged his big shoulders and said simply, "Can't."

She had been selfishly grateful for his mysterious exile, for his presence in the household was comforting to her.

"I heard you met the famous Major Khoury," Albert said

as he squinted at some overgrown daisies. "Heard a lot of fuss. Miss Delinda is a mite put out about it, I'd say."

She knelt down in the dirt beside him and examined the plant. "Look at this blousy thing. It really needs to be staked. See how limp it is."

"I've got the cure for it, an' it ain't staking," Albert cried indignantly and began rooting in his box—a converted toolbox in which he carried his gardening supplies. "And don't think I'm feeble in the head. If you're not going to answer me about that major, then tell me to take a leap into the Thames. Ah, now, I forgot, ladies ain't supposed to say such things, and that's what you are now. It's the delicate approach you'll be taking, being all fancy and such these days."

"I'm not," she protested. "I'm the same as I always was."

"Look at you. You look like a fine lady. Ah, girl, it does me heart good to see you done up fine. It's what you were meant for. What am I thinking? Get out of the dirt before you ruin your dress."

"It will brush off." She sifted the rich soil in her hand. "I miss the feel of the earth. I think I was meant to be a farmer."

"Well, you better get used to the feel of soft kid and fine silk, you know. 'Tis an earl's daughter you are. And don't look shocked that I'd know it. Not much happens around here that I don't get wind of sooner or later."

She didn't mind him knowing her parentage. "I look just like him. I've seen his portrait."

"Do you now? Well, it explains a good bit. I could never figure why your mother did as she did. She was harsh on you, she was. And look at them girls, what with all they have—they're as sour as lemons the both of them. You, now . . . you always bring the sunshine, I swear."

He put down his spade and came over to sit by her on the bench. "I tell you something. I like it when I see you with that fancy Lady May. It makes me laugh till I cry, I swear—her with her pink and feathers and you, tall and straight and proud."

"Albert, you've always been such a good friend. And you always take my side." They laughed together. "But Mother isn't a complete monster, you know. I cannot say I was ill-treated. I received the same things for my birthday as she gave to them, and at Christmas, I had exactly the same number of presents. I had dresses and dolls the same as the twins, and freedom enough to pursue my interests, eccentric though they may have been regarded. I can hardly plead an orphan's plight."

"Right you are," he replied. "You had a good home, if it weren't exactly perfect."

"Perhaps if I'd been less defiant, it would have been easier for me. But somehow I could never allow a word to pass unchallenged. I couldn't seem to help myself."

He was quiet for a long time. When he spoke, his voice came soft. "Aye, I never saw her mistreat you. Just . . . well, I got this one time stuck in my craw. I remember once, about oh, five years ago or so, I was working on the rosebushes outside the parlor. The damnable things were giving me a fit, I can tell you." His face twisted in consternation. "I couldn't get them pruned right. The doors were open, those Frenchy doors your mother had put in, and I wasn't paying no mind to what was goin' on, just cutting those cursed roses and slicing up me hands.

"Then I caught what she was saying. She was talking to you about marriage. And I remember as clear as day you saying, brave as can be, that you were waiting to fall in love."

Michaela nodded. She, too, remembered the talk.

"I remember how hot she was. She was having none of it, and she told you that love was a waste of time."

What her mother had said, exactly, was that love never amounted to anything. She had said it in such a sad and emphatic tone that the words, the mood of that conversation had stayed with Michaela.

Knowing now that Mother had once succumbed to the profuse charms of Woolrich, Michaela had to wonder if she had spoken from a broken heart.

"I was miffed, I was, thinking there were no cause for such words. But then you never seemed to mind your mum much. Except . . . well, you never did marry. I wondered many a time if you took her advice and gave up on your dream. A person's got to have dreams."

Yes, she had them, but she held them close to her heart, so close not even Albert would hear of them. She had always wanted a great love and everything that went with it. Children, laughter, long talks, and passion. And fights and glorious making up and dreamy days just being together, not even speaking, just . . . being.

Albert turned to look at her, and she gave him a smile in order to reassure him that she was quite content, even if it was a lie. Her secret dreams would remain hers alone.

"Sometimes I think your mum was afraid." He said it softly, his grizzled face gentled with emotion.

She was taken aback. "Afraid?"

"Of you, girl. Of you being so different and so strong-willed. Ah, I don't know. But I know your mother loves you, but it's a complicated sort of love."

On an impulse, she reached out and covered his gnarled, dirt-smudged hand with her own. She'd never done that before. She'd never touched Albert, nor he her. It was nice, though. He took her hand tightly in his own, and she felt comforted.

"She's different since you been staying at that Lady May's so much. Your mum don't seem to have much patience with them girls of hers anymore. She's had it with Delinda crying over Major Khoury—he loves me, he loves me not and all that bosh."

"She thinks Major Khoury is in love with her?"

"On Tuesdays and Thursdays. On Monday, Wednesday, and Friday she is certain he is smitten with you. And please don't insult me again by pretending you didn't hear me," he added with a lift of his brows. "Shame take you for trying that trick on me like I'm some old man loose in the brain."

"Albert, it isn't what you are thinking. It's . . ."

What? She had no words.

"Complicated," she finished and prepared for Albert's reaction.

Instead of the barrage of questions and challenges she expected, she received a slow look of speculation from the man. "Is it indeed? Well, my girl, that's an interesting thing to know." He nodded, chuckling as he rose and gathered his gardening tools.

"It's complicated," he muttered gleefully.

Chapter 6

Being a princess had its moments of pleasure, but there were others that were a deadly bore. Take this evening, for instance. Michaela might have liked to stay home and enjoy a book and giving her poor feet a rest from the punishing slippers that were in fashion but not practical for anything. Instead, she entered Lady Albright's spacious town house in Belgravia, an opulent residence made more so for tonight's soiree. There would be music and dancing and sumptuous feasting, which was wonderful, of course, except that the past three weeks had been dizzyingly packed with similar evenings of music and dance and sumptuous feasting.

"You aren't pining are you?" Aunt May asked, noticing her mood as she fussily adjusted a bit of lace on Michaela's bodice as they entered.

Mother snapped, "Stop fussing. You look fine." She said it to Michaela, but it was a curt message to Lady May. Two dogs wrestling over a bone.

"No," Michaela protested. "Of course I'm not pining. I suppose I'm just a bit tired."

There was no point in asking her observant aunt just who she was supposed to be pining for.

She *was* tired, it was true enough. The demands of the bon ton were many, most of them centered on nothing more important than appearances, she had found, and grasping at ever higher levels of social significance. Her sisters seemed to love it, but she . . . she wasn't bored, not exactly.

A real princess, she supposed, would have loved the endless fittings and hours at her *grande toilette*. And Michaela did, sometimes. But she was used to doing what pleased her, when it pleased her. She'd had more freedom when she'd had less money, and that just didn't seem right.

If it weren't for Lady May's charm and warmth, she might have actually been discontent. Oh, it was difficult not to love the woman; and May was so full of excitement over doing all of this for her, Michaela could be distracted from her restlessness. However, after the novelty of wearing gorgeous clothes for once in her life had eased, she couldn't say she cared for dressing formally every single day and adhering to a schedule of social demands that left less and less time for her own interests.

She was lonely for her old life, her old friends and activities. But she was certainly *not* pining.

Lady Albright leaned forward. "Why, isn't that Major Khoury coming in just now?"

Michaela whirled and saw Adrian just entering the room.

"Whatever is he doing here?" Lady May said, speaking the same thought that pounded in Michaela's head.

Lady Albright was sly. "I never thought he'd accept my invitation. How glad I am that he's decided to honor us."

Another woman drew up to them, holding up a lorgnette to get a better look. "I heard he is making the social rounds. He has his eye on a Parliamentary seat. He had better get himself married if he wants to win a general election."

Forcing herself to remain perfectly still, Michaela watched Major Khoury bow to a cluster of older men. Lord Appleton, a grizzled, robust man, slapped Adrian on the back fondly. As Adrian addressed him, he turned his head, his eyes unerringly finding her as if he'd been aware of her all along.

The air went out of the room. The pulse in her temple throbbed as their gazes held.

"Parliament, you say? I knew there had to be some explanation for his sudden appearance in London. After all, ever since Waterloo, he's been in seclusion."

"He's been recovering," a booming voice, which could only belong to the Baroness Schmidt, the wife of a visiting diplomat, sounded crossly. "He still has the limp. See him."

"It's rather dashing."

"I heard he had the melancholy."

The baroness's eyes flared wide open. "Of course he had the melancholy, you simple soul. He was at the most brutal battle of our time, and he was not only commander of many men who died on that field of honor, but he himself was wounded. A proud man does not take those things lightly and come home to traipse blithely among the bon ton."

"Oh, but he did just that," Lady Albright said, turning to Michaela. "He danced with you, didn't he, dear? As I heard it, he took to the floor, cane and all."

Michaela's skin felt heavy, hot, tingling. She felt again the weight of stares.

"Yes," Michaela answered, grateful that her voice was steady and strong, giving away none of the tumult inside her. Why did she have to lose such complete control of herself whenever he was about? She wanted to be cool, aloof, impenetrable. Most of all, she wanted none of these women to know how deeply she was affected by Adrian's presence. "But it was only a dance."

"Only a dance!" Twitters all around, and Baroness Schmidt smiled enigmatically.

Delinda made a sound that was suspiciously akin to a snort. Her mother glared at her. She whirled on her heel and stalked away.

Lady Albright's gaze was sly. "The major is elusive, and of course, it makes him all the more interesting. Oh, Major," Lady Albright called out suddenly, waving a gloved hand in the air. Aside to the other women, she hissed, "He is looking this way," then louder, to Adrian, she preened, "See, here is young Miss Standish."

If she could have turned to stone, if there was a way to melt right there into the seat, Michaela would have rescued herself from the humiliating sight of Adrian lifting his brow in her direction. He must think she'd put the ladies up to it!

He excused himself from the men and began toward them. The slight dip in his stride seemed exaggerated. Or did she only imagine the moments of his approach were drawn out, time slowed by her own mortification?

"Good evening, ladies." He bowed, his eyes darting to Michaela, and he inclined his head. "Your servant."

Michaela froze, forgetting everything about what a lady would do in this situation. It had been weeks since she'd last seen him, and in that time she'd spent untold hours mulling over their two meetings. Now that he was here before her, she was too stunned to recall any of the magnificently clever remarks she'd practiced.

She caught Lady May's expectant eye, and her back shot into a straight line. Grace and composure at all costs. And most of all, cool control—that was what was required. She said, "Good evening. How lovely to see you again."

"I *thought* you two had met," Lady Albright crowed.

"Indeed we did," he said. His gloved hand touched hers. His fingers moved in a caress that got the better of her and had her snapping her hand away. "I would never forget it, for it was indeed a memorable experience."

The ladies rotated their heads, exchanging looks among themselves to acknowledge this admission.

He continued, his honeyed voice grating across her taut nerves. "Our meeting that night is emblazoned in my brain for many reasons. Can I hope it has survived in your memory as well, Miss Standish?"

She hoped she didn't color. He was playing the audience, and at her expense.

Grace and composure.

"Vaguely," she sighed. "It was, after all, Major, only a dance, and there have been so many this season."

"Ah. The fickle female heart." His eyes narrowed fractionally, and he said, "I am certain I cannot hope to remain of import when you must have so many admirers. I thought to get some punch. Would you care for refreshment, Miss Standish? I would be happy to escort you."

The abrupt invitation was as artless as it was commanding. Michaela was aware of the wave of reaction around her as the ladies took this in. "No, thank you."

"Ah," he said, as if this were perfectly agreeable to him. He shrugged. "Then we can reminisce more on that first evening of our meeting right here, then. Now, I can understand that the dance was of no significance to you. As you say, there have no doubt been many, but there was the interesting misunderstanding following the dance that assuredly stayed in your memory—"

"I meant yes, I would like punch. I said no because I thought you were asking if I'd *had* a punch. I haven't. But I'd like some. Very much."

He grinned, his message sent and received. Drat the man and his insufferable arrogance.

"Michaela, I—oh! Hello Major Khoury!" Delinda's voice interrupted. She was slightly out of breath, most likely from having hurried over when she spied him. Behind her, a phalanx of her friends peered over her shoulder. "I didn't see you. Do you remember me?"

He bowed, "Indeed, Miss Standish, I recollect our having met. Will you excuse me?"

Taking Michaela's arm, he strode past the openmouthed, enraged girl, paying no mind to the flash of pure resentment she sent to their backs.

Michaela kept her smile fixed. "Your high-handedness is most unappreciated. And your humor." She gave him a lofty once-over. "Such as it is."

"Now how can you expect me to behave myself when you ignore me?"

His eyes were watchful of the women staring after them, and he smiled, forcing them to look away or appear gauche by staring. When they rounded a corner, he executed a maneuver so swift, Michaela didn't know what happened. She found herself with the wall at her back and his big body close enough to almost touch her.

He grinned, and now spoke low, with an intimate drawl

that stirred answering tremors from inside her breast. "And I don't know why you pretend you don't like it when you see me. Did you know your entire face glows with color, and your eyes snap green fire?"

Such poetry from this rough man struck her to silence.

His eyes slid like a caress over her features. "You have gypsy eyes," he murmured. "They are not docile or polite, not in the least. They give away every mood."

Her heart hammered. He leaned forward slightly, just the smallest encroachment, but she was immediately overwhelmed.

"And your mouth is a temptation. Your lips are cherry-red, as if you've just been kissed. I will tell you a secret about your mouth. It is absolutely—"

He broke off. Michaela almost shouted in frustration. What had he been about to say about her mouth? It was absolutely . . . what?

He stepped away. She felt the rush of cool air over her skin at the absence of his warmth, and she wanted to reach for him to bring him back to her.

A man appeared. "Miss Standish?" he said.

She swallowed, collecting herself for a moment before turning around. She recognized Lord George Halliwell, one of the men whom she'd met at a previous rout. His appearance at her side reminded her that she had promised a dance to him tonight. "Oh, Lord George," she said.

He beamed. "I was hoping for a dance this evening, if you've one free."

Placing a hand on his arm—an unforgivably forward gesture meant to aggravate Adrian, which, judging from the flash of fire in his eyes, it did—she bestowed an apologetic smile toward him and said, "Of course I do. I happen to be free right now."

His face lit. "Then may I have the honor?"

"Indeed, the honor is mine. Excuse us, Major."

She received little satisfaction for her ploy. Adrian merely executed a smart bow, giving her a glittering look that held a promise. His words confirmed this. "I look forward to our next meeting with a great deal of anticipation."

She inclined her head regally, covering the shiver. As she went to the dance floor with Lord George, she thought about that promise. If this was a battle of sorts—a battle of wills— then he was the more experienced, being a man used to battle. He was soldier. But she had a will of her own, and it was no trivial thing.

The day went to her, as it happened, for when she came off the parquet, she could not find him. Lady Albright was crushed, reporting that he had left and sending Michaela an accusing stare, suspecting she had had something to do with his preemptory departure.

Almost immediately the restlessness returned. The flash of excitement, which had seemed to fill her body with a snapping tension when Adrian had been present, was gone, leaving nothing of interest to divert her for the evening. She danced a few more times, made conversation with people who had nothing to say. Toward midnight, she overheard a dashing young man, standing in a circle surrounded by admiring men and fluttering females, opining in crisp nasal tones on the dangerous ideas of reform.

"And if the age of the climbing boy is raised, then who will clean the flues? And if the flues are left, then we shall all perish in fire, or freeze for fear of burning wood in the grate."

She picked a fight with the pompous fool just to keep herself from boredom, and when she had reduced him to sputtering indignation, she felt moderately satisfied. She pled a headache, which forced her aunt to send her home.

In the carriage, she was dogged by one thought. It wouldn't leave her, try as she might to master the direction of her mind. It was this:

What had Adrian been about to say about her mouth?

A few evenings later at Lady May's Park Lane home, her aunt mentioned that the gossips had latched onto the two of them as an item of interest. May seemed to be less pleased about it than was Michaela.

"I think it a mistake to limit yourself to one man so early

in the season," she warned as she sat overseeing the packing of her clothing. She was headed out to Turnbridge Wells for an off-season plunder of the springs there. A few of her friends made it their habit every year.

Watching the gorgeous clothing and finely made undergarments and accessories packed in the trunks, Michaela said wistfully, "I wish I was going with you."

May's face instantly registered her displeasure. Dorothy had refused permission for Michaela to accompany May on this trip. No amount of protesting from Michaela could change her mind.

"Cheer up, darling," Lady May told her. She sprang up from her chair and held out her hand to inspect a particular gown. "No, Jeannette, not this one. Fetch the blue velvet with the deep rose . . . yes, that one. I'll bring that instead. Now," she said, whirling to Michaela, "You feel denied, I know, and I do as well. I would love to have you with me. More so with this dreadful major hounding about you all the time. I tell you, I have no liking for him, Michaela. He is an intense man, a man with violence in his past. Men like that are dangerous." She made a face, her body shaking off a delicate shiver.

Michaela didn't voice the protests that sprang to mind in defense of Adrian. Lady May didn't know that he was kind, for example, and that he could be amusing, when he wasn't being exasperating and outrageous. And he was deeply engaging and fair-minded. He liked her ideas on the school, and there was a matching interest in helping the less fortunate, as well.

Instead of making her case, she simply said, "He is a man not to be trifled with, but I cannot say I think he is dangerous."

She had no fear that he would do her harm. She remembered his assurances about her reputation, and although he had taken wicked liberties with her, he had been meticulously scrupulous to avoid discovery.

But there was a deeper, more vague threat in him, something impossible to describe. Something that touched her where she was most vulnerable. As a woman, she had been awakened for the first time by his maleness, and it was a powerful tonic.

"But all this serious talk. You are young, yet!" May declared. "This is your first season, and it's only just begun. When your mother has tired of this tug-of-war with you, I will take you with me, and we will travel. Of course, Major Khoury is quite dashing, and his attentions a coup for you, him being so desirable in that devastating way some women find attractive. But he is but one fascinating man among many the world holds."

In the face of Aunt May's worldly attitude, she offered a provincial shrug. Not for the world would she admit her feelings and seem the fool. "I only dallied with him to make Mother angry. It wasn't as if it were some *grande passion*, or any such thing. *She* wanted him for Delinda, so I went for him."

Lady May pressed her lips together and said nothing, but her eyes were clear and beautiful, filled with understanding. "I know. So much misunderstanding there . . ." She trailed off and sighed. "But you mustn't take it too far. Major Khoury is not for you, darling. There is much you do not know about the world, of what can go wrong between men and women." She paused, and her lovely features creased as a shadow fell over them. "And a woman must choose her romantic interests wisely."

Michaela was silent, which Lady May took to be agreement and cheered. "Ah, but of course you cannot be thinking of any man seriously, you have so much to make up for all the years you were not able to enjoy the privileges that came with your birthright. We are being silly, aren't we, worrying about such things? Next week, you will meet a duke or a young viscount and, la, off you will be, swept away again with no more thought to this major."

As much as she missed her aunt in the ensuing days, Michaela was not saddened to be left to her own devices. She kept busy with books and resuming some of her old interests.

This afternoon she headed to the school where she volunteered. The day held only the simple pleasure of reading to the girls and taking them through a drill or two while their teacher caught up on some of her papers.

Her charity work with the school for the poor had led her to working in tandem with some like-minded instructors. Friendships had formed, and it pleased her to help them from time to time. After the demands of the polite world, it seemed like such uncomplicated bliss.

The girls were excited to see her. The school was a well-established educational facility for girls from good middle-class homes. Their education included reading the Bible, writing letters, needlework, and arithmetic, which they would need to run their own households someday.

"Which story would you like to hear?" she began once the teacher had gathered her things and left her alone with the class. "Elizabeth, you may choose a book from the shelf."

The story she chose was *The Little Mermaid*. It was one of Michaela's favorites. It had seemed to her that the little mermaid was silly, wanting to be human when she had such a splendid life in the sea, but she understood that feeling of not belonging where you are supposed to belong. She supposed the tear that came to her eye at the end was pure self-indulgence and not a very good comment on the fortitude of her own character. Really, she didn't used to be such a sentimental mess.

"That was fun," said little Martha, the youngest of the children. She was only six and had the most expressive eyes. "Please read another. I like it when you read. Miss Bonsby just reads it regular, but you do the voices and make it scary and silly and everything. It's like it's real."

The other children chimed in with their own sweet pleas.

And then another voice, a male voice, echoed the sentiment in resounding tones that at once silenced all the others. "Yes. Read another. You have a charming way with a story."

He was standing by the door, and in the throbbing silence, he seemed larger than life. Dressed informally, he wore a coat of fawn-colored wool and black breeches tucked into shiny Hessians. His cravat wasn't tied fussily. A simple knot, rather looser than was the popular style, was fashioned around his neck. Resting between his hip and his arm was a black felt hat, a plain one. He appeared casual and amused, as if enjoying every moment of her astonishment.

"I . . ." She stood, forgetting the book on her lap and letting it fall to the floor. "What—?"

"Am I doing here? I knew this was a passion of yours. You'd mentioned it, you'll remember. I was passing by and thought I'd ask after you, and I was in luck." He gave her a mocking look. "Here you are."

She didn't believe him. His finding her was far more calculated than that; she could see it in the crafty dance of his eyes.

Recovering, she said, "Ah, children, this is—"

"A friend," he supplied quickly, entering the room with three long strides, his cane swinging expertly to aid in his progress. He smiled at the bewildered class. "An old friend of Miss Standish's." He leaned down to speak for her ears alone. "Aren't you glad to see me?"

She turned her back to the class, not wishing the girls to witness her flustered state. "What is it you want?" she demanded.

"Firstly, allow me to inquire about your well-being. I trust you are not in any pain."

She was certain he was up to something. She answered tentatively. "I am not, sir."

"Or even discomfort?"

"I am quite well. Very well, I shall take the bait. Why are you asking?"

"I thought for certain your feet would be overtaxed by your vigorous and lengthy dancing with Lord George—so vigorous that you have disappeared for an age."

She fought against her indignation to find her voice. "It is incomparably vulgar of you to make reference to my body parts."

"I said feet. That is not vulgar to my mind. Unless of course your feet are unsightly."

"How dare you? They are not!" She cast a glance over her shoulder. Her students watched with avid curiosity.

"Bunions are nothing to be ashamed of."

"I am not ashamed!" she said, raising her voice louder than she wanted. The girls were craning their necks to try and see what was going on. She lowered her voice. "I have nothing to be ashamed of, sir."

"Good. Be proud of your imperfections, even when they are disfiguring."

"I do not have disfigured feet."

"Miss Standish! I am shocked. I believe you just uttered the word 'feet' in front of a male personage. What kind of example is that to set for these impressionable girls?"

She was stunned. "You think this is amusing? Well, as you have stated yourself, *Major,* you are a brute acquainted with the crass humor of males. I, sir, in case you have not noticed, am a female. This is the second time—no third!—that you have risked my reputation."

"You can't count the first time."

"I certainly can. You dragged me into a deserted room and kissed me."

"You are not recollecting accurately, Miss Standish. You beckoned me on that first night, even if you didn't know it at the time. You wished to be kissed."

"Please," she hissed. "The children."

"Unless they are equipped with phenomenal hearing, they are safe enough from our conversation."

"You know, Adrian, I do not find you entertaining, not in the least."

"And, by the way, I am adequately aware . . . dare I say, *painfully* aware at times, of your being female." He stopped. He gave her a look to burn and a long, slow smile. "You just called me Adrian."

"Did I?" She blushed profusely. "I didn't mean to."

"You did."

"Well . . . you told me to!"

"You said you would not. You said it was untoward."

"And it is."

He bowed his head, but his smirk stayed in place, the picture of gracious triumph. "As you will."

She made a face. "Why are we having this absurd conversation? I thought you were a serious person. A war hero is supposed to be a sober man."

"I usually am. I don't know what comes over me when I am in your company."

"Is it such a silly thing as teasing me that pleases you?"

"Oh, Miss Standish, let us not broach the subject of my pleasure, especially when it comes to you. And I must request you refrain from using the term *teasing*. I find it unaccountably disturbing. And smile, Michaela. You'll upset your students." Clapping his hands loudly he turned and strode toward the children. "Now, who would like to hear another story read by Miss Standish?"

The children erupted in a chorus of affirmatives. He sent her a look of appeal and pulled up one of the empty chairs as if he, too, were an eager member of the audience.

The classroom furnishings were fashioned smaller than most to accommodate the children's size. He puzzled over the thing for a moment before positioning the back end in front of him and, propping his cane to steady himself, swung his unhurt leg to the other side of the seat. He appeared quite comfortable in the end. He laid the ebony cane next to him and smiled pleasantly at her.

He should have looked absurd seated in the undersized chair, but the man's presence wasn't diminished. She stared back at him, her mind going over a score of resentments at his barging in here, his presumption, his taking cool command while she was caught effectively off guard.

She took in a long breath as she thought swiftly. She wished she had some way to turn the tables.

And then it came to her.

She smiled. "Instead of reading you a story," she said carefully. "What if I tell you one instead?"

The children agreed, ready for anything that took them away from their lessons.

"Make it about horses," Adrian called out. He turned to the girl next to him, who was staring at him with idolizing eyes. "I love stories with animals. Don't you?"

The girl's head bobbed slowly. She didn't even blink.

"Excuse me," Michaela said, "if you are going to be disruptive to the class, then I am going to have to ask you to leave."

"Ah. I shall behave."

If only that were true.

She opened her mouth, and instead of her own voice, she heard his prompt. "Horses."

She shot him an annoyed look. He grinned. "Please," he amended.

He really was like an overgrown boy. Huge, well-muscled, rock-hewn though he might be, he was pleased with himself no differently than a mischievous youth at a well-executed prank. He thought he had the upper hand, and he was graceless enough to gloat.

Well, she promised, we'll see.

"This is a story about a battle. A great and raging battle."

His look of pleasure collapsed into guarded alarm.

Michaela continued. "And a noble hero who, yes, indeed rode a horse, for it was his warhorse, of course. He, in fact, was a member of the famed and prestigious Horse Guards. He was known far and wide for his bravery and prowess, his skill in guessing the enemy's moves. It was almost as if he knew what would happen before it did. In addition to this attribute, he fought many battles and defeated his enemy by smiting him brutally with his sword."

Little Martha squealed, putting her hands over her ears. Adrian grabbed his cane and came to his feet, nearly toppling the small chair, and gestured to the girl. "You are frightening the children. I suggest you find another tale."

"Oh, I promise Martha will like this one. You see, Martha darling, the man of whom I speak—"

"Michaela!"

"Is none other than Major Adrian Khoury. Have any of you heard of him?"

He stood among a sea of raised hands as the girls twittered excitedly. Yes, indeed they all had.

Adrian's look promised dire retribution. She felt a swell of delight and savored every word as she said, "This *is* Major Khoury, children. He has come here so that you may meet him. Feel free to ask him any question you like."

There was a moment's pause as the girls digested this news. Then the room broke into a frenzy of noise: scraping chairs, excited voices, stomping feet as the class rushed him.

He managed to quiet them and get them settled back into their seats while Michaela watched, offering no aid. Finally, it was clear that the only way they would be appeased was with his promise that *he* would tell them a story.

"A story of the war!" one girl called. It was Annabelle, a tomboy with short-cropped hair and a gangly frame that was incongruous with both her feminine name and the frilly dresses her mother made her wear.

"A true one," another added. Sybil, the oldest girl, spoke as she fluttered her eyelashes shyly at Adrian. He tactfully pretended not to notice the blatant adulation.

He settled himself in his chair again, this time not among the class but at the head. The class quieted as he prepared to speak.

A moment of disquiet prickled along the back of her neck as she noted the tightness in him. The teasing cavalier was gone, and in his place was the face of the man who had inspired rumors of melancholy. His face was guarded, and she wondered if she'd gone too far in setting him to the task when she knew well it disturbed him.

Annabelle shouted, "Did you kill a lot of Frenchies?"

Adrian recoiled, but at exactly the same time, Martha squealed and clapped her hands over her ears, squeezing her eyes shut.

Michaela watched amazed as Adrian leaned forward and scooped her toward him. He settled her on his lap as comfortably as if he had snuggled children all of his life, which was, of course, preposterous. Leaning down, he whispered something in her ear that opened her eyes and put a wide smile on her face.

She wished she hadn't started this. It was wrong of her to allow spite to get the best of her, but he could be so provoking. . . . She was about to intervene when he spoke.

"Now, I fought Napoleon's armies, it is true, and am proud to have served my country, young lady. But I am not happy to have been forced to take lives. Many of the men who fought for Napoleon believed in their cause as much as we did ours. How many of you had relatives who fought in the war?"

Some raised their hands. One of the girls said, "My father fought at Waterloo. He lost his arm, but he is glad he fought. We are proud of him, too. He told us all about you, Major Khoury, how you fought with your own superior officers and broke ranks to go to the enemy's flank." She stopped and puzzled. "What is a flank?"

Adrian gave a soft chuckle, and his hardness seamed to ease a little. "The back of the troops; behind the enemy's line."

The wide eyes conveyed their admiration for such bravery.

Excited, Annabelle jumped out of her chair. "My father said that you dealt the Frenchies a mortal blow when you did that."

Adrian rubbed his steepled hands over his top lip, taking this in.

Stepping forward, Michaela said, "That is enough on the subject of war. It is unpleasant and decidedly *un*ladylike."

"You said we could ask any questions we wanted," Annabelle protested. She thrust a fist on her bony hip.

She sighed. "What you may not realize is that for the men who fight the wars, there can sometimes be bad memories at the losses they've suffered. War is not glorious, and it is not pleasant. It is serious business, young lady, and it is to be spoken of with deep respect for the gravity of the lives affected by it."

She was aware that Adrian was watching her.

"Why is it bad to talk about?" Annabelle protested. "My father says that Napoleon was evil and that he wanted to take over the world. We had to stop him. If we hadn't fought the war, what would have happened to England? To all of us?"

Sybil stood and said, "I, for one, am very grateful to the men who fought for us. I shudder to think what it would have been like to be a conquered race. My mother and sisters and I were so afraid when reports would come back that the war was going poorly. The worst day for all of us was when

Napoleon escaped his exile and marshaled his troops again. It was like a nightmare coming back when you thought you were awake and safe."

Everyone was silent. Sybil fought with her self-consciousness to continue. "Everyone spoke of it all the time, and we all prayed for the strength of our soldiers to protect us."

Marian chimed in, "It's true. We were all depending on the army to save us, Major Khoury."

"And kill scores of Frenchies!" Annabelle declared.

Martha squealed again, hiding her face against his shoulder. He cupped her head and whispered to her again, and again she relaxed as if he knew some magic incantation to dispel her worries.

He certainly had a way with women, Michaela observed. She knew from firsthand experience how much so.

"My goodness, you are a bloodthirsty one," Adrian said to Annabelle. "You might think differently if you ever had to face a live human in mortal combat. It is something momentous to use a weapon against a man, even if he is your opponent. But, as you say, there are things worth fighting for. One sometimes loses sight of it in all of the unpleasantness, but there are ideals, freedoms, even lives at stake."

He looked at the girls, each one in turn. "I didn't think enough about the women and children, the very way of life for which we fought. The battlefield is harsh, and the world at home seems too far away to even be remembered at times. I hear too much of the backslapping congratulations and not enough of the prayers and worries of those back here at home. I'm glad you reminded me of that."

Sybil blushed profusely as a few girls jostled her and giggled.

Martha looked up at him solemnly. "Do you feel better?"

"Do you?"

She bobbed her head. "I want those bonbons you promised now."

Michaela gasped. "You bribed her with sweets to not be afraid?"

He shrugged, absolutely unperturbed at her reaction. "It always works with my niece."

"That is . . . it is . . . "

"Effective," he supplied.

She was saved having to come up with a reply by the appearance of the children's teacher. Michaela explained as briefly as she could as she packed her things. She wished only to get out of the school and safely at home, putting as much distance between herself and Adrian as possible, as quickly as possible.

With the children still surrounding Adrian, she fetched her wrap and reticule, not even bothering to pull on her gloves before she bolted. She stood at the door, nervously wishing for Nora to come. The maid usually did errands and paid visits to her friends and her current beau while out and about with one of her mistresses. She always ran late and was notoriously unreliable.

Damn her, Michaela thought crossly. Making a quick decision, she hurried along the street, thinking to dash home before she had to face Adrian again.

He caught up with her just outside the small parish building. She considered for one giddy moment leaving all decorum behind and breaking into a run.

"Have tea with me," he said.

"How can you think I would?"

He fell into step beside her. "I'll call on you tomorrow, then."

"No."

"I'll come anyway. You won't refuse me."

"I will. I have no wish to be associated with you."

"And yet you cannot help yourself."

"You are too conceited. Have all of those adulating females gone to your head?"

"Can it be you were jealous?"

Jealous that every salon in Mayfair was vying for his presence, and every available woman vying for his eye? And she, a pretend princess, a woman he once thought a courtesan, for heaven's sake—was she supposed to believe he was interested in her?

What cruel fun was he having at her expense? Was this quid pro quo for the first night when he'd thought himself deceived?

"I am most certainly not jealous," she told him primly. "I was in actuality humiliated, and not for the first time by you. What were you thinking coming into the class like that?"

He shrugged, falling into step as she hurried home. "I missed you. You have been hiding at home."

"Hiding! Really. You say the most combative things. Aunt May has been away, and I have decided to pare down my social appearances to catch my breath, merely."

He gave her a cocky grin that spoke of his confidence that she was not telling him the truth. "Ah. So, your sudden reclusivity has nothing to do with me?"

"Oh! You are incredibly arrogant. No, Major, believe it or not, my life is not governed by my feelings for you."

He leaned closer, close enough that she felt the heat of his body, smelled the spicy, masculine scent of his skin. "Then you do have feelings for me."

"I am not going to have this ridiculous conversation with you any longer." She stopped in her tracks and faced him. "I wish for you to leave me now. If you do not, I am going to look for a constable to come and arrest you."

He chortled, very pleased with himself and not doing a thing to hide it. "All right, I suppose I've worn my welcome thin. I've had an interesting day, Michaela. Then again, every time I am with you, it is very interesting. You never disappoint me."

"Is that your good-bye? It is far too wordy if it is."

He bowed, suddenly formal, but mocking her all the while. "Your servant. We will see each other soon." Reaching out his hand to her face, he touched her jaw lightly.

To her chagrin, her body froze on the spot. She should have moved out of reach, or at the very least smacked his hand away. As it was, there was nothing she could do to stop him as his fingers stroked her cheek.

"And I shall look forward to it very much."

And just like that, with one touch, he lit a blazing trail along her taut, quivering nerves before dropping his hand.

She spun and hurried away. Her mind whirled with confused thoughts, images of the day: his gloating, his guardedness, the dawning of a thaw when the children had spoken to him.

What was she doing, giving him even the smallest consideration? She was playing right into his hands. She knew exactly what he was about—he was seducing her. He wanted what she had promised him the first night, what he had been furious to be denied. He thought it his right, and this game was nothing but another battle to be won for pride's sake alone.

She had taunted a tiger, and the tiger wanted revenge. And if she wanted him as well, so what? She was a lady, a virgin. She would not fall into his bed because he had a devil's grin. No doubt he was used to easy conquest when it came to women. He had a presence that women had to find difficult to ignore.

Nothing was going to come of the attraction. This she promised herself as she fled to the sanctuary of her modest home. He might try to charm her, he might try to use the traitorous sensations of her own body to lure her, but she would never give in to him.

Never.

☙ *Chapter 7*

In the smoking room of the Glenarvon mansion, a small circle of chairs were pulled up by the large bay window. Phillip Glenarvon presided over the meeting, his eyes crafty as he surveyed the men gathered around him. Adrian knew full well he was the one of most interest to the political master.

"You are not what I expected," Glenarvon said. "Perhaps because my own experience with men of the military had been with fops. Officers, in my experience, are merely younger sons whose families purchased their commissions to give them something to do besides frittering their allowance on gambling hells and bought women."

Adrian couldn't suppress a smile. This man's opinion was fairly accurate.

"You," Glenarvon said, holding out a beefy finger toward Adrian, "are the genuine article." His smile of approval didn't touch Adrian.

Rather, he felt the cold brush of dread, as if his fate were being sealed.

Glenarvon sat back, bringing his cigar up. "You have

fame, with your rather infamous part in the battles of Quatre Bras and Waterloo bringing abundant praise. The populace knows you."

He chewed on the end, then removed the rolled tobacco to take a generous portion of his drink, turning to the others. "That limp is excellent, just the right touch. In no way does it take anything from the bullish power of the man, and yet it bears the banner of his service. His *triumphant* service."

He smiled, turning back to Adrian.

He supposed he should dislike being discussed like a commodity, but it barely touched him. He felt a strange separateness from the entire proceeding, as if it had nothing to do with him.

Richard, sitting anxiously in one of the leather chairs, sat forward so as to be better seen through the thick eddies of smoke. "The common man loves him. They hold him a hero. He has none of the airs the landed gentry have a tendency to assume. His family is noble, and that lends him authority."

"No, it is his distinguished service," Glenarvon corrected roughly. "You mark yourself as a man of justice, don't you, Khoury? A self-made man, whose reputation was dug with blood and grit, and a small fortune made by a clever mind for investing. In short, gentleman, Major Khoury is perfect to run against Harris in the fall election."

Adrian supposed he should feel something at this pronouncement. Richard was beaming, hardly able to contain himself.

He was in this for good reasons, he told himself. He was a man of justice, just as the keen-eyed fox, Glenarvon, had said. What even Glenarvon's preternatural sight could not see, however, was what Adrian needed.

He needed to be whole.

Would serving as the common man's representative make up for all he lacked?

"You know," Glenarvon said, sitting back to give Adrian another one of his hard assessments, "when my veins start to hum, I know I have the possibility of something great in my sights. But you aren't sure, are you, Khoury?"

"I will do what I have to."

"Spoken like a soldier," Glenarvon replied approvingly. "Does your dedication extend to a fast marriage? Because, as I see it, your single status is the largest obstacle to the campaign. No single man is going to get the elector's votes. Family means stability, someone the electorate will see as reliable and steady."

Richard interjected, "But his war record already tells the . people that. And he has family—his brothers, my wife, my children. He is bred from one of the oldest families in England."

"I very specifically mean a wife and children. It represents a personal stake in the politics of the land. That's what was wrong with the House of Lords—men making decisions for parcels of land they haven't even been to in their lives. Now, you, Khoury, can be a man of the people, a man of progress, of change. That is what you are, it is how you will be elected, but you have to look the part, every bit of it."

Adrian sat forward, zeroing his attention on Glenarvon. "All the people need to know is that I am committed to social reform, and even more so to political evolution. What the devil difference does it make if I'm married?"

Glenarvon nearly laughed. "My God, you actually *care.*"

"Indeed, I do, sir," Adrian said, his eyes narrowing. His body itched for motion, but he held himself in check as he rose and stood facing the man who had the ability to manipulate his chosen protegés into major political appointments. Becoming an MP was the first step to being a force in government. Appointments to committees, especially the coveted Treasury, could mean the difference between having a lackluster career and being a major policy-maker. "And if you do not care as well, then we are mismatched."

"Sit down, Major Khoury," Glenarvon said. "You have something that in this business of politics can be a liability. You have vision. The problem with vision, you see, is that it has to be shared. You alone, you can do nothing, even as a member of the House of Commons. But ten men . . . why, you could change this country. The shared vision is what's needed."

Khoury smoldered. He was used to command, never good

at taking orders. Now, however, he was in the unenviable position of being in a realm he knew little about, and he was forced to acknowledge Glenarvon's unquestionable superiority in these matters.

"The first task at hand is to find you a wife. The right wife, one who will reflect the values you will stand for. A man of the people, that is what you are. That is what is going to get you elected."

Glenarvon fell silent, watching. Adrian struggled with the surge of bitterness. He thought of his friends—the men he'd fought with and respected—and he thought of their widows, especially Sarah Trent, wife of the man who had saved his life, and of her tiny child who had been orphaned because of him, and he sat there and took his schooling because it was what he owed.

"He knows this," the elder brother, Richard, said. "We have been working on that problem."

"I heard about some girl who wrote a letter to the newspaper?"

Glenaravon paused, waiting for Adrian to supply Michaela's name. When he didn't, the older man shrugged and went on. "That would not be the wise choice. Anyone controversial or outspoken would be unwise."

Richard piped up. "I had a widow in mind. One with children, so as to make an instant family. This would be excellent for the image you are speaking about."

Glenarvon cheered. "Children would be excellent. Blond children would be best. They appear cherubic. Are the children blond?"

Richard appeared at a loss. "I am afraid I have not seen them."

"Well, see if you can find a woman with blond children. A boy and a girl." Glenarvon lunged forward, inspired suddenly. "Devil be damned, a brilliant idea just occurred to me: make her a war widow. By God, we'll shove the war hero aspect so far down their throats, the electors will be sobbing for a week."

Adrian came to his feet and sprang toward the window, suddenly unable to breathe. All this damned smoke!

Rage blazed for a moment, then was checked. His hands curled into fists, and he fought with himself—to be the man he wanted to be, to be weak and take what he needed, and back and forth again.

"Adrian?" Richard said. He was close, just behind him.

Without a word, Adrian strode out the door, his wide shoulders knocking a pair of men standing slightly in his path back a step or two.

Richard turned to Glenarvon. "I'll go talk to him. He'll be fine."

Glenarvon took in a breath, paused, and let it out heavily. "See that he is. I'm not wasting my time any further unless he is tractable."

Michaela gazed out the window at the gathering clouds as she waited while her sister, Delilah, dallied over the sprigged muslin and the striped cotton at the drapers' shop on the Strand. It was a fashionable place, and they were selecting some very special material for a ball given by the Duke and Duchess of Kent to which all four had been invited, taking place later in the month.

In the street, people quickened their steps, taking heed of the threatening storm. She and Lady May had already selected her gown, but she had come on the outing rather than stay at home, as her aunt was still in the country with friends.

"What do you think, Mother?" Delilah asked.

"Oh, just pick something, would you?" Delinda snapped, and for once, Michaela was in complete sympathy with her.

"It's going to storm," she said to her mother.

"Yes," Mother said, "it looks dreadful outside. We do not wish to get caught in a downpour. Please Delinda, make a choice."

"I'm Delilah!"

Mother made a soft sound of annoyance and chopped the air with her hand. "Just choose!"

"I cannot make up my mind."

"Oh, bother," Delinda declared, and strode up, angrily jerking one of the bolts off the table and shoving it at her twin. "Just take that one. I'm hungry. I wish to go to the tea garden now."

Delilah frowned, still uncertain. "I want this to be a special dress. I never look good because I always let you rush me. But I just don't have an eye for these things."

Michaela leaned her head back against the pane of glass and rolled her eyes to look out into the street again.

"Michaela? Could you perhaps advise me?"

She turned back to her sister, not sure if she had heard correctly. Michaela looked at Delinda, then at her mother. The former was scowling, the latter watched without expression.

Delilah, who rarely spoke to anyone besides her twin, spoke again. "You always look so nice. I just thought maybe you would help."

It took a moment for Michaela to recover from her shock. "I have no taste for fashion, believe me. Lady May speaks to the modiste and makes all the choices."

Her sister cast down her eyes. "Oh. I see."

Before she knew it, Michaela rushed forward. "But I may have picked up a thing or two. Let's see. Let's hold the fabrics you've chosen up to you and see how the color reflects off your complexion. The modiste is always concerned with how a color or pattern goes with one's skin."

Mother strode closer to listen but did not interfere.

Holding up the sprigged fabric, she said, "This is pretty. A safe choice. The style of it is all the rage."

"Then I will look like all the other girls."

"Is that what you wish?"

"I was thinking if I chose to have a dress made up in this," she said with barely repressed excitement, pushing the butter-yellow and tan stripe, "then I would be very unique."

The shop assistant stepped forward, eager at this sign of resolution at last. "That would do very well indeed."

"Only, I don't know if it will look ridiculous."

"Of course it will," Delinda snapped. "Choose the sprigged muslin, and it will be like mine."

Michaela whirled, and before she could stop herself, she said, "Perhaps she doesn't wish to be like you."

"That's enough," Dorothy said, stepping between them. Taking hold of Delilah's chin, she peered at her daughter. "Hurry and choose, please. It is not the end of the world. It is a dress."

Michaela said, "I say the striped. Fly or fail, it will be a statement, will it not?"

Delilah frowned. Then she looked at Michaela and smiled, as if sharing some daring move. "All right. That is, if you agree, Mother."

With a speculative look at Michaela, Dorothy nodded.

"I cannot believe you would take Michaela's advice over mine!" With a harumph loud enough to raise the dust from the shelves, Delinda whirled and presented her back to all of them.

Dorothy's gaze narrowed on Delinda. "Michaela, would you please go on to the tea garden and order us a pot? It will save us all time. Our tempers are suffering from hunger. We will finish making the selections for the trimmings and be right along."

Michaela got the distinct impression that Delinda was about to receive a long overdue dressing-down. Too bad she wasn't going to be allowed to witness it.

Michaela stepped out of the shop and into the busy street. The sky overhead was low and threatening, a swollen gray mass that appeared ready to burst a deluge upon those below at any moment. Trust her to leave her umbrella at home when she would undoubtedly need it.

Cautioned by the weather, the open carriages and pedestrians were hurrying down the street. Michaela glanced about quickly to get her bearings. She stepped out toward the street to better read the signs hung sideways above the storefronts, searching for the tea parlor.

The sight of Adrian standing just a short way across the cobbled street, speaking with several men, was a surprise. He looked over and saw her just as she spotted him. In that instant of being caught off guard, she felt a surge of joy blossom in her chest, filling her with a quick, liquid-hot pleasure. Impulsively she raised her hand and waved as her face broke into a smile that hid nothing.

With her hand over her head flapping like some demented bird, she realized her mistake as soon as she saw the droll pleasure on his face. Michaela dropped her hand.

What was she doing? She was a lady of quality, not a scullery maid hailing an old chum from down the road. Mortified at her lapse of decorum, she began to walk swiftly in the direction away from him, hoping he would not try to intercept her.

She should have known better. When she heard footsteps behind her, she knew he was not going to allow her to get away from him so easily.

She didn't turn, didn't even pause as he drew up to her. "Please go away."

"Don't be rude, Michaela."

A cold raindrop plopped on her forehead as she paused, spun, and inclined her head to him. "Hello, Major. Goodbye."

He caught her before she could turn back around and continue running away from him. He said, "Surely you don't mean it, not after that enthusiasm all over your most expressive face when you saw me."

"I didn't mean to do that. I began waving before I realized what I was doing. Do not read so much into it."

"You lie terribly, do you know that? Your chin gets stubborn, as if you are daring me to believe you."

"You are impossible."

"Yes," he murmured, "That, you see, is precisely the problem."

"What?"

"The impossible."

"And now you are speaking in riddles."

"I have no doubt I am sputtering the incoherent rantings of a madman. Which is exactly what I am, what you have rendered me, Miss Standish—mad as a hatter. It is absolutely terrifying, is it not, what comes over us whenever we are in each other's company?" Sighing, he looked up, surveyed the street. "I swore I wasn't going to do this again. I admit I've enjoyed our little battle of wits, but I hardly imagine it can continue without one or the other of us resorting to murder."

"I know you regard this as some sort of lark. No doubt it amused you enormously to have sport with me."

He paused, genuinely thoughtful. "Why do you insist on thinking it thus?" A sudden rush of raindrops made him draw closer, as if he were going to protect her with his body. "Let me get you out of the rain. Where are you headed?"

"Greer's Tea Garden. My mother and my sisters are back at the dressmaker's, and I'm to meet them there."

He gave her a speculative look. "Greer's?" He pointed behind them. "It is that way." He hunched against the incremental increase in the storm's intensity. "Haven't you an umbrella?"

"No, I do not," she shot back miserably as she reversed her direction and trudged onward. She was wet and getting more so by the second.

Halfway down the street in the wrong direction! And worse than any of this, she sounded bitter-tempered and shrill when he was being charming enough to melt a polar ice cap. "If I had one, do you not think I'd use it? Or do you imagine I have it secreted in my garter, where all the ladies of polite society keep theirs? It is the latest rage."

Beside her, he said, "I should like to see how you retrieve it."

The heavens opened up, and the rain began to gush in earnest. It was one of those sudden soakings that left one drenched within moments. Even an umbrella wouldn't have helped much, not with the wind kicking the downpour into sheets of stinging water. His hand clamped around her upper arm, and he gestured to an alcove where an entrance to one of the shops was set back from the sidewalk.

"Get inside," he said.

"I should get to the tea garden." She headed again into the deluge.

She began to rush in earnest, trotting through the rapidly filling puddles. Her kid shoes were immediately sopping wet, and her sodden skirts flapped around her knees.

"Come in here," he shouted over the storm. He was as wet as she, his fair hair darkened by the water, falling in points over his brow.

"No. I'm going to the—" She cut off as a crack of lightning and thunder burst overhead. She flinched, almost falling against him in fright. Pulling away, she cautioned herself against such a disastrous impulse.

Along the street, people were huddled against the rain, hurrying past. There was a sense of mild pandemonium as open carts cleared the area and pedestrians found their way indoors.

"Don't hold a grudge, Michaela. Don't you get weary of this bickering?"

She sighed, and her voice lost its stridency, sounding more plaintive than she would have wished. "What am I to do when you provoke me so well?"

"This is ridiculous. You may be the most stubborn woman I have met in my entire life, but even you cannot wish to continue this in the middle of such weather."

She allowed him to lead her to a covered doorstep. The cessation of water pounding on her was an instant relief. As she wiped off her face ineffectively with a soggy handkerchief, she said, "You think I'm stubborn because I don't do your bidding. You cannot command me as you seem to be used to doing. I will not be toyed with, and I am not a soldier in your regiment, *Major Khoury.*"

"Oh, Miss Standish, I assure you there is never confusion about that." He gave her a slow, insolent perusal. "You look nothing like any of the soldiers in my regiment. I am afraid a fellow would fare rather poorly with your aspect."

She fumed as he opened the door, setting a small bell atop the frame to tinkling. She had no choice but to enter, not unless she wanted to seem more churlish than she had already made herself.

Warmth enveloped her as she stepped across the threshold, and the click of the door behind her was punctuated by another ear-splitting crash of thunder. She jumped, backing into him.

The comfort there was like a fast-acting drug. She stiffened her spine against the lingering effects and put her attention to their surroundings.

Upon the walls were landscapes and portraits, still lifes

and architectural sketches all in carved frames in wood and gold leaf. Michaela glanced around as she peeled off her gloves and twisted them together, wringing water from them. It seemed they had entered a small art gallery.

A young boy took shelter on the stoop they'd vacated. Opening the door again, Adrian called to him, "Boy, come here." Producing a coin from his pocket, he flipped it to him. "Run up to the dressmaker's on this street. There is a lady inside with two daughters who look exactly alike. Tell her that their sister is soaked through, having got caught in the storm, and that Major Khoury is taking her home. You'll get a devil of a soaking, but there is another piece of gold for you if you come back and tell me that you spoke to them. Two if you can tell me what the lady is wearing so I know you've really done the errand as I've asked."

The lad smiled. "Aye, gov'ner. I can do it, I can!" He dove into the rain.

Michaela, who had been flapping her skirts, commented dryly. "This is turning into an expensive adventure."

He looked at the way she had taken to shivering. "We need to dry off by a fire. I'll speak to the shopkeeper."

A voice called a greeting, and Adrian turned to the man who had come out from behind a curtained doorway.

"Come in, then, come in," the man said, beckoning them closer just before he ducked behind the curtain to return within moments with a large, soft blanket. Adrian took it and drew it around Michaela's shoulders, wrapping her up tightly.

"I'll build up the fire, sir," the man said to them. "Back here, then."

Adrian nodded gratefully at the man's eager hospitality. "That would be much appreciated."

The man held back the faded velvet barrier, welcoming them into the personal area set up like a cozy drawing room in the back of the gallery.

"I'll make tea as well," he said, rubbing his hands together.

"Thank you so much," Michaela said. "It is kind of you to

open your private sitting room to us. It is dreadful outside, and we were quite desperate to get dry."

"No trouble, no trouble, my lady. My name is Oliver Rye," he said over his shoulder as he hunkered down to see to the fire.

Adrian introduced Michaela, then himself. Mr. Rye reacted to his name.

"Not *the* Major Khoury. Is it truly?"

"I suppose it is," Adrian replied with a wry look. "Although I can't be certain the one whom you have heard tell and the man in the flesh is anything remotely similar. But I am aware there are some . . . stories about the recent battle that mention me by name."

The man's eyes went wide, his face lit with excitement. "Well, I'll be. It is an honor to meet you, sir!"

Adrian's response gave no doubt that he wished nothing made over his reputation. Mr. Rye seemed to sense this, leaving off directly. He busied himself to stoking the fire to life, shaking his head and muttering, "Wait until I tell them down at the Pierced Egret."

Adrian relaxed. "You have a few pints at the Pierced Egret, do you?"

"From time to time," Mr. Rye replied with a salty grin. "Do you know it?"

"By reputation."

"You have some lovely paintings out there," Michaela said. The blanket and the stoked fire were doing the job of warming her. "They are exceptional, those that I saw briefly when we came in."

"Ah, I love this little gallery." He finished, then stood and hung the kettle. "Do you like paintings, Miss Standish?"

"I do, but I am afraid I am not learned in the arts. I go to the Royal Academy to see the exhibits whenever I can."

"Ah," he said, settling himself in a well-worn chair, "it's books for you, I'll wager. Those novels that are all the rage, no doubt."

"Oh, yes," she laughed, nodding happily, "horrid ones, too."

"And what of you, Major, do you read the horrid novels?"

"I don't have the vaguest idea of what they are, sir."

"Adventures featuring specters and heroines in grave peril."

Michaela sat forward excitedly. "And usually, the hero is very dark and brooding, and you just know he is awful, but the poor woman trusts him because she doesn't know there's danger, and the ghosts are just the most dreadful things, rising up, and it's wonderful."

His eyes glimmered with something soft as he regarded her. "I see I am missing quite a good read."

"I think they are more of women's taste," she said, "I also like Byron. I thought 'Don Juan' was incredibly funny. Did you read it?"

"I did. Rather a racy choice for a young lady." Adrian chuckled. "Which is why your mother forbade you to read it. But you did so anyway."

She was astonished. Catching Mr. Rye's chortle, she tossed her head. "Well, it goes to show what you know. She did not forbid me to read it."

"Then you didn't ask."

"Her feelings about Lord Byron are well-known, and so I just kept it sort of a little bit of a secret. A harmless one."

Mr. Rye got to his feet. "Let me show you a painting you might like. See to the tea, will you, if the pot boils before I return."

Michaela rose when the water began to roil, setting the leaves to steeping and laying out the cups, which Adrian watched with that half-veiled gaze of his. Somehow, the atmosphere between them had shifted. The fire seemed to be having a salubrious effect on thawing the coolness between them.

"See, each one is a story of color and shape and line," Mr. Rye chirped as he hurried back into the room with a few canvases under his arm. "It's in the light the painter depicts, the shadow and how it falls on the subject that creates a mood, evokes emotion, as words might in a novel. Each painting tells a story, you know, as much as the written word. You just need to use your imagination."

"Using my imagination was never much appreciated," Michaela observed sourly.

"Excuse me for saying so, in case it insults anyone you hold dear, but only a person devoid of an imagination would ever fault a person for possessing a rich one. Imagination in my estimation is by far the best attribute any person can possess. It gives that person the ability to create, to enjoy things in a realm others can't fathom, and it's that power that frightens those that don't have it. They know they're missing something, and they know it's something wonderful. So they pooh-pooh it, they demean it."

Adrian was impressed. "Well put, Mr. Rye." To Michaela, he added, "Miss Standish here has an excellent mind. She has a score of inventive ideas about the poor that challenge people to rethink what they know and consider the possibilities of something better. I'd say that is imagination at its best, wouldn't you?"

Mr. Rye was pleased. "Well, then perhaps you two will enjoy this little game I play. Take a look at these."

He turned one of the canvases around to reveal a small painting. It was of a man reclined in bed, eyes closed. He had dark hair and a beard. On a bedside table, situated behind him, were a few odd items. The dark blanket and shadows clustered in the background provided the means for the scarlet of his bedclothes and the white pillow to stand out in contrast.

"Now," Oliver said, obviously pleased with his game, "what do you see?"

Michaela studied the painting. "A sleeping man." She looked up to her host. "Is it a portrait of someone famous?"

"No, no, just a man, an ordinary man." He held up an instructive finger. "But he is a man with a story."

"He is ill," Adrian said. "Or wounded. He looks rough. The red of his nightshirt gives the hint of blood."

Michaela tilted her head, considering the work. "But he is not thin or wasted looking. See the breadth of his shoulders. He is a strong man."

Oliver nodded, "Actually, the man was injured and permitted the artist to paint him as long as he was quiet and did not disturb his convalescence. He is a laborer. His beard gives him a rough look, as do the details—what you can see of them—of the humble room in which he sleeps. See there, the objects on the table. A book, water, a vial of something which is probably medicine, and something red, but what? There is no way to know."

"It looks like a lady's reticule." Michaela pointed. "See the tassels. He had a female caller, and she left it behind."

Oliver grinned. "Yes. It could be, couldn't it? Now, look at the picture, and allow your imagination to tell you the story."

As Michaela concentrated, Adrian pointed a finger abruptly at the painting and said, "He sleeps sitting up. He fights his infirmity. He hates being confined to the bed."

Michaela added, "He loves the woman. She came to visit, just before he fell asleep. She was so upset at his having been injured, seeing him a convalescent, that when she left, she forgot her reticule. It is red, as is his clothing. That signifies the connection between them. Maybe she is someone wealthy, of a higher class, but she cares for him, perhaps loves him. And he . . . see how peaceful he looks. He's handsome, comfortable with himself. He's just seen the woman he loves and now he rests, contented."

Adrian was incredulous. "You gleaned all of that from a red reticule? My goodness, you *do* have a formidable imagination."

She gave him a haughty look, belied by a pleased smile. "Aside from the figure, which is the focal point, it is the most significant thing about the composition. That is why it, too, is scarlet. Am I correct, Mr. Rye?"

"There is no correct or incorrect. What does the painting mean to you? That is what matters. You see a great love story. Perhaps it is part of your own thoughts. Major Khoury sees a man who hates his infirmity, as he himself knows he would feel."

The man hadn't meant to blunder, but she saw Adrian's hand go to his thigh and rub the heel of it against the muscle. He must have lain, quite like this man, alone in a bed, to recover from whatever injury had left him with the slight limp in his gait.

Oliver Rye continued. "Do you know, Miss Standish, that this painting sat outside for six months, and all the swells and the lovely ladies that promenade the Strand came in here and passed it by. They saw a sleeping man, and with all the blacks, browns, and reds used to compose the depiction, not a very attractive painting at that, certainly nothing to grace their fashionable drawing rooms."

"It isn't a very pretty picture," she agreed.

"But it is a powerful one. Now, here, look at this one."

Eyes wide, Michaela took in the vista on the next canvas. Flushing scarlet, she murmured, "Oh, dear."

Naked nymphs danced across the canvas, their alabaster skin glowing in the subtle light. Rounded bottoms and tiny pink nipples, shaded crevices between lush thighs created a rampant decadence of pastel color and florid flesh.

Squinting, Adrian regarded the work of art. "Now, that is a story I'd like to hear. But perhaps another time, when we do not have to be concerned with Miss Standish's sensibilities."

"Oh. Oh, yes," Oliver said, embarrassed. "Sometimes, I get so caught up, I forget myself. If Margaret—my wife— were here, she'd fairly box my ears, I daresay."

"It is a gorgeous painting," Michaela supplied softly as he tucked it away.

"Quite right, a superior work, to be sure, but one mustn't dwell on the story with that one." He grinned sheepishly as he quickly rearranged the canvases.

The last painting was of farm laborers, a study of blues, purples, and tan—not unpleasant but earthy. It showed a man with a scythe in the foreground, his wife, young and pretty, with a sleeping babe in her arms transacting business with another man, payment for the work her husband had just done. The setting was a dusty courtyard piled with bundles of wheat.

The scene was nothing dramatic. The man with the scythe had cut wheat. He was tired. His wife collected his pay.

And yet the very simplicity of it, the ordinariness, incited all kinds of ideas in Michaela's mind.

They discussed the use of color to convey mood, and the symbolism. Mr. Rye had some very exciting ideas, which Michaela enjoyed discussing very much. She soaked up the way Mr. Rye analyzed the work.

Adrian, too, was taken by the exercise. He pointed to the man with the scythe. "Look," he said, "how he holds his head, his back straight. He is detached from the others. His exhaustion, his dignity . . . you can feel it."

Michaela liked the way he saw things in the picture, as she did. He was not reluctant to express views. It emboldened her, and Mr. Rye eventually coaxed her into offering her interpretation of the story of the painting. Unable to help herself, she launched into a long tale of intrigue to explain why the laborer seemed so reticent, but supplied a happy ending.

Adrian and Mr. Rye laughed approvingly when she concluded. "Perhaps you should think about writing some of those horrid novels yourself," Adrian observed.

"She'd be the rage," Mr. Rye agreed. "Here, we have neglected our tea. The pot should be ready."

Michaela smiled, feeling a flush of warm pleasure at their praise. If she had told these things to her family, she had no doubt she would have been scorned for being odd. Yet, these men seemed to admire her ideas. Adrian, in particular, glowed with approval.

She found she liked it when he looked at her like that.

Chapter 8

Michaela studied Adrian as he bowed his head over his tea, blowing to raise tiny ghosts of heat off its surface. His eyebrows were pulled in tight over the bridge of his nose. It wasn't an elegant nose, either. It was nicely shaped but largish, with an angle to the bridge.

His was not a beautiful face but a memorable one, one that wore pain in small hints around the mouth, the eyes. It touched a tenderness in her breast and a longing to know—

"On a rainy day like this, there's nothing I love more than a cuppa and some quiet moments to enjoy the stories on these walls." Oliver Rye stirred his tea, laying the spoon down on the saucer. "Unless, of course, it's to share it with fine folk such as you."

Michaela forced herself to shift her attention from Adrian. "You mentioned your wife, Margaret. Isn't she here?"

His pleasant expression didn't alter. "Lost her a few years back. She was a fine woman, she was. A very practical sort," he added fondly, settling back to reminisce. "Used to say I had bats in my belfry, looking at paintings all day. But sometimes . . . well, sometimes she'd sit with me, and we'd stare at a good work. She knew what she liked. When one hit her, she was useless for anything else, same as me. The paintings, they talked to her, too."

Michaela's eyes stung. "You must miss her."

"Ah, that I do. But she's with me." He thumped his chest and smiled.

"Did you have any children?"

Adrian spoke softly. "Michaela, perhaps he doesn't wish to—"

"No, it's all right, sir, truly. No children, miss. Had a few babes, but they didn't last. But her sister, now, she had a child, and when she died, young Tabitha come stay with us. We raised her like ours. She's a good girl, got a position up at a big house in the West End, now. And what of you, miss? Do you have a big family?"

"I have sisters, both older." She turned to Adrian, taking the opportunity to indulge her curiosity. "What of your family, Major?"

"You can use my name. You've done so before."

But that was in private.

"Can you fathom this, Mr. Rye? He retains the rank, which is something most men would be proud of, yet dislikes anyone to use it."

Mr. Rye opened his mouth, but it was Adrian who spoke first. "Not anyone. You."

"Sometimes," Mr. Rye interjected smoothly, "a thing can take on different meanings. It depends on the situation . . . and the person. It was like that with my Margaret. I could take a ribbing from anyone, but if she were to criticize me, it felt like a betrayal. She was my solace, you see, the one I came to when the world whipped my hide. I counted on her to see the good in me."

"How lovely," she said. "It is a great gift to have had such happiness."

"Aye, Miss Standish, that is true enough." His smile encompassed the both of them.

The chiming of the bells signaled a patron had entered the shop. Mr. Rye rose. "Let me just go and see who that is."

Adrian said, "It might be the boy I sent to the drapers. If it is, he will be looking for this." He fished out the promised reward.

"A generous offering. I'll see to it, if you like."

In his absence, Michaela turned to Adrian. "This is not quite proper, is it?"

"Being alone? One cannot always manage to have interlopers about."

"Why do you dislike it so when I call you Major?" she blurted.

He pursed his lips, taking his time to respond. "Because when you saw me the first night we met, that was what you saw. It was *all* you saw: *Major* Khoury, the war hero, dare I say even as I despise the fact of it, something of a legend and as such a superior pawn in a very particular game you were playing. You were not interested in me as a man. So, when you call me by my title, it is like you are crowing over a conquest. It insults me."

"But you cannot expect me to call you Adrian. Not in front of people," she said.

He leaned forward. "Then say my name now, here, in private where it is just us two."

She twisted her head, unable to withstand the way he looked at her.

"Michaela, why do you rebuff me when I know you want me as much as I want you?"

The earnestness in his voice wrenched her heart. "I do so because it is expected, is it not? This game we are about— you provoke, and I demur."

"It's not a game. It never was."

"Revenge then, for that first night. You felt I had deceived you somehow."

"I felt cheated," he clarified. "And I still do. I want you, and your eyes and your flirting promised me things I cannot even describe. But I don't wish revenge. It is simply that I cannot seem to bear it when you ignore me. Do you know why I came to your school that day? Because at Lady Albright's you gave me the cut. A very good, well-executed cut, and it nearly drove me to distraction. I couldn't resist, you see."

"I seem to remember you telling me that I frighten men off."

"I said most men. I am not most men."

"Why did you say that?"

"Did it hurt you, Michaela? Did you think I meant you were undesirable? Far from it, but your looks aren't the fashion, are they? You don't have the pallid, soft kind of beauty that make men feel larger, stronger, more capable. And your mind isn't the simpering sort that inflates the male of the species' sense of superior knowledge and evokes protective feelings for the inferior female. You challenge, Michaela. Even your features declare you to be of bright mind and forward thinking."

"But I have known many men who were not dandies looking for sweet misses to dangle on their arm. Intelligent men with the same ideals as me. If it is not too much of a conceit for me to tell you that I know some admired me, even sought my opinion."

"But none of them ever kissed you."

She jerked her chin up, wondering too late if he would spot the defensive gesture. The damnable man saw everything. "And what of you? Why is it I do not seem to frighten you off as well?"

"I have fought enemies for my very life. I was nearly thrown into military prison several times for countermanding orders I thought were idiocies uttered by idiots." The corner of his mouth curled upward. "I think I can manage one strong-minded female."

"But you make it seem like some great laugh, and at my expense. You came to the school and teased me—"

"As I said, it was because of the cut."

"And today?"

"Running into you as I did was completely a fortunate happenstance, I promise you. I did not arrange it. But don't think I would be above such a tactic. If I wish to see you, I will do so. Now, there is something I wish to know." He hesitated, as if reluctant to ask. "When you first saw me today from across the street, you looked as if . . ."

She ducked her head, embarrassed.

"You seemed pleased."

She folded her arms over her chest. "Before I could remember what a pestering trial you were, I did feel pleasure at seeing a familiar face."

He laughed softly, and she joined him.

Adrian rose and went to the fire, taking up the iron and stoking it to revive the flames. "I think Mr. Rye may have a sale," he said, taking a peek through the curtain. "Some intrepid customer in dire need of art is keeping him well occupied."

"I wonder that he can bear to part with any of his precious paintings. He seems to love them so much."

"I can see why. Particularly the rampant nymphs. I was sorry we didn't get to exercise your imagination on that masterpiece."

She shook her head in exasperation. "You do seem to favor being incorrigible."

He grinned. "It is my curse. I was known for being incorrigible since I was a boy."

"You say that with pride."

His eyelids lowered to half-mast. "I am most proud of the attributes that cause others to take offense. You might say it is my nature to be objectionable."

"You cannot mean that."

"And yet it would appear so."

"Can appearances not be deceiving?"

He angled his head, pleased, and asked, "I believe they can."

What did he mean? Some riddle. She was so very curious about him.

He was not a man to invite confidences. The deluge had forced them into a truce, and she might have pressed on but for the way the companionship was easy between them for once. They lapsed into a comfortable cessation of words, but the warmth of their companionship lingered. The crisp snap of the fire, the soft drone of the voices in the other room brought relief from absolute quiet but made no demands on either one.

Eventually, Mr. Rye returned with the message that the boy had returned and reported the ladies sent word back that they were heading directly home. He'd been given his reward and sent on his way.

When they were finished with their tea, Michaela rose and asked to be taken home.

"Have you dried sufficiently?" Mr. Rye inquired.

She looked down at her dress and fluffed the still-clinging material. "Well enough to go forth for another drenching."

Adrian was aware of a sudden reluctance to part as he rose to thank Mr. Rye for his uncommon kindness. Pressing his card into the man's hand, he said, "If I can ever be of service, you must call on me to return the favor."

As he escorted her to his carriage, Michaela peered at him reflectively. "I do not think you care to be indebted."

"I prefer balanced relationships. I don't like to have anyone depend on me. I may disappoint them."

"How could you?"

He opened the door and pulled down the step. He handed her inside, then climbed up to sit across from her.

"I don't think you could," she went on. "Disappoint, I mean. Have people expected so much of you in the past that you would dread such a thing? And how strange that you would care so."

He bowed, not wishing to argue. For once, he'd let the belief stand that he was what people said. It mattered, he found, that she thought well of him.

She gave her direction to the driver. He could have, but he didn't wish her to know he had already acquainted himself with where she lived. They didn't speak much on the ride home. He was glad. Somehow, the mood wasn't ripe for words.

In Mr. Rye's back room, something sweet had brushed up against the nether regions of his soul. He felt a hint of the kind of peace he had known briefly as a boy, but not for a minute since.

When they arrived at the small house, a respectable residence in a modest neighborhood kept neat with trimmed shrubbery and an ambitious amount of spring plantings along its borders, she turned to him. "Thank you. I suppose it was very fortunate that I saw you today."

"Don't give me that suspicious look. I assure you it was quite by chance."

"You were kind to take such good care of me, especially when we haven't always been on the best of terms."

"It was not so very much. I doubt you would have been swept away by the storm if not for my intervention. You would have fared well enough without me." He took her hand in his. "But it did make for a pleasant afternoon."

"Yes. I thought Mr. Rye the most charming man."

"And there was that painting of the nymphs," he added with an evil grin. It made her laugh. It was a sweet, dear sound.

He didn't wish to let her hand go. What folly was this, what stupidity. He released her at once. She bid him farewell and the coachman handed her out. He forced himself to sit back, look ahead, not at her retreating form. But each breath was tainted by her scent, a softly feminine aroma that lingered in the air long after she had disappeared inside the house.

He wanted her.

He *would* have her.

In the swaying interior of his coach as it headed toward his apartments in St. James, he made a decision.

He would move heaven and hell to get her into his bed. Now, all that was left was the simple matter of forming a plan.

He couldn't simply approach her with the proposition, not as he would another woman with more worldly experience. Damaged by the dirty little secret of his past he may be, but he was no fool. He could see Michaela's quality. She was not Frances.

Was that the reason he had pursued her like no other woman? Yes, she was a cut above in every sense. It had taken nearly all of his forbearance to keep his hands off her.

He wanted her, indeed more so for all of the time spent

getting to know her, her singular and quirky charm. But now, instead of thinking of a quick, satisfying affair, he was of a mind of a more permanent arrangement. A few times in Michaela's bed would do nothing to douse the desire he felt. Therefore, he might be able to convince her to become his mistress.

If she could overcome her moral objections—the middle classes could be peculiarly provincial about these things—he could imagine many entertaining interludes. He hadn't ever wished to linger after lovemaking, but he could see that with her, he might enjoy those lazy hours indulging in all sorts of discussions, savoring them almost as much as the time he would take teaching her the pleasures of the body.

If he had thought a moment about her fierce mama and watchful aunt, he would have realized how foolish the idea was, even if she was willing. But his mind was too happily occupied with the optimistic thought that she might agree. She was, after all, a woman of forward thought, and her slightly advanced age, her intelligence, as well as her exposure to a cosmopolitan lifestyle almost insured she would not harbor the sort of notions of romance and love he was incapable of fulfilling.

For he was not a man to delve too deeply into sentimental matters. Lust he understood, and understood it well. Love . . . well, thank goodness Michaela Standish had all the markings of a woman of a much more practical mind.

"I am worried about Michaela," May said.

She sat with Robert in the drawing room of her town house. Glad to be home after her short foray to Turnbridge Wells spa, she had told Robert nothing about the restlessness that had prevented her from enjoying the yearly romp. She had never failed to have a wonderful time with the group of fun-loving women who'd been friends since girlhood, but this year she had returned early, begging off with excuses of commitments she didn't really have.

When Robert had expressed surprise at her premature return to London, she had dismissed it as having to do with

Michaela. It was true, but only part of it. She had also missed him desperately.

He was looking tantalizing right now, his large body hunched in one of the delicate chairs she had spent a small fortune to acquire when she'd decorated the room to her taste. Relaxed, he read quietly, oblivious to his surroundings, all except for the tray of freshly made tarts on the table beside him. He was systematically devouring them one by one.

In response to her statement, he nodded and grunted. This was typical when he was absorbed in a book.

When May said softly, "Robert?" he summoned himself out of his reverie and looked up.

"You weren't listening," she chided with a smile.

He closed the book. "True. What is it you were saying?"

"I was attempting to speak to you about Michaela." Frowning, she didn't notice when he took the tray of tarts onto his lap, giving it his full attention and began to eat with gusto. His body was trim, fitted with lean muscle, and yet he consumed more food than anyone she knew.

"She is not her carefree self of late," she proceeded. "When I called upon her to announce I'd come home early, she was so pensive I thought she'd quarreled with her mother. She denied it, and it occurred to me it could be the melancholy. I worry, you see, because Wooly could be like that at times. He would shut himself away for hours, sometimes days. She is not like that exactly, however. She is more . . ."

"In love," he said and popped another morsel of tart into his mouth. "She's probably in love."

"In love? That is impossible."

"Why? Are there no men paying her court? She is a very lovely young woman. I would imagine there are many men who would be happy to romance her. One of them caught her fancy, that's all there is to it."

"You are not to notice that she is a lovely young woman. You are not to think of her in that manner, do you hear me?"

"Why, May, are you jealous?" That twinkle in his eye never failed to set her pulse to racing.

She tried to ignore the climbing heat the cursed man

could invoke with that look. She replied primly, "You know I am wildly irrational when it comes to you. Since I cannot have you, not publicly, I tend to be a bit possessive with what I am able to lay claim to."

He grinned, brushing the crumbs from his hands. "Is knowing me privately not enough?"

"Your conceit is showing, Robert. No man is that good in bed that a woman can forget all her other needs."

What had made her say that? She had never voiced any discontent with their relationship, and she didn't like doing so now. It made her sound grasping.

He put the tray back and, reaching out his long arm, he ran his hand along her shoulder.

A cascade of shivers flowed over her flesh. He knew it, too, his expression gloating. "I thought you enjoyed our very nonpublic meetings."

She gave him an admonishing smack on the shoulder. It sounded as crisp as a snap. "Stop laughing at me," she said coolly, doing very well in hiding her reaction to his touch. "I am trying to have a serious conversation with you. And what do you know of young girls in love?"

"I was young once, and I knew some girls who were in love."

"In love with you, you mean."

He grinned again, enigmatically silent.

"I don't think Michaela is in love." She picked up one of the tarts, pinching off a corner of sweet crust and sampling it. "There are men, of course, always in attendance whenever she is at a rout or a dinner party. . . . Oh, no."

"What?"

The tart was poised just before her mouth as she mulled over her thoughts. "She absolutely cannot be harboring a tendré for Major Khoury."

"Why not? He is all the rage, isn't he?"

"He is absolutely wrong for her. She could never pine for a man like Khoury. He is so serious, even surly. And she is so young. She's only just begun to make her mark on the ton. Wooly would be so proud of her, of what she has only begun to do."

Robert pursed his lips. "She is not Woolrich, May."

"But she is—"

"She may look like your brother. I'll grant you the resemblance is startling. She may even have traits that put you to mind of him. But she is her mother's child as well. More, though, she is her own person." He frowned. "And you have a grudge against the major. Why?"

May chewed on the inside of her lip and frowned. "He puts me to mind of someone. I think he will prove unpleasant in the end, for all of his dashing charm and mystery. No, Robert, I do not like him."

Robert handed her a glass. She took it absently and drank the wine without tasting it. "Do you really think she could be in love?"

"I don't know. I am tired of the topic in any event." He reached for his book, which he had placed on the table. May placed her hand on its cover, preventing him from opening it. He looked up and she cocked one brow.

His hand twisted, fingers capturing hers. "So," he said, "are you determined to speak about love, May?"

Pulling on her hand, he guided her out of her chair and firmly nestled her onto his lap. He buried his nose in the curve of her neck and murmured, "Then I shall speak about love." His hand closed over her breast and she gasped with the sudden rush of pleasure.

"It is a very special language." His hand moved slowly. Her head fell limply to his shoulder. "It needs no words, nor even a voice."

To show she understood his language perfectly, she slipped her hand down to his lap. "Ah," she sighed, nuzzling the salty musk of his smoothly shaven cheek, "but it does help to use one's tongue." Which she did, to great effect.

He ground out an unintelligible word, and she turned her face toward him for his kiss. He obliged, covering her mouth, then drawing away, whispering against her lips, "I see you are fluent yourself."

A little while later, when his book lay on the floor and he was splayed on his back in the middle of the Aubusson carpet, May gazed at him. He was a man, full-grown and seething with virile energy, but in this vulnerable moment, with his sooty lashes fanned against those aristocratic cheekbones, his mouth lax and soft in sleep, he looked heart-wrenchingly like a boy.

He was as silly as one, too, she thought, laying her head against the firm give of his shoulder. Imagine him boasting he knew anything at all about women in love.

How ever could he, when he didn't even suspect that her own heart was hopelessly lost?

Whenever Adrian dreamed about the battlefield, it was always the same. Part memory, part cruel fabrication from his own haunted conscience, he relived some version of the moment when Paul Trent died.

Fatally wounded, falling slowly, slowly, as if time had stretched like a giant pull of taffy so that each second was transformed into a minute and a minute to an hour, Adrian watched helplessly.

Tonight, as he sat breathing harshly in the silence and the dark, waiting it out until his pulse slowed to normal, images from the nightmare sizzled like live electricity along his nerves. Fragments flashed like small explosions in his head, leftover trauma reluctant to retreat into the shadows again. He remembered the sheen of Trent's hair, wet with blood, plastered to his head. And the way the big, capable man's hands were limp at his sides, not coming forward to break his fall, because he was already dead. On his face was the same expression of shock Adrian had seen so many times on men's features when they saw their end before them.

The solid sound as Trent hit the ground beside Adrian had yanked him cold and unprepared from sleep. Wiping the sweat from his neck, his forehead, his chin, he lay back down, staring up at the ceiling.

How he hated remembering. Sometimes it hurt, actually hurt, like a crushing weight on his chest. As his body cooled, he felt the chill of the room.

He liked it cold at night, preferring to burrow under blan-

kets than to have a fire smoldering in the grate. The window
was open. The air had grown damp.

Folding his hands behind his head, he closed his eyes. No
more Paul Trent. No more of any of the others under his
command whom he had seen lying cold and stiff on the
ground. He breathed a sigh of relief and turned to the bedside
table.

What time was it? Squinting, he read the face of the clock
in the dim light. Five? Too early. Ah hell.

He rose and dressed, sparing his valet having to come at
this ungodly hour. He had not had the services of a gentleman's gentleman for years when he'd served on the Continent, and under worse conditions than prevailed in his
bachelor's quarters in fashionable St. James. He could certainly manage to shave himself and tie a cravat.

Famished, he surprised the house cook, who was busy at
her baking. Cajoling her into a fresh loaf of bread piping hot
from the ovens, he helped himself to an apple and a hunk of
cheese from the larder. She was strict about the rules, but the
woman was in awe of him, and it was one of the few times
he used his reputation for gain.

He reflected that civilian life had made him soft. He'd
known hunger for days during the war, learned how to put it
out of his mind.

What had made him think of that? He didn't like to think
of the war.

It must have been the dream. It sometimes left him disconcerted. A sudden recollection of Michaela telling her class
that war was filled with tragic loss grabbed him.

She had said it without artifice, without affecting false
sympathy. She had said it as if she might know something
about the matter. Some women had played that tack, and
he'd been ashamed of the spark of hope inside him at the
possibility that someone might understand the darkness inside him. Or at least not be afraid.

But their platitudes had been but preludes to flirtation,
and he'd taken the tarnished offering and left with the knowledge that he was truly alone; the nagging questions and the

horrid sense of guilt that lived inside him could not be shared.

What made it worse was that he was actually *admired*. England's citizens, even those who had lost loved ones in the torrid battles, lauded her heroes. The sadness of the loss was not to be dwelled upon, never to be spoken of. It was nearly treasonous to suggest the war had been anything less than glorious.

"War is not glorious."

The sound of Michaela's voice, the memory of it, rang like a ghost in his head. He felt his heart twist.

How had she known?

Her face came into his mind. *"It is serious business, young lady, and it is to be spoken of with deep respect for the gravity of the lives affected by it."*

How could she comprehend that? He hadn't known it, not until Quatre Bras when fate had struck a tragic lesson. He, for all of his life had been brash, even frivolous. Fools had seen it as bravery. It was merely nothing to lose.

He hadn't cared about death except in that one fatal moment when it came to call. His own men had saved his life.

Which was how Paul Trent, as good a man and soldier as Adrian had ever known, had fallen. In a way he'd taken his commander's place. Adrian came to think of it like that. Trent had died, and his young wife would never see him again, never lay their baby in his arms, and Adrian, who had nothing, lived on.

He returned home. To nothing. No, not nothing. This wretched burden of clawing shame that he had not been the one.

He should have been the one to die.

He had thought he would face death bravely. But when the moment came, he'd been afraid. The indestructible, brilliant, irascible common man's champion, Major Khoury, war hero and legend . . . was a fraud.

Rubbing the heels of his hands over his face, he tried to scrub away the morose thoughts. Old wounds didn't bear examining, but for the fact that Michaela Standish had somehow spoken of them without ever meaning to.

He worked for a few hours at his desk, answering correspondence and reading the political pamphlets being circulated by various factions.

Consulting his watch, he wondered if Michaela would be taking the air in Hyde Park today. Perhaps she rode or was driven in a fashionable curricle.

It didn't bear too close an examination, the lightening in his mood as he decided he would at least see if she were out. He shrugged on a coat and placed his hat on his head.

When he didn't find her in the park that day, however, it left him disgruntled. A curious reaction he didn't like at all. Perhaps it was best if he cooled his heels a bit before pursuing her. It would clear his head.

Yet, he had the strangest, most discomfiting sensation that he wasn't ever going to know a clear thought regarding Michaela Standish.

❦ *Chapter 9*

Michaela's dance card was full on the night of the Earl of Breamore's *grande fête*. The Mayfair mansion of the highly fashionable couple was stuffed full of notables. It was difficult for anyone to maintain their ennui when the prince regent himself made an appearance. He congregated with the men in the billiards room, took a turn or two on the dance floor, then made his exit.

Breamore and his countess then proceeded to strut importantly about the party, doing their best to act droll and unfazed, as if Prinny dropped by nearly every evening.

Michaela found this amusing, but truth to tell, she was awfully impressed herself. Breamore's heir, the Viscount of Wickam, approached to claim her for the dance he'd reserved in the beginning of the evening. He was very handsome, tall and blond, resembling some possible Norse ancestor, and had a great love of fun.

"I think he is ridiculously fat," Wickam observed as they picked up on the topic of the evening: the prince regent. "I rather think the sausages at the buffet had more of a shape than he."

He said it drolly, without any real mischief, and she allowed a laugh to escape before she could catch it: He grinned, then turned her around the dance floor with relish.

Thus encouraged, he went on, "My father is a friend of his, but one of the type who loves to run to all his other friends with, 'The prince said this,' and 'The prince said that,' and going on and on about it until everyone within earshot is reaching for a vinaigrette."

That made her laugh again, and she lost her footing. He caught her in his arms and righted her. "Clumsy of me. Do forgive me, Miss Standish. Now, as I was saying, good old Prinny . . . ah, yes, I was about to comment on his costume. Did you see it? He thinks himself the height of fashion, I can tell you, but if I see one more bow on that man . . . well, *I* might need a vinaigrette."

They took another turn together, this one working quite nicely. He regaled her with more amusements, and she found she was able to keep the steps of the dance well enough as long as she wasn't laughing too hard.

"See how you've improved," he praised when they went a space without a stumble.

"I only just learned. My aunt taught me just recently. My mother found it scandalous and wouldn't allow me to learn until she found they were permitting it in more and more ballrooms. Even the Almack's patronesses allow it these days, with special permission. I am afraid I need more practice. I am better at the quadrille."

"Ah, then reserve that dance in advance at your next rout. I shall wish to see this spectacular vision of artistic movement."

Giggling, she realized she was having a wonderful time. Wickam might be handsome, charming, and a relative stranger, but she somehow sensed she could relax with him. His flirtation was harmless, meant only to amuse, not seduce. There were no dark currents here, no feeling of dizziness and excitement and frightening physical sensations to confuse her. Like Adrian.

And just as she thought of him, she spotted him on the edge of the floor among the crowd watching the dancers. His hands were on his cane, propped squarely in front of him, and he was peering straight at her.

Her body reacted violently with a deep, visceral heat.

"You know, the worst thing about Prinny," her partner was saying, "is that he adores the French styles. He fashions his hair like Bonaparte. Don't you think that's the epitome of the ironic?"

Wickam whirled her, and she had to shut her eyes to keep herself from feeling too light-headed. She scolded herself hotly, despising the strong feelings that were already coursing through her.

She couldn't help herself. She sneaked another peek. Adrian stood, arms crossed over his chest, staring blatantly at her and fuming like Vesuvius.

"I think someone should tell him Bonaparte was defeated," Wickam went on, shaking his head sadly. "By his own armies. I suppose they don't as he might decry the loss to men's fashion."

Michaela struggled to attend her dance partner. After the interlude with Adrian at Mr. Rye's gallery shop, she had been looking so forward to seeing him again. But he hadn't so much as sent a note in all of this time. He had promised to call. All right, she did say she wouldn't receive him, but whenever had her denials stopped him before?

She had begun to think she must have imagined the cozy intimacy of that afternoon. Perhaps only she had thought it memorable. After all, she was brought up with no real knowledge of his complex world of the blue bloods. They were a different breed, she had learned, with odd ideas of fidelity and devotion that would never be found in her heart.

It was her conclusion that he had realized how mismatched they were and moved on to more likely candidates for the wife of an MP.

"There is a man who could tell him," Wickam declared, having finally noticed Adrian. "Why, it is our famous Major Khoury. Perhaps he is the man brave and brash enough to apprise our regent that it is unfashionable in the extreme to emulate the man whom you have just defeated in war."

She found her voice. "Yes. I see him."

"He looks disgruntled."

She sighed. "It is a common ailment with him. Dyspepsia, I think. Do not be discouraged by it."

"Ah. Are you a friend of his?"

How odd, when put like that. She would have liked to have answered differently, but she said meekly, "We are acquainted, although I haven't seen him in a while."

"Then when our dance ends, let us go see him. I wonder what he thinks of Prinny."

"Oh, I doubt the major has much patience for Prinny's follies."

"Ah, but he does entertain us—the prince regent, I mean, not the major."

Michaela replied dryly, "Oh, the major has his amusing moments as well."

"Drat," Wickam said. "There is my father signaling to me. He probably wishes me to meet someone, and I know what it is about. Another of his potential brides with which he harasses me mercilessly. How tiresome he is, parading eligible women before me, and always when I am having the best time."

"I am flattered," Michaela said at the implied compliment.

"The man wants grandchildren. How do I know this? I have ears, do I not, to hear him proclaim it at least four times daily? And I am only seven and twenty, hardly the age for a buck of the ton to be forced to settle down."

"It is not such a great age, but not too young, I think. And an old man likes to know his family is settled, his line of succession secured. He may be just feeling his age, my lord."

He looked surprised for a moment. "All the other girls I know always agree when I wish to paint myself blue. You aren't like the others, are you Miss Standish?"

She blushed. "I am like any other girl, I am sure."

He shook his head. "You are not. I am honored if you would allow me to call you friend. I like a person to tell me what she thinks without trying to soften the blow, so to speak. We are all men in my household, my brothers and my father and I. I could use a woman's honest point of view."

"I would be happy for you to call upon me, my lord, at your convenience."

"I shall. Now, for this evening, advise me, please. I am a free spirit, but I am a good son. What is to be done, to please a father or please my recklessness?"

"Why don't you just go meet the girl first? If you find her agreeable, there is your solution right there."

When he grinned, his blue eyes sparkled. "You are a genius."

"Your father is growing impatient."

"One more thing. What do I do if she is not agreeable?"

She smiled at him. "Why, run, my lord."

Wickam laughed, bowing over her hand before hurrying off. Michaela chuckled to herself as she turned, almost colliding with Adrian. They were in the middle of a crush, and the press of the crowd trapped her.

He had been standing very close. They were even closer now, a problem she remedied with a swift step backwards, but it wasn't as far as she would like.

His smile was cynical. "Is that your new beau?"

"My beau? Wickam?" The knowledge that he was jealous was so sweet, it left a pleasurable throb in her stomach. She said, "I don't know. I think he's very pleasing."

"I saw you laughing," he said. "I wanted to call him out on the spot."

"Well, that makes sense. It *is* a hideous offense, and anyone making me laugh should pay the ultimate price." Scowling, she made to brush past him, but he subtly blocked her with a strategic step. "You are showing your brutish side again. I was all set to be pleasant to you when next we met, but you make it impossible."

"You bring out my worst, have you noticed? Perhaps it is your low opinion of me."

She snapped her fan open, fluttering it in agitation. "Can you read thoughts, then?"

"I daresay, if I could read your thoughts at this moment, my sensibilities would be positively assaulted."

"I didn't know you possessed sensibilities. You've certainly never demonstrated any sign of them thus far."

"I don't know why I like your acid tongue, but I do." He flashed a demon's grin full of dark heat. His eyes swept her, from her bared shoulders to the silken hem of her dress. "It only makes me want you more."

"Ah," she said, closing her fan with a punctuating snap, "what a treasure that is to me."

"Now you are just attempting to annoy me."

"You were already annoyed before we had exchanged a single word. And without cause. You've not bothered with me in a good deal of time, and are now put out because I've found pleasant companionship."

"I know. I'm incorrigible. You've told me so before."

"Lot of good it did."

They made their way through the crowd, conversing in hushed tones and pleasant demeanors that were in complete contrast to the barbs flying between them. They were thus engaged in their pretense when a man crossed their path.

He was tall, barrel-chested, with a great mane of salt-and-pepper hair. The moment he saw them, he reacted strongly, recognizing Adrian, his arrogant features twisting in an expression of disdain.

In turn, Adrian's body tightened. She felt the subtle wave of enmity emanating forth like a wave of heat. He proceeded past him with exaggerated indifference.

"Who was that?" Michaela asked, unable to keep her curiosity checked.

"Why, Michaela, I had no idea there was anything amiss with your powers of sight. That was a slug dressed in a cravat and tailcoat."

She arched a delicate brow to give him an imperious look. "Does the slug have a name?"

"Shepston." She waited, but he provided no other information. "He is the Earl of Shepston."

"And may I gather you do not like him?"

"I loathe him. And he loathes me."

Tossing her head impudently, she teased, "It is no wonder if you display the same lack of manners with him as you do with me."

He flashed a smile, throwing off the scowl. "How am I supposed to react when I catch you flirting outrageously with another man? You were doing it on purpose, were you not, hoping to get a rise out of me?"

"Of course I was. You have seen through my guise. Everything in my world is done for the sole purpose of how it will affect you. You are the center of my universe. I was only having a good time for the purpose of annoying you."

He laughed. She was only teasing now. "Ah. Well, it worked," he assured her.

She paused, staring at him. "If you really are jealous, you have no right to be, you know. You have sent not one word while you've been off wife-hunting!"

"What? Wife-hunting? Who said . . . Ah . . . the gossips have had at you. And it is *you* who are jealous."

"I am not! Everyone knows a politician needs a wife. It is no matter to me, of course, but it hardly puts you in a position to be possessive."

"How would you like it if I came into this ball tonight with another woman on my arm?"

She sputtered for a moment, then announced, "I need refreshment. If you will pardon me."

This time he allowed her to pass. She made her way to the refreshment table. Again, he dogged her, his fluid use of his cane not impeding his ability to keep up.

"I missed you like mad," he said casually over her shoulder as she placed several petits fours on her plate. The calm words nearly took her knees out from under her.

She fought for control. "You did well enough that you didn't seek to remedy the situation by calling. Not that I would have received you."

"And you fared well enough without me, I see. I doubt you spared me a thought for all your pretended indignation. You were having a fine time, cozy with that Wickersham fellow."

"Wickam," she corrected.

His voice took on a husky tone. "Come with me outside."

"No. I will not."

"Come, Michaela." He was a man who was not used to having his wishes defied. In fact, it was damned hard not to obey. "We can stroll the garden. It's quite acceptable."

"Why should I go with you?"

"Because I am beside myself. I saw you, laughing and flirting, and all of my careful cautions flew, and I found myself quite out of my head."

"You must be out of your head indeed, sir. At last we find a topic upon which we can agree."

"I need to talk to you, away from everyone." He was lying. It wasn't a desire for conversation that burned in his eyes. She felt her resistance crack and crumble like porcelain dashed against stone.

"Come with me out to the garden. I assure you, you are quite safe."

She would never be safe from him. She had this as a clear thought, and yet when his gloved hand pulled hers through his crooked elbow, she allowed it.

After her dance with Wickam, she should have rejoined her family. She murmured this halfheartedly as a token protest. He ignored her, and as soon as the words died on her lips, they were forgotten.

He was skillfully riding the edge of propriety, and she wasn't sure whether to protest. Oh, she was tempted. True, he was being unforgivably forward but not insultingly so. And he was doing it in such a way that no observer could tell, not from the even tone of his voice, not from his correct motions, what she was certain were his shocking intentions.

But she knew exactly what he was doing. And what she was doing, too.

She did not protest as he pulled her outside, for this devil had taken possession of her, and even if he were leading her straight to perdition, she could not have raised a finger to deny him.

She did not feel her feet hitting the ground or the touch of those whom she brushed up against as they worked their way free of the throng, and out to the night.

The air was thick, moist, filled with verdant smells of foliage unfurling tentatively amid the seductive beckoning of milder temperatures and longer days. There was fever in her flesh, and the caress of the chilly air on her bared shoulders and arms felt wonderful.

"Here," he said, and they strolled a way, quite respectably, her hand on his arm, in silence. But as she suspected, they were barely clear of the lighted torches along the house when he pulled her safely into the shadows, away from prying eyes and into the nooks and crannies built to harbor couples seeking privacy.

There was nothing gentle or romantic about either his touch or his kiss. His hand captured the back of her neck, and his mouth descended over hers roughly.

The warmth he breathed into her seemed to melt her bones, and she became loose-limbed in an instant. The feel of his soft lips moving over hers, his tongue stroking alive her passion, left her gasping. She clung to him, sighing weakly, as he drew back.

She tried to pull away, but he had her fast. "What are you thinking? Why did you do that?"

"Because it's been driving me insane not to." He touched the wisps of hair that curled over her face, traced the outline of her ear. She shivered.

"You like it when I touch you." As if to make his point, his deft fingers brushed chills over her neck. His lips were at her forehead, pressing small kisses to her temple. "I need to touch you. It is why I stayed away, you fool. I knew I wouldn't resist."

She opened her mouth, but nothing came forth. Instead, she twisted her face, turning it upward so that he could kiss her again. He framed her face in his large, callused hands and possessed her mouth.

His hand slipped to her waist. Grasping fingers dug into the swell of her hips, his long legs braced so that when she leaned against him, she was secure. The rigid line of him against her thigh told her he was aroused.

She felt a bolt of excitement, chased away quickly by shame. She pulled back, confused. Something inside her reacted to the evidence of his desire, but she'd been taught to fear and dread sex.

How did one reconcile that to the delicious eddies of sensation pooling in the valley between her thighs and making her breasts throb?

"You do that to me," he said huskily, knowing full well what she had felt. "Every moment I am in your presence, every time I think of you."

"I didn't mean to. You can't blame me for that."

He chuckled, his breath fanning over her face. "Of course I blame you. How can I not when you make me mad to touch you?"

A small sound escaped her, and she felt her muscles melt, leaving her pliant and weak in his arms. She pressed her hands tentatively to his face, feeling the powerful jaw, the thick cording of his neck. "I want to touch you, too."

Persian silk could not be as soft as his lips. She moved her cheek against his, marveling at the combination of textures. His chin was rough, his throat silken.

His hands cupped the back of her neck, and he stared down at her fiercely. "My God, your curiosity is the most potent aphrodisiac I've known."

She dug her hand in his hair and brought his head down to hers.

He took what she offered, trailing hungry kisses down the graceful column of her neck. He murmured, "You are nothing I want in my life, Michaela. But I can't get you out of my mind."

Her tone bore the depth of her insult as she stiffened in his arms. "Neither are you. You are arrogant and uncaring, and you give orders imperiously."

"You are very rude to me," he said. She heard the smile in his voice. Her skin prickled as his teeth grazed the skin just under her ear. "I put up with much disrespect. I am unused to that."

"That is because you are obnoxious and contrary." Her head suddenly felt too heavy to support. "I don't know why I even speak to you."

His hands smoothed over her shoulder, leaving her feeling

suddenly, deliciously exposed. "You are so beautiful. But I've known beautiful women before."

Her back arched. His fingers hooked inside the neckline of her dress, and he hesitated as if he were considering his next move.

She said, "You aren't even kind. You amuse yourself cruelly at my expense."

He withdrew his fingers, and she felt disappointed. Running one fingertip lightly along her collarbone, he left her paralyzed. "Your skin is only as soft as any other woman's. Surely it is merely my imagination that makes it seem that I have never felt anything as the feel of it."

"You have dreadful manners. Too many years in your regiment. You are coarse and insolent."

"You are too stubborn." His lips brushed hers, and hers answered.

"Your mockery never fails to infuriate me."

Leaning closer, he touched his nose to her hair. "Anyone could use that soap and she would smell the same. It is not unique."

"No, it is not," she whispered. Her eyelids drifted closed. He kissed her again.

The hand on her hip slid up her back, tracking tightly the curve of her spine. "I could find a hundred women as tall as you are. Some move as you do, with a dancer's grace. It would not be impossible to duplicate."

She smiled and felt hot tears on her lashes. "It is a nuisance, anyway. I am always towering over everyone. And my dresses cost extra for the added material. And I am not graceful, not at all."

"I like your walk." His lips brushed her forehead. She could feel his breath on her skin, lifting wisps of her hair. "You look like a gazelle."

She laughed softly. "I don't know how well I favor being likened to an animal."

He bent his head, his mouth just a hair's breadth from her own. "A beautiful, graceful one . . . yes, you like it."

He kissed her again. Yes. She liked it. She liked all of it. All of him.

She twined her hands around his neck, holding tightly, wanting more. Wanting this wonderful, soaring feeling to never end.

He murmured something, a swear word, but he said it so soft and rough, it was like an endearment.

Suddenly, he seized both of her hands, and his expression was grave. "I'm stupid from thinking of you, of scheming ways of finding you, how to be with you. Do you know what I mean, Michaela? I want to be with you."

She thought she did, and her heart soared. How she yearned for his nerve-racking presence, his rumbling laughter, the way his eyes grazed her with passionate looks. She pined. All right, she pined.

"Yes," she said, answering on a breath buoyed with joy.

He was about to say something else, something she desperately wished to hear, when the sounds of people nearby shot them to alert.

"I thought I saw him out here," a male voice said. The voice called, "Adrian?"

A muffled sound issued from deep down Adrian's throat. An epithet again, but this time nothing gentle.

"Where the devil did he go?" the man said. "I swear, my brother came this way. I saw him myself."

"Terrance," a female voice chided, "perhaps you were mistaken. Or maybe he's gone back inside. It was horrible getting through that crush, and we might have missed him."

Adrian bent to whisper to Michaela. "My younger brother, and his fiancée, if I'm not mistaken."

She felt a slam of chilly air as he stepped away. His abrupt absence left her to rely on her own strength, which felt questionable.

"Come with me," he said, and once again he was in command. He proceeded out of the alcove and down the path. Somehow she managed to will her body to move, to take his direction, and she followed.

"Terrance! Indeed it is you. I didn't expect to see you here tonight." Adrian's voice was cordial, steady, betraying nothing of the passion that had made it rough and low only moments ago. Michaela stood shivering by his side.

"I thought I spied you," Terrance replied gleefully. "I told Connie it was you. We have so been wanting to see you."

Terrance was obviously a Khoury, his face bearing a resemblance to his brother, but his youth and rangy build gave him an entirely different aspect. The men greeted one another warmly.

"This is Miss Standish," Adrian said. His voice was not precisely unfriendly, but Terrance, who no doubt knew his brother well, seemed to notice. He looked back and forth between them. Michaela felt her face flame.

"I am delighted to meet you," Terrance answered. "My fiancée, Miss Constance Perlmutter."

They murmured their greetings, and Michaela supposed she made a better show of it than she thought, for all seemed fine.

Adrian turned to Constance. "Terrance does nothing but talk of you. Are you chilled? It is rather cool out tonight. Terrance, shame on you for being so lax. We should take Miss Constance inside."

Michaela walked along with them, numb and dazed and trying frantically to appear unfazed. Looking up, she saw the stars winking above her. She felt as if she'd just been among the heavens.

And she wanted to go there again.

What wicked thoughts were these, what insanity? Whatever had happened to her pride? He had wooed her with an insulting offer, and she had melted like an ice princess in the arms of a fiery demon.

"Miss Standish?" Terrance's voice was full of concern. "Are you well?"

"Oh, yes, of course, I . . ." She paused, thinking she wasn't well, not at all. She was as confused as a bedlamite, and overwhelmed. "I think I should find my family. They are probably looking all over for me. Will you excuse me?"

ℌ *Chapter 10*

When the Standish women returned home that evening,
Michaela wanted desperately to flee to her room. Before she
could, she caught Delilah staring at her.

"Are you all right, Michaela?" she asked shyly.

"Yes, of course. Why?"

"Your cheeks are scarlet, and your mouth is bloodred."

Shocked, Michaela clamped a hand over her lips. Her reaction, spontaneous as it was, gave her away. She darted a
look to her mother and other sister, but they were occupied,
Mother complaining about her feet and Delinda relaying the
gossips she'd accumulated throughout the evening.

"I am tired. I shall go to bed at once," Michaela said and
spun on her heel.

"Michaela," Delilah called, running after her.

Michaela stopped at the top of the stairs, closing her eyes
against the dread of what was coming. Her sisters loved to
torment her. She braced herself, knowing she had only herself and her artless stupidity to blame for the ribbing she was
about to receive. "What do you want?" she demanded.

"I am worried. Did something happen. Is it Major Khoury? What is wrong?"

"Oh, of course, you are probably beset with concern." She heard the sarcasm in her voice. She strode purposefully down the hall, meaning to discourage the girl from further curiosity.

But for once, her shy sister was not dissuaded. She kept in step. "I didn't mean to pry. I know you think I don't care, but I do. I don't wish you to be overset, and I can see you are."

"I am sure you do. No doubt you wish to go now and impart every detail to Delinda."

Delilah's eyes glimmered suddenly, as if tears had sprung to them.

Oh, no, this was too much. Now she was going to pretend Michaela's words had hurt her!

"I thought I might help."

There was, amazingly, a pang of regret upon that wan face. Steeling herself, Michaela refused to offer an apology. She did, however, pause at her bedroom door. "You don't have to go. I just wished for some privacy. I . . . I didn't mean to be rude."

Delilah hesitated. "Did something go wrong tonight? You don't seem happy."

Michaela entered her bedchamber. She didn't say anything when Delilah followed her inside. She had never invited her before, although the twins had made free with her room frequently in the past. "I had a busy evening; that is all."

"You can only mean Major Khoury. I saw him. His eyes were on you all night when you were with that handsome fellow."

She sighed. It was impossible to deny it. "Yes."

"It is rather obvious you two were enamored. Don't worry, I didn't mind." She sat on the edge of the bed. "It was rather funny to see Delinda's tantrums finally set Mother's teeth on edge. I think she's realized she's created a monster. I know you only set your cap for him to vex her in the beginning, but I think you two really do suit. Please don't mind about Mother pushing him for one of us twins. It's at

Delinda's insistence. She won't give up the hope that she still might secure his interest."

"Yes, Mother is quite consumed with your prospects," Michaela said, ashamed of the bitterness in her voice.

"She worries about us because we are older, and because Delinda . . . well, she can be difficult. In a weak moment Mother promised her she would be the first to marry, and I am afraid she is holding her to it. And I am no good at meeting new people, and she keeps pushing me. I think it is I who vex her the most, actually."

Michaela shook her head. "I can't believe you are being so nice to me."

It was Delilah's turn to look uncomfortable. "I'd like us to be friends. I mean, I don't suppose you need friends, you have so many. But since we're sisters as much as Delinda and I, I thought . . ."

"I don't have so many friends that I cannot use another."

Delilah plucked at Michaela's coverlet. "Why, who would have thought you gave a fig for us? You always fought Mother tooth and nail. As for Delinda and I . . . well, I didn't suppose you could abide us in the least. We have been horrid at times."

"I suppose we never got on very well. And as for Mother, I didn't think of it as me fighting her. I thought it was her fighting me."

Delilah laughed, and after a moment, Michaela's shoulders relaxed and she laughed, too.

"I envied your courage in opposing her as you did. I never had it myself. You always knew just what you were about, and you never gave an inch."

"Goodness, no." She stared amazed at Delilah, realizing just how differently they had both seen the same situation. "You can't have thought I was confident."

"Of course you were. You were so beautiful, and so exotic and interesting." Delilah shrugged, twisting her plump fingers together. "Delinda and I only made fun of you because we were jealous. Or at least I did. I'm so ashamed of it now."

Michaela came to the bed and sat down next to her. "I

never knew you felt that way. I thought you regarded me as a silly twit, or worse, a mortal enemy."

Delilah smiled. "Surely we were not that bad, were we? Oh, Michaela, I truly am sorry now. Can you forgive me?"

"Delilah, you've made me very happy. It is wonderful to me that we can talk like this. It's really all I've ever wanted."

"Mother says you don't need us any longer. I think that makes her sad."

"I cannot imagine that."

Delilah's voice turned wistful. "I don't blame you. Lady May is so lovely, and she knows so much. She loves you very dearly." Growing excited, she sat straighter, becoming almost pretty with color in her face and her brown eyes round and animated. "I think she has a wonderful way with clothes. I love her daring! Imagine, wearing pink feathers! She always has the most outrageous things in her costumes, things that would be ridiculous on anyone else but on her, and yet it only accentuates how softly feminine she is. I wish I had such a flair."

It was difficult to believe she was actually having this girlish conversation with Delilah, but she was. She felt poignantly happy. "It is really her modiste who is the genius. Oh, Madam Bonvant is absolutely wonderful, Delilah. She is like a whirlwind, tossing material here and there, decrying this design as outré, praising another, and all while I can make neither heads nor tails over any of the mishmash of it all, yet in the end, she produces the most gorgeous clothing."

"It sounds like so much fun."

"I will ask Aunt May to take you with us. You would absolutely love it. I know you are looking to make a change of wardrobe."

"Oh, I would like to, very much." She was excited, then halted. "I want to ask you something, a favor. My name . . . I hate it. I've been thinking about this for a long time, and I think Mother had to be delirious when she decided on those names. I mean *Delinda* and *Delilah*?"

"You don't like your name?"

"It forever links me with Delinda, as if our looks don't do that enough already. I wish to be my own woman, and so I am going to choose my own name. I'd like you to call me Lilah from now on."

Michaela laughed. "That's a lovely name. All right. Lilah. Oh, that will take some getting used to, but I daresay it will be easier when you look completely different, which you will when we get you an entire new wardrobe."

The distraction with Delilah had settled her brain a bit. She felt more herself already, less undone. Mother had always said that the best way to get one's mind off of one's own problems was to help someone else.

She said, "Let's speak to Aunt May about it right away. We'll call on her tomorrow."

Delilah—Lilah—beamed back at Michaela. "Yes, let's do."

Michaela recognized Adrian's carriage the moment she exited the school the following afternoon.

He lounged outside, taking in the street scene and deliberately not turning toward her, although she could tell he knew she was there. Her heart thundered as she approached, knowing she was tempting the devil himself, but she wasn't able to help herself.

"Did you not wish to come inside?"

"And have to face that bloodthirsty lot again? No, thank you."

She laughed.

"I came to give you a ride home, Miss Standish."

"I do not think I had better. My maid should be along soon, and I enjoy the walk."

"Nora is already at home. I sent her away."

"You what?"

"I told her that I was a friend of the family. You really should look into hiring better staff. She's a flighty creature. She never asked a question, just bolted, happy as a lark for the time to herself."

"You cannot simply—"

"Afraid your morals aren't strong enough for the challenge?" he said lightly, stepping aside and gesturing toward the door. They both knew she was going to accept.

Sauntering up to him, she gave him a haughty look. "I am more afraid of yours failing, sir."

"As well you might be," he murmured. The softness of his voice raised gooseflesh and a pleasant tingle along her spine.

With a toss of her head and a light, "Hmph," she allowed him to hand her into the carriage. He climbed in and sat down beside her instead of taking the seat opposite.

"It's rather a tight fit," she protested. He only smiled and squeezed closer.

He checked the ties of the curtains over the small windows, satisfied with their privacy. "One of my favorite things about this carriage. The tight fit." He pulled her to him roughly.

"Get properly into your seat," she demanded. She pushed ineffectually against his shoulders.

He didn't budge. "I thought you would never come out of there. What were you doing, reading the *Iliad* to those poor children?"

She never had a chance to answer. His mouth smothered the clipped retort she'd been about to utter, but she didn't mind. The aroma of spice and musk, the rock-hard feel of his body, the hungry fire of his mouth taking possession of hers tipped her into a free fall of sensation.

His hands felt like brands of heated iron, burning into her flesh clear through her clothing. He cupped her chin, holding her face still as his tongue plundered her mouth. From deep in his throat came a low rumble of satisfaction.

She clung to him, helpless as he moved down to attack her neckline. She could feel the knotted muscles of his arms ripple as his fingers worked with amazing dexterity with the buttons of her dress. Once he had spread the unfastened flaps of her bodice, he splayed his ungloved hand over her throat and chest. His warmth filled her, as if flowing from him and into her.

His lips moved against her hairline. "I waited for hours."

She struggled for breath. "I had to take Delilah—"

He cut her off. "Damn. I don't care." He laughed with diabolical glee. "I have you now. I would have stood here for days to gain this."

His mouth trailed down the straining tendons of her neck, nibbling lightly. Her strength fled, and yet her arms clasped him tighter with surprising urgency. Her fingers dug into his hair, and she arched her neck to give more access to his delicious attentions.

The sway of the carriage tumbled their bodies together on the seat. His strong hand cupped her buttocks and brought her onto his lap.

The feel of his iron-hewn thighs against her bottom shocked her. He chuckled at her gasp, and then gave no respite as his fingers opened her gaping neckline and he kissed the hollow at the base of her throat.

She fell against him, her anxious fingers working to open his coat. She wanted to be closer, to touch him and feel him. Her hands flattened against the plane of his chest, and in her palm she could feel the sure and steady thrust of his racing heart.

With a swift movement, he tugged at the front of his shirt. She heard the tiny sounds as onyx studs flew in every direction. Then his warm hand enveloped hers and slid it into the gaping fabric.

The texture of his flesh was like velvet. So warm. Underneath, his muscles quivered, hard muscles that pulsed with virility and strength so foreign.

"I've never touched a man."

He answered with a groan, and that emboldened her. She was fascinated with the texture of him, the shape of muscle, how differently he was made from her. Hungry, she moved, feeling the flex of sinew as he shifted, gathering her more tightly to him.

"I've waited a long time for you, Michaela," he said, his words staccato syllables ripped from him.

She'd waited longer, she thought. All of her life to feel this way, to be held by a man and loved as a woman. Wanted, desired at last, for herself, odd or not.

He held her captive while his kisses blazed a trail of fire down to the swell of her breast, fear and excitement blending inside of her. She whimpered, torn with knowing she should not be allowing any of this to take place, and yet when his fingers brushed the sensitive peak of her breast, she lost all interest in denying him anything. He stroked her again.

She felt the forbidden touch all through her. Her heart fluttered like a mad bird. Her toes curled into the unforgiving soles of her expensive slippers, the silk stockings suddenly decadently soft against the sensitive flesh of her thighs. Every nerve ending danced, and she fell back in his arms, surrendering to mindless pleasure.

In a few swift moves, he undid the buttons to expose the upper curves of her breasts. The kiss of air on the sensitive flesh curled sweet coils of delectation in the pit of her stomach. Glancing down, she saw herself, her bare skin gleaming like lightly veined marble, the stiffened peaks taut and pink, visible just below the lace of her chemise. Adrian gazed, too, the expression on his face tight and tense as he cupped her tenderly.

She reached for him, gripping his thick shoulders tightly and drawing him back to her. The dark intensity in his rugged face speared her, leaving her defenseless as he kissed her again while his hands squeezed her breasts lightly. His other hand rapidly shirred up her skirt.

His voice was urgent, muffled against her skin. "We can go to my apartments. I'll tell the driver . . . in . . . just a moment." He nuzzled her neck. "Just one more moment. One more kiss."

He moved, taking her under him. The solid mass of him settled pleasurably over her, and her womb contracted in a spasm of welcome when she felt the hot, hard sex rubbing against the apex of her thighs, jolting her with primal recognition, even through layers of clothing. Her hips rose of their own volition to create friction she craved without knowing what she was doing. She knew only that she desperately needed to feed the ache . . . there.

He groaned, a sound of delicious torment. "Don't . . . not that. I can't . . . God, not here."

He pressed into her again, and she realized they were mimicking the act of sexual congress.

She twisted, gasping for breath. Clutching at sanity, she fought against the vortex of his power, her own responsiveness to the way he touched her, kissed her skin, teased alive nerves to send her spinning out of control.

He said something she knew was a prayer, the same prayer for prudence, which was not granted. She cried out as his hand slipped inside her undergarments and molded to the round shape of her derriere. Pressing her hands against his shoulder, she pushed.

"No!" she said, thrashing her legs. "Stop. Please."

He looked at her, his hand growing still. "Did I hurt you?" He leaned his forehead against hers, his eyes clamped shut. "I didn't mean to. I'd never hurt you. I want to make you feel good, I promise, Michaela, please. I need you so much. . . ."

She hesitated. Then the naked want in his voice coiled beckoning fingers against her heart.

"I want to ask you to be my own." His free hand touched her. Her ear, her cheekbone, her chin. "I would provide for you. I would give you whatever you wanted. A house near the park, your own carriage. I would give you your own household, and you could command me, I swear it."

She stopped, a cold feeling creeping into her bones. Was he asking her to marry him?

"And I shall keep you all to myself. I would visit you often. God, I don't know how I'll leave you, how I will even think of it. We'll have a long time together to get to know each other, perhaps take a trip. It will be like a honeymoon."

Her heart stuttered. *Like* a honeymoon.

But not a honeymoon.

She yanked back, staring. Her face burned.

"Michaela?" Rolling his cheek into her neck, he sank his lips to the sensitive curve. She bucked, pushing aside the slick wash of tremors this sent through her torso.

"No. Please." She pushed again. His chest was like a wall. He caught hold of her wrists, holding them away and staring down.

"Let me go," she said.

"Jesus, Michaela, you cannot be serious."

She bucked, this time without any passionate intent. He

threw himself up and off of her with a sound like a wounded bear. Then he twisted away, turning his head into the side of the carriage as if he didn't trust himself to look at her. In the silence, his breathing was as ragged as if he'd run ten leagues.

"I'm sorry," he said, jabbing clawed fingers into his hair. "I frightened you. I didn't mean to. I did that badly. I think I was overcome."

Michaela was busy stuffing her bosom into her dress, still unable to speak.

He glanced over at her, a slight glimmer of hope in his eyes. "Let me take you to my apartments. I want to—"

A sob rose, and she bit it back, camping her jaw down stubbornly. She wasn't about to make the situation worse with blubbering, but her body throbbed, and her heart stung.

He moved toward her. "Michaela."

"No!" She shrank back. "Don't touch me."

"I won't hurt you."

"I am not concerned about you hurting me." But she was—not her body but her heart. "I do not fault you. I am much more horrified by my own inadequate response to this . . ." She shot her hand out expressively. ". . . groping. I was quite vulnerable, I will admit. I will not go to your rooms, Adrian, and you disrespect me to even ask."

He was silent. She barely scraped together enough self-possession to add a haughty edge to her voice as she asked, "Would you please take me home? I am quite humiliated."

Regarding her with a wary eye, he drawled, "Oh, good. We are going to argue. That should keep us occupied and safely away from . . ." He mimicked her hand action. ". . . groping."

She slapped his hand, scowling. He chuckled.

"Don't act the prude, Michaela. It doesn't suit you. I tasted your hunger for me."

She blanched, feeling her entire body melting under the flame of mortification. How dare he taunt her!

"Why are you so afraid of passion?"

She jerked up her head. "I am the daughter of a notorious rake. I daresay passion is in my nature. However, I am not a strumpet. I am not so undisciplined, so uncivilized, so *un-couth* as to spread myself in a carriage for a man's pleasure. Or even my own. I value myself too much to risk so much for an afternoon's diversion."

"And what of a more permanent arrangement?"

Her eyes flared. Thank God he didn't guess how she'd misunderstood. "You insult me to even ask. I will not dignify the disgraceful offer with a reply."

Forked brows dived toward the bridge of his nose. His nostrils curled. "I am afraid I cannot seem to give up the idea of it. I cannot let you go. And despite this little show of pique—" He paused, smiling knowingly. "—you don't wish me to."

"You act as if that is all there is to it. What both of us want, and there it is. We simply fall into bed."

"What else?" He inclined his head, his eyes studying her. "Love? Pretty words and promises of forever? Little fool, those things don't exist. You've been too sheltered, left too long to yourself to dream these childish dreams."

His mockery riled her temper. "That is a callous notion. Haven't you ever been in love?"

His face shifted, suddenly forbidding. "What a stupid question."

She cocked her head, intrigued. "Are you a fraud, or a jade, Adrian?"

He leaned closer, renewing his wicked grin. "Neither. A realist, that is what. And a pragmatist. I want very much to make love to you."

A sharp thrill stabbed her like a lance. She covered the sensation with a toss of her head. "This is an unsuitable conversation, and pointless in any event. It is plain to see we do not suit."

"I thought we just demonstrated that we suit very well. No. Do not give me that suspicious face. I didn't plan this to seduce you. I wouldn't take you cheaply in a carriage. I can't say what it was I was thinking exactly just now. I had to see you, that was all. And then, what with the kiss and then it didn't seem possible to stop. . . . You will most likely never believe me, although I swear it is completely the truth. I wished to speak to you privately, that is all."

The lulling motion of the carriage slowed.

He lifted the curtain and glanced out of the window. "I told the driver to go around to the mews. The coachman will see you to your door."

She gathered her gloves and reticule and without thinking, said, "I suppose I should thank you for the ride, but as you attempted to deflower me in a moving carriage in the middle of the afternoon on the streets of London, I hardly think it appropriate."

She caught him off guard, and he laughed.

He threw open the door for her. "But I failed. Nothing is broken. Your virtue is intact—bruised, perhaps, but basically unbroken. And I have managed to survive your blasted good sense and righteous rebuff."

She paused at the door, turning to give him the benefit of a very direct look. "I tell you again, we do not suit, Adrian. That was made very clear today. We are at odds and ends. I have no doubt you think this merely a lark, but I would appreciate it very much if you would cease this relentless and most immodest pursuit before you ruin my reputation."

He matched her stare. "I wish I could."

Chapter 11

A dreary, damp day in late May could prove as cold as De-
cember. The wind coming off the Thames had a bite, and it
turned London into an unseasonable fit of chills.

When asked why she was so inclined to remain at home,
curled by the fire with a book on her lap, Michaela blamed it
on the weather.

The weather, however, did not explain why she stared for
long periods at the same paragraph when trying to read or
why her pen stood poised over an unfinished article while
her thoughts took to the winds, flying hither and yon to subjects that made her heart compress. It was not the reason why
she did not go to the school. How could she venture out
when she was terrified of putting herself in the path of
Adrian Khoury once again?

Though, it was likely he had lost interest when he found she
was not game for his disgraceful proposal. He had probably
gotten a good laugh at how ridiculous she had seemed fleeing
the carriage like a mouse scurrying from a famished cat.

When she thought about her own behavior, she wanted to

crawl into a corner and never emerge. She'd allowed him to pull her into shadows, kiss her, take unthinkable liberties— ah, but that was just it. In his presence, she could not think properly. Her reason betrayed her, and the smooth, impassioned words he murmured in his husky voice were so persuasive, they seemed true and real. But they were not. They were merely seduction, meant to bring her to his bed, to disgrace and ruination.

She should really be more angry about it. She was. She was angry, very angry. And yet it excited her inexplicably. What was wrong with her?

It came to her that the reason she couldn't apply herself to her old pleasures was because she wasn't the same person any longer. It was too late to retreat to the comforts that once eased her so well, for she had been changed. Her very self was altered so that she didn't fit into her old life.

A message arrived one day after more than a week of restless pondering. It read: "I can hold out no longer. I wish to see you. May I call?" It was signed, "Adrian."

His handwriting was unpracticed and bold, not at all beautiful. She held the piece of paper he had held, riding a spike of joy, and then a plummet of grief.

She penned her reply: "Major Khoury—There is little point in our association. Please discontinue communications. Good luck in your future endeavors."

She didn't send it for hours, deciding a thousand times each way until at last, just as Thomas was leaving with the post, she handed it to him.

That was the end of temptation.

The matter was settled, she thought as she wandered back into the parlor, curling into her chair again and opening her book.

At tea, she hadn't turned a page.

Sometimes, Adrian thought as he waited in the hallway of the Standish residence, *a man has just got to swallow his pride and admit he's wrong.*

In his breast pocket was the message he had received this

morning, telling him not to come. He never was any good at taking orders.

God knew he'd done everything he knew how to do to avoid this moment of reckoning. Since the day he'd nearly ravished her in his carriage, he hadn't set eyes on Michaela Standish, even going so far as to visit Shepston-on-Stour, ostensibly to check on the refurbishing of his house. He'd been determined to master the raging emotions he'd come to regard as a wretched weakness.

And yet, here he was. His brave foray into independence hadn't lasted very long.

He placed the package he had brought with him against the wall as he waited for the housekeeper to announce him. Michaela's name was written in block letters in the corner. He would leave it there in case he was thrown out on his proverbial ear, and maybe, if she found it later, then maybe it would make the difference, and she would relent.

He was shaking. Damn it to hell, he was actually shaking! Ah hell, he'd done worse things, hadn't he? Hadn't riding headlong into a bloody melee been worse?

He'd known fear; they were old friends. He'd grown used to it, perhaps. Once on the battlefield, he'd crawled among dead bodies when he'd lost his regiment and found himself surrounded by the Cuirassiers. Whenever the elite French soldiers passed close by, patrolling the battlefield for injured to be taken prisoner or executed, they stuck their bayonettes into the stiffening bodies. Adrian had lain stock-still, face-to-face with a dead man, his breathing so loud—at least to his own ears—that he feared it would give him away. How he had managed to stay as still as the grave—literally—when he was imagining the cold kiss of that blade any second, he couldn't say.

If he had defied his instinct to run in order to survive that particularly horrific experience, why was it more than he could bear to wait while the housekeeper who had taken his card returned with the pronouncement of whether Miss Michaela Standish would receive him?

He'd gone over the scenario a thousand times in his head: Just how would he react when she turned him away cold? He

might spin on his heel and storm out loftily, or he might demand she see him. There just was no way to tell. He'd never
been predictable.

It never occurred to him that he would be accepted. Thus,
when the housekeeper returned and informed him that he was
to be shown into the parlor, he was somewhat dumbfounded.
Then he gathered his wits together and followed the woman.

Mrs. Standish was present in the parlor with Michaela and
the two other girls. He could never tell them apart, so he addressed them both as "Miss Standish," as he did Michaela.
But he lingered over the latter's elegant, slender hand, cool
and fine in his grasp after the pudgy heat of her two sisters,
and attempted to hold her gaze, catch her mood. She was
closed to him, however, being merely polite and absolutely
refusing to meet his eye.

"Please have a seat," Mrs. Standish said.

She gestured to a settee, and Adrian took her direction.
The moment he sat, he noticed an abrupt change in
Michaela's demeanor. She sat straighter, her chin tilting as if
something were suddenly amiss.

He was at a loss until he noticed with whom he shared the
furnishing. One of the twins, decorated like a birthday present with bows and geegaws all over her head and chest, simpered at him. "Tea?" She offered him a cup, leaning forward
and fluttering her eyelashes.

"Yes, thank you," he replied, coming toward her to take
his cup from her. In truth, he found this vision of decoration
alarming. He was not a follower of fashion, but even he
could see this hideous apparition was grossly overly orna-
mented.

But one very curious thing happened—for the second
time. As he eyed the gaudily dressed girl with carefully concealed antipathy, Michaela grew restive.

"Cream?" the bedecked twin asked, scooting forward to
reach the small pot. Her shoulder brushed his arm. He
smelled the cloying perfume of flowers. Lots of them. Like a
funeral.

Michaela's head shot up. Her eyes narrowed.

He took the cream in his cup, stirred as thoughts ran rampant in his head. He hadn't come here to devil the woman, quite the contrary. But sometimes the good Lord put something so perfect in one's path, it seemed a sinful waste not to take advantage.

He reclined, feeling as pleased as a cat with feathers sticking out of its mouth. As he did so, Michaela matched his action, and he detected a sigh of relief, but her eyes were still wary.

"Sugar, Major?"

"No, thank you."

When the gaudy sister offered him the sugar cup, he smiled at her, and he could have sworn he saw Michaela's lip twitch, as if she wanted to curl it in anger.

Warm pleasure washed over him. It was easy to make small talk with the Standishes and ponder this interesting development at the same time. The twin who sat next to him did most of the talking, anyway. He was only required to nod every so often.

The twin—what the devil was her name?—was saying, "And then we went to Cavanaugh's. Do you know it, Major? It is simply the most charming inn, just outside of London. Oh, what a day that was. I was wearing my yellow frock, which everyone says is absolutely stunning. It has feathers all about the neck. . . ."

He could feel Michaela staring at him, but when he looked at her, she jerked her chin up and quickly looked away.

So she wanted it to be that way, did she?

"It sounds fascinating, Miss Standish." Shifting in his seat so that he was facing the garrulous girl, he said, "Do tell me more. I love feathers."

And there it was. Out of the corner of his eye he saw Michaela's reaction, and he knew he'd been right.

It was small of him to tease her, but it did his ravaged pride good to see her squirm. It was just recompense for the hot, tempestuous nights of frustrated tossing and turning for want of her, for want of wondering where she was, if she was dancing at some society affair, and if so, in whose arms.

He'd known that hell too often since he'd caught her carrying on with that Wickersam fellow.

"Well," Delinda was saying, basking in his feigned attentions, "I ordered a pot of tea and so did my sister, and the man there said, would we like to share it, and I said no and Delilah said yes *at precisely the same time*." She erupted into delicate twitters.

He laughed enthusiastically. He thought they were going to have to peel Michaela off of the ceiling. She glowered at him openly now, all subtlety gone.

"Don't leave me in suspense," he said, leaning even closer to Delinda. "You must tell me how it ended. One pot or two?"

The rage on Michaela's face was so intensely gratifying, he wondered how it had come to pass that he had sunk to these new levels of perversity. Not that it troubled him. He was enjoying himself too much for his conscience to bother him.

A footman appeared in the doorway, a salver in his hand with a small, rectangular card lying upon it.

Mrs. Standish picked up the card and read it. The corner was bent, signaling the person was waiting for a reply. The woman looked up. "It is the Viscount Wickam."

There was a small hesitation. Adrian understood at once. Two suitors calling at the same time was an awkward situation.

Michaela leaped up at once, her face unabashedly triumphant. "Send him in, Thomas." She whirled, touching her hair and doing her best to appear as pleased as she could be, but the look she sidled to him gave her game away at once.

He settled back to enjoy the performance.

The lanky viscount, whom he had mentally dubbed "Beanpole" when he'd seen him dancing with Michaela at the Breamore ball, strode into the room with aplomb.

"Your servant," he said, sweeping a low, dramatic bow before Michaela. She replied by placing her hand over her throat and behaving as if this was the most magnificent show of masculine worship she had ever witnessed.

Adrian shifted, suddenly feeling an uncomfortable climb in his temperature. He almost sneered at the sloppy way that hideously long body folded with rather too much grace to be masculine. How could she be impressed with that foppish show?

Winniwick said, "I am honored you have agreed to receive me. How I've been hoping you would not turn my impertinent self away. It's taken me all this time to work up the courage to brave my poor fears and land on your doorstep."

With a flourish, he did another weird bow.

"Oh, my," Michaela exclaimed and emitted some strange laughing sound. It was nearly a twitter, but it sounded wrong coming from Michaela. "Oh, I assure you, my lord, the honor is uniquely ours."

He could have shaken her at that moment, especially when she tossed a look his way that showed she was aggravatingly pleased with herself.

The fellow greeted the rest of them. His face was open and pleasant. Grudgingly, Adrian could find no fault with him, other than the fact that he was unnaturally friendly. Perhaps he was simple. The thought cheered him.

"Major Khoury!" a voice said, calling him back. It was Delilah. No. Delinda. The one with the bows.

Apparently with Michaela making a fool of herself over Wickahoo, Delinda had decided he was a prime target for flirting. But flirting had its uses.

"Pardon my rudeness," he said, and an eye on Michaela as he slid slightly closer. "What was it you were saying before we were interrupted? I was simply enraptured."

"Come sit by me, my lord," Michaela shrieked, waving Wickerwig into a chair.

Delinda said, "Um, Major, do you like dogs?"

"I like them very well. What type do you have?"

"Oh, we don't have any. I have an allergic reaction to dog hair. I turn red all over, and my eyes water like a primed pump."

He blinked away the revolting image. "Ah, perhaps a cat is your pet?"

"Roughish creatures. Michaela used to keep one in her room as a child. He shredded everything and . . . well, he was none too clean."

"Then . . . why did you ask if I liked dogs?"

"Oh." She looked panicked for a moment. "I was just making conversation. You know, so I could get to know you better. I very much want to do that. Get to know you."

He had to move away. The smell of overripe chrysanthemums was simply too much. He cursed his sense of smell, for if not for it he would be able to cozy up nicely with Michaela's sister. He wished to present the most taunting image possible to that infuriating female who was right now gushing disgustingly over that overly long, freakish Wickerham—

Michaela's voice cut into his thoughts. She wasn't speaking to him, however. She addressed herself to the viscount. "How is your father, my lord? Did his friend please you the other evening?"

Beanpole responded with a chuckle as if this was some shared joke between them. "He did indeed have a few acquaintances to whom I was presented, but none so charming as you." He looked to Mrs. Standish. "Did you pass a pleasant evening at our ball, Mrs. Standish? I thought it highly diverting. I was so sorry to have to miss you since."

Oh, now the cheeky fellow was trying to coax his way into Mrs. Standish's favor.

"I had a delightful time, my lord. As did my daughters. All *three* of my daughters."

Wishywashy looked absently at the twins, first the resplendently beribboned one next to Adrian, and then the quiet one who sat alone in a chair. "Ah. Did any of you manage to meet the prince at our fete?"

Adrian frowned. The prince had been there? All he had noted was that Michaela had been there, and in the arms of another man—this man.

Mrs. Standish preened. "I could never claim to have met him, I confess, but I did see him, and he was not even as far from me as you are seated now, my lord. It was such a thrill."

Wickywick glanced at Michaela with a conspiring expression, as if they shared some secret amusement. "Major Khoury, did you happen to notice how like Napoleon he styles his hair?"

Michaela stifled a laugh. Adrian replied, "I didn't notice, but now that you mention it, he does favor the same style."

"Ah," Winkerham pronounced, holding up his index finger, "this is the very topic Miss Standish and myself were discussing, and it was put forward, Major, that a man like yourself may be needed to remind the prince which side of the war he was on. Namely, the *winning* one." He laughed. Michaela laughed. The other two girls and Mrs. Standish laughed.

"Very amusing," Adrian said without inflection.

"Oh, my lord, you make my sides ache!" Michaela declared. Her eyes glittered shrewdly. She cast a look his way to make certain he was annoyed.

"Oh, speaking of the war," Delinda chirped, "I would love to hear of your days in courageous defense of our great nation, Major, battling foes bent on the destruction of civilization, selflessly sacrificing your liberty, even risking your very mortality in service to the monarch and all his loyal subjects."

"No," Adrian answered. "The war is something I do not discuss, not ever. Will you excuse me, please."

With that he rose and in the gaping silence, took exactly four thumping strides to Michaela. With a warning glare at Wickerbocker, he said, "I would like to see the gardens. Mrs. Standish"—this over his shoulder and slightly louder to address the elderly woman—"do I have your permission to have your daughter show me the gardens?"

"I don't . . ." Mrs. Standish said, her voice trailing off uncertainly as she looked to her daughter, trying to gauge her wishes and no doubt thinking to intervene for her.

Michaela stood and faced him, nearly nose to nose. Her eyes snapped, and he felt his blood heat instantly. "It is all right, Mother. Come, Major. I have a good deal to say to you, and I wish some privacy for it. I don't know if you will enjoy our stroll, but since you have asked to see the gardens, you will get everything you have coming to you and a bit more in the bargain."

She stalked off, leaving them all gaping. Adrian was on her heels, leaving behind the embarrassed silence.

As he could have anticipated—in fact any less show of spleen would have constituted a profound disappointment—she stomped down the short hallway. He watched her for a moment, admiring the sway of her hips, the way her skirts swished like a waterfall about those long legs. His groin tightened, and he cursed himself, following at a leisurely pace.

Throwing open the doorway under the bend in the stairway, she turned to him with her hand on her hip and posed with magnificent arrogance. He could easily imagine her with gold hoops in her ears, bare feet peeking out from under skirts with colorful scarves hung in an uneven hem, the gypsy, in her element, dancing for him.

"Here is our garden. You best come quickly. I intend to have my say and be done with you." Then she disappeared outside.

He grinned, taking his time. The brightness of the day was a sharp contrast to the inside of the house. She was halfway across the small lawn by the time his eyes adjusted. She stood squarely. Lord, she was a virago, her face flushed, eyes flashing, and the sumptuous mouth he was aching to sample once again red and pursed and looking delectable.

"Now there is no one to hear what I am about to say to you, no one to scold me for my wayward tongue. Therefore I am free to tell you what I think of you."

"Well, well," he said drolly, mainly because he knew it maddened her, "I'll wager it is not much." He jerked his head toward the door. "Do you favor fops like that in there, then? Wickywack?"

She lifted her chin. "Do you refer to Lord Wickam?"

"Whatever his name is, it is no matter to me," he quipped. "If you prefer the company of bowlegged men who obviously sleep with paper curlers in their hair—"

"How dreadful of you to insult the man. He's done nothing to you except call on me, and why should he not? Oh! You have no concern for the feelings of others, which you toy with like . . . like . . ."

"A child?" he supplied helpfully. "They play with toys."

She jammed her hand on her hip. "Do you think this is amusing?"

He donned a sober expression. "Indeed not. I take dressing-downs quite seriously."

"How remiss of me to forget I am dealing with the great insurrectionist, Major Adrian Khoury. You do not like it when someone tells you that you are wrong, that you're acting the jackass, or that you might have blundered exceedingly."

"There is no need to get personal."

She choked. "It is quite personal. For me. But for you, it is simply recreation—and that, sir, is the precise nature of the problem between us. To have asked me, as you so glibly did, to be your mistress—"

"All right, Michaela. I've had enough tirade, and I've patiently heard you out. You are angry, rightfully so. Frustration impedes my brain, I've learned, and I confess I was less than discreet and abysmally unfair to you. But now it is time to settle down. I must speak to you about something of the utmost importance."

But she wouldn't settle down. What had made him think she would?

"My God, your conceit is boundless, telling me when I am to be done being angry! It is only outdone by your arrogance and the swelling gall." She finished with a look that would have done an empress proud.

The torrent of words might have angered him, except that it was everything he knew she would say and . . . if he were completely honest with himself, had a right to say.

He bowed his head, the low chuckle rumbling in him, getting louder until he was laughing outright. She stopped talking, and he was sorry because her articulate expression of his faults was rather remarkable. She had a formidable vocabulary and a vivid imagination, and combined with her inflamed temper, she was quite a force to be reckoned with.

Why that made him laugh harder, he didn't understand. He covered his eyes with his hand and shook his head, leaning back against a small tree.

"Why are you laughing?" she demanded. Her tone was wary, guarded. She suspected she was the butt of some joke.

It was a while before he could speak. When he got himself under control, he wiped the tears from under his eyes and drew in a breath to steady himself before saying, "I must marry you."

The silence was expected. It fell hard, dead air like lead all around them.

"Did you hear me, Michaela? I wish to marry you."

He stood before her, wanting badly to touch her. Only now, he realized he had wished to do this differently. There had been times between them that had been tender. Tender would have been better. "Will you accept my proposal? I will speak to your mother and do this properly in every way, but first I wish to know if you are amenable."

"Is this a horrid joke?"

"Not at all. I fear the only way I will be contented is to make you mine."

"You are mad."

"Distressingly so. Now, will you agree to the match?"

She made a small sound, a helpless kind of sound, and spun away. She didn't flee as he feared, but only walked off a way and stood with her back to him.

He followed, not able to keep himself from touching the nape of her neck, wanting so much more that his body throbbed in time to his heartbeat. There were other words locked far away. The pressure of them pressed against his ribs. He felt her shiver, and his body raged, an explosion of sudden and overwhelming desire igniting in him.

"I will be good to you," he said hoarsely. "I swear I will, Michaela. I will not play you false. I can give you a good home, and I will endeavor to make it a pleasant one. I know you have no cause to trust what I say is true, but I keep thinking of that time in Rye's gallery. Do you remember what it was like, by the fire, with pleasant conversation?"

There was a moment's hesitation, and she answered, "Yes."

"It can be like that, then. We'll make certain of it. It is what I want. Do you think you would—?"

She whirled, confronting him with an expression not of outrage as he'd anticipated, but pain. "What of my family, and my father—my real father I mean? I am Woolrich's by-blow, a middle-class girl."

It would have insulted her to pretend he didn't know what she was saying. He might himself detest that sort of snobbery, but it was real enough in the public arena, and he was, for better or worse, in the public arena.

If she were a shopkeeper's daughter, a maid, anything less than she was, he still would have to have her. He was insane enough with this fever of desire to marry her no matter what her circumstances.

But he, who never explained himself, could only shake his head and tell her, "I don't care."

"You don't care—just like that?"

He stepped forward, taking her face in his hands. Her eyes searched his, anxious and frightened. "No. Just like this." And he kissed her.

It was like drinking after days in the desert. The sweet touch of her lips filled him, fanning fires that he had kept banked for far too long. She fell into him, and he indulged in the temptation to slide his hand up the curve of her back.

She kissed him back, and his skin prickled, alive. He had to have her. Ah, there was no cure for it. He had to make her his.

His. That one word reverberated inside of him, for he was hollow, waiting to be filled, completed only when he at last took her to his bed. She'd be a wonderful lover—all that gypsy passion and fire. He'd tasted it, too briefly. He wouldn't be satisfied until he had it all.

"Say yes," he whispered against her lips.

It was a simple equation, even logical. He had decided he had to have her. The only way he was going to have her was as a wife. He needed a wife. She could be that wife. Very simple.

Even logical.

He stood, trembling, barely breathing and telling himself he was not anxious about it.

Say yes, Michaela.

For a moment, one terrible moment, he thought she was going to refuse him. The tactician in him went into action. His fingertips brushed the inside of her wrist, and he felt her shiver. Then, he folded her hand in his two and said, "Michaela. Please. Do me the honor of becoming my wife."

She lowered her gaze, disconcerted, and he prayed, actually prayed for angels to touch her mind.

He was trembling.

"It's what I wanted," she admitted at last. She raised her gaze to his. "Go speak to my mother. I will marry you if she gives her consent."

After Michaela and Major Khoury departed, Delinda fled the room in a burst of loud sobs, shouting, "You promised I would be the first!"

Delilah, who was doing her best to be known by her new name of Lilah, could not believe it when Mother rose, her face an alarming shade of red, and excused herself, quite forgetting propriety by leaving Lilah and Wickam unchaperoned.

Wickam, however, seemed to enjoy the entire spectacle immensely. "I say, you Standishes are an entertaining lot. I've never been so tickled in my life. Imagine, Khoury stomping out of here like that, dragging Miss Michaela off with him. It titillates the imagination to wonder what they are doing out there, does it not?"

What she imagined was his implied slur against Michaela snapped her into a tight posture. "Is your imagination so easily provoked, my lord?" she replied tartly. "It speaks of a despairingly dull existence, should that be the case."

He blinked, looking her over. "Well, I declare, you are a spitfire," he said approvingly. "I thought you rather shy, not having said anything the whole while."

Lilah stared at him. "You may be a lord, but I have never met such a rude man in my life."

"Good gracious!" Wickam declared. His eyes danced. "I fear I am smitten!"

"Stop it at once. I will not tolerate your ridicule."

"I swear it . . . er, what was your name again?"

Drawing herself up, she said, "My name is Lilah. My given name is Delilah, but I no longer wish to be a part of 'Delinda and Delilah,' known at times collectively as 'the twins' as if we weren't two separate people, and so I've decided to choose my own name."

His blue eyes flashed and he grinned. "I like it. And, Miss Lilah, I like *you.*"

"What is more important is *I* like it. And you are preposterous with your sarcasm."

"What a termagant you are! 'Tis not sarcasm but true admiration you hear in me. I like an outspoken woman."

"My lord, I am not the outspoken sort. You had the right of it when you took me for a shy person. I barely spoke in the past. It occurred to me, very recently, that I had opinions. And then, I found I liked voicing those opinions, and having my say. So I am resolved to speak my mind and keep my peace no longer."

"And make up for lost time, I'll wager. Pray tell me that I may escort you to the opera this week? I have a box at a superb theater on Drury Lane, and the current performance is a stirring rendition of *Aida.* Please say you will come."

"To the opera?" This stopped Lilah. She'd never been asked out with a gentleman before. But she wasn't certain if she liked this odd fellow, not yet.

But, oh, to go to the theater on the arm of a viscount . . . even if he were a bit forward and more than a little irreverent. Yet, he was very handsome, and his engaging personality had no doubt charmed many an unsuspecting female.

In every way, he was her superior: good-looking while she was plain, rich while she was very much not, and titled while she was simply a poseur circulating on the edges of the bon ton by the good grace of her sister's birthright. Why in the world would he have an interest in her? If she said yes as she curiously wished to, she would just be one more fool who had fallen for those heavily lashed eyes and chiseled features.

"I think not," she said at last, although it pained her. She would have dearly liked to accept. "I am going to leave you now and will send the gardener in to show you out. I would appreciate greatly your not telling anyone about the scene you witnessed here this afternoon. It is not typical of my family, and we've spent a good deal of time cultivating a respectable reputation. Please do not diminish it by spreading gossip."

Undaunted, Wickam's blue eyes twinkled charmingly. "An intrigue, eh? Just you and I and a secret to be shared." Abandoning his teasing mien, he sobered and rose, striking a respectful bow. "I shall take my leave of you and utter not one word of anything that transpired here today. I am your servant, Miss Standish, and by my spotless behavior, shall convince you of my genuine intentions." He gave her an audacious wink and added, "I mean to take you to the opera."

It was Albert who remembered the parcel Adrian had left in the center hall. He brought it into the drawing room where Michaela sat alone.

Wickam and Adrian had gone, and everyone else was resting after the eventful afternoon. Adrian had promised to speak to Dorothy at a later time, when the situation in the house had calmed down. So, for now, his proposal was her secret, and she hugged it to herself.

She was hopeful her mother would agree to the marriage. She certainly approved of Major Khoury. But the promise that Mother had made to Delinda that she would be the first to marry, troubled Michaela. Surely Mother wouldn't hold to that, not under the circumstances. It was a silly rule. What if Delinda never got a proposal?

The thought was too horrible to bear. Poor Mother, if that should ever happen. She suddenly realized this was probably why Dorothy had taken such a staunch stance on Delinda's prospects being given priority. She didn't wish to be left with an unmarried daughter, of course, but moreover, she didn't wish to be left with an unmarried *Delinda*.

"Miss Michaela, the major left this in the hallway for you." Albert grinned broadly as he brought in the parcel.

She rose, instantly intrigued.

"Set it down, Albert. Come, help me open it." She tore through the paper with anxious hands. Goodness, she was nervous, or excited perhaps.

She gasped when she saw it was the painting they had seen at Mr. Rye's gallery, the one of the sleeping man, reclining in his shadows with his lover's red reticule on his bedside table.

Michaela murmured, "Oh, my God!" and covered her face with her hands.

A laugh came from behind her. It was Delinda, sneering from the doorway. "It is the ugliest painting I ever saw. And depressing. What a wretched gift."

Michaela staved off the tears threatening, touching the canvas with reverence. "I think it's beautiful. It tells a love story."

"What? That is ridiculous. How sad that this is what he thinks of you. Now I am glad I didn't get him. My fiancé shall regale me with presents of jewelry and flowers so that I will bask in their perfume. It will be so much more romantic than a *painting*."

"You already have enough flower perfume on your person to rival the gardens at Buckingham."

With an insulted huff, Delinda stomped off.

Albert grinned at her. "Does this gift please you, my girl?"

"Oh, it does. It is a fine gift." She stared at the painting, smiling until her cheeks hurt and tears pricked her eyes. "It is perfect."

A few sharp words sounded from the hallway. Delinda and Mother were having a quarrel. It ended quickly, and her mother entered, her face clouded. "What is that?" she asked. Her voice sounded weary.

"It's a betrothal present," Michaela said without thinking, gazing at the painting. "Adrian brought it. He must have forgotten to give it to me."

"A betrothal present?" Her mother's voice was cold.

Michaela turned, cursing herself for her stupidity. She was so enraptured with her gift, she had not thought to be discreet.

"Has he spoken?" Dorothy asked in an urgent voice.

"He said he would speak to you within the week. He thought it prudent to wait as today was rather a hectic scene."

Dorothy was stiff, her eyes darting in tandem to thoughts she didn't speak. She was troubled, and Michaela knew why. A sinking feeling began to pull at her heart. If Mother had promised Delinda that she would be the first to marry, then she might withhold permission until such time as Delinda became engaged.

And when would that be?

No. That was too medieval to contemplate. She decided she was being overly emotional. Considering the day she had had, and this recent surprise of the painting—could Adrian really be this sentimental?—it was understandable she was overreacting to her mother's natural concern.

"Come, Mother, look at it," she said, turning around the canvas. She was determined not to let anything spoil this moment. "See how it tells a story. . . ."

ℰ *Chapter 12*

"You what?" Lady May exclaimed. She had rushed to the Standish house as soon as Michaela's message arrived, and it showed in her appearance. There was no question that her toilette, usually so carefully applied, had been rushed.

Mother and the twins were resting after the excitement that day, so Michaela and May were left alone in the front parlor.

Michaela's smile, brilliant a moment ago, dimmed. She had been so looking forward to telling her aunt the news. "I accepted Major Adrian Khoury's proposal of marriage. It is to be announced next week, after he speaks to Mother."

May appeared appalled. With her hands fluttering at the feathers at her throat, she cried, "How could you?"

Michaela was taken aback. "Not you, too. Why do you object?"

"Because he is . . . he . . . Oh, Michaela, you don't believe yourself in love with him, do you? Oh, Lord. Robert was right."

"Robert?"

Lady May looked a bit startled, as if she hadn't realized she'd spoken out loud. "Did I just say Robert?"

"Who is he?"

Her aunt was nonplussed. "Merely a friend. You don't know him."

"What was he right about?"

"About disaster, darling. Now tell me. Are you under the foolish impression that you are in love with this man?"

Michaela bristled, but tried to answer honestly. "I feel something for him, something very strong, very compelling."

May forced herself to calm. "Tell me what you feel."

"I don't seem to have control of myself when I am around him," Michaela explained thoughtfully. "I feel so many things, and I am confused and irritable, but I get hot and shivery at the same time and it is very pleasant. When he kissed me, I felt like I was flying over mountains. I can't stop staring at him, and even when I force myself to look away, I *feel* him."

She broke off, realizing all she had just said. Blushing, she cast her eyes downward.

Aunt May waved her hand, dismissing such wasted emotion. "It's desire, Michaela. Just as I suspected. Good lord, you should not get pie-eyed over it, and certainly not base such a momentous decision as marriage on a bit of fire in the blood. Take my word for it; the lust will die in time. Oh, do listen to me, darling, he is not the man for you. I can tell these things. You are so much like your father, and I know you would never be happy with him."

Michaela felt her happiness plummet in the face of Aunt May's objections. "I don't believe I can be contented without him."

"Yes, it feels like that, but it will pass. A man can make a woman believe anything if he tells her he loves her. But it is quite different when in time other things replace you, even other women."

She looked away, disturbed. Adrian hadn't spoken of love. She knew she loved him. Maybe she'd always known it, but at some point she couldn't define, the conscious knowledge slipped easily over her thoughts, and she'd ac-

cepted it without it even being any sort of revelation. But he
had not even hinted of harboring any deep feeling for her. He
had spoken of want, of desire, and pleasant companionship.
That wasn't the same.

She refused to be undone by these trivial doubts. She
knew he loved her. He wanted to marry her. He'd given her
the painting.

But he hadn't said the words. Not even hinted of what it
was she meant to him.

Funny it hadn't seemed such a glaring omission until now,
and the seed of doubt burrowed into her mind.

May sighed. "Come. I don't want us to quarrel."

"Neither do I, Aunt May, but I don't know what else to
do. I love you very much, and do not wish to displease you.
You have been so kind to me, given me a great deal, but how
can I simply obey without really understanding why you are
so against this?"

There was a moment of hesitation as Lady May seemed to
be mulling over a decision. "I think I need to tell you something about myself, Michaela. I've never told anyone. Come,
sit here. You are as stubborn as Woolrich ever was, I declare.
I fear you will not heed me unless I can make you understand."

The two women settled on a plush settee. Lady May
touched a strand of hair, swiping it out of her face, and
Michaela could see her hand was trembling. "When I was a
young woman, I had many admirers, but I married Lord
Matthew Hayworth. I selected him out of the others because
I thought him dashing. He was dangerous and moody, but I
was caught in the romance of it all, the challenge, you see. I
fancied myself in love, and he with me."

She sighed, a look of pain crossing her lovely features,
and she continued. "We were wild back then. Oh, you think
Prinny is decadent, but twenty years ago, it was more than
you could imagine. More than I *want* you to imagine. But we
wanted each other with feelings that were nearly ferocious, if
you will pardon the term. I assure you, it is not exaggeration."

Michaela listened patiently. It was obvious this was a

difficult subject upon which her aunt spoke, for the strain showed in the fine lines suddenly visible on her drawn face.

"I married him, and for a while we were contented. He fell into melancholy and became surly, one moment angry and the next brimming with charm. I thought I could save him from his torment, provide love that would even out his moods. But he was ugly when in a foul mood, and in time, it got so bad that we would fight viciously, sometimes violently, and then we would come together afterward, when he was weeping with apology, in an explosive night of lovemaking. I am speaking frankly, for I want you to understand that we never resolved any of the problems when we made up. It was just that passion got the best of us. He was obsessed with me, and I with him."

It was shocking to imagine her small, dignified aunt, the inimitable Lady May who always seemed to have all matters in her life well in hand, in such a relationship. "What happened?"

"When the fighting became too much and the loving less and less, I found I had lost my feeling for him. He was angry all of the time toward the end. His reason was gone, I think. The melancholy took him over. It was as if the madness I had thought so exciting at first had rotted his heart, and in its place was a morass of hatred. He became cruel, and I despised him, but he was my husband and by law, I could not leave.

"He could command me at will, which he did. He removed me from my friends, cut off my funds, all but imprisoned me. He became my jailer, not my husband any longer, and I was trapped for what I thought would be the rest of my life, bound in matrimony to a madman who had complete power over me and everything I did."

The memory seemed too much for her. May fumbled for her handkerchief, but Michaela produced hers first and held it out for her. "Oh, Aunt May, I am so dreadfully sorry. I cannot imagine you in such a life. Could you not get a bill of divorcement?"

"He was wealthy, with friends in government, and he did

not wish it. I was defeated soundly when I investigated that route."

"Then you were fortunate that his untimely death released you, as wicked as that sounds."

"Yes. I was very fortunate. More fortunate than you know. You see . . ." She paused, swallowing convulsively. "Matthew did not die of a firearms accident as is commonly thought. A physician friend of his family's faked the death certificate, and took the body out to be disposed of before the magistrate was called. Well-placed payments to the county officials did the rest. Michaela, Matthew shot himself."

Michaela gasped. Lady May focused on her niece and she spoke with hard seriousness. "He had sworn to me that he was going to kill me dozens of times, and I believe that had I been alone with him in the house that night, he would have taken me with him. But Wooly had come to get me, you see, defying Matthew's right as my husband to keep me where he wanted. He rescued me, and as it turned out, it was more than just another sound beating I escaped from that night. The melancholy finally defeated Matthew. In despair, he finally put an end to his misery and mine."

Michaela found she had tears in her eyes. "I am so sorry, Aunt May. What a dreadful thing to have endured. But what has this to do with Major Khoury? Surely, you can't think he would do any such thing."

"But you really don't know him, do you?" May's eyes were keen as they pinned her niece. "There is always potential for madness when a man possesses a passionate nature."

"He isn't like that. He is often kind and amusing."

The look on May's face spoke of how little she thought of that defense. "And then there is all those years he was at war. These things haunt men. Think about the way he retired his commission and returned home, becoming nearly a recluse before deciding to join the living again, seeking a career in politics. Did you ever wonder why he hid himself away for all of that time?"

She shook her head, protesting, "I know the war makes him sad."

May pounced on that. "What if that sadness harbors

something darker, something not even formed yet that would
blossom once you and he were bound together for life?"

Michaela couldn't think Adrian would ever be a brute.
No. It was impossible to imagine.

Yet, how many people choose wrongly? Like Aunt May,
they found themselves somewhere they never planned to be.

A cold finger traced a shivery path along her vertebrae.
"Do you really think that could happen?"

Impulsively, May reached out and grabbed her arm. "Yes.
Not that it will, darling, but that it *could.* He is a man of intense feeling, a man of secrets, a man no woman will ever really know. Men like that are dangerous."

The word hung in the air. Michaela was stunned, reeling,
confused. She trusted her aunt and had relied on her astute
wisdom. However, nothing of what she had told Michaela
seemed to have any bearing on Adrian. Michaela simply
could not entertain the possibility of him turning into a monster like Matthew Hayworth. However, there was a single
nagging doubt, and that left the door open for other doubts to
rush in. How well *did* she know Adrian Khoury?

And how much did she know of men at all? Surely, her
aunt knew leagues more, having lived a full, rich life with
many experiences. Whereas she herself had lived her life
with her nose stuck in a book. Lord, she'd never even been
kissed before!

"Besides," May said, her voice persuasive, "there is no
terrible hurry. What harm could come in at least waiting? Ah.
I see by your expression the idea pains you. The heat of lust
creates a sense of urgency. Are you in such a rush to get into
his bed that you would risk the whole of your life for a
night's pleasure?"

Was that right? Michaela gnawed on the inside of her
cheek. In her mind was the clear recollection of his reassur-
ances, his promise that he would be a good husband. Those
gentle words had seemed to pierce something deeply embed-
ded inside of her. Her dream, but only half the dream. She'd
dreamed of great love.

He hadn't spoken of love. Oh, yes, he had. To scoff at it,
ridicule it and anyone who was fool enough to think it real.

"Maybe you are simply so hot for him, you cannot think of anyone else. In time, when your blood cools, you may think differently. Affairs are a reality, as much as society would like to quell it. Sometimes you have to have the man if he is in your blood. And sometimes the having is all it takes to douse the fire enough so that you can think clearly again."

It was outrageous to suggest that she give herself to Adrian outside of marriage. Aunt May couldn't be hinting at that, but Michaela was suspicious she was trying to sway her in some way.

"You think that passion is just fleeting? It doesn't last?"

"Rarely. Darling, it is not wrong for you to feel this way about Adrian Khoury; he is a magnificent man, elemental, powerful. Any woman would desire him. If you are in lust, then admit it and don't fool yourself it's anything else."

Michaela frowned, thinking a million jumbled thoughts. May came to her, laying a hand on her shoulder. "This is why you must think clearly and take great care. Considering the consequences, which I know myself to be dire, I ask you . . . I beg you, Michaela, to choose well in the matter of a husband."

Adrian was alone in his apartments. He reclined in a tufted leather divan drawn up to the fireplace as evening fell outside the window. It was his favorite time of day, in between the afternoon's activities and the whirl of London nightlife. The warm air forbade the cheery comforts of a fire, but he still liked the scent of woodsmoke that clung to the charred stone.

He was tense, which defied reason. His proposal had been given and accepted. They would make the announcement at a ball coming up within the week. Then he would have that which he most desired.

But he remained agitated. The need for Michaela had not been mitigated. It was a compulsion inside him, insisting on fulfillment. He didn't like compulsions. He preferred the clean, sweet freedom of nothing to lose that had comforted him for so long.

There came the softest of knocks to intrude upon his unpleasant thoughts. He thought at first it was a trick of sound until it came again. Someone was rapping upon his door. James, his valet, had the evening off, so he went to answer.

Michaela stood in the hallway. The recognition took a moment, for she was completely enveloped by a cowl and cloak that had to be suffocatingly hot in the mild night air. It was a rough garment, wool and dung brown. He had never before seen her with such an ugly article of clothing and belatedly he realized she was hiding under it.

"Ask me in," she said urgently.

Dumbly he stepped aside. She moved past him quickly, a cloud of her scent trailing behind to ensnare his senses. It was quite maddening the way she did that.

"We need to talk," she said. Turning, she drew off her cloak and threw it across the divan. It fell into a shapeless lump. She didn't bother to right it.

She was dressed for the evening in a pale green thing that was the most sinful arrangement of material he had ever seen. The low décolletage hurt his eyes, perhaps because they strained painfully to catch a more thorough glimpse of tantalizing creamy flesh displayed prominently among the rushing.

What was she doing here, at this hour, alone, and dressed to make a man drool?

"May I offer you something?" he asked, determined to be patient. He sauntered to the small sideboard. He kept spirits decanted for guests. "Some sherry? Wine?"

She declined. She was very nervous. Looking about the room, she took in her surroundings with anxious, darting glances.

He advanced, feasting on her scent. Never one to pass on a windfall of good fortune, he immediately began to compute the possibilities. "Would you like to sit?"

"No one knows I've come," she blurted. "I fooled my mother by saying I'm with Aunt May, and Aunt May believes I am remaining home tonight."

He nodded, as if understanding perfectly. "Very clever."

"I had be alone with you," she explained. "To speak plainly. I have to speak of things that are . . . unconventional." She colored so gloriously he stared in appreciation. She was flame, this one, from her flesh to her heart.

"You see, we could be making a terrible mistake."

"What mistake?"

"Marriage."

He felt a jab of irritation. "Why ever would our marriage be a mistake?"

She stammered, "Because the only reason you wish to marry me is because you wish to . . . um . . ."

"Make love to you."

Scarlet flamed more deeply over her smooth, unblemished skin. "We must think of whether or not we suit." Her voice sounded as if invisible hands were choking the air from her lungs. "There is more to a married life than . . . than . . ."

"Bed."

Her color went to vermilion.

God help him, he was enjoying this. "And you have a solution?"

"I do." She took in a quick, bracing breath. "Marriage is a sober institution, a lifelong companionship that once undertaken, is not to be broken. We will be tied to each other for life, longer. Even into death. For all eternity."

He saw the fine sheen of sweat begin to glisten over her skin. Her eyes widened emphatically. "We will be trapped into utter misery."

"You have been reading far too much Dante," he said drolly.

"Don't make fun of me, Adrian. We should both take a good long time to think on this, really think."

With a sudden fierce frown he nodded, as if agreeing to this.

She caught his sarcasm. "You think this is amusing? You know what I mean. You said yourself you cannot keep hold of reason when you begin to feel . . . stirrings."

"Ah. Trust you to use those admissions against me."

"But I am afflicted, too. Don't you see, that is just the

problem? We are swept away, caught up in something powerful, but not necessarily good. Therefore, I propose we postpone the announcment of our engagement indefinitely."

"Your solution is unappealing, and I reject it," he said, swiping his hand impatiently at her. "I have a better one. I think we should sleep together."

"Yes, I know you think we should, which is why you asked me to marry you. Is it the *only* reason?"

"Well, husbands and wives sleep together. Doesn't that appeal to you?"

"Of course it does. You are changing the subject. I cannot . . . sleep . . . with you. Not now."

"Why not? It is simply to see if we suit." He shrugged, as if this were purely an academic argument he was putting forth. "And it would be an excellent way to see if we are merely caught up in the heat of frivolous desire."

She knew he was mocking her. She regarded him with suspicion. At least he thought that was what it was, but when the silence lengthened, he determined she was actually thinking about it.

"I see. It is to test us. After all, we haven't had a smooth time of it. It's hardly even been a courtship at all, not conventional in the least and full of squabbles so that I might not even know how I feel about you."

His tongue could barely form words. "You are considering accepting my offer?"

"Well . . ." Her brow was furrowed with consternation. "It isn't the same as before because we are engaged. Almost, anyway, and this is not just for pleasure. It is for a more . . . useful purpose. It is a test of sorts, a kind of experiment."

He didn't like the sound of that. While he was sorting out why he suddenly had a bad taste for what she was saying, she continued. "Aunt May suggested that perhaps it is merely the lure of the forbidden that has us caught in its snare, and once we have a taste of each other's . . . um . . . well, when we each know the other's true nature, we will find ourselves disillusioned. So, if we are simply in lust, as Aunt May puts it, then we will know it was all—"

"Your aunt?" Suddenly, he didn't feel so smug. "You've discussed this with her?"

"Oh, we talk about everything. Lady May is very worldly. She might have been hinting that we go further and see, purely for purposes of edification, whether we really wish to marry. She doesn't think we should, you see. She thinks our being intimate will completely dampen our desire for one another, and then we can avoid disaster."

Anger hit him in the chest like a fist. *It was Lady May's idea?* How dare she meddle in *his* relationship! He managed to remain calm, at least calm enough not to snap at her. "So *you* have come here to seduce *me*?"

"Why no." She frowned. "It was you who suggested it. But now you say it as if you object."

What degree of idiot would he be to repudiate Michaela's offer, no matter what the circumstances, and yet his pride rebelled. He wanted to howl with the unfairness of it. Here he was with Michaela offering herself to him. It was the very thing that had obsessed him since laying eyes on her. And he couldn't. Ah, trust the maddening chit to find the most unacceptable, offensive means to give him exactly what he wanted so that it was impossible for him to accept.

"As an experiment to debunk the idea of marrying me, then yes, I do object."

She blinked, stunned.

He raised his hand, and his fingers flexed, itching for a touch. "For the love of Christ, Michaela, get your cloak on and get out of here this instant."

"But . . ."

"Has it occurred to you that your well-meaning aunt is a lunatic? What sort of woman sends a virgin to be deflowered by her fiancé in order to persuade her not to marry him?"

"She didn't send me to be deflowered. You are being rude and disrespectful. And stop acting the prude all of the sudden. You were ready to devour me when I came in here. You asked me to be your mistress, for goodness' sake. Have you forgotten that?"

"I don't like outsiders meddling in my life," he replied sourly.

"I just thought we could get it out of the way so that we'll both know if—"

"Get it out of the way? Why, so that if it's just desire, we'll have the whole mess out of our systems and just go on with our lives? It's a stupid idea."

"You've no need to be so insulting. I only wanted to avoid a terrible mistake."

"See, that is the trouble. You've evidently decided I am a mistake. I see now." What did he see? He was talking without any connection to logic or reason. He was panicked was what he was, because he wanted desperately to take the tainted fruit with which she taunted him.

"You aren't listening to me," she said, getting that mulish expression on her face.

"You are playing with something that you have no idea how dangerous it is."

"*You* don't understand. I am serious."

He groaned. Part of his mind was screaming for him to shut up and get his trousers off. Incredibly, he was standing and talking to her like an actual rational person when all he wanted to do was bury himself inside her and ride them both to ecstasy.

"This is absurd, even repugnant. I am not a stud to prove myself with you. I am telling you I am not getting caught up in . . . Put your cloak on this instant."

The sight of her décolletage had suddenly become too much.

"Oh, dear," she said, biting her bottom lip. "Why do you have to make everything so difficult?"

"That's right. I don't want to take part in your twisted 'edification' exercise." What a liar! His body was trembling, and if the truth be told—which it would not—he was afraid. This woman terrified the daylights out of him, because somehow she had gotten the power to reduce him to a quivering mindless mass dominated by thoughts both impure and lofty; thoughts of lust, yes, and more.

Whatever the "more" was, it forbade a meaningless toss, an experiment on the purity of their lust, or whatever godforsaken reason she had. "Now, leave," he commanded.

If he had ever ordered his regiment with that tone, they would have laughed at him. It held as much bite as a puppy's yap. Michaela just stared at him, her eyes luminous green, uncertain, even hurt.

"I will not," she said. "How dare you order me out. You make me feel like some cheap, brazen hussy—" She broke off at his hiked brow. Scowling, she stamped her foot. "This is the worst thing you've ever done, Adrian Khoury!"

"I've had enough of this," Adrian said. "I withdraw my offer of marriage."

He went to the cloak, picking it up and handing it to her. His body protested every movement. He just wanted her to get the hell out of here before his baser self got the best of him.

She reached for it, avoiding his eyes. He held on to it a moment until she finally lifted her gaze, and indeed she did look pitiful.

"When I make love to you, Michaela, it won't be under the direction of your aunt or for any silly reason meant to disprove what we feel. You made me a promise that first night we met. You made it with your eyes and with your mouth and in every provocative movement of your body. I intend to collect all I am owed."

His fingers uncurled, releasing her cloak. "I will do it my way, however, as a man does these things in his own time. Oh, maybe some might not care how they get it. The devil of it is, I do care. So our first night together will not be a test. It will be you and me, as we were meant to be from the first."

She gaped at him, her eyes as round as pennies, her mouth slack. And then, to his utter shock, she seemed to fold. Her hands slid up her arms. The cloak draped like brown wax. She hugged herself tightly as a great, gulping sob ripped from her, and she stood squarely in the middle of his library and began to bawl like a child.

℘ *Chapter 13*

May paced her boudoir. Robert, standing with his legs braced, watched her. His eyebrows were drawn into a tight line, a sign of his displeasure.

"I cannot believe you disagree with me when it is obvious I am in the right," she cried.

His tone was quieter, with grave dignity no stableman ever mimicked so well. "What could you have been thinking, May? I would have never thought you would do such an outrageous thing as this."

"I am trying to save her!" May declared, spinning to face him. "It isn't Adrian Khoury I object to, not exactly. Actually, I admire him. He is exactly the sort of man one is drawn to as a lover, but a husband—no!"

She found herself squarely in the sights of his discerning eye.

"You are rather passionate about this, and you've always been very careful to display only a droll attitude before. I wonder what it is that has you so up in arms."

She deliberately attempted to lighten her tone. "It is just

too soon for Michaela to think about marriage. I wish to travel with her, show her some of the Continent, especially Paris. We will go to Rome, then Venice, where my friends let romantic villas overlooking the canals. Ah, but Salzburg and Vienna are also gorgeous, and the splendid parties they give there are unmatched anywhere in the world."

Robert regarded her stoically. "Are you really that selfish, or are you merely dissembling? God, I hope it is the latter. I would hate to think you so shallow that you would forbid your niece's happiness to indulge your own preferences."

"I am thinking of her!"

"Indeed? And what does Michaela want?"

"How can she know? She is too young. That is the point." She stood before him, hands on hips. She didn't care a fig for his towering height, nor was she intimidated by his massive male form dwarfing her petite frame. "How can she know what is a good choice for her? She is too inexperienced, too foolish, too full of dreams that the world can break like so much glass."

His eyes narrowed, but she was too far gone to take heed.

"And if you think I am being selfish, what of men who drag wife and children to other countries, or live in the city when the woman loves her horses, or the country when she pines for the excitement and society of London?"

She felt the heat stinging her cheeks and the grip of emotion touched her voice as she continued. "When it comes to selecting a husband, a woman must choose wisely, with all care and sensibility. Passion is a poor match with marriage. A husband must be tractable and weak, a man to be managed. It is the only way a woman can protect herself."

In the face of his watchful gaze she wondered if she had given herself away.

When he spoke, it was with a sharp-edged tone. "I sometimes wondered what it was you saw in me. You, Lady May Hayworth, the supreme socialite. Every man over forty and half of them under the age would sacrifice a limb for a chance for just one night with you. So . . . why dally with a man who is merely a stable owner, who mucks out barns and greases rods on carriages for a living? Why did you choose me? I always wondered. And I think I have just realized why."

May had never thought of herself as choosing Robert. It had always seemed to her, rather, that the tall, insufferably handsome and deliciously enigmatic proprietor of the finest carriage house and stables in London's West End had selected *her*.

He leaned forward, smiling without any pleasure in his eyes. "I suppose there could be nothing safer than an underling. A man of horses, not of title, would be easily *managed* by a woman who is, I have just discovered, afraid of the opposite sex."

Her laugh was the cultured trill those of her class affected for superiority. "I am not afraid of you or of any man."

"You are afraid of Adrian Khoury. That is why you do not wish for Michaela to care for him. And least of all, to marry."

"How dare you presume to analyze me."

"Listen to your haughty response: *How dare I.* You are without a doubt to the manor born, through and through—complete with the innate knowledge of how to deal with a mere commoner like myself." He touched his forelock, a gesture of fealty. But his eyes were all challenge, not backing down one whit.

"And yet," he continued softly, "I have *dared* a great deal, haven't I? I've touched you. Kissed you, made love to you. I've advised you and listened to you and scolded you. I've praised you and asked your opinion and labored over long discussions when we've had different points of view. I've been your friend, your closest companion. But in the end, I can be dismissed, and I can be effortlessly *managed,* for I am not a lord and therefore not husband quality for a lady such as yourself. It is the perfect relationship for a woman who is, unless I am mistaken, hiding from the past."

How did he know?

How long had he known?

"Oh, that is rich!" she countered. She felt like the fox cornered by a snarling hound, ready to fight for her life. "A 'mere commoner like myself'—that is rich. If you are not noble born, then there is no aristocracy to be had in all of

England. My God, do you actually believe I'm that daft? If there is anyone hiding from the past, it is not I, Robert. You are the one with all the secrets, and if I've respected you and not mentioned them, then please know it was not from stupidity, but tact."

His expression shifted like a shutter being closed against a storm. Pressing her advantage, she struck a saucy pose to punctuate her words. "We pretend, you and I, and we have from the beginning. Neither one of us is a fool. I thought that was understood. I've left you your secrets, and you've never challenged mine. We both knew the limitations from the beginning, and we like it that way."

"Do we? Do we, really, May, or do we settle for a half existence because it's the best we can do?" For a moment, a look of anguish crossed his chiseled features. "Two cripples, cobbling together some semblance of a life—that is what we are."

"How gauche of you, Robert, to turn into a romantic on me."

She wanted to appear lofty and sophisticated, scorning his earnestness, but she feared he could see right through her. His eyes, instead of flaring with rage, softened. He said, "What happened to you?"

She made a small sound. She couldn't move, not even when he reached his large, callused hands out to touch her face. "Won't you tell me? Let us change the rules right now. Someone did something terrible, didn't they, and they wounded something inside of you. Don't take that out on Michaela. Leave her to live her own life. Help her, guide her, but don't scheme. It will end up badly."

She slapped his hand away, and he seemed to come to his senses. All warmth fled.

It dawned on her what she had done, striking him like that, and fear hit her in a reflex of memory. For an awful moment, ten years fell away, and she was looking up at Matthew, at how his face would cloud when she had gone too far and his fist would curl at his side moments before the pain.

She clung to reason that told her this was Robert, who had

never struck her. He *never* would. Despite the undercurrents
of mystery, she had always felt so safe, so sane with him.

But logic wouldn't be tamed by the rampant emotions
gripping her. She prayed fervently that he would just go. She
felt raw and frightened, and she wanted to be alone.

Whether he sensed her state or simply left of his own ac-
cord, she found him gone when she looked up. He had been
so silent, or perhaps she'd been too involved in her thoughts.

May eventually pulled herself together. She pretended for
a full ten minutes that she was glad. Who needed him? What
wisdom could she count on from him? *He* might be crippled,
but she certainly wasn't.

Then, as she began to calm, she grew afraid. First afraid
that she might never see him again, that perhaps he would
not forgive her. And then afraid that it should hurt like this.

When had she given him the power to hurt her?

The only possible way to outdo yourself after throwing your
body at the man you love and having him reject you,
Michaela thought miserably, is to stand in his home sobbing
as loud as you possibly can.

But she seemed absolutely helpless to stem the tide of
emotion that racked her. "I can't believe you're sending me
away!" she wailed. "Why does this keep happening to me?
Does no one ever want me? Am I so terribly flawed?"

He stood, watching her carefully. His face bore no expression, none whatsoever.

"I don't have anyone. There has not been one person, not
a one, who ever knew me, I mean really knew me. I don't
want to go my whole existence without that. I didn't come
here on some stupid impulse. This is important to me. I need
to make sure before we pledge ourselves that it isn't simply
an itch that, once scratched, would subside."

She drew in a shaking breath, not daring to peek and see
his dispassionate regard. She wished she would just shush,
but she seemed as unable to stop the words coming out of her
mouth as she had been the sobs that had come before. "I
don't suppose you would understand. I am sure your family

was wonderful. It would have to be, wouldn't it, because you have such marvelous confidence. It was different for me. I never knew who I was, how I fit into my . . . Oh, you must think me a dreadfully whiny fool."

Still he was silent. She continued with emphatic gestures. "It was terrible, all of those years feeling as if I didn't even belong in my own family! How could she not realize how she showed favoritism? I didn't imagine it. It was my father she saw when she looked at me, and it made her angry. Or sad. Oh, I don't know. I think she was afraid of me? Albert told me so, and I think he was right. I felt that, didn't I? Don't people hate what they fear? We fought all the time. I just wanted love. All my life, I just wanted love."

She stared at him, at his blank face and cold eyes. "Is that all, then? You are saying nothing? I suppose you don't appreciate me spouting all of this untidy personal information. I wish I hadn't. You probably think me hysterical now. Why can I never play by the rules, accept things for what they are? What is so terrible about the rules of marriage? We marry and mate until we tire of each other, then lapse into cold coexistence. The best we can hope for is cordiality." Her eyes filled with hot tears again. "I don't think I could bear that, Adrian. It might be different for someone who has known security in their life, but I couldn't go back to being invisible, unwanted."

Squeezing her eyes shut, she stood and took the ensuing silence. Punishment, well-deserved, for her outrageous behavior. Why had she said all of that—as if he cared?

Her flesh crawled in humiliation. She heard him moving. Maybe he was calling the watchman to cart her to the asylum, or the coachman that brought her to haul her away before she flooded the apartment.

She felt something cold and hard being pressed into her hands. She opened her eyes. It was a tumbler. It was filled with brown liquid.

Looking up, she saw Adrian's inscrutable features cast in shadow in the dim light. "It's Scotch whiskey. Sip it slowly."

She drew it to her lips and wet them. Even this slight kiss

of the smoky substance burned. She swallowed convulsively, spreading the fire.

He moved away to lean on the mantel. Not looking at her—and for that she was grateful—he waited patiently as he studied his own glass. "Take more."

The next sip of the Scotch burned less.

"Do you not get on with your mother?" he asked.

She bowed her head, filled with a mix of feelings. She found herself saying, "I thought Mother would be different after Lady May came into our lives. After all, once I found out who I was, the association to Woolrich brought great fortune to us all. She always idolized the fashionable and rich, longing to be back among her peers. Now she could. Because of me—her *mistake*. That night, at my first ball, I felt like a princess, but she said nothing, not one kind word. And then she wanted Delinda to meet you, so I tried to get there first. And I did."

He gestured, indicating she should drink. "Slowly," he clarified. "Just sip it."

She obeyed. Swallowing, she continued thoughtfully, "It is stupid, at my age, to worry about such things."

He drank, shielding his face in the glass. "I don't suppose hurt has an age limit."

She tried to hide behind the rim of her glass, too, but the fumes of the Scotch brought her, sputtering, up for air. She put the glass down and pressed her hands to her temple. "I would have wagered a few moments ago that this evening couldn't have gotten any worse, but I was wrong. Here I am prattling on about things you can't have any interest in. I am very sorry. I . . ."

She pivoted, wanting to turn away, but a swift movement of his hand captured her arm, keeping her where she was.

"Really, I appreciate your listening, it's very polite." She pulled, but his grip was as immutable as iron.

She said, "Well, if you will not allow me to leave, will you please *do* something because I really think I need you to *do* something to keep me from dissolving right here in front of you."

He eyed her, careful, face devoid of expression. "What do you need?"

She groaned and turned to go. "I need to leave, to be alone. I am terribly embarrassed and—"

"Stay," he said, a soft command.

He turned her slowly, his fingers capturing her chin and tilting her head back. He wanted her to look at him, but she couldn't yet. He let her go, sighed, and to her utter dismay, placed his arms about her. She was all at once enveloped in warmth.

"Thank you," she whispered.

"For what?" He coaxed her to the sofa and placed her upon it. Then he took her glass and put water in with the Scotch, sat down, and handed it to her.

"You are taking very good care of me."

"I've given you a drink you didn't like so far. That is not much."

"You listened. You didn't ask me to explain all of that nonsense I spouted, and you couldn't have understood much."

He picked a strand of hair out of her eyes. "Maybe I understand."

She smiled shakily. "I'm so sorry about what happened before. I wouldn't blame you if you thought quite ill of me for throwing myself at you like that. My suggestion that we . . . It was outrageous."

"It was my suggestion. I have to tell you, however, that I found the entire conversation the most exciting I've had in my life."

She was astonished. "But you were so angry."

"Because I couldn't possibly take what you offered, Michaela. Not that way."

His hand around her shoulder caressed her exposed skin. Whether from that or the spirits, she began to grow warm. His smile was cool, his eyes full of intensity.

She laughed nervously. "If I didn't know better . . . I'd think you were trying to seduce me."

"You know me well enough to recognize the signs, I imagine."

"You can't mean to. You only just turned me away."

"I turned away a plan, a passionless plot to satisfy intellectual curiosity. A test without any feeling to it. That is no way to find out about lovemaking."

"And now I am weak and shivering, and you can be the strong one."

His face was shrouded, his eyes darkened into pools of crystal brown. "No. Now you are Michaela. The woman, as it happens, who has my desire."

She sighed. "You are right. It didn't feel right before, did it?"

"You were trying to be something you are not."

"And now . . ."

"And now this," he murmured, touching her lightly along her jaw, "is what we are. I want to make love with you, not couple with you in some perverse experiment. I want you to feel. Not think."

She said, "You just wish to be the one in charge."

"Oh, I assure you, I am anticipating the delights of having you take the lead. But never without passion. It makes it all the sweeter, doesn't it, when we have the power to make the other weak with pleasure?"

She tried to struggle against the blissful lethargy that held her spellbound. "Are you sure about this? I mean, if you continue . . . well, Adrian, I think this is leading to trouble."

"Ah, but of course it is. I knew you were trouble the first time I saw you, Michaela Standish." He touched his finger to the full pad of her bottom lip. "Michaela, named for the warrior angel, ready to do battle. Are you as fierce in loving as you are in fighting, angel?"

That was nice. It burst a sweet warmth inside her. His smile deepened, and he asked, "Do you wish me to make love to you tonight?"

Her stomach plunged, then climbed, a pleasant ride of excitement. "It is what I came here for, after all."

His look grew dark. Her blood felt thick, pumping sluggishly. "Say it."

"You are trying to command me again."

"And you are a coward. Say it."

She bit her bottom lip. "I want you to make love to me. I do. No test, not for any purpose but because I need you, and you need me."

He smiled. "Now that," he muttered, lowering his head, "is something I can oblige."

His kiss was wonderful. It always was. Soft and tender, then deepening quickly. His arms came about her, strong and sure. She clung to him, caught by a surge of emotion unleashed by the night's events. The kiss was like air to starved lungs. It was invigorating, sparking her to life.

Her heart pounded, filling her brain with the passion-heated blood rushing through her. She closed her eyes tight, hoping he wouldn't remember he was actually angry and that he'd refused, less than a single hour ago in this very room, to even touch her.

He groaned, murmuring, "I want you. I waited for so long."

The feel of his hand on her breast shot liquid fire to her core. She arched, surprised, filled by the sensation of his touch. Through the cloth, his fingers stroked, awakening a response.

He found the front of her gown relatively easy to unfasten with a few dexterous motions. He gazed at the flesh he'd exposed, his eyes hooded. "You're beautiful," he said and then said it again, then again, then kissed her, and she kissed him back.

His hands stroked, awakening her body. She lay back on the settee, not having the slightest care for the rough texture of horsehair underneath her. He leaned over her, kissing her neck and shoulders, then down farther to taste the creamy flesh where the rise of her rounded breasts began. She stared at the ceiling, thrilling under the difference between his gentle bites, a lick, a kiss—each one evoking a separate sensation.

He laid his mouth at the base of her throat. His hands were beneath her skirt, engaged in a shivering encroachment up her thighs. She closed them, overcome suddenly by modesty.

"Open. I promise you will like it. I will only touch you. It

will feel good; I swear it." The urgency of his voice was
deeply erotic. The power of sex had him in its grasp.

She parted her legs, and his hand found the center of her.
Patiently he explored the pleasure to be gained by clever
strokes just so. She gasped, whimpering with confusion as
she throbbed with a need for more.

"Dear Christ, you are wet. Hot."

"Yes," she cried as he stroked again.

"You like it. I know you like it."

"Yes."

"Say it."

"I . . ."

"I command you," he murmured, and she could hear his
smile, sense he was teasing, and that he wasn't, too, and it
added to the excitement, his arrogance, his unqualified confidence at his ability to make her do as he wished.

His hand paused only fractionally before she bucked and
said, "I like it. Please."

"More?" He pushed, filling her with two fingers. His
thumb settled over the most exquisitely sensitive spot in the
front of her sex.

"Have you known pleasure?"

She lay, dazed. He pulled back to stare at her. "Have you
touched yourself here?"

His thumb glided over moisture-slick folds, finding her.

Nodding, she bit her lips, moaned slightly.

"Tell me."

"Yes! Yes, I did. I . . ."

"Did you come?"

She thrashed her head from side to side, emitting a low
moan.

He bent his head and suckled a nipple. She reacted violently to the new assault of sensual delight, squirming violently under him.

"Stay still," he said, blowing cool air over the moist flesh.
Her skin was impossibly tight and hot. Like a fever.

"Do that again," she rasped.

"Good," he said, a smile in his voice. "You are understanding. I want to please you, Michaela. I wish to know how it feels for you. You must tell me everything you want."

She tilted her hips. "I like this. Please don't stop."

"I won't, not now, love."

She felt the building pleasure, writhing with what her body demanded she do to maximize her pleasure.

"Did you come?"

"What?"

"When you pleasured yourself, did you come?"

"I don't know . . ."

"The pleasure, the intense pleasure that climbs and peaks to great satisfaction." He was speaking quickly, softly, his voice as rough as sand.

"Yes. Not . . . ahhh."

"Not like this?" he supplied when she couldn't speak.

She nodded, and he chuckled wickedly just as she reached her fulfillment. She let out a small scream, her eyes flying wide, staring into the triumphant, smoldering depths of his as pleasure burst inside her, fracturing her and filling her at the same time.

She fell back, limp. Closing her eyes, she lay without modesty. Her heart hammered violently, shaking her all over.

He pushed her skirts out of the way and shifted, his body over hers. She felt the hot ridge of flesh along her thigh. Mindlessly she opened her legs, wide enough to accommodate him. He entered her in a swift, sweet motion. Her sensitive inner flesh clamped tightly around him, welcoming this new penetration.

"It doesn't hurt?" he inquired.

"No." She'd been prepared for pain. Even May had cautioned her not to allow the initial rending of her virginity to discourage her from relaxing afterwards and "enjoying the ride," as she put it.

"Good. I want you to enjoy it." He pushed in deeper.

"I do. Oh, yes, I . . ."

"Tell me if you want me to enter you like this . . . or this." He tilted his pelvis, bringing his angle of penetration upwards on the second stroke. Her wordless response was all he needed. He leaned upwards, gathering her knee in the crook of his elbow, and thrust inside her again.

She threw her hand over her closed eyes, only to have it ripped away.

"Look at me," he said.

He was magnificent. He still wore his shirt, but it hung open. His broad, muscled body gleamed with sweat. She could see the ridged flat of his abdomen, a trail of coarse hair leading to where she refused to look. Where their bodies joined.

He leaned down to kiss her. His breathing hitched and he grunted, then jerked hard against her. He thrust mightily to fill her, stretch her, and then again. Exquisite pleasure filled her as he rocked her body hard with the intimate stroking of his body.

He'd . . . come. Wasn't that what he'd called it? Like he'd made her do.

She felt a wash of joy. They'd shared this pleasure, made it between the two of them. Hugging him close, she laid her cheek in the curve of his shoulder, feeling the blissful feeling of a deep, deep joy.

May had been wrong. This was not just passion. This *was* love. She felt it all through her. The sweet peace, the floating warmth all through her body, the fading eddies of pleasure in her limbs. This was surely real love.

And hadn't he grasped her tightly and seared her with his wild look of yearning? Oh, he loved her, too. This she felt to the core of her being.

She wanted to weep, but she didn't want to make a sound. The next moment, she wanted to laugh, but turned her smile into a kiss against the slick, masculine flesh. He smelled good, the clean sweat mingling with soap and man.

This was the feeling she'd waited all of her life to have. Love. Pure, unsullied, uncomplicated—hers! She belonged right here, in his arms, completed by him, filled by him.

"I am sorry I was so cross with you earlier," he murmured.

"You anger easily with me."

"You vex me."

"I don't mean to."

"Yes you do."

"All right, sometimes I do." She smiled, burrowing closer, and sighed. "I don't believe Aunt May's theories proved to be correct."

"Give it time," he said, amused. "Perhaps you'll tire of me yet."

She felt a fierce and sudden certainty that this would never happen. But a doubt made her say, "Or you me."

"I don't imagine you'll be too much of a bore, at least for a little while."

She could tell by his tone he meant exactly the opposite, but she gave him a jab in the ribs with her elbow, just the same.

He cupped her head in his wide palms and turned her face to his. "So, then, Miss Standish, do you still wish to marry me?"

A shadow crossed her face, and his eyes flickered. "What?"

"I do wish to marry you, Adrian. I just don't know if Mother . . ."

"What is this? Why in heaven would your mother object? You told me she was determined to get me for one of her daughters."

"It was for one of the twins."

"Good God!" he exclaimed. "One never speaks, and one looks like a birthday cake!"

"I've come to discover Lilah is very dear. She is just shy and was always overshadowed. And Delinda, while not exactly sweet-natured, is terribly insecure. She only brags and calls attention to herself so boldly in her dress because she . . . oh, all right, she's disagreeable. Which is why Mother has to marry her off first, so she doesn't get stuck with her."

"She told you that?"

"I sort of figured this out on my own. In any event, Mother has made Delinda a promise that she would see her married first, as the firstborn, and that part is indeed fact. If she abides by that promise, she could deny us."

"I am certain your mother will pose no obstacle. I do not tolerate obstacles."

"You do not know Mother," Michaela said darkly.

He peered at her. "This upsets you."

"I have been clashing with my mother since I was a babe in arms. I dread that this may degenerate into the same kind of contest of wills that has beset our relationship in the past. And if she absolutely refuses—"

He tightened his arms about her. "I will take care of it, then," he assured her, and his tone brooked no doubt. "I don't wish you to worry about this another moment."

She closed her eyes and smiled, drinking in the protective warmth enveloping her. "Mmm. I do not wish to go home."

"Then do not," he murmured, his lips brushing her hair.

"But of course I must go home."

"Stay with me. I'll let a town house for us. We can't live here, in these bachelor's quarters."

"Adrian." Untwining her arms, she twisted to face him. "I have no wish to be parted from you. But I must go home."

"To face all that turmoil. Why would you wish to do that?"

"And the alternative?" she inquired pertly.

"Gretna Green is not *that* far."

"You wish to elope?" She gaped at him. He seemed to be completely serious.

"Would you be disappointed in not having a large wedding with all of your friends and relatives in attendance? I, for one, would be glad to be rid of the entire business, but most men care nothing for the ritual in which women place so much importance."

"But what of your career in politics? Couldn't something like this reflect badly on you? If you lose the election because of making a bad marriage, and in a bad way, it would be terrible."

"I have never given a fig what people say or how something looks, good or ill. I am not about to begin now."

"But we haven't even announced our betrothal."

"That's the most delightful part of eloping. All of those formalities and traditions no longer hold." His eyes held hers as his hand slid up her arm. "Why are you coming up with all of these objections? It can be like this, Michaela, together like this. We can spend days and nights lingering in bed with no one to tell us a thing about it."

"I wouldn't mind eloping," she said tentatively. The words brought a vibrant chime of delightful sensation. Yes. She liked the idea. "And as for the big celebration, who would be there to smile? Mother will be vexed, even if she permits it, and Delinda will weep, and Aunt May . . . well, the less said about that the better. Who wants all those frowning faces at their wedding?"

"Not I," he said with a winning grin.

She laughed. "Then, yes, let us elope."

His grin stretched wider. "We can be off in a few hours. Before daylight, before anyone comes searching for you. By the time they find us—" His head dipped to hers for a kiss to seal the bargain. "—you will already belong to me."

✾ *Chapter 14*

"'Pon my word, it's Miss Lilah Standish."

The effusive declaration came from a tall blond man who paused before Lilah and Delinda as they strolled the promenade in Hyde Park. With a pointed toe and a lavish wave of his arm, Viscount Wickam dipped into a low bow. "Your servant."

Lilah felt an instant rush of blood rise to heat her cheeks. She managed, "My lord," and then Delinda jarred her with a well-aimed elbow, and she indicated her twin. "Er . . . Viscount Wickam, do you recall my sister?"

Delinda simpered, offering her hand. Wickam was polite but didn't linger over it. Turning back to Lilah, he said, "I am relieved that you haven't given me the cut, Miss Standish. When you refused my flowers, I thought perhaps you were put out with me."

"I did not refuse any flowers from you," Lilah said.

"But your reply was quite specific. And colorful. I am sorry to say I was quite vexed. Ah, but therein lies the challenge that boils in my blood. I am afraid it has only made me more determined."

"My lord!" she said, resuming her pace, remembering manners. A gentleman may walk with a lady and converse with her, but they must never stand about like ruffians plotting a reticule snatching. He quickly positioned himself on the street side, a show of courtesy.

She said, "I am certain I do not know what you are talking about."

"There was a misunderstanding, then. How relieved I am to hear it. Now my heart can beat again."

"If you think I should be flattered by your silliness, you do not know me very well."

"I must admit you are correct in that regard, for I do not know you half as well as I would like. Now, how to remedy that appalling condition? I have it. We shall deepen our acquaintance. That's the cure, by God. Shall I call on you?"

She didn't answer him.

"Oh, don't mind her. She's often cross," Delinda said, batting her eyelashes at Wickam. "I am afraid I am the one who got the easy nature between the two of us."

Lilah could hardly believe her sister's treachery. But Delinda had never made any bones about her self-interest, so it should not surprise her.

Wickam pointedly ignored Delinda's interruption. "Allow me to propose a hypothetical, if you will, Miss Standish. If I were to call on you one afternoon, say in two days or so, when you've had an opportunity to mull over this chance meeting and see how much you wish you'd been more welcoming to me, would you be amenable to receiving me?"

"Oh, I know I would," Delinda cut in. "So, if you were to pay us a visit, Viscount Wickam, I daresay one or the other of us would be happy to entertain you."

He placed a mild smile in place for courtesy's sake. To Lilah, he said, "Your sister says she would not refuse. Would you?"

"I would never be outright rude to you, my lord." A devil made her add, "Without proper provocation, that is."

She was feeling giddy with exhilaration. Was this timid Delilah exchanging quips with a peer of the realm? She didn't know herself suddenly, for she was now Lilah, an outspoken person, her own woman.

He turned to Delinda, leaning forward confidentially. "It gives one hope, does it not, when one sees the object of their affection being reasonable? I say, Miss Standish, does she ever speak of me kindly?"

Lilah said, "I do not know why you are speaking about me as if I am not present. I am still standing right here."

"I see you," Wickam said. "Indeed, I can scarce see anything else."

"Then you can speak to me directly."

"But you are pruning your face up and looking so disagreeable at me, so I thought perhaps your sister might be more congenial."

"Indeed, one of us is as good as the other, isn't that true?" Lilah stomped off, surprising both Delinda and Wickam.

She instantly regretted it. A glance over her shoulder confirmed that he was still speaking with her sister. Wickam caught her eye and tipped his hat, giving an abbreviated bow this time before hieing off again with his trademark jaunty walk.

When Delinda caught up to her, Lilah was stewing. "Don't you think a man like that grows weary of women throwing themselves at him? You were making a fool of yourself."

"I hardly agree," Delinda said with a haughty lift of her nose. "He is probably paying attention to you to make me jealous. I think he is in love with me."

Lilah rolled her eyes. "Like Major Khoury? Perhaps when he returns from his elopement with our sister, whom he strangely chose to marry instead of you with whom he was madly in love, he can see to the forming of a society of lonely hearts pining for Delinda Standish, and the viscount may join."

"You dare mock me. Of course, Major Khoury saw I was nowhere near ready to settle down so soon after making a splash on the polite world, so Michaela snapped him up. Don't be so full of yourself, *Lilah*. How I hate that ridiculous name! As if the one given to you by our mother wasn't good enough for you. I knew you would get a bad case of conceit if you knew that a viscount had been sending you gifts."

Without breaking her stride, Lilah said, "So that is why you sent the flowers back."

Delinda was so taken aback, she forgot to play coy. "How did you know?"

"I didn't. I only guessed. Did Mother know?"

"Of course not. I was only thinking to save you the trouble of doing it yourself. I realized, of course, that you couldn't abide the man. And the bouquet wasn't so grand, in any event, not nearly as fine as he boasted."

"And you didn't tell me."

"I knew you would be vexed."

"Vexed?" Lilah paused as they came upon the carriage, which had been waiting on the corner. Their packages had already been loaded by attendants. She waited while the coachman hopped down and pulled down the step. "I don't want you to ever meddle in my affairs again. If you do, I will make you exceedingly sorry."

Delinda looked affronted. "My, my, Delilah, aren't you suddenly prickly. Quite the lion after so many years the lamb. One might think you actually liked the attentions of this foppish viscount you go to such lengths to scorn."

Lilah took the step and flounced into her seat. She was done with this ridiculous conversation, determined not to speak to or even acknowledge her infuriating sister for the entire ride home.

Adrian waked out of sleep to the awareness of a soft, pliant breast cradled beautifully in his palm. It belonged to the slumbering form of his wife. She was moving, making soft sounds like a mewling kitten as she slept. He felt the bed shift, and the mound of flesh that fit so neatly in his relaxed hand rubbed. The rose-colored tip tightened. He grinned, deciding if he should allow her to sleep on or give in to temptation.

It really wasn't a contest, and he didn't waste any more

time resisting the urge to continue the friction. She had started it, after all.

Her head lolled, and her eyelashes lifted.

"Your hand is on my breast," she said sleepily.

"I believe that in this case it was your breast in the way of where my hand was lying."

"I apologize in that event," she said, and smiled a lazy, sultry smile that made his throat go completely dry. "I trust my breast getting in the way of your hand did not disturb your sleep."

"As a matter of fact, it did."

He didn't cease his gentle, slow caress. She squirmed, her eyes glazing.

"Now you are taking advantage," she said breathlessly.

"Are you making complaint?"

"I am enjoying every moment of it, my husband," she assured him.

He experienced the same small shock at the word "husband" as had been happening since the speedy ceremony just over the Scottish border. It jarred him pleasantly every time he heard it.

He liked marriage. It was so much better like this than shackled to some dough-faced widow, even if she did come with blond-haired children in tow. The chief advantage, of course, was privacy. He definitely liked the privacy.

Bending down, he kissed her, taking his time. His abrasions to her sensitive flesh became rougher, quicker. She sighed, drawing up her knee to cradle his hip.

He had learned in this short week of matrimony some of what she liked. To his delight, she had proven an eager, unself-conscious lover who was willing to experiment. Although he had taken it slowly at first, she had not balked at any of the new things he had introduced.

She had also proved curious, and quickly learned a few of the things he liked in bed. This she demonstrated with her hand when she found his sex engorged.

She made a delighted sound at his state of readiness. "I shudder to imagine the dreams you were having to wake you in such a state."

He bent to kiss her breasts, flicking at the nipples lightly. She moaned and twisted in his arms, wanting more.

"I was dreaming," he said softly, "of a bold woman who nearly accosted me at a ball one evening. She plied me with her attentions and green eyes with a gypsy slant that made me lose all sense of myself."

He moved lower, putting his tongue in her navel, and she grasped his head in her hands. Sliding his palms down her side, he rode the curve of her hips. He followed with his mouth, kissing her, tasting her flesh on his tongue, until he delved into the dark curls covering her center. He stopped, skating light fingers up the inside of her thighs.

"Those eyes made promises. Of nights filled with erotic fantasies a man would crawl through a desert to know."

His fingers found her. She was already wet. And hot. Michaela was always hot inside.

She reacted, and he grinned. He loved her like this. She abandoned herself to lovemaking. No woman he'd ever been with had laid herself before him so freely, taking and giving without artifice, pretense or games.

Well, maybe some games. He definitely liked the sorts of games he and Michaela played in bed. She was more than his match, even with her inexperience. It whet his appetite for the future.

He let her lie, panting, waiting, quivering for what he would do next. He said, "She was a woman meant for pleasure." He showed her that, and she arched, throwing her head back and giving herself to his play. "But she was a woman of mystery. She refused to give in to her real nature."

He rose up and drew her legs open. Kneeling before her, he cupped her buttocks and brought her hips up to meet his jutting erection.

Poised at her entrance, he waited just one indulgent moment, taking it all in.

She was magnificent: flushed, her mouth slack, her green eyes glowing with desire. His body thrummed with unbearable excitement at the mating about to take place.

Her legs folded around his hips, and she pulled him into her, her arms reaching as she whispered breathlessly, "You poor man. You must be in need of solace. Come, let me ease you."

Yes. His body slid into the sweet comfort of her body. He leaned down and tasted her mouth, his hands roaming where they might as they rose swiftly together in passion.

He came hard, feeling her orgasm under his, clutching her tightly as pleasure splintered like fragile glass inside his body. When he was spent, he collapsed, bracing himself on his elbows to keep from crushing her.

He curled together with Michaela. The silence of the room was broken only by the soft sound of their breathing, the occasional whisper of skin against the fine cotton sheets.

She said, "And then what happened?"

"I woke to find her in bed beside me. So I ravished her."

"What a splendid dream, Adrian."

"Hmmm."

"Are you going back to sleep?" She sounded indignant.

"No," he said groggily. He was lying. His body was replete, and sleep sounded wonderful.

"But we have to get up. It's back to London today. Don't you remember? You promised."

"Nonsense. It's not Tuesday."

"Indeed, it is not, it is Wednesday, you lazy oaf, and you promised that Tuesday was the day we would return. So wake up."

"But it is your fault. You insisted we take that scenic hike into the hills when we were in Kingston. Then our clothing needed to be laundered."

"Because you pushed me into the lake."

"I told you to undress. You wouldn't listen to me."

"You were a bully. That water was freezing."

"You didn't complain very long, as I recall." He pulled her in tighter, resting his lips to hers, feeling her smile against his. "We passed a very pleasant afternoon while your clothing dried on the rocks."

He rubbed his leg along hers. If their lovemaking hadn't exhausted her, he would be more than happy to oblige her again. Michaela sometimes craved several climaxes before she was spent. Adrian delighted in her ravenous appetite for the pleasures he was more than capable of supplying.

"Why are you in such a rush to get back to London? It is filthy, and the humidity can wilt granite. It is so much more pleasant here, where we can do what we want, when we want."

"You are spoiled and lazy already."

"I admit it. I cannot recall the last time I didn't have someplace to be, some obligation or demand to command my time. I find this—" His hand took another bold liberty. "—entirely more pleasant."

The ploy to distract her didn't work. She pushed against his chest, saying, "You said I was going to meet your family. If we keep them waiting, they will think it is my fault. They dislike me already, most likely."

"They don't know you, so how can they dislike you?"

"Then they dislike the idea of me."

He tried cuddling. "When they meet you, they will be as captivated as I."

"Get up and take me home."

His hand covered her breast. She pushed it away. "You are too tired to make good on any promises, so don't start that again."

"You know me so well after a mere week of marriage," he argued. "I'll have you know I can pleasure you even in my presently depleted state."

He saw the glint of interest in her eyes. He grew hopeful. If he could get her to relax, enjoy the pleasuring ministrations he was happy to provide, she might be amenable to a nap afterwards.

He brushed his fingertips in the soft down at the top of her thighs.

"That is it, you lout," she exclaimed, sitting up. The peaks of her breasts, he saw with lascivious interest, were taut. Her body was willing, even if she was pretending not to be.

She whipped back the coverlet and stood. Retrieving her shift, she slipped it over her head. The fine lawn concealed nothing, only draped bewitchingly. She didn't bother with any other clothing. God knew, after the days and nights they had spent together, she couldn't possibly have any modesty left.

"You are taking me home today."

The game, however, was not over. He leaned back, hands folded behind his head. "What if I say no?"

She donned an equally arrogant pose, and countered, "Then I will secure a separate chamber and remain out of reach."

"You wouldn't."

"I would. I will."

"I would crook my finger, and you would come running back, begging for me to take you." He made his voice sound especially haughty, just to get her temper up.

She opened her mouth in exaggerated horror at his boast. "I would refuse you to the end, even if you begged piteously for want of me."

He shrugged. "Then you would leave me no choice. I would tie you with silk bindings and blindfold you. Then I would take the softest piece of silk you own and feather it all over your body until you were one touch away from fulfillment. Then I'll wager I'd hear no more nagging about London."

She narrowed her eyes. "You would?"

"Indeed, yes, my gentle wife. I would enjoy it, too."

"You wouldn't dare." Her eyes danced eagerly. It was an invitation if he'd ever heard one.

"My God, Michaela, you are a wanton. What a perfect match we are. Now, come back to bed."

"I am getting dressed. Then I am going to London if I have to hire my own coach."

"I will take you to London. But first there is the matter of the condition your little game has left me." He glanced meaningfully down at the sheet covering his hips. "I am afraid your prancing around in that absolutely fetching chemise and challenging me with erotic images has created a bit of a problem."

"I don't trust you," she said, gnawing on her bottom lip.

He loved when she did that. It drove him insane, those even white teeth plying the plumpness of her reddened flesh.

"I shall come and get you," he threatened, making his voice as dark as possible. "Is that what you want?"

She smiled and sauntered over to the bed, placing one knee on the edge. "Perhaps that is what I want." She gave him a look that sent a new rush of blood to his nether regions. "But I am prepared to hold out until you agree to take me to London immediately afterwards or I am going to—"

She didn't get to finish her sentence, for Adrian surged forward, catching her wrist and bringing her down beside him with alarming speed.

They didn't speak for a long time. When they rose, they wore secretive smiles and cast veiled glances at one another as they dressed. And true to his word, Adrian took her home.

It was strange what came over Adrian as soon as he and Michaela came within view of the huddled rooftops of London. The chimney pots spewed smoke, mingling with the acrid smell off the Thames, and the smog it created stung his eyes.

It had not pleased him to come back here. He experienced no sense of welcome, nothing to bring anticipation to his heart. In Scotland he would rather be, lost in a fantasy, feasting on carnal delights. The past week and a half had been a dream of forbidden pleasures.

It occurred to him at that moment that there was not a single thing he was looking forward to of his ordinary existence. He seemed to have all he wished for bundled in a smart traveling habit on the seat beside him in the carriage. He supposed, he realized with a shock, that he didn't much like his old life.

Michaela, on the other hand, was glad to be back. He had taken a suite at a hotel in Hanover Square. They settled in. Then it was time to face the families.

The call on the house in St. Alban's Crescent went better than Michaela had hoped. Lilah was happy for her. Mother was as well, surprisingly. She seemed relieved, and Michaela realized that by taking matters into their own hands, they had spared her a difficult decision. As for Delinda, she took an unexpected tack. Appearing indifferent to the new couple, she spoke rapidly and at length about her various admirers. She was sending a message, no doubt, that she would be following swiftly into the life of a wedded woman.

Michaela found she could be charitable to her, and even to Aunt May, whose stiff reception they received next. As they were leaving her Park Lane home, Michaela broached the subject of Adrian's family with her husband.

"I sent word to my brother's home here and received a prompt reply."

"Do they wish us to call?" Michaela asked eagerly.

His look was inscrutable. "I said I preferred to take it gradually. Richard has said that he would come tomorrow afternoon for tea, if that suits you."

"That would be fine. But why—?"

"Trust me," he said, sotto voce. He didn't look at her, staring instead out the window, his jaw set. "In matters of my family, it is best to be cautious."

She got no more clarification on that cryptic comment, not even when she applied herself to the task of cajoling him most ingeniously. Adrian refused to budge, but Michaela enjoyed the effort in any event.

The following morning, she fluttered about nervously before Richard's visit trying on various dresses and casting them off. She chided Adrian for his cravat, which was knotted the same as he always did, and complained about the sparse spread the hotel sent up for their repast. But when Richard arrived, she transformed. Composed, smiling beguilingly, she was formidably charming as she sank into a deep curtsy before the marquess.

Adrian smiled at Richard's reaction. He had not met Michaela before. Upon seeing her for the first time, he blinked in astonishment as she dazzled him with a winning smile and a flash of green eyes.

Adrian understood the reaction. Michaela's beauty had only grown in the short weeks of their marriage. He himself still felt a sweet, weak feeling inside him when he looked at her. But to see his wife affect his brother, who had once taken so much from him, stabbed a sharp, satisfying feeling into his breast. It was immediately followed by remorse. After all, Richard hadn't been to blame. Why had he always regarded him as a rival? Male pride?

"I am honored," Richard said as he bowed low over Michaela's hand.

Adrian felt a surge of proprietary pride.

Michaela presided over the tea expertly, pouring out without spilling a drop, conducting light conversation, the sort women do, to make everyone feel at ease.

"You are coming to the house, of course," Richard said, looking about. "You cannot mean to stay here. You must come live with us until you return to Shepston-on-Stour."

"Of course we mean to stay here, at least until I let a town house."

"Nonsense. We've plenty of room at ours."

"We do not wish to impose." Adrian's tone was definite.

Michaela cast him a curious look.

Richard was insistent. "But you must. Frances has the children here. She came when she heard of your elopement." Turning to Michaela, Richard explained, "My wife is very anxious to meet you. She wants me to inform you that she is hopeful you two will come to look upon one another as sisters and wishes to have you to dinner as soon as you are settled."

To his horror, Adrian saw Michaela seemed pleased at the idea. "I am looking forward to making the acquaintance of the entire family."

"That's ridiculous," he cut in. "They will hardly see one another, let alone grow close. They will meet eventually, yes, but we do not have to make a production of it."

"Frances said you would say that."

"Then she has more sense than you."

Michaela watched this interchange like a spectator at a lawn tennis match.

"Come, Adrian, stay with us. It is as much your home as it is mine."

"Michaela and I desire our privacy. Besides, I never felt at home there." What he didn't say was that this was especially the case if Frances was in residence. "My mind is quite made up on the matter."

A movement caught his eye, and he looked over to find Michaela's eyelashes sweeping downward, her face composed but not so much that he couldn't see that she was upset.

Richard was disgruntled. "Then at least come for supper. I'll have Frances arrange a convenient date and send a man round to give you the particulars."

As much as he would have liked to thwart the prurient interest of his sister in-law—which was exactly what was behind this false show of familial welcome—he had no good reason to refuse the dinner invitation.

It put a bitter taste in his mouth, but he agreed.

"I almost forgot," Richard said, placing a packet of correspondence on a table as he pulled on his gloves in preparation to take his leave. "Your solicitor brought these around when you closed out your rooms in St. James. I said I would bring them to you."

Adrian eyed the pile of letters with little enthusiasm. "Thank you."

As Richard picked up his hat and strode toward the door, he reminded Adrian of the series of meetings set for the next few days. Glenarvon was in town, he said with a meaningful look. They had a great deal to discuss.

Ah. The marriage would not meet with the approval of the political master. He had gone against the express advice on the kind of wife he needed. Not that Adrian cared a whit for that. He'd always done what he pleased.

But a twinge of conscience pulled at him. In the past, the consequences had been his, but his obligations now were different, deeper. He thought of Paul Trent, and he thought of his wife, Sarah, the condition he found her in when he'd returned home. And how he had vowed to make certain veterans of wars and their widows were protected, that servants had rights and could not be exploited, that progress would encompass all the classes of England. He'd been an ambitious fool. To some degree, he still was.

"I liked him very much," Michaela said, coming to slip her arm through his when Richard had gone.

Disengaging his arm, he moved away, feeling unsettled.

This was why he hadn't wanted to come back. Like a mantle unseen, but felt keenly, the responsibility he'd accumulated layered onto his shoulders.

"Do you think I made a good impression?" she asked.

"You don't need his approval or anyone else's."

He regretted the words. He felt agitated. He repressed the unsettled feelings. It was certainly not Michaela's fault he was so restive, and he wouldn't hurt her, not intentionally.

"I suppose I am grouchy pining for Scotland. It will be easier for me when we are in Shepston-on-Stour." He gave her a quick embrace. "As for the impression you gave, I am certain it was stellar."

"I thought your brother a lovely man. I am very much looking forward to meeting the rest. He and his wife have two boys, and a little girl. How charming; I adore children."

The last thing he wished to do was dwell on his family. Holding up the packet of correspondence, he added, "Forgive me. I have work to do."

"Oh," she said. "I am sorry, I didn't realize I was keeping you. I should take a ride to the house and see Mother. I'll leave you to it." She kissed him fleetingly and smiled before making her exit.

He brought the packet of letters to the small desk provided in the suite, filing through them. One had caught his attention. It was from the village of Shepston-on-Stour, which was within an hour's ride from the huge house he'd purchased in the sleepy district.

Opening it, he saw by the introduction that it was written by a solicitor, Mr. Horace Brown, under the direction of a James Chivers, who identified himself as a smith, an illiterate, who was using the services volunteered by the good Mr. Brown.

Adrian read on, his brows knitting together more tightly with each sentence. Tipping his head back and forth, working the tension from his neck, he closed his eyes against the sudden wave of weariness.

His obligations and commitments had not abated during the haze of lust he'd been steeped in for the last few months. He had gotten selfish. Enamored of the sensual delights of his new wife, he'd lost the cutting edge of determination to put Shepston on notice for his feudal abuses of power.

As he shuffled through the remaining letters, he vowed marriage was not going to inhibit his ability to serve the people, those common folk who had represented the best of the fighting men he'd known. He felt strongly about Michaela, a closeness born of desire and a natural need to protect and care for her, but he was not going to abandon his other ambitions.

Ambitions? No. It had never been about ambition.

It had been duty.

With his demons resurrected and pealing like a chorus in his head, he wrote several letters and called to have them sent to the post.

Michaela entered the room cautiously. "Am I interrupting?"

He smiled, leaning back in his chair and scrubbing his hands over his face. "Come in. I could use a rest."

"You seem tired," she said, coming to his side.

He held out an arm for her. Grasping his upturned face in her hands, she kissed him. "Do you need a nap?" Her smile held an unmistakable meaning.

He took her fingers, twined them in his. "I have more work to do. I am afraid the distraction of a wife—getting her, wedding her, and bedding her—has taken its toll. I have neglected my duty."

"Hmmm." She rubbed enticingly against him. She wanted to make love.

"Michaela." He set her away from him firmly. "There are important matters I must see to."

"Oh, I know. You are a very important man." She giggled. Spying an open letter he had been studying when she came in, she touched her finger to it. "So, tell me, then, who is this from?"

He frowned. "A smith from my district. They are in a spot

of trouble out there." He folded the letter and slid it under the others.

"Is there anything I can do to help?" she said.

He grinned. "Do you have your pen at the ready to write more letters to the newspaper?"

"I would write a treatise if it would help," she said. "To every newspaper in the country. So, what is the trouble? Tell me, and I will come up with a brilliant solution for you."

"It is my problem. I will deal with it. Let us speak of more pleasant things."

The rebuff stung. "I didn't mean to pry."

"You didn't. I am sorry if I am being a brute. I am just busy right now." He indicated the pile of papers.

"I shall bother you no more. I will wait to see you at dinner."

But when dinnertime approached, he stuck his head into her dressing room and informed her that he had an appointment and he was going out.

Seated at the dressing table, brush poised, she stared at his reflection. "At this hour?"

"Lord Glenarvon is in Town for the next few days. He wishes to meet with me. I have to go. I will be busy with him for the duration of his visit. I don't suppose you should expect me home much."

She was crushed as the plans she had been making for their first evening out since arriving back in Town crumbled. "I had hoped to go to the theater. There is a production of *Love's Labor Lost*."

"Go on, then, if you are set on it."

"But I wished to go with you. You told me you liked Shakespeare."

"I do." He was growing irritated. "But I have these meetings. Now don't bother about it. Ask your aunt or your sisters. I need to go. I'll see you when I return."

She was about to tell him that although she was on speaking terms with her aunt—barely—and her sisters, she could hardly insinuate herself *alone* into their evening plans. Even inviting them to accompany her would be unacceptable. It would be too embarrassing. She had gambled everything on him, on their being together. Wasn't that what had driven them to run off to marry before anyone could nay-say them?

She had risked her good standing in every other relationship to run off and marry him, and as a result, she felt isolated and a bit unsure of herself just now. She needed *him*.

Didn't he realize that she needed him now more than ever?

Chapter 15

Michaela wondered if Cinderella languished in her castle after she and Prince Charming wed. Did she sit and read, or sew? Did she visit the indigent? Just how did she keep from going mad in those long hours when her husband was off doing state business? She would really like to know. She needed a few ideas.

Later on that first week, she paid a call on her aunt. She left after only a short while, nearly in tears because of the stilted atmosphere that pervaded the room as they searched for topics upon which to converse. They never before had been at a loss for words with one another, but Michaela understood May was deeply hurt by the elopement.

She was cheered when she arrived back at the hotel by an impromptu call from Lilah. They shared a few laughs about the status of all of Michaela's acquaintances and how people reacted to the news of her sudden marriage. The cheerful visit lent a small slice of brightness to her day, but the sameness of the hours was restored soon after her sister left, rush-

ing out in a hurry against Michaela's pleading for her to stay
in order to avoid a gathering thunderstorm.

Adrian returned just before supper, soaked to the bones.
She rushed to help him as he stood dripping all over the floor
as he gingerly removed his coat, brushing off his comment
that he would call his valet.

"It was sunny as the desert when I departed this morning.
I am going to change." He went into the small dressing room
and exchanged his wet things for a dressing gown and fresh
trousers while she fussed over his clothes. "You don't have to
do that," he said when he returned to see her spreading the
garments to dry. "Call someone to see to it."

"I don't mind. Do build a fire, Adrian."

He fetched a few split logs and hunkered down to feed
them into the fire.

She'd come to know his closed look to see he was in one
of his pensive moods. Something troubled him, and it was no
small worry. It had been much the same each evening when
he arrived home after calls and meetings in the homes of political dignitaries. The few hours spent with her before dressing for the evening and going back out were usually
characterized by this subdued mood. Then he'd return late,
smelling of cigars and faint traces of spirits.

The worst of it was, she knew he was miserable. Sighing,
she glanced down at the book on her lap. Tonight, she didn't
mind his silence for her own worries were on her mind. She
couldn't stop thinking about her aunt and how different their
visit this afternoon had been from the gay times they had
spent in the past.

Roused out of her thoughts by feeling the book sliding
away, she looked up to see Adrian kneeling in front of her,
pulling it off her lap. She was surprised. He was smiling.

The sight of his face made her feel instantly better.

"You were fathoms away," he said.

"It was a boring book."

He glanced at the title. "Mrs. Radcliffe is usually one of
your favorites. Something is troubling you. I've been waiting
for you to tell me. Now I've run out of patience."

She sighed. "It is of no import, not greatly. I suppose I am feeling badly about the state of things with Aunt May and myself." She told him about the visit.

"You weren't going to tell me," he observed when she had finished.

"I didn't wish to bother you."

He was silent, thoughtful. Then he took her hands and folded them between his. "I know I have been busy. I've neglected you. I assure you, that is not my wish."

She wouldn't argue with him. He had been dreadfully absent of late, and she felt the loss of his presence keenly.

He shrugged. "As for you and your aunt, it is important you make it up with her as soon as you get the chance. Believe me, one should not allow family problems to fester. They transform into long-term resentments, and then it is too late by the time you realize all you've lost."

"I do not think she wishes to. I am afraid her disappointment in me has put a breach between us."

"Michaela, affections are not so fragile as to break when a strain is put on them."

"I have never known them to be different," she said.

He took her chin in his fingers so that she was forced to meet his gaze. "You refuse to be cheered."

"Perhaps you best leave me," she said. "I am afraid I am not going to do anything but sulk. I don't wish to be happy. I want to pout."

He smiled softly. "That bad, eh? Come here."

Standing, he drew her up with him. He arched one brow, as if taunting her, and tugged her toward the doorway.

"Where are we going?"

"Just do as I say."

"I—"

"No objections. Didn't you vow to obey, wife?"

She felt a tide of pleasure. "I did. But I trusted you not to abuse the privilege."

"I doubt you will have complaint," he said.

She allowed him to lead her into the bedroom, where he undressed her. Performing each motion slowly, he removed her dress, then her undergarments. He lingered on each stocking, caressing each long limb slowly. "Now lie down," he directed, easing her over onto her stomach.

Michaela clutched a pillow under her and lay her head on it, sighing contentedly. Behind her, Adrian spread his hands over her back and began to stroke deeply, kneading and rubbing down the length of her back.

"Relax," he commanded.

She grunted, lulled instantly by the movement of his hands. His touch always stirred a primitive response, but this was different. He eased the tension from her with his strong, capable hands, and she faded into contentment. The weight of her concerns were knuckled away as each muscle received diligent attention.

"What are you doing to me?" she asked groggily. His fingers lightened, rippling shivers over her skin.

"This was taught to me by a master in the art of sacred massage when I was in the army, stationed in the country of Moravia."

His voice held a teasing tone. Lifting her chin on her fist, she acted puzzled. "Moravia. I've never heard of it."

"An exotic country. Not many people know of it. It's nestled in the Carpathian Mountains, well up in the most remote parts of the European continent. It's mysterious, a well-kept secret. Only the most privileged and accomplished are allowed to visit there and learn their ancient secrets."

"I see." She smiled lazily, then went as limp as overcooked asparagus as he found a knot under her shoulder blade. "So . . . tell me why this is considered sacred."

"Oh, you'll see."

His hands dipped on either side of her chest, stroking the sides of her breasts, delving to the undersides and into the sensitive length inside her arms. A coil of pleasure sprang to attention in the pit of her stomach.

"No." He spoke softly as she moved sensually against his touch. "Be still. This is the good part."

"Are you certain this is sacred?"

"It cleanses the body of all tensions. But you must relax."

"I cannot. Your massage has taken a decidedly different turn. Not exactly relaxing."

"Sometimes an alternative tension can be helpful in combating the original tensions. Allow me to demonstrate."

He slipped his hand under her belly, then down until she gasped. Then he withdrew, leaving her disappointed.

His voice was soft at her ear. "Like fire fighting fire, that sort of idea."

"Fire . . . oh, I think I feel the fire, Adrian."

His hands delved under her once again, then eased, gliding over her quivering flesh to her buttocks and down her legs. "There? You feel the fire there?"

"Oh, a bit higher, I think."

He tickled the back of her thighs until she squirmed.

"Not there!" she cried, dissolving into giggles.

"I think I know where," he assured her, and lay down next to her. He had removed his clothing. How he had managed that while attending to her so assiduously, she couldn't imagine, but then she'd been in a half-stupor.

The press of his naked skin along the back of her was delicious.

She leaned back to feel more of him. He reached around, toying with her until she grabbed his wrist and moved his hands where she needed them. Within moments, she was caught in the flames he had spoken of, forgetting everything else but the feelings coursing through her.

On his side, he spooned her in front of him, murmuring instructions for this new exercise in erotic experimentation. She obeyed, unable to object. The way he was manipulating her body, commanding her senses, left her in no position to argue. She was hot and weak, completely malleable. She stretched out along the cool sheets.

Pulling her buttocks to his hips, he slid inside her from his position behind. This new and pleasurable sensation instantaneously aroused her. Her hands clawed the sheets, and she arched to give him more access. His hand nestled in the soft curls between her legs, exerting enough pressure to make each stroke exquisite, building her to quick climax.

He was gentle, then rough when sensation claimed them both. She clutched the arm wrapped around her, easing back into him as they quieted. He stroked her hair. "Better?" he inquired.

"Mmmm."

"This is an excellent argument to justify my refusing the invitation to live at my brother's house, is it not? We can hardly slip upstairs whenever we please when we are in someone else's domain."

"It might be more comfortable for you. After all, they are familiar surroundings."

He rolled her onto her back, cradling her in one arm. With the other hand, he touched her collarbone, tracing its line. "It would be very uncomfortable. My brother's wife and I do not get along."

This was a tremendous relief. Michaela had thought it was her reputation—a controversial, letter-writing, illegitimate daughter of a legendary rake—which had made him reluctant to bring her to meet his family.

Existing family tensions were to blame for his keeping them at a distance. "I can't imagine any woman not being utterly susceptible to your charm."

"I have no charm," he stated.

"You do. It is subtle, granted, but potent."

He lifted a brow and scowled, but his lips twitched. "I have no artfulness with women."

"And that is exactly your charm—simply your strong nature." She rolled her eyes dreamily, and her playing won her a real smile. "It is quite stirring, you know. It was what made me fall in love with you."

He reacted as if she'd said something contentious. This puzzled her. She understood he might be taken aback by the abruptness of her pronouncement, but it could hardly be a shock to know how she felt. He had to know she loved him.

And that she wanted desperately to hear those same words from him.

Because he *did* love her. How could she feel it, know it, sense it all through her being, if he did not? How could he not when he made such sweet love to her, when it went past bodies and into a realm far too metaphysical to describe? If that was not love, what was?

The coldness in him frightened her. "What is wrong?" she murmured. "Did I say something wrong?"

"No, nothing. We should dress. It's later than I thought."

"I didn't mean anything, you know." Oh, traitor to her heart, it had certainly meant everything. But her pride had her now, smarting painfully from the slap. "I know you hate sentiment."

"It's not that. I'm famished, and dinner is nearly served." He rose from the bed and began to pull on his trousers.

More slowly, she followed. "Please forget I said anything."

He sighed. Tying his trousers, he came to her and laid a hand on her cheek. He looked pained, troubled. "Oh, Michaela." He seemed like he wanted to say more, then shook the words away, deciding against it. "We are honest with one another. That's what I value so much about this. We are married. I am pledged to you, and I promised to be a good husband, and so I shall be."

"But you do not love me?"

"I have a deep caring for you, Michaela, you know that. Why quibble about a word? Once it's spoken, it does things. It makes people fleetingly happy, but it also has the power to make them enduringly miserable. I am satisfied with our life. We enjoy each other, we are good together. But when one speaks of love, then easy companionship becomes a state of demands and obsession and dissatisfaction. I simply have no taste for the word or the emotion. My experience has taught me it is a quagmire. Let us do well enough without it, as we have."

"It doesn't always have to be that way."

He gave her a sage look, as if he knew better but would charitably hold his tongue. She didn't wish to argue. How could one argue for emotion against such systematic logic?

She felt as if she'd been stung by a fury of wasps. She nodded. Traitor to her heart, yes, indeed she was to so meekly acquiesce. But to rain ideals upon him for which he had no use was unthinkably humiliating.

As she was dressing, she thought about what he'd said. Reason told her that he was a soldier, a seasoned war hero, a self-contained man. No fawning lover, he was strong, and with that strength came certain attitudes, she told herself, that try a woman's emotions at times.

She was learning quickly that he was very much a solitary man. His feelings, for the most part, he would not share. Not even with a wife. He was a generous lover, and she was absolutely confident—this she told herself emphatically to help drive the point home—that with time he would feel comfortable in telling her the things she longed to hear.

Needed to hear. For a woman who had never felt loved, it was her most cherished wish to know, feel, taste, hear those precious words. The great love she'd always yearned for to chase away the cold years of her upbringing.

It wasn't so terrible for now. Adrian was caring and wonderful and sexy. But . . .

But sometimes, she was more than a little bit lonely.

The fact that Adrian had told Michaela virtually nothing about his family, other than that he didn't get along with Richard's wife, made her all the more nervous to meet them. As they entered the fine mansion situated in the heart of Belgravia that was the London home of the marquess, she was nearly shaking with apprehension.

From the tense silence of her husband, he was far from easy himself. She wanted so much to ask him what it was that made this evening so difficult, but she could not. Adrian did not talk about himself, and to ask only brought tense rebuffs and frustration.

Adrian greeted the footman warmly. The elderly servant smiled, welcoming him with a great deal of pleasure as he showed them in. Such familiarity with servants, she had learned since coming to know something of the nobility, was not typical.

They entered the drawing room together, with the footman announcing the Major and Mrs. Adrian with aplomb. The first person she saw as she entered the drawing room was Terrance. "Here is our new sister," he said, and came to clasp her hands.

Michaela was so grateful for this kind greeting she nearly burst into tears. She managed not to as she was greeted by his fiancée.

Then Richard came to her, kissing her cheek, then drawing her forward to the woman seated in a small grouping of furniture by the hearth. The mild weather made the fire unnecessary, and yet not only did it burn, Richard's wife was nestled close up to it as if the evening were one typical of mid-January instead of early spring.

"Frances, my dear, this is our new sister. I told you she was charming."

Frances extended her hand. Michaela took it. It was cold. "Michaela, how lovely it is to meet you at last," she murmured. Her gaze was bold, taking in every aspect of Michaela's appearance.

She couldn't help but shift a bit under such intense scrutiny. Frances was elegant and self-possessed. More handsome than outright beautiful, she had hair the color of sand and large, well-shaped brown eyes. Her mouth was painted vivid pink. She was dressed in an elegant gown. Now acquainted with the telltale mark of a good modiste, thanks to Aunt May's tutelage, Michaela spotted it as a very expensive article of clothing.

Frances slid her gaze to Adrian and allowed her eyelids to droop, lending a sultry appearance to her face. "Adrian. How good it is to see you. It's been ages."

Holding her hand out, she curled her lips slightly, as if daring him to take it. He did, bowing over it. "Your servant."

Her eyes flashed.

Terrance burst the tension with his good-natured inquiry about when exactly dinner was going to be served as he was starving.

Frances turned to her husband. "Have Charles check on it, will you, darling?"

Richard turned to do this, and Frances gestured for Michaela to take the chair near hers. It was uncomfortably warm in the room. Michaela would have preferred some distance from the fire, but she couldn't refuse her hostess's invitation.

She turned to look for Adrian. He was speaking with Terrance.

"How was your wedding trip?" Frances inquired.

"It was lovely." Michaela perched on the edge of the chair.

"I am certain you were a lovely bride. How sad that we couldn't be there. But I suppose that is what you desired. You must think of yourself first on your wedding day, and have what you like, no matter how it affects anyone else."

Frances spoke in a frigid tone, and Michaela knew she was being chastised.

There was something about Richard's wife that unsettled her. The way her eyes bored into her, the false half-smile, as if she were mocking Michaela even as she played the doting hostess.

Adrian came up just then and excused himself from the room.

"He is probably off to find Richard for more secret whispering about the election. Those two," Frances said, laughing musically and fluttering her hand gracefully after them, "are impossible. They have done nothing but run from meeting to meeting all week. You'd think they'd be tired of it." In a more droll voice, she added as she adjusted a curl at her temple, "I know I have."

"Yes, it is quite exasperating," Michaela agreed. She wanted desperately to loosen her neckline, but as it already dipped dangerously low, she couldn't do much to relieve the stifling heat.

Frances smiled at her, seemingly oblivious to her discomfort. "I want us to be friends, Michaela. I've been so looking forward to meeting you ever since the first rumors began to circulate. Of course, we were all of us simply stunned that the great and reclusive Adrian Khoury"—here her voice dipped into a sardonic tone—"had finally taken an interest in a woman." Frances smirked. "But, of course, with the election imminent, we knew a marriage was forthcoming."

Suddenly, she didn't want to be here with this woman alone. She was caught in a no-win situation. If she said nothing, Frances would think her meek. If she spoke up, she would risk sounding defensive and give Frances the satisfaction of knowing she'd gotten quite effectively under her skin.

Casting a look to Terrance and Constance, Michaela heard Frances laugh. "Oh, they'll be like that all evening. They are oblivious to all the world. Love. I myself find it insufferably rude."

"I think it's charming," Michaela said to cover her disappointment that there would be no rescue from that quarter. Where was Adrian?

"It seems the desertion of both of our husbands leaves the two of us to amuse ourselves together. Oh, but we have so much to talk about, catch up on. Tell me, Michaela, do you enjoy the ballet?"

"Yes, I do. I have only been a few times."

"Why so, if you enjoy it?"

"I loved to go to all theater, but the expense was prohibitive." She clamped her mouth shut, damning herself for stupidity.

"Imagine, the daughter of that fine dandy, Woolrich, not having money for a night at the ballet. Oh, don't be alarmed, Michaela. Yes, I know about your parentage. Richard told me all about you. I can be trusted. Believe me, I am the soul of discretion."

Frances turned to examine her shoulder, stroking away imaginary specks of lint on her dress. She said, "When I want to be," then turned back to Michaela, and her smile brightened. "We were talking about the ballet. You will have to come with us. We take a box for the season."

Even the sublime pleasure of ballet dancing would be ruined in the company of this woman. And Adrian would forbid it, thank goodness. Michaela made a noncommittal sound.

"How are you and Adrian getting on? He is such a moody man. I hope you are a patient woman. You will need the fortitude of a saint to manage him, I swear."

"I enjoy my husband immensely," she said. She had some satisfaction in seeing Frances's face redden.

"The *Quarterly Review* even ran a piece on the two of you," Frances said. "That bastion of Tory opinions is keeping a close eye on our Adrian, and his new wife is, as you can imagine, of much interest. He is the favorite of the party for the fall election, and they want their man to win. I daresay, this all worked out unbelievably well for him, the timing of it all—a very fortuitous marriage indeed. Even the ploy of the elopement made it seem so genuine and romantic, it can hardly be revealed as a political move."

Michaela's spine straightened, and she now understood a very important fact about this evening. She hadn't been invited here to be welcomed into the bosom of the Khoury family. This woman was her enemy for some reason she didn't know.

Frances was making very certain to sow the seeds of doubt and unrest, and given the state of Michaela's uncertainties with Adrian, they were finding fertile ground.

But Michaela had plenty of practice in the trading of barbs, living with her resentful sisters for all those years. "You are mistaken, Lady Frances," Michaela replied as tartly as she could muster. "The marriage was anything but politically motivated." It was perverse of her, really it was, but once she spied the sour look on the other woman's face, she simply could not resist adding, "I assure you, we eloped for . . . other reasons."

Recovering, Frances's mouth curved slowly, and her eyelids drooped. "I imagine Adrian had many reasons for the marriage. I know the man quite well. Oh, dear. Didn't Adrian tell you? Oh. I suppose he wouldn't." She donned a pretense of demure secretiveness. "He is so very private."

"No. He didn't mention you," Michaela said, giving the woman back some of her own vinegar.

As Frances opened her mouth, unquestionably to make a crushing retort, she was interrupted by Adrian sauntering back into the room. Richard was behind him.

"She is too young for jewelry," he was saying.

Adrian shrugged good-naturedly. "No woman is too young for jewelry."

"You spoil that child."

"I had promised her a bauble, and I could not go back on my word."

Richard came toward his wife. "Frances, I caught him in the nursery again, keeping our daughter awake and giving her some gaudy piece of nonsense I just know she will insist on wearing as if it were crown jewelry and embarrassing us horribly." Turning back to Adrian, he wagged his finger. "What that child needs is discipline, not baubles."

Adrian grinned. "I agree. But that is *your* job."

Frances scowled. In the midst of the men's light banter, her response was noticeably chillier. "I do not approve of your indulging Samantha as you do. It is making her wicked and defiant."

"Don't be jealous, Frances," Adrian replied, not looking at her. "It's unflattering on you."

Richard explained the situation to Michaela. "Our daughter, Samantha, has a *tendré* for her uncle, I am afraid, and Adrian encourages her shamelessly. Actually, I think he likes it. And . . . well, she is a bit put out since your marriage, as she wished to marry her uncle herself. I try to tell my brother that he has to be the one to set her firmly in her place, but he refuses to do it."

"I told you, it is not that I refuse. I simply cannot. I swear, when she pins me with that look of pure appeal, I cannot think properly."

Frances cut in sharply, "I hope you do not say such balderdash in front of her. She is a mere child and impressionable. It will swell her head."

Adrian did look at Frances then, just for a fraction of a moment, and Michaela was shocked at the naked animosity in his face. His voice was similarly cold. "Giving a child affection does not swell their head."

"You just love the fact that she adores you," Richard declared with a good-natured laugh.

Adrian shrugged and smiled. "The child has shown herself to be an excellent judge of character."

The brothers might be enjoying their banter, but Frances was seriously annoyed. She didn't seem to like Adrian paying attention to her daughter. Michaela wondered if she actually were jealous, just as Adrian had said.

Happy to be able to accomplish two things, opposing Frances and allying herself with Adrian, Michaela piped up cheerfully, "I think all little girls thrive on the idea that they are special. It can only help her confidence to know that her uncle loves her."

Richard flung his hand approvingly at her. "Ah, then, I am

chastised. Oh, I was meant to tell you all that dinner is served, by the way. We can go in."

"Tell your brother and that fiancée of his," Frances said as she stood and whisked past them all. "He has been grousing about his stomach since he arrived."

But Terrance, who had been oblivious to the flying tensions and other aspects of human interchange for the entirety of the evening, apparently had a keen perception for the announcement of food. His head up, it being previously bent to hover very close to Constance, he shouted, "Food at last! Saints be praised, let's go, Connie, before I faint from hunger."

With that, he grabbed her and marched her out of the room. Frances had gone ahead, still visibly miffed. Richard seemed to be the only one inclined to observe courtesies, and he chatted amiably as they proceeded into the dining room.

Richard took one end of the table, Frances the other. Defying convention, Terrance put his hand on Constance's back and nearly pushed her to the seat next to his on one side of the table. He ignored Frances's glare as he fluffed his napkin and attempted to look as innocent as possible.

Adrian laughed softly at his brother's antics and pulled out the chair next to him at Frances's end of the table for Michaela. She wished there was a tactful way she could refuse the seat next to the spiteful woman, but she had no choice but to comply silently.

The six chatted as the soup was brought out. The tensions previously noted ebbed considerably, largely due to Terrance entertaining them with quips and amusing stories about some of his less-than-intelligent friends at university, where he was attending his last term.

When he could be pulled away from mooning over Constance, he was a charming fellow, Michaela found. Too bad he wasn't more in evidence in the parlor. His presence would have been a welcome distraction.

Their hostess was now silent, but Michaela could feel hot waves of ill feeling coming off her as they progressed to the next course. Michaela wished she could forget the things she'd said to her, but she couldn't help herself from ruminating over the sly insinuations Frances had made about Adrian and a past they two had shared.

The implications were dreadfully obvious.

Frances said to Richard, "Michaela mentioned she loves ballet. I told her she must come with us."

Adrian did not look up from his plate. "Michaela shall be very busy in the upcoming weeks. The election makes demands on all of our time."

"Then you have decided to go for the seat?" Frances asked sharply.

"It doesn't seem I have much choice," he murmured.

"It is going to be a spectacular victory." Richard beamed. "Harris does not stand a chance."

Michaela wondered what Adrian had meant: He didn't have a choice?

With a hollow feeling of unpleasantness, she realized she didn't know many things, even come close to knowing, about her husband.

Constance erupted in a jarring bout of giggles right then, which she immediately attempted to stifle. "Oh, pardon me," she said, but her eyes sparkled as they slid to Terrance, who smirked back, leaving little doubt there was some playing going on between the two of them under the table.

Their plates were taken away, and the next course served.

"I knew you would agree in the end, Adrian." Frances smirked at her husband. "I know him better than even you, Richard, for all of those years we were together when you were off at university. If you would only listen to me, you would find yourself much better prepared to deal with him. A woman knows these things, don't they, Michaela, dear?"

Michaela stewed as the next courses were served, trying her best to keep her thoughts and feelings masked. Frances, she was certain, was attending closely, lapping up any sign of discomfiture like a cat at a saucer of fresh cream.

"After all, Adrian and I used to be inseparable, the two of us," Frances continued as she picked at her fish.

Michaela bared her teeth in a semblance of a smile. "You already mentioned Adrian and you knew each other well."

"Oh, indeed we did. He was the first boy I ever danced

with." She put a delicate hand to her throat. "Do you remember those country dances, Adrian?"

"No, I don't," he said with finality, and silence fell.

The tension between the two of them pulsed in the room. The only ones who had not been aware of it were the lovers across the table. Eventually, even they were affected. Terrance stopped piling mushrooms upon Constance's plate against her protestations that she hated the things, and raised his brows.

"You remember those days, don't you, Terrance?" Frances asked, seeing his interest and picking up the conversation.

"They are inscribed in my memory and give me nightmares to this day. I particularly recall playing hide-and-seek, and a crueler version there never was, Connie, dear. Why, they'd make me go hide, and there I'd sit for hours, sometimes falling fast asleep, and when I'd wake up, I'd go and find *them*. They'd quite forgotten all about me. They were always doing that, going off without me. I began to take it personally for a while."

"That's enough reminiscing, I think," Adrian said brusquely. A servant bent next to him with a platter, and he selected fare for his plate. "It is boring and rude to Michaela and Constance, since it excludes them."

"Oh, I am sorry, pet!" Terrance declared, taking Constance's hand in his, his face drawn in lines of repentance. "I didn't mean to make you feel awkward."

"Oh, no. I don't mind. Oh, poor, poor dear," Constance said in response, peering pitifully into his eyes. "Did they mistreat you?"

Seeing he'd won her sympathies, he nodded forlornly. "All the time, I am afraid."

Their heads came together again as she cooed comfortingly to him. Richard's booming voice filled the void. He spoke about some of their mutual acquaintances until Frances clapped her hands to summon the servants to clear the course.

Michaela felt Adrian's eye on her. She looked up. He was as mysterious as he'd ever been. She, however, was blazing angry.

There were depths to these waters he had not prepared her

for. Never had he given her one hint of this barrage of subtlety and spite that thrived in the bosom of his family.

One thing she knew for certain, and that was that he and Frances had shared much in their past. It was clear that the two of them had once been lovers. And tonight Frances was taking great pains to make certain Michaela knew it, short of coming outright and giving details of their bed sport. She felt like a supreme fool.

The meal eventually came to an end, and the ladies retired. Constance excused herself to "powder her nose," and Michaela was once again left to Frances's tender mercies as they strolled into the drawing room.

She groaned silently at the sight of the fire blazing afresh. Walking into the room was like entering a suffocating embrace. Frances took her spot by the blaze, comfortably settling in. Michaela drifted to the window, trying desperately to catch a draft.

She couldn't breathe. She felt as if the air in the room was being consumed by the greedy fire, which had some supernatural connection to the malicious woman curled next to it.

"Adrian is not himself tonight," Frances mused. "He hasn't been for a long time. Not since . . . well, since Richard and I married. I am afraid Adrian didn't take it very well."

Michaela refused to give this woman one more moment of satisfaction. So, her reply was, "These are lovely lamps."

Frances's eyes narrowed. "They are old; they came with the house. I don't care for them myself, but Richard won't let me touch anything. It is all hallowed, you know. Ancient Khoury heirlooms, down to the dust layering the books in the library." Her tone was rancorous again, making her discontent with her present life apparent.

"Old families can be full of quirks."

"They can be a bore."

Really, she was terribly unpleasant. And Richard seemed a splendid fellow. A shame he had such a wife. Michaela wondered what he saw in her, then supposed it was her beauty. She certainly had a presence.

"Adrian thinks so, too," Frances said, her tone oily with

mischief. "He cannot abide the old houses and the entire tradition of it all."

"Perhaps that is why he joined the army."

Frances looked startled, even delighted. "That is not why
he purchased a commission. He never told you?"

Michaela cursed herself for having said anything to give
her advantage. Constance entered at precisely that moment.
Michaela excused herself, hurrying into the hall after receiving directions to the privy, located in an old powder closet.

It took a supreme struggle to recompose herself. When
she had done her best to repair her face and gather her wits,
she went back into the parlor.

The men had come in during her absence. Constance and
Terrance were already cuddled on a settee as if they'd been
separated for ages. Adrian stood with his hand braced on the
mantel, looking lordly and disgruntled.

She approached him. "I hate to end our evening early, but
I am not feeling well."

"The food did not disagree with you?" Frances cut in,
overhearing.

"No. It was a fine dinner. I am only fatigued."

Adrian placed a hand on his wife's arm. "We will leave
immediately." He was obviously ready for the easy excuse to
leave.

Despite his prompt response, it seemed to Michaela an interminable amount of time before they were out of that house
and away from that spider. The night air felt blessedly cool
after the stifling heat and constriction of that woman's crafty
gaze. Michaela breathed it in, wishing it would magically
ease the boiling pressure in her head.

It helped, after a few moments of freedom. She began to
feel better, but a dull ache was left behind.

It was pain. And fear. Because she knew the reason her husband could not love her. He was in love with his brother's wife.

𝒟 *Chapter 16*

Michaela wasted no time in making the accusation.

"You were her lover," she said once they were in their hotel suite.

Adrian looked at her as if horrified and astonished at her outburst. This angered her more. The hypocrite was going to play the innocent!

She folded her arms across her chest. "Does Richard know?"

He recovered his shock, his face clouding. "My God . . . I wouldn't have thought you capable of such vile suspicions, Michaela. I never slept with my brother's wife."

"Are you going to try to tell me that you never made love to that woman?"

His face twitched. He was hiding something. "My past is none of your concern," he said.

"As if that is any sort of an answer."

"It is no sort of an answer, as you have no right to ask the question."

"I am your wife," she cried.

"And as such, you may have a care with whom I sleep from the day of our marriage forward. But the past is not relevant."

"It is when I am confronted with one of your past lovers. Oh, Adrian, why can you not simply tell me? Do you have to shut me out until I want to scream just to get one answer from you?" A thought struck her. "Unless, you feel guilty. Is that it? Did you cuckold your own brother and now you cannot bear to admit it?"

His snarl was frightening. "This conversation is finished. You must be overtired. Call for your maid to help you to bed."

"Don't you dare dismiss me." She skittered round on him, blocking his path. "Very well, if I have the wrong of it, then tell me what is the truth. Why won't you tell me? What could be so awful?"

"Nothing awful. I bear no shame. But I do not explain myself."

"Ah, the Khoury legend."

His jaw worked.

She threw up her hands plaintively. "Is that why you block me at every turn when I try to draw close? Is that why you never talk to me about anything of consequence? I had no idea you were decided on submitting your name for election, and I am your wife! Then you take me to dine with one of your former lovers without any kind of preparation. Does my opinion, my *feelings* mean so little to you?"

"I was the one who wanted to refuse the invitation. I wanted to avoid the whole ugly scene."

"It is your family. How can you avoid it? Is that what you've been doing all these years—avoiding her?" She remembered something Frances said, and looked at her husband in careful speculation. "Is she why you bought a commission? You ran to the war to escape her because you couldn't have her. Childhood friends, childhood sweethearts. Did you always love her?"

His jaw worked, and he looked thunderous. "You wish to hear the sordid tale? Do you see how she wanted this? Don't you see, little fool, you give her exactly what she craves. By listening to her, you have fulfilled her purpose. I thought you wiser, Michaela."

"Apparently, I am supremely stupid, for I am unaccountably disturbed by the fact that your sister-in-law is your former lover. *And* she is still in love with you, which is plain to see. And you . . ." She paused, watching him closely. "I think she hurt you very much. It still hurts to look at her, doesn't it? Do you know, Adrian, you didn't look at her, not unless you had to, and then only a glance."

"I loathe the woman. I have to wrestle with myself to keep from wrapping my hands around her throat when in the same room with her."

"Such passion," Michaela said spiritlessly. "No wonder you can't love me. Your heart is already taken."

His scorn was scathing. "You are being ridiculous. That imagination of yours, reading into things that you know nothing about."

"You owe me an explanation, then, Adrian. I deserve one. If not out of love, then out of respect. So meet my eye and tell me here and now that you not being able to love me has nothing whatsoever to do with Frances."

He scowled. But he didn't look at her. "I don't explain myself."

"A very useful rule. Is it pride or shame that keeps you so righteous?" She began to turn away, then something awful came to her mind. She spoke slowly. "Tell me something. Is the child yours?"

He recoiled at the suggestion. "Good God, no! I never touched her after she married my brother. You will not relent until you hear all the details. If you need to hear the admission of what you already know, then, yes, we were lovers. Since childhood, we played together and as youths fell into lust. Not love, Michaela, although we didn't know the difference at the time."

"Did you plan to marry her?"

He looked away. But it was enough of an answer to raise a lump of grief in her throat.

"My God," she said. "If she was your love, how did she come to marry your brother?"

His expression changed, the arrogance gone in an instant. "When Richard returned home after years at university, he fell in love with her. He didn't know about us. Frances was different then, lively, pretty, not virulent like you saw her tonight, and she flirted with him until he was eating from her hand. He asked her to marry him, and she wanted to be a marchioness. She wanted to be wealthy and as my father firmly believed in the principle of primogeniture, I had nothing. It was then I saw her for what she was: a prime bitch."

He stroked his thumb and forefinger along the corner of his mouth, flexing his jaw. "She proposed to marry my brother for the money and title, and that she and I remain lovers. I was disgusted, and wished to be through with the lot of them. I wrongly blamed my brother for my misery, and hated her. Terrance, the only one I gave a damn about, was at Eton, happily ignorant of the morass of immorality and betrayal that had taken over the ancestral home. So, I bought a commission, wanting only to get as far away from them all as I could."

He ran his hand over the back of his neck, working away the tension the memories brought across his wide shoulders. "I was young, only nineteen. I was enamored of my misery, of the unfairness of it all. I had not yet mastered the concept of mind over emotion.

"It took a while to understand it was Richard, not I, who deserved pity. He might not have known about Frances and me in the beginning, but he's had to have guessed since. As you saw, Frances is hardly the soul of discretion. But he has never said a word of it, or against her. So we all move like players in the maddening farce my family has become. It would be amusing if it weren't so humiliating."

His eyes focused, and he blinked, seeming shocked that he had said so much. He curled his mouth in a cruel smile. "I hope that satisfies your curiosity. You have split me open and examined my innards. What perverse pleasures you take in dissecting me."

Her hand fluttered to her throat. "You act as if I had no right to know."

He didn't answer. The look he gave her was closed, denying her everything.

"So this is my fault?" she snapped. "I had the impertinence to ask you for an explanation—what heresy! The great, the arrogant, the proud-to-a-fault Major Adrian Khoury explains himself to no one. Why, we should have that inscribed upon a lintel and hung over the door to our home. Oh! I may say *our* home, may I not? That isn't too presumptuous of me, I hope."

She felt eerily calm all of a sudden, cloaking her rage in confidence. She wasn't afraid of him any longer. What could be worse than all he'd just told her? "I believe I understand now the terms of this marriage. Namely, silence is all that is required of me. Oh, except in the bedroom. You don't like silence there. Those little noises you get from me seem to please you."

He jerked his head away, irritated. "Don't be crude."

"Do I misspeak? You want no companionship from me, you seek to share nothing of yourself. You are self-contained—What was it? A master of will over emotion."

He threw up his hands. "Please pardon me for not weeping on your shoulders over my troubles."

"You see it as womanish, weak to share your life with another person? You never really wished to be married, not in the sense of a shared life, a warm, fond companionship—all those things that marriage means to me. You wish to exist exactly as you have as a single man, but with one significant difference. As my husband, you may avail yourself of my body."

"You are my wife; do not degrade that." He reached for her, perhaps wanting to be conciliatory.

The moment he touched her, she went stiff in his arms. "How utterly irrelevant this conversation is. I am mad to vex you with such trivialities as my inconvenient emotions are. I see now all we really need from each other is sexual gratification. Forgive me. I suppose I am not yet a master over my emotions."

Spinning on her heel, she went to the bed. "We've been wasting all of this time when all you wish from me is this. It is, after all, the only time you pay me any mind. It is thought-less, presumptuous, even, to keep you waiting."

She began to remove her dress.

"Your facetiousness is not appreciated," he said evenly. But his eyes watched her hands as they worked at her dress fastenings. "And you are not at all as cutting as you'd like to think. You are acting like a child."

"Oh, I assure you, there is nothing childish about what I am planning to do. I am undressing for you, husband, like a dutiful wife. Unless you would like to do it? You've enjoyed that in the past."

His eyes narrowed. "This game does not amuse me."

"What a pity. It is all for your amusement, after all, is it not? This marriage is nothing if not amusing—when we are in bed, that is."

She finished shedding the simple empire-style gown.

The expensive silk rushed against her legs to puddle in an elegant green pond at her feet. She stood in it, like Botti-celli's Venus rising from the sea, poised and confident and in a finely sewn chemise and pink silk stockings.

She lay back on the bed, holding out her arms to him. "There," she sighed, giving him a sultry smile. "This is more like it. All of that looking at you while I was vertical was so strange. Here. Come and be horizontal with me, and I shall feel very familiar."

He didn't move.

"No? Oh, perhaps you would like me to undress further." She undid the ribbon at the neck of her chemise.

"Michaela. You are taking this much too far." He looked horrified at her lying there on the bed in a parody of erotic subservience, but his eyes blazed, betraying him. It excited him to have her play the whore, even if he didn't want it to. "Get up off the bed."

"What is wrong? Has the passion died so soon?" She glanced meaningfully at his trousers. Seeing the evidence of his interest, she smiled. "Ah."

"What exactly are you trying to prove? That I want you? Yes. I desire you. That is no great ambition. You are the most desirable woman I have ever seen." He paused, cocking his head to one side. "Or is it you are trying to prove your power to make me want you?"

"I am being your perfect wife." She spread her arms out over the sheets sensuously. "I am being what you want, Adrian, all you could desire. It is my duty, isn't it? It is what you married me for."

He stood as if carved of granite. Michaela didn't feel seductive or sensual as she lay in front of him, waiting for him to make his choice. She felt terrified.

If he rejected her, she'd be humiliated. But if he didn't . . . if he crawled into bed and lowered himself into her, she'd be right.

And that was much worse.

"Well," she taunted, unable to stop herself. "Why do you hesitate?"

And then, Adrian smiled.

Something in that smile quickened a beat in the pit of her stomach. It pulsed pleasurably in the long silence that ensued.

He lowered his hand to his trousers, and he began to unfasten them.

She felt very vulnerable all of a sudden lying in front of him. She was no longer afraid, or perhaps she was a little. She was excited now, too, and the fear only heightened the emotion.

Her heart banged hard against the wall of her chest as he stripped quickly.

"I am a fool," he muttered. "Arguing with you when you are waiting for me, willing to play a little game. I don't need games as a rule, but this pretense . . . why, that is an especially delightful fantasy no man can resist. What do you call it? It is a sort of invigorating slave-and-master theme. Ah, no. Don't move. I like you like that. This was an excellent idea. A good row stirs the blood."

She did move, realizing she had taunted him too far. But he caught her hands and bore down until she lay again on her back.

The surge of exhilaration she had felt when she was the one wielding the power was gone. Now he kneeled over her, his nude body magnificent. His aroused sex jutted out like a delicious threat. The hard musculature of his upper body flexed as he shifted, leaning down so that he was pinning her on four sides.

"Comfortable?"

Her eyes stayed locked with his. Her teeth caught her bottom lip, and he touched it, rubbing his fingertip along the soft pad.

Some impulse nudged her. She might be able to get the better of him yet.

She opened her mouth and slowly swirled her tongue around his finger.

His eyes flared wide, then narrowed. "An impudent slave," he said with approval. Determination prodded her to close her mouth around his finger and suck.

His eyelids grew heavy as he watched the act. She didn't look away, wanting to witness her power.

Because this was, of course, only about power.

With a push, she sent him on his side, then back. He rolled over, his eyes glittering in anticipation.

A surge of exhilaration tingled inside her as she knelt beside him, viewing him as he had her. His body was taut, not a spare inch of flesh on the powerful frame. He wasn't an elegant man. He was hard, hot, solid. A warrior.

Her own softness gloried in the difference as she slid her hands over the feverishly hot skin. Looking relaxed, she sensed expectation in him at high pitch. There was the slightest intake of breath when she reached for him, closing her fingers around his turgid shaft. It pulsed in her palm.

Bending, she kissed the tight skin of his abdomen. It was like silk against her lips. Her tongue delved into his navel, then she flicked her tongue over his flesh again, moving lower.

Thrusting his hands in her hair, he ripped out her pins, letting them fall around them with soft little pings. Into this delicate music exploded a harsh epithet when she took him in her mouth. His hips moved to augment her teasing and bring him wholly into her possession.

Groans ripped from him, as if he begrudged her even that

much communication. It was his defeat, and he loved and hated it.

She felt his hands on her shoulders and was lifted up. Tossed on her back, she found herself staring at him.

"As tempting as you are, this is not the game I desire."

"It is my game." She tried to rise, but he pushed her back down. She tried to rise again. He placed his hand instead over the juncture of her thighs.

She stopped. He pushed upward, and a burst of pleasure scalded every nerve.

His look was unadulterated triumph. "This game is to prove me a knave. Do you think I don't know it?"

"It is to be what you desire."

"You were always what I desired."

One last flagging spark of rebellion gave her the strength to push his hand away. It was ineffective, however, and he parted her and began the gentle, light motions to flood her body with paralyzing sensations.

This was all wrong. She didn't want him to pleasure her; she wanted to show him . . . what? His hand moved so deliciously, so irresistibly, and she couldn't think until the world exploded and she lay quivering underneath him.

He withdrew. She lay, waiting. With weakened arms, she reached for him. Even in defeat, she craved him to fill her. She had no illusions that the emptiness inside her would be filled with his manhood, but she wanted it nonetheless. She wanted it so badly she was trembling.

Why did he hesitate? She opened her eyes.

He hovered over her, his breath fanning her face. She ran her hands down to his hips, pulling them forward as she opened for him. His erection prodded her entrance.

He made a low grunt, and suddenly he was gone. She blinked at the empty air above her, the sudden chill at the absence of his warmth. It took a moment to comprehend he had risen off the bed. The sound of rustled clothing told her he was dressing.

Sitting up, she pulled the covers over her. His back was to her. Squeezing her eyes shut, she cursed herself for what she had done, what she had given. They had played a game, and she had lost.

There were no words in her. Words were from anger, and that had gone. What was left was choking, cloying grief.

He left without speaking, without looking at her. She stared at the door, not wanting to accept or believe what had happened. She'd been bested; she'd been defeated.

She had no power over him; she never had.

Days later, Adrian sat in the damp, drafty parlor of his sprawling house in Shepston-on-Stour. He had a whiskey in his hand, but he wasn't drinking it. Spirits had never worked for him. Generally, the result of imbibing was a fuzzy feeling that led to a queasy rebellion of his stomach. It had been a joke among his troops, most of whom prided themselves on their consumptive abilities. It had been how they took a measure of a man, but with their major, a different standard had been adopted.

His performance with his wife, after which he had fled the city like a debtor put to flight, was a poor showing indeed. He had disgraced himself. And . . . and he had hurt her.

The hardness in him roiled, looking for release. It was her fault. She shouldn't have asked so much. She . . .

It was his fault. Pathetic halfling that he was, he had cheated her of what she desired, what she deserved: a real husband to dote on her and ply her with pretty phrases. A man who was free to feel the things she wished him to feel.

A footman came in to say that Sarah Trent had arrived.

"Send her in," Adrian said, rising.

A small woman with brown hair and large blue eyes entered. She was very pretty, especially when she smiled as she was doing now. Adrian embraced her.

"Thank you so much for coming home, Major," she said.

"Sit down. How is Margaret?"

"Big," the woman replied, beaming at the mention of her two-year-old daughter. "And naughty. She says nothing but 'no' the entire day through."

"It is her father in her, for Paul Trent was truly the most ornery man I ever knew."

They laughed.

Adrian said, "I remember when he walked five miles with no boots because the men had played a trick on him and taken the damned things to get a rise of him, and do you think he would even *mention* it? He was a stubborn man."

Sarah leaned back, remembering. "He may not have made a fuss of it to you, but I certainly heard all about it in the letter he wrote me that night. I believe he detailed each and every one of the scrapes on his poor feet. His mother got busy right away knitting him more stockings, thick ones, and we all made a terrible fuss. I am sure he enjoyed it very much."

They laughed again, reveling in the memory of a man they'd both loved.

"I take it Shepston has things bad off for these people," Adrian said at last. "I know you wouldn't have written for me to return unless things were dire."

"Not so bad lately. I didn't ask you to come to the county to talk about the situation with our squire, not this time. There is something else, rather important, that I wish to speak to you about." She lowered her gaze to her hands twisting on her lap. "I've . . . I've found someone and I'm thinking of . . . well, he's asked me to marry him."

Adrian was surprised. It was strange to think of Sarah remarrying, but she was an attractive woman and young. After a moment, he asked, "Does he treat Margaret well?"

Sarah broke into a tremendous smile. "You know I would have no stock of him if he didn't. He's a wonderful man, Major. I want your blessing."

Taken aback, he said, "You do not need my blessing, Sarah. It's been over two years since Trent died. Anyone would understand your wishing to marry again."

"Paul thought you were the best man he'd ever met in his life, and I want you to tell me it's all right. It would be like he's saying it. Please, Major Khoury, tell me what you think."

The wife of the man who had given his life for Adrian's looked to him with a blend of hope and anxiety. Adrian said, "My God, of course you have my blessing. I only want you to be happy. And the best for that little girl of yours." He stopped, thought, then added in a careful voice, "And I know Paul would want the two of you to carry on."

For a moment, Sarah said nothing. She just closed her eyes. Her chin quivered a moment, but she didn't cry. "Thank you." she whispered. Opening her eyes, she smiled brilliantly. "And thank you for all you've done. And not just for me and Margaret, but for all of Shepston-on-Stour. We so badly needed a hero, our own private hero. Shepston had a wicked hold on this county, and no one to stop him before you came."

"The earl is not vanquished yet."

"But he is tamed. You did that, and no false modesty will change the fact. I don't know how, but you set your cap to stop him, and you did."

When Adrian had first come to the village to find Sarah and give her the message he'd promised Trent he would, he had found an abomination feeding off the good people of the county. It was their earl, their landlord and master.

His rents were outrageous, leaving so small a portion for his tenants after he took his share that the people were near starving. It was his right to set the rates where he pleased; that was the law. The people had no recourse in the courts, and no one could leave. Where would they go? A cottage and a few acres are hard to come by.

Shepston was the stingiest of all the lords in granting his land rights and cruel to anyone caught trespassing on his land. It didn't matter if folk were starving. Soon after his arrival, Adrian learned that a boy of only eight years was caught snaring a rabbit. Shepston was calling for him to be taken to the corrections house. Then, suddenly, the boy was home. Adrian couldn't let the matter rest. He went to visit the family. They were not eager for it to be known, but he guessed that his sister had gone to the big house, into "service." Shepston's reputation made it clear what kind of service the earl was interested in.

That was how he got involved. He had known from Sarah that she had been let go without a reference for refusing the earl favors. Such a situation was not uncommon for any attractive woman working in the earl's employ, either directly or as a relation to a man who worked for him. So many had to succumb; he'd put them or their family out if they didn't. And they had nowhere to go. How does one get a position when they've been let go without a reference?

He'd simply done what had to be done. He hadn't solved the situation of the despotic earl, but he had contained him for now, turning his own vices against him.

"Shepston is more hated around here than Satan himself." She gave a small laugh. "Some say he *is* Satan himself. But we have great faith in you. If you routed Napoleon, you'll get Shepston yet." Sarah's blue eyes danced.

He shifted uncomfortably, and she laughed. She said, "Is it true you are going to run in the election this fall?"

"My brother and I wish to serve in Parliament together. There are issues of reform, progress, and social change, Sarah. You seem disturbed at the idea."

"Well, it's just that the House of Commons is in London. It isn't very far away, I suppose, but I always felt we need you right here. I know England needs to change, but sometimes that can take a very long time. And I don't think we can spare you."

"Are you telling me you think I will lose the election?" he teased.

"I think you will win in a blink, and no mistake about it," she assured him.

"I will not abandon this county," he promised, his gaze holding hers.

She sighed. "It is a relief to hear that from your lips. I hope your new wife will like it here. Everyone is so looking forward to her coming. It is the hope that she will fall in love with our hamlet and make you live here instead of London."

The idea of a bucolic existence with Michaela in this peaceful, happy town hit him like a pleasant jolt. But his wife was now, even as he sat here conversing with Sarah

Trent, making the social whirl back in Town. The gossip rags had published all the details.

After they shared tea and more talk, Sarah departed. Adrian reentered the room after seeing her to the door, his eyes dropping to the pile of London papers on the desk in the corner.

It was his habit to have them sent from the city while he was in residence at the sprawling home he'd purchased after returning to England, "moldering" as Richard liked to say, in his country domain. They'd called him a recluse all these years, but Adrian had found that the quiet life had suited him after military life. It wasn't so odd, was it, to like clean air and a slow pace, days of riding, reading, mulling about the house overseeing its restoration?

He kept abreast of the government and other happenings as a rule, but his interest had been in the society pages. The recent ones had carried glowing notices about Michaela Khoury.

So, Michaela wasn't sitting at home any longer. She went to parties dressed, it was said, in resplendent gowns. She danced. So many dance partners, many of whom were enumerated in explicit detail. She was, in short, doing quite well without him.

He'd asked her to come with him after receiving Sarah's letter asking to see him the next time he was in Shepston-on-Stour. It was just the excuse he needed to flee . . . er, see to matters he'd been putting off in Surrey. Michaela refused him. They were still not speaking after that awful, insane night and the stupid argument over Frances, and he had thought it best to go on without her.

All right. He'd run away. She'd laid herself out before him to prove her point. The damnable fact of it was, even though he'd pulled back at the last moment—some grand gesture to deny that what she had said was true—she had been right.

Of course she'd been right, damn her. She'd more or less called him a cold-hearted bastard, and he was. He *wanted* to be.

Or at least he had for a very long time.

Needing action, needing motion, he sprang up out of his chair, walked three steps. His leg ached after being inactive, bringing him up short, and he wondered what he was doing. There was nowhere to go.

He was a liar and a fraud. He'd rejected her, but he hadn't meant it. He was not cold, not immune. Oh, part of him still loved the strength, the iron hardness of being a soul closed to all emotion. But he wanted something else suddenly: the things she'd wanted.

He loved the way they could talk. He was afraid of intimacy.

Peter entered with a discreet knock. The old man had been the butler since the days of the old marquess from whom Adrian had purchased the house. He served his new master with respect combined with a fondness that broached the boundary of his position, but Adrian didn't mind. "Sir, dinner is served."

"I'll just take a tray in here, Peter, thank you."

"Very good," he said, frowning as he closed the door. Peter tended to worry.

Adrian sighed, reluctant to be left alone. He didn't wish to return to his thoughts. Perhaps Peter would like a game of cards, he wondered, then tossed out the idea. He was not fit company for anyone, not even the patient and loyal servant.

No one liked being reminded that he was an imposter. What great thing had he ever done to deserve anyone's admiration, for God's sake? The truth of it was humiliating. He had been a lovesick boy who had run away from the world, off to the glory of war, and found he'd done well. He was no hero. But he'd been good at being a soldier, a tactical expert whose opinions were sought by his superiors. He'd risen quickly to his rank of major and gained a reputation of being fearless in a fight.

His men had loved him, and their families honored the sacrifice when they had died to save him. They deemed it a worthy sacrifice, for all they knew was the brave and brash legend, not the real man who had been faced with death and found himself no longer brave and brash, but afraid. . . .

An imposter, no hero.

God. He hated that particular memory. It had been an ambush; the French had a few brilliant tacticians as well, it seemed. The French Imperial Guardsmen had him dead to rights. He'd been outnumbered, struck down. He had felt his strength draining, the blood pouring out of his leg. He'd prepared himself to die, opened his mind to it, the fear chasing him all the way. And all the years that he thought himself too bitter to care whether he lived or died proved to be a lie. He'd wanted to live. He was terrified of death. He wasn't brave at all.

And when his men had arrived to save him, he'd been *glad*. What sort of man was glad to live when it meant others had died?

And Michaela wanted intimate conversations and warm companionship with *that*? No. She was better not knowing. Her anger, even her rebellion, he could bear. Her disillusionment, he could not.

He sank down on a chair and rested his head in his hands. Why did he suddenly feel he was coming apart?

Damned woman, splayed out for him, beckoning him in that voice devoid of intonation. A whore at her craft?

No. A woman, a siren, a lover begging to be reassured. She'd been vulnerable and pleading, and it had punched a hole right through him. He had told himself he'd not taken her because it would be giving her what she wanted, proving her point. The truth was she was everything he wanted, and he couldn't let himself take it.

She'd had him wrapped around her little finger, and all the stomping out of rooms and running to the country wasn't going to change that.

Still, he had decided to wait before going back to London. They needed a longer cooling period. He needed to sort out the confusion in his head. The blight of their last parting burned, and he was eager to put things right if he could. But he had to think it through, figure out what he should do. . . .

But when he rose the next morning and sipped coffee

while perusing the previous day's paper, he found another reason altogether to return early.

"Peter," he called, rising so fast he jarred the table, setting the china clattering, "pack my things. We are leaving for London in an hour."

Michaela got no notice that Adrian was arriving home. When she heard the door to the hotel suite open and close, his heavy footsteps, distinctive with the slight pause caused by his limp, she knew he had returned. The knowledge filled her with a jolt of happiness. Then she grew apprehensive as she waited for him in the bedroom, where she was dressing to go for a drive with Lilah.

Her heart kicked like a mule in her chest. Her hands were clasped to keep them from trembling. She was so nervous! How silly, when it was only Adrian. One would think Attila the Hun was advancing into the private recesses of the suite, not her own husband.

He entered the bedchamber without a pause or a knock. He was windblown and rumpled from the long ride, his hair tousled, his face abraded by the wind to a ruddy tan, indicating he had ridden instead of traveling in comfort inside the carriage. How like Adrian.

She couldn't find her voice to speak the quip tickling the tip of her tongue. He looked too delicious, mussed and raw like this, and she wished overwhelmingly to reach out her hand and touch him.

Only now did she know how much she'd missed him.

He said nothing at first, and neither did she. Crossing the threshold with his hesitant stride, he filled the room with his presence, squeezing out the air until there was none left to feed her lungs.

He was angry.

Then he raised a brow and spoke. "Madam Khoury."

"Adrian," she breathed.

He smiled, but it was a devil's smile. "You have kept quite busy since I've been gone." Holding up something in his hand, she saw he held some news clippings. "The newspapers are full of your exploits." He dropped them onto the table. "I have read them with tolerance, but my patience has its limits."

Michaela was aware of the notices. She refused to look at them, keeping her gaze trained on him. She hadn't had any "exploits" since he'd gone. She'd been reckless, and that on purpose, yes. But the rags liked to pick a darling and follow their every move. Since she had begun to appear in public without her husband, she had become that darling, attracting all sorts of attention and speculation. It had suited her purposes to have Adrian read about the wonderful time she was having, and she'd played into a bit, but she'd done nothing wrong. She'd just been very conspicuous.

She opened her mouth to say so when it occurred to her that she needn't defend herself.

"It's been a fine time on the old Town for you, hasn't it?"

She shrugged. "A girl has to have some amusements," she replied blithely.

When her husband cannot be bothered.

"I did not know you enjoyed cards. Your losses were noteworthy. Seventy pounds, the *Tattler* reported."

"An exaggeration." She gave him a droll look. "It was half that."

"Still quite a lot."

"Why are you concerned, Adrian? Can we not afford it?"

"It is of no consequence. Thus, if you wished to annoy me that way, you'll have to lose at least ten times that to get my notice. However, I am more than passingly intrigued by the fact that you were caught dancing three times with the same man in a single evening." He held up a clipping, which she could barely see as he had crumpled it in his fist.

She gave a mulish expression. "He was feeling lonely that night. His wife was with her lover, making no secret of it, and we thought that turnabout was fair play."

"And the following evening you were spotted coming home in time for breakfast."

"I went to Gwyneth Hasbrow's house. There were quite a

few people there, it was well chaperoned, and it is not all that unusual for a musical evening to last until morning. No one left until well after dawn. The papers are just making it seem sensational."

He tossed a newspaper onto the small table by the bed. "Are you having an affair with Wickery?"

The accusation was a shock. "If you mean Wickam, no. He is my sister's beau. Or, rather, he would like to be. He does nothing but pine for her." Recovering herself, she said, "Why all of the interest suddenly? I thought questions were not in order, married or not, or does that apply only to you, my husband?"

"Ah." He was guarded, taking her measure. "I wonder, Michaela, if you are being petulant or . . . have you come to the conclusion that you actually regret our rash marriage?"

"Do you?" she shot.

He narrowed his eyes, and their intensity burned. "I have enjoyed the fruits of our union."

Oh, the bastard! He was making fun of her, diminishing her with mockery. Her own temper flamed. "Such as they are."

She was rewarded with a satisfying blanching of his too-hard features.

Ah, but Adrian could always do her one better, and he recovered quickly. "Well, what do you expect when you choose a husband only to spite your sister? What a dashed inconvenience to find yourself leg-shackled to me when you could have done so much better." He jabbed a finger in the direction of the discarded paper clippings. "You might have had a title, Michaela, and a fortune to boot. Just imagine the exquisite shade of chartreuse your sisters would turn should you have been free to receive a duke's suit."

She sputtered. "You are being an ass, Adrian."

"I am only speaking my mind."

"I wonder if you even know your own mind."

"I'll tell you what I know," he said. "You have obviously been dedicating yourself to making a spectacle so that you are sure to be written up in the gossip pages. Are you intending to make me jealous, or just dog me with scandal as a form of retaliation?"

"I have been enjoying myself, doing as I please, when I please. I cannot help it if people talk. And I hardly care if it disturbs you."

"After all," he said slyly, "turnabout is fair play, eh?"

She tossed her head, refusing to answer.

He went on. "If you couldn't get my attention one way, you'd have it another. So if all of this was not for the express purpose of annoying me, then I don't know you. And my dear, I *do* know you enough to know that these past nights were probably the hardest work you've ever done. Your idea of fun, dear wife, is lying about in front of a fire with a new book. You like your own little world. Your societies for the poor and your books and picture gazing . . . that is what you enjoy. You are about as unsuited to the fast-paced life of a society darling as I am suited to the priesthood."

"Oh, really!" she exploded, her rationale fleeing in the face of his dead-on insight. "Well, for your information, I could care less what you think—just as you don't give one damn about my feelings."

He tsked. "A Khoury never resorts to petulance. I am sure you will one day make the family proud, a full-fledged mule head like the rest of us. But I am afraid for now I cannot tolerate it, my sweet wife."

She jammed her fist on her hip. "And what do you think you can do about it?"

"I shall tell you what I *will* do. I am taking you with me."

"What?" She could barely sputter out the words, so great was her shock. "Where?"

"We are returning to my house in the country, where you will learn to behave as a proper wife should. I have had enough of London, enough of all of this interminable society nonsense, and enough of the political machine. You and I are going home."

She was momentarily stunned; then her confidence returned and she scoffed. "You cannot do this. You would not."

"I can," he said, his voice low and full of menacing promise. "And I will."

The seriousness of his tone convinced her he was not bluffing. It flustered her. "It is just as Aunt May said! You fling orders about as if you think I am required to follow them. You are too used to command, but a wife is not a soldier. You cannot force me to go, to leave London."

"A good wife is an asset to her husband, just as a soldier is a valuable asset for his commander. Like a soldier, you can obey or choose insubordination. And like any soldier, you will deal with the consequences."

She stared at him, amazed. "Well I choose insubordination, you autocratic beast. You can court-martial me later." She whirled and made for the door.

"Stop at once," he barked.

On a wild impulse, she turned back to him, clicking her heels together and executing a sharp salute. "Yes, Major."

His eyes flared. He looked murderous in that moment.

"Do you have further orders, sir?" she shouted in clipped syllables.

His nostrils flared. His lip curled. He was not pleased.

He waited a long time before responding, seeming to be torn between rage and self-control. "I am having your belongings packed and removed to Shepston-on-Stour. If you wish to oversee the process, then you may stay. If not, there will be no complaints when we arrive home."

"Understood, sir."

"Stop that ridiculous parody this instant."

She slid her feet apart and placed her hands behind her back. "Is that an order to go to my ease, sir?"

His nostrils flared again, and his lips curled, but this time there was a hint of amusement in the gesture. "The term is 'at ease,' soldier. And yes, go ahead."

"Much obliged, sir."

He sauntered up to her, his eyes raking over her as if inspecting her and finding her lacking. "I find myself in a new and disconcerting predicament, soldier. In all my years of military service, this is the first time I have become aroused by a subordinate, even a rowdy, undisciplined one such as yourself."

She looked up at him. "Permission to speak freely, sir."

He hiked up a brow. "A little late for that. But in the spirit of things, then yes, soldier, speak your mind."

"Go to the devil," she said in her own voice, the strident tones of her playacting gone. "Or anywhere else you please, but you will go alone."

Chapter 17

Dorothy Standish hesitated on the doorstep and felt herself hurtled backward through the years. It was a heady remembrance, looking at the Georgian facade again, remembering all the things she had forbidden herself to think about in the intervening time.

Afternoons when she should have been shopping, or at tea with an acquaintance, she had crept to rendezvous with Woolrich in this house, to become someone else. . . . To become Mellisand—what a silly affectation that had been!—a pet name Woolrich had had for her.

He had read poetry to her and listened raptly as she played the harp in the music room. They laughed and lazed about, he in a casually belted dressing gown and she clad only in her chemise. The fading afternoon sun spilled wanton light into the room where they had made love before she'd dress and go home to her real life.

Raising the knocker, she let it fall. When the footman answered, she handed him her calling card and agreed to wait.

It was Lady May herself who returned, bustling with a crisp swish of her abundant pink skirts.

She always looked lovely, Dorothy noted, and not without a touch of jealousy. Of course, she had the money to dress well, and the confidence that came from wealth and privilege. No wonder Michaela adored her.

Lady May held out her hands for Dorothy's. "What a delightful surprise. Don't you look well!"

For some odd reason, the woman's effusive and seemingly genuine display of warmth and welcome touched her. She wasn't quite certain what she was doing here in the first place, but it all came together, or apart, as it were, as her shoulders slumped and she felt a long-denied weariness pull on her limbs.

Lady May reacted strongly to this show of distress. "Is it Michaela? Has something happened? Oh, God, I'll never forgive myself my wretched pride."

"There's been no harm done," Dorothy rushed to reassure her. "At least, not the way you are thinking, but, yes, I have come because of Michaela."

"Come inside." May hurried her past the formal sitting room, into the cozier, more intimate environs of her private withdrawing room. Dorothy looked about briefly, taking in the comfortable seating and colorful cushions. With the lovely framed landscapes on the wall and cheerfully patterned drapery, the atmosphere was restful and unassuming, a room for relaxing. This was May's private parlor.

"Shall I ring for tea? No? Please sit. Now tell me what has happened."

"Michaela is unhappy," Dorothy responded as she sat. "Not the usual as one could expect for a newly wedded woman adjusting to marriage. It is different. I have never seen her like this. The child had more spirit than was good for her. Now she is despondent, and as a result seems to be rather reckless in how she is coping with these troubles. She is doing things I've never known her to do. I am more than worried for her."

May said, "Yes, I read the papers."

Dorothy drew in a long, labored breath. "She has been to

see me, and has asked if she may come home. She wishes to leave Major Khoury."

May's head shot up. "I see. May I ask why you have come to me?"

"Because I said no." Dorothy lowered her eyes and summoned her strength. "You are the only other one to whom she will go. She loves you very much and thinks much of you. She will try to seek refuge with you."

May blinked, sitting rigidly with her dainty hands folded on her lap. It was an uncharacteristically demure pose. "You are mistaken. We have not been close lately."

"I did not wish to refuse her," Dorothy blurted. "I had to; she cannot run from a marriage after only a few weeks. Lord knows, if I thought it was best, I'd have taken her back in an instant." She sighed, her face falling into a deep frown. "And now she truly hates me. She has no idea why I had to deny her. The child already thinks I dislike her. It isn't true. I love her dearly, but it was always so hard with her."

"She has much of her father in her. Stubborn. And, yes, reckless."

She had prepared herself to remember, but the force of it took Dorothy off guard. "Being back in this house . . ."

May laid a reassuring hand on her arm. "I know it must be painful for you."

"It feels . . . strange. Warm, bittersweet. And painful. Yes, it is still painful." She sighed. "We are grown women, so we don't have to pretend with one another. I was in love with Woolrich, but he didn't love me. Not in the way a woman wishes."

"Yes," May said, nodding, "it was his way to love many woman, but none too deeply."

"When he found out I carried his child, he patiently explained to me what must be done. He was so . . . dispassionate about it all. He'd had other affairs, other children. It was a crushing and cold realization to understand he didn't feel the same as I did."

"Oh, Dorothy. Wooly never meant to hurt you, I am sure."

"He never meant harm. But he did harm." She shook off the anger. "Michaela always sensed something different in herself. She asked me once about it. I was unprepared, and I struck her."

"I know you have a troubled relationship." May came to sit beside Dorothy. Ignoring the way the older woman shrank into the settee, she firmly took her hands in hers.

"I had my girls. My twins. I know it was wrong, but I poured myself into them. They were comfortable, easy to understand. They thought as I did when Michaela . . . she was just so *foreign*."

Very gently, May said as she squeezed her hand, "I am sure you tried your best."

Dorothy shook her head. "I should have done better. I wish I had. Now I've completely lost her. I have wanted to explain all of this now that she is a married woman and she knows about her father. I thought perhaps there was a chance that we might understand one another at last. I have so wanted that, but I have not found the words, the right time. . . ." She pressed a trembling hand to her lips. "I thought she wouldn't wish to reconcile, not when she had you now."

May said softly. "I am afraid I, too, have let her down gravely. I . . . I spoke out of turn against Adrian, and she has not forgiven me."

"You opposed her marrying Khoury?"

"I did, yes. I suppose some of it was selfish. I had only just found her. I didn't wish to lose her so soon. And I had . . . other concerns. I worried about him, but I think I was wrong. It seems that way, gratefully. With all of their troubles, he has behaved honorably, not at all what I had feared. In the end, I made her quite unhappy and all for nothing."

"We must help her now. You must not take her in when she asks you. Khoury is taking her to the country. She does not wish to go, but she must. She loves him, you know, and he dotes on her, although he'd put out his own eyes before admitting it. They are two stubborn, prideful people, and they are making a botch of this entire thing. I tell you, I feel this in my heart, in my very bones. I have done so many things wrong, I am determined to do this thing right. She must have the man she loves. If you take her in, she may never reconcile with him."

May's anguish was apparent as she wrestled with Dorothy's request. "I cannot refuse her if she asks me to come here. This goes against every instinct." She stood, walked to the opposite side of the room, then returned. "Why does he have to take her away? How will we know she is safe?"

"Major Khoury must keep her safe now."

Pausing, May's petite body stiffened. Touching her fingertips to her lips, she closed her eyes. "I want to rescue her if she needs me. But . . . I've recently been told by someone whose wisdom I trust that perhaps my instincts are not wholly accurate in this instance. Perhaps you are correct, and she needs to work this out on her own."

Dorothy stood, confronting her. "Then you promise?"

Lady May hesitated, then nodded. "I'll do as you ask. But if I ever feel she is in danger, I will not turn her away."

"I concur. Thank you, Lady May. And . . . thank you for all you did for Michaela. For all of the girls, really. I admit I resented it more than a little bit, but I thought I was losing her to you, and I was jealous."

May was astonished. "But Michaela loves you. Your approval is everything to her. No one can replace a mother."

"Even such a mother as I've been?"

"How could you be so terrible?" May reassured her with a smile. "Look at what a wonderful girl she has turned out to be."

"Yes. You are right. She is wonderful. And she deserves to be happy."

May's eyes narrowed. "Oh, she will be. I will be watching to make sure of it."

It was a cold, damp day that saw the master and his new bride arrive home.

When Michaela entered the gigantic mansion, which Adrian had only referred to as a "house," she gaped at the half-wrecked monstrosity. Her mood upon leaving London had been grudging. She was angry as hell at him for high-handedly ordering her to leave the city, and let him know it. She answered none of his attempts to engage her in conversation, refused even to look at him, giving him the cut with relish.

Nor had she spoken when their carriage pulled to a stop in the half-circle drive and she alighted, nor when her husband led her into the house. But this time it was not spite that held her tongue, but awe.

In the huge entryway that led into a cylindrical center hall, there hovered a domed ceiling overhead, presently under scaffolding and numerous canvas coverings. The walls were painted gentle hues and hung with Renaissance paintings. A row of columns formed a series of embrasures. On the floor, chipped marble was laid in an intricate pattern, and a Persian rug was carelessly tossed at the foot of the wide, sweeping staircase.

She turned a slow circle to take it all in.

He gestured to the ceiling. "I'm having a mural painted. The fellow thinks he's Michelangelo painting the Sistine Chapel. The damn thing is taking as long, I fear."

The butler and housekeeper, an energetic couple—he tall and lean, she tall and round—made an appearance then, and Adrian made the introductions. He then fired off a few instructions, saying he would show his wife around the house and then escort her to her room when they were through.

"Adrian," she breathed when they were again alone. "Are we are rich?"

As he peeled off his gloves, he replied, "So you've decided to speak to me."

She gave him an arch look. "I was snubbing you."

"You were sulking like a child. Which is surprising, since this is not so bad a place to come to."

Pointing a finger, she squinted at him. "The problem was never the house. It was you. You must have simply everything just your way. And by the by, what did you say to my aunt May to get her to refuse to allow me to stay with her? It had to be something especially horrid, for otherwise she would never deny me sanctuary from a bully of a husband taking me away from London."

"I have not seen your aunt. I spoke to no one but you about the state of affairs between us. And I certainly didn't threaten anyone."

"You threatened me. That is why I am here."

"Besides you," he corrected absently. "Do you wish to see the master suite?"

"Ah, so that is why you have brought me here, to lock me in the bedroom so you can ravish me at will and there is no one to whom I can call for help."

"I am your husband; no one can save you from me," he replied, his eyelids hovering at half-mast. "As for ravishment, I don't force myself on women. In fact, I have even been known to refuse willing ones, when they are merely playing games."

She bristled, the humiliating memory of his rejection rankling. Turning her attention to the house once again, she inspected the montage of old and new.

The polished banister on the staircase gleamed in the dreary daylight, but the carpeting was worn through, some of the stair rods broken and brittle with rust. The chandelier overhead looked like a medieval relic, but the walls boasted what had to be a fresh coat of creamy paint.

"Come, Michaela," he said, holding his arm out to take her hand, which she snatched away. He smiled patiently. "You have been sulking the entire journey here. I wouldn't have thought you such a poor loser. Why not make the best of it? Come, I will show you the house."

She made a hard harumph but followed him as he took her through the rooms. Her fussiness was merely a ruse, and he knew it. She couldn't give in easily, and certainly not because the house was—or rather would be one day—magnificent.

His voice, when he spoke of the place, was almost boastful. "If you think this is wretched, you should have seen it when I purchased it. It was a moldering wreck."

"Then why ever did you buy it?"

He made a face, pursing his lips, then shrugged. She

waited a long time, and when he didn't answer, she went through the morning room to the doors to look at the terrace beyond.

"Ah, I have trod on hallowed secrets again," she murmured when he joined her. "I have unwittingly touched on some memory or other thing that I have no right to know and must not ever mention. Do make a list, so that I won't keep pestering you. When we are done eliminating subjects, we might have to keep ourselves to discussions of the weather for the rest of our lives."

Adrian saw she was angry, and she was hurt, too.

Laying a hand on her shoulder, he felt her stiffen. How many times had his touch made her weak and pliant? He longed for that, craved the freedom to let his hand roam.

"When I returned from the war, I located the widow of a man I had known. Her situation, which was rather dire at the time, brought me into the status of things in this district, and I became involved rather quickly."

She turned, her curiosity as pure as a child's. "Why, what had happened?"

"The village of Shepston-on-Stour is almost completely owned by the earl, and he . . . well, he is not a kind fellow. He is greedy, depraved, and someone had to stop him."

"Oh, the man we saw at the ball. I remember. My aunt knew the Earl of Shepston, or rather knew of him. When I asked her about him, she said that she always made it a point to snub him, and told me to give him the cut. She said he was a lecher."

"He is a man of great appetites, and his appetites require money. The law says that any landowner can set the tax rate on his lands, taking whatever portion of the crops he deems his due. Shepston bleeds his tenants dry, and the effect is like a series of domino tiles, for the farmers' poverty depresses all the services in the area. The hamlets are impoverished. The people here are fighting for their lives."

Her eyes were keen. "Is that why you wish to go into politics? You wish to take on Shepston?"

"I have already made it . . . less comfortable for him to

continue as he's been. As for seeking Parliament, it seemed the right thing."

"And you always do the right thing."

She was making fun of him, but he sensed an undercurrent of admiration. "There are many issues involving reform I would like to advance. Schools for the poor, for example, would be a social improvement I could enthusiastically endorse."

"Ah, a bribe. Very well, you are bent on projects in which I happen to share an interest, namely the betterment of social conditions—" Her lips twitched in approval, while she raised a nicely arched brow. "—but must you do it from this cave?"

He laughed. Even with the pull of the tensions running between them, he could enjoy her company more than any other woman he had ever known. The very air seemed to thrum with energy, and his nerves crackled with pleasant tension.

"The house is not so bad. I thought it showed promise. That was why I purchased it. It seemed, with a spot of work, to be a rather grand place. I liked the location. Given the rather complicated state of affairs between myself and my family, it was a good enough place to settle. If I ride on horseback, I can travel to visit them in a day. And then I became involved in the project of transforming the house and found I rather liked it. I often found myself laboring alongside the workers."

They had made their way through most of the first floor, and he took her into the library. It was the room he spent all his time in, so it was the only one that appeared lived in. The fire had been lit, and it felt pleasant as they entered.

"I see. While all of London wondered what had happened to their hero, you were here, plane and saw in hand, playing the village carpenter."

"Some days. I oversaw every aspect of the alterations to the place. I worked with an architect, of course, but kept a close eye on the transformation so that it would be exactly as I envisioned. What I foresaw in my plan for the house was to try to restore the beautiful appointments of the Tudor style that neglect and misuse had marred, but I am obsessed with dispelling the gloom, to bring light into the place. For that, I've employed artisans to work their craft in the hopes that one day the house could be a place a person might reasonably feel comfortable."

"You enjoyed it, didn't you?" She looked at him strangely.

He had a tendency to become enthusiastic in his plans for the house. It was the first home he'd known since childhood and that word, *home,* had sparked ambitions in him he hadn't known he'd had.

He'd probably been too effusive, so he shrugged. "It was helpful during a difficult time. It felt good to use my hands, work hard. I am used to that."

"It must have been terribly expensive."

In truth, the work cost him plenty, but he hadn't minded. It was rather a sad comment on his life that he had little else upon which to spend the small fortune he had made when he had invested his modest inheritance in New World trade. The market was shy after the Colonial war, but he had known that if the Yanks were strong enough to defeat England's army, they were strong enough to become a formidable trade power. He'd been proven correct.

"This library was one of the first rooms to be done over. The dark paneling was stripped and then rubbed with lemon oil until the natural wood tones gleamed. I did most of that work."

She looked about. "New draperies? They are lovely brocade. Did you choose them? Somehow, I cannot see you poring over bolts of fabric, and putting together colors. It is thought to be a woman's strength."

"If you wish to know if I had my mistress do the decorating, the answer is no. I have hired someone to make those choices. A man."

"Oh."

"I never kept a mistress, Michaela."

"It is of no consequence to me," she said with a toss of her head. "I am not to bother with your past."

"Michaela . . ."

She stood, denying him whatever fumbled apology he'd been about to make, and pointed to a spot over the tiled fireplace. "I would like to hang the painting you gave me in here. As this is the most progressed room, I suppose we will be spending most of our time in here. It will double as our withdrawing room, if you don't mind the invasion."

He looked at his desk, piled high with correspondence, all buzzing with the tedious developments in the latest legislative proposals. By the hearth was his favorite chair, a table beside it piled high with newspapers he had neglected while tending to personal business.

None felt as inviting as the idea of finding her here each evening.

"Not at all. Let us see what you can do to improve the place."

The sound of raised voices in the hallway diverted his attention. Dennis, one of the footmen, was conversing loudly with someone.

"What is going on here?" Adrian stepped out of the library and drew the doors closed behind him. Dennis was having a bit of a tussle with a man. They stopped immediately as Adrian barked his demand, and Dennis swung round, his face red. The man stopped as well, standing with his rough woolen cap in his hands. He was a laborer, Adrian saw. Poor, but well turned out for all of his obvious lack of coin. His homespun garments were neatly mended, his boots scuffed but clean of mud.

"You said for me to come see you, my lord," he said, standing on tiptoe to address himself to Adrian over Dennis's height.

"Ah, Mr, Chivers, isn't it?"

"That's right, me lord," Chivers said.

"You are not to address me thusly," Adrian corrected edgily. "I am not a lord."

"Begging your pardon, then, sir." He said it, "sair," with the harsh accents of a Cockney. "I don't mean to be disturbing you or nothing, but I got to talk to you, like I said in me letter."

"Yes." Adrian nodded to his man, giving the sign for Dennis to relax. He seemed disappointed, as if he had been looking forward to throwing this ruffian out on his ear. "It's all

right, you can show Chivers into the estate office. I'll see
Mrs. Deiter and have her bring tea."

"Tea, sir?" Dennis sounded scandalized.

"Do you object to civility?"

Chivers spoke up. "Sir, I don't need nothing a'tall."

"Nevertheless, I'll order a pot brewed. I could use a
cuppa."

It took only a moment to tell Mrs. Deiter to bring in a
tray, and another to fetch the flintlock from his desk in the library, check it, and place it in the waistband of his trousers.
He had lived with a weapon at his side for too long to think
of going into a situation where a man was obviously agitated
without the solid feel of his pistol pressed against the small
of his back.

Although he was as English as they came, he was not
under the delusion that a cup of tea was always enough to
soothe the savage beast. Mr. Chivers had seemed very irate,
and the tone of his letter had been less than cordial.

He entered the estate office, a small, humble room with an
outside entrance as well as one connecting it to the house,
used in the house's glory days to collect rents and administer
to business concerning tenants and other neighborhood concerns. Its walls wore chipped paint, the beams dark with age
and neglect. He hadn't gotten around to this room yet in the
refurbishing process, but he thought he might keep it humble. Making a grand statement of wealth would be in poor
taste, he thought, when one was meeting with those who had
lesser means.

"How may I help you, Mr. Chivers?" Adrian asked as he
moved to take the seat behind the desk.

"Me girl is Alice."

Adrian paused, looking at the man, then slowly he lowered himself into the chair. "I see. You know, then, that your
wife came to see me."

"She's not me wife. Her husband left her and her kids.
Drinks too much, he does. Took off, and no one's seen him in
three years. Me and her, we're together now. I'm more of a
husband and father than that rotten bloke whot's left her
without a farthing."

"That's admirable of you to help her."

"She ain't a charity case, sir. I love her. You need to know how it is. We try to be like a respectable family, with everything except the blessing on us."

"I understand that. I am of the opinion that not all marriage is made in heaven, and thus not all a blessed union. I believe Parliament will loosen its restriction on separations and divorces in time, so that good women like your Alice will be free to marry again, making a union like the one you share legal."

Chivers looked at him warily. "I heard you had some fancy idears."

"How can I help you, Mr. Chivers?"

Chivers thrust his hand into his pocket and drew out a fistful of coins. He placed them on the desk. "The problem, sir, is that you already have."

"You are referring to the money I gave to Alice?"

"I am." Chivers's eyes glistened with challenge. "I came to return it to you, sir, with all respect and tell you that she ain't a loose woman. She has me to take care o' her, and the kids."

Adrian nodded, considering what he should do. He didn't reach for the coins. "Are you under the impression that something . . . untoward occurred between myself and Alice? Something of a personal nature?"

Chivers looked bullish. "It happens, don't it? Some lords o' the manor think it their right."

"I am not such a man," Adrian replied.

"Beggin' your pardon, sir, but we don' know much about ye, do we, being that you're new to the neighborhood."

Sitting back, Adrian gave him a hard stare. The man was visibly uncomfortable under the intense scrutiny, shifting slightly in his seat, but he didn't relent. Adrian asked, "What did Alice say when she told you about the money?"

"She didn't tell me, I found it. Cried, she did, and begged me not to come. I could see she was ashamed, she was, an' I was more determined to set things straight. I mean to fight for her, even though I'm just a smith and you're a fancy toff

She's just a relief from boredom for you, but she's me whole life."

"She is lucky to have you. Listen well, Chivers, I take no offense at your coming here. You are a good man to challenge me on behalf of the woman. Allow me to allay your fears. I never had any improper relationship with Alice. Surely she told you that."

"What else would she say?"

"That she came here to apply for a position. I had nothing to offer her, since I was leaving for London for an extended stay. She was in the process of explaining how she was upset because she was having to send her children to her mother for keeping until she was on her feet when she began to weep, for her mother, as you know, lives in another village. She was prepared not to be able to see her children for long periods of time, but she had to find work. It seems Shepston turned her out without a reference, a trick he's known for when his female staff don't allow him the liberties he likes."

"Shepston isn't worth a damn, and I wouldn't have her there one day more after what he did. She'd have none of it."

Adrian looked at him gently. "Then what makes you think she would come to me and offer me what she denied him? Either a woman can or cannot trade on her body. You have to know she didn't earn that money on her back."

"It's just that she was so overset, I was afeared she'd done somethin' desperate. I told her we wouldn't split up the family, not for nothin'. I'd take care o' things." His face transformed, his agony apparent. He was young, Adrian saw with some surprise, but the cares of his life had worn on him. "It ain't fair, it ain't, sair. I work hard, an' I do good work. Ask anyone."

Leaning forward on his elbows, Adrian asked, "Why can't you make a living?"

"Shepston allows each cottager to keep enough crops for his family, none to sell. With no income, how can a man pay a smith? How can he pay for anything? He does without, that's what he does, and the smith does without as well. Oh, I shoe their horses and mend their metal. What else am I going to do with me time? But I get only what they can spare, an' it ain't enough. It's hard on a man, not to provide for his family."

Adrian saw the frustrated pride, the impotence against unfairness, and he felt the same emotion seep into him. Chivers looked at him, his lips drawn back in a snarl. "It's Shepston, sair, he's takin' it all. Who's to stop him?"

Adrian rose. "I will. In the matter of your Alice, she and I came up with a solution of sorts. I loaned her the money, which is repayable through either direct payment over time should things improve for you, or by a debt of service when her oldest child is of good enough age to look after the others for a few hours a day. She said that might be in a year or two, and I told her that would be fine. In the meantime, she assured me she had an excellent hand with baking, when she had the sugar and the eggs for it, and as it happens, I have eggs and sugar as well as a monstrous sweet tooth. When I am in residence, she is to bake for me."

"Is that why she's been bakin' up a storm?" Looking down at his rough, scarred hands lying limply on his lap, his face drew into deep lines. "I didn't believe her. I thought, 'No one would give blunt away like that.' I should have trusted her."

"Well, you favor me with more charity than I possess. I did not give her the money. I expect payment. I made sure my investment was sound. I found Alice was well regarded, and then of course that business about Shepston pricked me good, but in the end, it was the children, you see. They should not be separated from their mother."

"You'll get your money back, sair," Chivers vowed. "I'll see to it."

"I know I will, or I'll get its worth in biscuits. I particularly favor shortbread, if you would tell her for me."

Chivers stood, his eyes on the money he had laid on the desk. "It's honest then?" When Adrian nodded, Chivers visibly relaxed. "I thank you, sair, I surely do. I see you know something about how crazy a man gets for a woman."

Caught in midrise, Adrian paused, then straightened, waving his hand casually. "It is an affliction we all face at one point or another. Quite normal."

Chivers exited through the door leading outside. Adrian bade him farewell, locked the door behind him and blew out the torch that had illuminated the dingy room. As he went to the door leading back to the house, he saw the thin line of light under it blocked by a swath of shadow just wide enough for a lady's skirt.

He crept softly until his hand was on the knob. With a quick turn, he unlatched the catch and pulled it quickly inward.

Michaela stood in the hall, eyes wide, mouth in a soft little O, staring at him like a child caught with her hand in the biscuit jar.

He raised one brow very slowly.

He could almost hear the wheels in her fast moving brain clicking to wheedle her way out of the predicament. While she searched, her face assumed a defined casualness that was so phony he almost laughed.

He waited.

Finally she said, "Did . . . er . . . you want supper served in our rooms or in the library? Mrs. Deiter asked me."

"The library will be fine temporarily."

"All right." She turned.

"Michaela," he called, striding out to join her, "you weren't *spying* on me by any chance, were you?"

"Spying? No, of course not. I was wondering if you wished me to tell her the library or the bedroom."

"Did you hear anything while you were wondering?"

Her blush reminded him of how she looked in passion, the color high and her eyes sparkling with vibrant color. "I wasn't eavesdropping."

"The door is thin enough for sound to transport. You must have heard something."

"Oh, maybe something about sweets."

He smiled, looking ahead of them, not at her. "I cannot abide sweets," he confessed. "I send the ones Alice makes to the children's home in Banbury with the milk wagon."

Stopping, she stared at him in amazement. "I heard you tell that man you loved sweets. In fact, you loved them so much, you had to have them, and therefore Alice was earning her money by supplying them for you."

"My God, you make me sound as desperate for sugar as an opium eater is for the poppy." His eyes narrowed. "It proves you *were* listening."

She got that mutinous expression that always drove up his blood. "How else am I to find anything out about my husband? A woman has to have tricks when denied the most fundamental consideration. And I am completely unashamed of it. I am, however, curious, and although I know I am to mind my place and not ask such impertinent questions—" She drew in a breath, her sarcasm giving way to sincere interest. "Why did you give that woman the money?"

"She needed it. It was only a pittance, for God's sake. One might think I gave away half my fortune."

"It was enough to save her from having to send her children away so she could work."

"What was she to do? Would you have had me deny her?"

"You know I would not. That is not my point at all, Adrian. It just . . . It just is a very grand gesture."

"It was not a gesture. The woman needed help. And you are well versed in the needs of the poor. Sometimes, one must intervene. It is not such a great thing to see the logic in this."

"Yes, of course. I just didn't know you took your beliefs so far. Not many do." She sounded impressed, as if she hadn't suspected his charity would extend to becoming personally involved with indigent folk. In a way, it rankled that this would surprise her. What must she think of him?

What else but what he'd shown her thus far? And that was not much. It was simply against his nature.

Disgruntled at these thoughts, he said, "Well, it proves how little you know me."

Her face fell into strange lines. She appeared sad and resigned, but there was a hardness in her, too. "Yes," she murmured. Her chin jerked upward. "I quite agree."

The air was heavy again, all the playfulness of their cat-and-mouse game gone.

He allowed her to have the last word, stepping back as

she stalked past him. He watched her go, dropping his gaze to the sway of her hips. They weren't sleeping together, not since that last debacle. The choice to remain lusty strangers was his. Her accusations that he hadn't wished to share his life, only his bed, still remained fresh in his mind.

Damn and damn, the bloody witch was right.

He'd tried to marry without changing anything about himself or his life. What a comfort he had once thought that was. Now, however, he was filled with a briny feeling of dissatisfaction and unrest. What was so godforsaken wonderful about his wretched life that he had to preserve it, anyhow?

That evening, as he dressed for dinner, he eyed the door that connected their suites. What a stupid idea, mistress and master suites connected discreetly.

But the door stood, large and solid, a symbolic barrier that was more than polished oak and brass knob. If he couldn't follow the siren's song pulling at his soul to test whether or not she would refuse him should he open it, he had only himself to blame, for he had made these absurd rules as much as she. Perhaps more. Perhaps his foolish pride had dictated no other recourse.

And the little vixen was going to make him pay for that folly as often as she could.

Chapter 18

The grounds of the house were as neglected as the interior had been, but as Michaela strolled the walled gardens and beyond to the lawns rimmed with tender green undergrowth and bristling buds on the forest trees, she saw promise. She wondered if she could coax Albert here to bring the gardens to life. He was a wonder with planting and landscape, and she would dearly love the man's company.

Resolving to speak to Adrian about it, she breathed in deeply of the moist air. When Adrian had insisted she come to Surrey, she'd been afraid she wouldn't like it, but it suited her. Even the house was not terribly daunting, not after Adrian explained his plans for the remodeling. Michaela had liked his ideas very much.

Who would have thought the rough and brazen man who'd carved a legend for himself from war would appreciate the gracefulness of line and space? He had an aesthetic side to him she had never suspected. It only made her itch to know more.

The sour feeling came, as it always did, a rough awakening out of her dreams. He held her at arm's length, so what could she know of a man who did not wish to be known?

And what of herself? she thought, and her shoulders slumped. She'd been no ideal companion, either. She'd allowed her hurt to make her less than pleasant. She'd been petulant and argumentative when she really only wanted to get his attention. But who would wish to pay attention to such a wife? He must think very little of her these days.

She had to have a care. This wasn't an enchanted castle in a fairy-tale wood. It was too easy to believe in possibilities here.

Oh, but it was lovely. It lifted her spirits, this place. She might have been happy if things were different with Adrian. There was an ache inside her, but as much as she missed her family, she suspected that her loneliness was incurable, for she pined for the man who lived under the same roof.

"Care if I join you?" Adrian's voice reached her, rousing her from her thoughts.

She turned to him. His appearance surprised her, for he was dressed simply. One might think him a laborer if they didn't know differently, with his rough cotton shirt and wool trousers tucked into a well-worn pair of boots. Ah, but his arrogance would always give him away. He wore it without any rancor, simply a subtle air of confidence, and it would have elevated him to noble status had he been dressed as a beggar.

She ducked her head to hide her reaction to him. "No, please do." They began to stroll together, with no particular destination.

In companionable silence, they wound their way through the garden. Michaela stopped a few times to examine a plant. Adrian asked if she knew plants, and she talked about Albert and how she would help him in the garden. He listened quietly as she commented on that shrub or that perennial, seeming interested in what she had to say.

Two other people might have felt comfortable clasping their hands together, walking side by side without any self-consciousness. They might have bent their heads together as they strolled; Constance and Terrance came to mind, their immature and sweet infatuation terribly poignant. Like anyone else in love, they might have sought a casual touch to tide them over until they could find the privacy to allow their impulses to reign free.

But they did none of that as they came out of the garden and followed the path into the wood.

Adrian gestured to the line of trees. "There is a stream farther up, with a rocky bed and a waterfall. Would you like to see it?"

She nodded.

They walked for a stretch. Then Adrian asked, "Michaela . . . are you terribly unhappy here?"

Unhappy? She wanted to wail her unhappiness. She wanted to tell him to hold her, beg him to open his arms, his heart, and love her as he had once loved Frances.

She did like it here, though. For a girl who had lived all her life in the city, she felt an immediate sense of welcome in these pastoral lands.

Her reply was evasive. "It is lovely, true. But I miss London."

"You must yearn for your family. Perhaps we can have them for a visit. Why don't you write to them? London will be heating up. The country is restful in the summer months."

"Thank you." She couldn't look at him, because she was a coward. "I think I would like that."

"Michaela, you don't need my permission to ask your family. I would like to be consulted, of course, about your decisions, but this is your home, too. I want you to think of it that way."

"Yes, thank you." She smiled, surprised that he would have such a care of her feelings. He certainly hadn't when he'd all but dragged her out of the city. Yet, that had been a good decision, she saw now. It felt *right* in this place. "I would be happy and proud to show them your home."

The look he gave her was warmed with a smile. "Our home. It is ours."

"Yes," she said, and returned his smile.

They found the path, his touch warm and tingling on her

skin as he helped her over some tangled roots. Her skirts snagged on the bracken in a narrow area.

"Do you wish to turn back? It is rougher here than I thought."

"No. I can manage."

He turned, holding her hand in his broad, strong one, the raspy touch of the calluses in his palm creating eddies of sensation up her arm.

Since their arrival they had existed in cordial awkwardness. They'd shared no signs of affection, not even the most casual touch. The door between their two suites had remained closed.

They hadn't been intimate since she'd laid herself out on the bed for him, when she'd tried to hurt him into loving her.

It was clear that she had broken something deeply held between them that night. She had used passion as a weapon. She deeply regretted how she had lashed out at him but didn't know what to do to make it right.

She heard the gurgle of water, the steady swish of the falls. The clean tang of moisture assailed her nostrils, and her feet moved more quickly. They broke through the trees to find the area open to the sky. A wide throat of the stream churned white and frothy as it tumbled over the rocks and spilled in stages down to the swirling bottom. The depths eddied as the fast-moving water calmed before flowing more decorously downstream.

Around them, wildflowers peppered the underbrush, cropping thickly there, thinning to sparse clumps as the thicket took over. Honeysuckle was strong in the air. The sight of larkspur and foxglove and candytuft and other things Michaela couldn't identify surprised her.

"It looks like a garden," she said, pointing to the flowers.

"I thought maybe someone had tried to cultivate the spot, but I don't know much about such things."

"It's been neglected for a while, overgrown and all out of its borders . . . or maybe it was meant to look like that, sort of an enhancement of the natural arrangement of wildflowers. This is lovely, Adrian."

He said nothing, but when she peeked a glance at him, he

was looking out over the stream, his face very still. His eyes were soft, and he was at ease.

Blinking, he looked over at her, giving her a half-smile in self-conscious apology. "I am sorry. What did you say?"

"You do love it here, don't you? You even love that awful house."

She thought he might get that closed look he favored when she asked something he didn't wish to answer. Instead, he raised his eyes, his smile a slight twist of his lips. "I like it here," he replied softly.

"Then why in the world would you wish to go to London and serve in the House of Commons?"

He continued to scan his surroundings, as if filling himself up on its peace. "Obligations."

"To whom?"

He walked a short way to a large, rounded boulder perched on the bank. Carefully, in deference to his slight infirmity, he stepped over the mud and sat, then held his hands out to her.

"Come. It is a picturesque spot."

She was so tempted. What was it about him today that was different? Something was missing, a hardness, a distance. He seemed vulnerable. And she wanted to be near him.

Stepping closer, she took his hand, and he helped her avoid the mud and settle next to him.

Her back rested against his chest. He felt so solid, so rock-hard and strong. Sometimes she just wanted to melt into that strength, give over her own will.

"Good men," he said. She didn't know what he meant, and then recalled her question.

"Men you fought with." She spoke softly, for it seemed a hallowed place, like a church. "You still think of your fellow officers and all the soldiers you knew."

"The highest quality soldiers I met were simple men: laborers, farmers, tradesman."

She leaned back, feeling so wonderfully warm. Klaxons of alarm went off in her head, but she ignored them. It felt too good to relax into him.

"Do you know something? I don't think you wish to be a

Member of Parliament, Adrian." She twisted to look at him, and he gazed down at her thoughtfully.

"And what makes you say that?"

"Because you hardly care about this election. I wonder if you are serious about it or just going through the motions. You hardly talk about it. You never go to meetings or any of the things men of politics are forever doing, except when you have to, and then you are as prickly as a porcupine, I swear."

He made an impatient sound, but offered no denial.

"When I worked with the charities and various societies I belonged to in London, most of those people lived a public life every day, all day. And . . . well, I think you would be a terrible politician. It seems to me that it requires the ability to get along with people. And those that do that sort of thing thrive on it. They eat, sleep, *breathe* that life. You do it grudgingly."

"You do not think I can get along with people?"

She could feel his breath over her ear, along her jaw. "I think you have other strengths," she said with measured diplomacy that brought a low rumble of laughter to him. It vibrated from his chest into her body, and she absorbed it greedily.

"Which are?" he asked.

"Determination. Honor. Honesty. And sometimes politics requires a reserve of the truth, compromise, and a certain degree of canniness I don't think you'd approve of."

"And how do you know this?"

"Because I ran into the same problems in London with the various societies and charities I helped: the Society of the Improvement of the Conditions of the Poor and the Society for the Promotion of Aid to the Poor. The people who know the way politics operates always get the best results. They simply have a knack for it. It was a knack I didn't have, so I used what I could: my pen."

He paused. "There is a man like that. Lord Glenarvon is a political master, a man who manipulates men in power. Richard brought me to him for the election, and he agreed to manage the campaign."

"With the reputation you have of being insubordinate, I

don't imagine you would like your career being manipulated, even by a master."

"I was not insubordinate," he replied. "I cannot submit to fools, Michaela. But you are correct about my stubbornness or pride or whatever it is. I can't submit to Glenarvon, although he is no fool. I have had enough of that, and I don't wish to follow any more orders."

"Is it truly that terrible?" she asked.

"Well, you decide. They wanted me to marry a widow with children—blond children, at that. And any widow with towheaded offspring would do. That was when I began to suspect, although I didn't declare it then, that I was not made for a political life."

"What? They can't have been serious."

"Oh, they were. However, I did as I pleased. I married you."

"Oh. I didn't know. I am sorry I created problems for your political aspirations."

"The damned truth of it is, Michaela, they didn't start out being mine. It was just something I thought about for a while, and it suddenly had a life of its own. My brother was the one who wanted it. It's his dream to have us both in the Houses of Parliament. He pushed it, and it seemed like a good idea at the time. I don't suppose I had anything else to set my mind to. When I married you, I realized I couldn't exist in the confines of what they wanted from me, or I'd suffocate."

The sound of the water was rough music as he lapsed into silence. When she didn't say anything after a while, he jostled her gently and inquired, "What is it?"

She sighed softly. "That is the first time you've ever said that something good came from our marriage. That it meant something to you besides just . . ."

"Sex?"

"Yes."

The low, sultry tone of his voice was persuasive. "But that is good, too."

Shivers ripped over her, sweet and sharp. They hadn't made love in such a long time.

"It's not enough, Adrian," she said. It was barely a whisper. She closed her eyes, hoping he wouldn't touch her and hoping he would.

He never answered her. The mood fled, chased away by all the things she couldn't say and he wouldn't. She sat up, hugging her knees. She felt cold without him.

He didn't touch her again except to lend a hand as she climbed down the rock and leapt over the mud to join him as they walked back to the house. Up to their separate rooms with that damned door between their suites a mocking reminder of a situation neither one knew how to remedy.

May cursed silently to herself when she saw Robert lounging in her parlor. She hadn't thought to give orders to her staff to refuse him; she hadn't thought she would have needed to. The man was insufferably proud, so she never imagined he would have deigned to step foot in her house again.

It seemed she was wrong about Robert Carsons—or whomever the devil this man was.

She was not some swooning deb, for God's sake. Squaring her shoulders, she tilted her head back and gave him her most imperious look as she entered the room.

He didn't seem uncomfortable, not even now with her pinning him with a glare that had sent other suitors into sweating apology. Damn the arrogance of the man, but he stood as Zeus might have, arrogant and silent.

"What can I do for you, Robert?" she said crisply.

Without waiting for a reply, she moved to the sideboard. She said, "I must say, you have terrible timing. I have friends coming this afternoon, and it might prove awkward to have you here when they arrive."

She was lying. To keep her hands busy, she went to where his favorite whiskey was still decanted in one of the crystal containers. She removed the heavy stopper and poured a glass, her shaking hands clanging the neck of the decanter against the side of the tumbler.

"You are lucky to find me home," she went on. "I am usually so busy these days. Why, with Michaela married and off to the country, I have my life back, and I've jumped into the fray, as it were, with both feet." She brought him the glass.

It was only after he took it that she realized what she'd done. It was such a mindless thing, something she'd done for him every evening when he'd come through the door, tired and silent. He'd always nursed the drink, let it unwind the knots in him before he was fit to speak. The routine was so deeply entrenched, she'd enacted it again without knowing she was doing it.

"Well, look at that," she said in an attempt to laugh off the action. "I suppose old habits die hard. I am such a creature of habit, which brings me back to the issue of some of my new habits and the matter of my . . . er . . . visitor."

She felt cheap, trying so thinly to goad him into showing jealousy. She wasn't even making much sense, but yet her mouth continued to spew words despite her best efforts to rein in her fleeing self-control.

"I suppose you forgot something important. Tell me what it is, and I can send Millie to fetch it for you from upstairs. I don't know why you didn't just dispatch a messenger, as it would be best, you know—"

He moved, and her words cut off. She felt a sudden thrill of fear as he placed the tumbler on a table and ate up the distance between them in three hard strides. His powerful hands snatched her by the waist, trapping her.

For a moment, she wanted to slap his hands away. Her pride balked, but it was no match for the desire for him. His eyes gleamed, deep blue and filled with emotions that tore the bottom from her world, sending her free falling.

With a jerk, he had her up against him. She gasped, clutched at him now because her legs had gone to water and she didn't have a will any longer; she only had need. And then the need was no more because his mouth came down and took hers.

Her body felt like it was being crushed, and yet she wanted to be closer. Small sounds she never meant to make trembled in the back of her throat. He cupped the back of her head, trapping her. His mouth slashed over hers, his teeth, his tongue melding with hers.

Abruptly, he broke away. "Now," he said, his voice a barely audible rasp, "tell me to go away, May. Send me away. Go on, if you can."

She struggled for breath, hesitating only a moment before falling into him again. He captured her in his great arms. She'd missed this, dear God, she'd missed him. Whatever had kept them apart seemed suddenly so unimportant, so irrelevant, she couldn't summon anything but the need to kiss him.

How could she have cared about anything when there was this, when there was sweet completion in just knowing he was here, with her?

"No more questions," he muttered. His lips feathered kisses across hers as he spoke. "Nothing but this. If that is all you wish from me, then so be it. Keep your secrets, keep it just you and I. It doesn't matter. It's so good, May. It's so good."

She cried softly, reaching for his mouth, hungrily devouring his kiss as he bent over her. "Yes," she managed. "We should have never said all we did. It was wrong. We can have our secrets. What does it matter? We won't ever speak of it again."

"Yes. We'll just go back to the way we were. Nothing's changed. It's all right. I swear it, May, it's all right."

A low twist told her this wasn't so. No one could take words back once they were spoken. The truth of their lies to one another had been exposed. But she couldn't bear to think that. She loved him, she loved him, and she would hold him to her, no matter what, until the end of her days.

She loved him.

"Nothing has changed," she swore, and he cupped her face in his hands.

"May . . ."

"Here," she whispered. "Now . . ."

His hands obeyed. She let him do as he would, reveling in the swift capability he had to divest her of even the most intricate of gowns. His hands on her bare flesh were like hot brands. His smell was of man, of horse, of sweet spice that was only him.

"Now," she commanded again, her voice quivering. She didn't require foreplay, she required him filling the void his absence had left.

She worked fervently to undress him. When they were nude, he pressed her down onto the carpet, laid over her, and entered her. His hands cupped her buttocks, cushioning the rough brush of the carpet threads on her sensitive flesh and thrusting her hips up to each of his penetrations.

Her world exploded. Stellar heat flowing into her as he poured himself out with a harsh cry.

It was her name.

Michaela entered the village of Shepston-on-Stour from the west via Marysgate, an interesting relic of a cathedral stripped now of its stained glass and religious motifs. However, the Caen limestone stood grandly, making an impressive entrance directly onto the square.

Shop fronts surrounded her on four sides, with a small opening opposite Marysgate, where a green of fertile grass and a few trees served as a park. The Tudor styling of the older buildings was interspersed with some brick fronts and whitewashed edifices incorporating a few modern touches. It was all very charming, Michaela decided as she alighted from her carriage.

Adrian had gone to visit his brother at their country house for a few days. He had told her he thought it best if she didn't come with him. They both understood Frances was the reason and, not wishing to interfere with Adrian seeing his brother, of whom she knew he was very fond, she agreed he should go alone.

She had handed him a few old baubles she had found in her trunk. "Here," she had said, "take these for Samantha. I know you enjoy surprising her with treats, and she might like these for playing dress up."

He had been touched, she thought.

She laughed. "I don't know if you spoil her because it pleases you or to annoy her mother. But I know it would please me *that* it annoys her mother."

When he grinned, it was the devil-may-care smile she had lost her heart to. "If it accomplishes two most desirable ends, why question motivation? I shall let Samantha know they are from her new aunt," he said as he tucked the few items away. "It will go a long way toward forgiving me for marrying."

"Perhaps she can come visit us, and stay for an extended period." Michaela quickly added, "*Without* her mother."

Adrian had laughed and, to Michaela's surprise, gave her a quick, chaste kiss.

It was their first kiss since the horrid night.

Shaking the memory, Michaela focused on her surroundings. She had been looking forward to coming to the village. She'd been wanting to investigate the neighborhood since she'd first arrived.

Her companion for the day was Diane, her new maid. Adrian had hired her from the village. After they alighted from the coach in the square in the center of town, she stood beside her mistress and brushed out her skirts rather dramatically. Michaela understood at once this was for showing-off purposes, and smiled, amused. Diane wanted everyone to know of her change in status.

"Over there, ma'am," Diane said, indicating a row of shops to her left. "That's the inn. Beside it is the haberdasher's shop."

"Very good," she replied. "I believe I will have a walk round, first. I am thinking of asking Major Khoury if we may host a dinner party to meet the neighborhood folk, and I might find some treasures in the shops to brighten up the house. Lord knows it needs it."

She began to stroll, lingering some places, pausing to step into a shop at others. Her main objective was to meet the people, and she was nervous. She wanted them to like her, she found, and wondered why she was so anxious. It soon became apparent that she need not be. Once a shopkeeper or assistant found out her identity—which was not long, Diane boasted this fact loudly as soon as they entered any establishment—the proprietors and other villagers were fairly bowing and scraping to her.

She learned that Adrian was regarded as some demigod in these parts, and there were frequent references to Shepston. Every time the name was mentioned, noses wrinkled and lips pursed in mute disdain.

A group of Diane's friends approached her, filled with excited interest at her new position. Michaela dismissed her, telling her to have her visit and then afterwards, meet her at the local inn for tea.

She proceeded on her own, taking her time, which is how she liked it.

One particular shop proved especially intriguing. Its shelves were filled with the most unique and unusual items. The stuff was a montage of different eras and styles. Some of the items were old, obviously rescued from various houses. There were also new pots for ferns and locally crafted items. She thought of the dreary house that was in dire need of brightening up, and began to sift through the assortment of treasures.

She liked a pair of statues, two Greek-style cherubs, which would look well on the mantel in the library, one on each side of her painting. She picked them up daintily and was surprised to find nary a smudge on her white gloves.

As jumbled as the place was, it was certainly clean. The cause was revealed when Michaela spied a woman running a dusting cloth over some items in the corner.

She took the pair of statues to the woman. "Excuse me, may I ask you the price of these?"

The woman smiled politely and replied, "I'll have to get my husband. It is his shop."

She didn't say it, but she was of course wondering why the woman was kept in the dark as to the prices in her own husband's shop.

The woman laughed, sensing her thought. "We are only newly married, three days ago, to be exact." She ended with a giggle.

Michaela shifted the statues to free a hand, extending it. "I am Mrs. Adrian Khoury. A pleasure."

The woman appeared surprised. "I had heard the major had returned to the house. You are his wife."

"Yes, I am," Michaela said. "I have been meeting everyone today. I hope I shall keep all the names straight. May I ask yours?"

"Oh, ma'am, it is a wonderful honor to meet you. I am Sarah Trent. Rather, I was Sarah Trent, which is how you may have heard of me. Now it is Sarah Morten. Paul Trent was my husband."

Michaela gathered that Paul Trent was deceased, as his wife had just remarried. The question remained, however, why she would think Michaela would recognize the name.

"Has the major not mentioned Paul?" She looked stricken. "He served under the major. They fought at Quatre Bras."

"I see," Michaela replied, keeping her composure. There was some significance that Sarah assumed she knew. Pushing aside the scald of having to admit how little she knew of her husband, she explained. "Please do not take offense at my not recognizing your name. The major finds his war memories rather painful. He does not speak of them to anyone, and if your husband fought with mine, I would not know of it."

Sarah's frown was angry, then thoughtful. "I had hoped he would feel differently in time."

Michaela shifted the awkward burden of the cherub statues again. Sarah exclaimed, "Let me take those! Here I am blabbering, and you're left holding them. They came from Shepston Manor, you know. He's selling off everything these days."

Michaela allowed her to take one, and she placed it on a table. Michaela put the other one beside it.

"I wonder if it would please my husband to have these in our home."

Sarah appeared shocked at the idea, then she laughed. "I daresay it would be a trophy. He might enjoy it at that. Well, Mrs. Khoury, you may not know it, but you are married to a real-life hero."

"I know," Michaela said. She knew she didn't sound much impressed.

"Not for what he did in the war. Many men were heroic." She gestured to the corner of the shop. "Come and have a seat. Donald put some seats by the hearth. Usually the men get bored, while the women want to pore over every shelf, so it comes in handy."

"I shouldn't take you from your work," Michaela said, but it was only a token resistance. She very much appreciated this woman's overtures of friendship.

When they were settled, Michaela said, "My husband has not spoken about his experiences in war."

"Ah. I see. If he is reticent—and I believe I know why—then I shall tell you a bit of it, but only because Paul would want that. You see, my husband was one of the major's soldiers. He thought the sun rose and set on Major Khoury. He wrote to me often of the major's brilliance, for he was a great tactician. But more than that, he fought for his men. He respected them and refused to put on airs. And they respected him—no, more. They loved him."

Michaela nodded. "I know it still haunts him, his days on the battlefield. I suppose he felt a great responsibility for the death of your husband and the others that died at Waterloo."

"It wasn't Waterloo, ma'am. It was Quatre Bras. You see, Major Khoury led one of the four brigades sent by Prince William of Orange to confront the French army. They were suicide missions, all four. They were sent by the prince against Wellington's orders. He got his snoot up . . . that man! . . . he had no business even being anywhere near that battlefield—a noble playing war without a single idea of what he was doing and men's lives on the line."

She bit off the last words, her pain in her features before she reined it in. She composed herself and continued. "Before Wellington arrived and salvaged what was left of the troops, the army sustained terrible losses. My Paul died that day, and Major Khoury was wounded with the injury that gave him his limp."

"I thought he fought at Waterloo," Michaela said, confused. "There is a story that is famous of how he peeled off several men without orders and stung the enemy's flank. It is said he was nearly court-martialed except the maneuver was a resounding success."

Sarah's face was pinched. "All of that is true. What no one knows is that he did it with his leg nearly in shreds. He told no one about the injury until after the following battle. He kept it secret, wanting desperately to be with Wellington when he faced Napoleon at last."

Michaela couldn't speak for a moment. All she could see was Adrian with his face drawn in determined lines she knew so well, injured and in unspeakable pain. It was easy to be-lieve the story. "But how do you know this if your husband died at Quatre Bras?"

"I learned it from one of the soldiers who came to me after the war and told me everything, about Paul, and about Major Khoury. The major was pinned by three soldiers, French Imperial Guardsmen. He had been wounded. Like jackals, they were closing in for the kill when Paul arrived with three other men." She smiled sadly, bravely. "I was proud to know Paul went in there like that, to save the major he was proud to serve. He was a big man, used to the heavy work of a tanner. He would have had no fear. But God chooses our time, and it was Paul's."

"My God, my God," Michaela murmured as she digested all of this. Her heart was splitting as she thought of Adrian, wounded and awaiting the mortal blow, saved by a man he would have thought it *his* duty to protect as the commanding officer.

How well she knew him, after all.

She was mindful that this woman still grieved for her hus-band, clearly a beloved companion. "I am so sorry for your loss," she said.

Sarah seemed startled. "But that was a long time ago. I had my mourning. Now I remember only the best things about Paul. Thanks to your husband, my daughter and I are fine."

Michaela's chest ached. *Adrian, why didn't you tell me?*

"He helped you?"

"Why yes. And others. For myself, I was in a terrible state when the major came to find me. I had been at Shepston Manor, working in the kitchens, but I got promoted to parlor maid right after having my daughter. I curse the day I was promoted, for I caught the earl's eye, and when I would not do what he wished, he sent me off without notices."

She spoke without demurring. Her gaze was direct, un-apologetic. Michaela admired her. Indeed, the woman had nothing to feel ashamed of and didn't bother with silly pre-tense.

"The major found me in a bad way and acted immediately. At first he gave me his charity: a house here in the village and money for food. He found me a position. Then, as I began to tell him how things were around here, he took an interest. He bought the house and declared open warfare on the earl. I—".

"What?"

Sarah bit her lip. "I don't think I should say any more. The part of it that has to do with me is my story to tell, but the rest of it is not. The major should tell you his plans."

Michaela didn't protest. She felt that perhaps she had too much to think upon as it was.

"Well, then, let's find the price of these statues, shall we?"

Sarah located her husband, and Michaela purchased the cupids. After they were wrapped in brown paper and tied with string for easy transporting, the two women said a fond good-bye.

She was almost to the door when she spotted another item. It was a portrait, one of somebody she didn't know and yet that thoughtful profile, that particular expression, made her smile. She had it wrapped and paid for it and left the shop.

Her heart felt tender; her head was brimming with confused emotions. She was angry to have to learn such intimate details from a woman who was a stranger to her this very morning, but she was grateful as well. Adrian's generosity, his deep commitment to what was right, struck a resounding knell of admiration. But if he were such a caring man, why did he hide it, as if it were all something to be ashamed of? Did he feel guilty about Quatre Bras? Was this a shame that burrowed him into such resolute privacy?

She thought for a long time about the things she had learned, but came to only one conclusion. That was that she might never understand the man to whom she was married.

✍ Chapter 19

At Richard's house, Adrian was first greeted by Samantha, who had pushed herself to the front of the group assembled in the hall. Perhaps assaulted was a better term. She looked like a little storm.

Ignoring her frown, he scooped her up. The tiny child remained rigid, staring at him with the clearest eyes, as her mother frowned and her father tried to bite the sides of his cheeks to keep from laughing.

"You have neglected me dreadfully," Samantha said.

"I know it. That is why I have brought you extra special presents."

"Adrian!" Frances cried sharply.

She hated it when he petted and spoiled her child, and Adrian damn well knew it. It wasn't, however, his reason for doing it. Just an added benefit.

Frances was shushed by a quick command from Richard.

Adrian asked, "Do you not wish to see what I have brought you?"

The child was dubious. "All right," she said at last.

Adrian lowered her to the ground and produced the pretty necklaces and earbobs Michaela had given him. They were cheaply bought, perfect for a child to toy with.

Frances sneered cuttingly. "My goodness, they are paste. Samantha, you already have better than that in Papa's safe."

"They were sent by your aunt Michaela," Adrian said to Samantha, ignoring his sister-in-law. He was much calmer than he usually was in her presence. The sound of her voice could set his teeth on edge and his jaw to aching from the constant clenching. Now, he simply paid her no mind. "She thought you might enjoy playing dress up with them."

"Are they real?" she asked. Ah, her mother's daughter— the mercenary.

"No. They are merely baubles."

Samantha looked at the offering, then slid a sly look to her mother. "I like them," she pronounced. "But I still want to marry you."

"Well, I will speak to your aunt about it," he said.

That pleased her. She examined her gift. Adrian said, "Also, we thought you might come to stay when you are older and your parents will allow it."

Samantha thought that was an excellent suggestion. She raced off to look at herself festooned in her new jewelry.

"Really, Adrian, those cheap things are not fitting for the child of a marquess."

He looked at Frances. Really looked at her.

She was the same as he remembered. She hadn't changed. She was still beautiful in her way, but it was a cold, dead sort of beauty. It didn't move him. It was colorless. Where Michaela sparkled, this woman was brittle. Michaela had temper; Frances was merely full of bile.

"You cannot even look at her, Adrian."

Well, he looked now. He looked his fill and wondered what he had been afraid he would see all of these years. There was nothing there except a fool of a man who had been too embarrassed to face the fact that he had loved wrongly. Fate had cheated him of having that love, and thank God for it.

"As a child of a marquess myself, I believe it to be fitting amusement. And Samantha likes them. It would be small of you to deny her." That was all he had to say to her. He turned to Richard. "I would like to speak with you privately."

"Fine," Richard replied. "How long are you staying? Where is your man?"

"I will return home on the morrow. I am only going to stay the night."

Richard was disappointed, he could see. He would be even more so when he heard what Adrian had come to tell him.

They went into the room that to Adrian's mind would always be their father's lair. It was the library. The books were old and moldy and unread, the chairs old leather, split in some places and worn thin in others. Richard's affection for the past, for tradition, for the reverence of the family went deep.

He told him of his decision not to run in the election for the district seat in the House of Commons.

Richard seemed to be expecting this. He asked, "Is it Michaela? Does she require you to give up your dream?"

"Michaela does not know of my decision. It is not my dream, Richard. It was yours."

"You wanted to help, really help. Make a damned difference."

"I think there are many ways to figure into the scheme. Large ways and small ways, and I'm done with big-scale heroics. I will see to making improvements where I can. I find that much more gratifying. Parliament isn't for me. Politics isn't for me. I think I knew it all along, I just didn't want to admit it."

Richard jerked his head, staring at a landscape on the wall. "All right. I think I knew your heart wasn't in it. It was just thinking of Father, how proud he would be."

It was a sly effort. "He is proud, Richard. You are a fine Marquess of Granville."

He snorted, then laughed genuinely. "I want to ask you a question."

"Ask."

"Do you plan to hide from my wife the entire rest of our lives?"

Adrian froze. He spoke carefully, stiffly. "I hide from no one."

"I know you cannot abide her, and I know why. Frances is about as subtle as a Viking. I cannot say I blame you in avoiding her. She gets nasty when you're concerned, but then, you're the one she really wanted all along."

Adrian was at a loss. He kept his counsel, and his brother continued.

"Frances's shortcomings were made evident to me a long time ago. Unlike you, I have simple requirements in a wife, and Frances meets them satisfactorily. She is a good hostess and avid social climber. A man in politics can make use of that. If she is sometimes indiscreet about her infatuation with you, I can overlook it."

"You do not seem angry."

"Not at you. The very fact that she sparks like a riled cat whenever you are around is enough proof for me that you have not betrayed me."

"No," Adrian answered with fervent sincerity. "I never betrayed you, Richard."

"Good and well," Richard proclaimed. "Then let us be done with this ridiculous awkwardness."

"Then you do not mind she has a pining for me?"

"Lord, why would I? Oh, you mean, that she is not in love with me? What a romantic you've become. I have a very delightful mistress with whom I share a unique affection. She is quite content with the arrangement, and therefore, so am I. It is not the ordinary dalliance. As for Frances, I will speak to her. And you are not to avoid me or my children any longer. I'll never hear the end of it from Samantha if you do not."

The excuse of his daughter was thin enough for both men that they shared a smile.

"And that dope of a brother we have as well—he and his charming fiancée will be made welcome." Richard nodded, his hands coming together as he began planning. "Now that you are not going to Parliament, I am going to go to work on him." Richard leaned back, looking smugly content. "I like the idea. He has that way with people, and Constance is a popular girl, from the right family. . . ."

Adrian rose to refill his glass. He was in a mood to celebrate. "Before you plan the boy's entire future, you might ask him first what he thinks."

Michaela was beautiful.

That was Adrian's first thought when he entered the library. He had startled her when he'd opened the door. She had been sitting at his desk, writing. Now, she unfolded her graceful length and stood, her eyes wide and welcoming, her mouth curved in the slightest hint of a smile. She was pleased to see him.

"You are home."

The three simple words settled warmly upon him. She rounded the desk. "I didn't know to expect you so soon."

Heat infused him, and he thought of what she would do if he just reached out right in this moment and pulled her to him in a long, hungry kiss. He said, "I concluded my business quickly. I didn't wish to be gone long."

He turned his attention to his surroundings. The room was different, cozier. He never noticed things like furnishings or bric-a-brac, but the obvious difference in his surroundings was apparent, even to him. She had been at work. She must have scavenged all over the house to improve the room, and it showed in the tasteful touches he hadn't been able to accomplish, not even with help.

"I am famished," he said. "I shall check in the kitchens to see if there is anything to eat."

"I'll call Millie and have her fetch you something. You sit. You must be tired." She hurried to the door, pausing to glance over her shoulder at him. "Or do you wish to bathe and change?"

Not unless you come with me.

"Later." He pointed to the papers on the desk. "What were you working on?"

"Oh, nothing really. Some correspondence. The Society of the Improvement of the Conditions of the Poor asked me to write an article for their new pamphlet they are printing for the election. I was just jotting down some ideas. Do not worry. I will continue to do the work anonymously."

"I see no reason why you should. My sensibilities are far stronger than to worry over other's opinions, if that is a concern."

She smiled slightly. "But the election."

"I am not running in the fall election, Michaela. I think you know why."

"Why? Oh, no, was it because of what I said?"

"No, of course not. You merely observed what I was too thick-skulled to admit. I am not a man suited to talk and more talk and coffees and all-night sessions where everyone smokes cigars from the colonies and just . . . *talks.*"

"So you do not wish to go to Parliament?"

"I feel like I've been released from hell. No, I do not wish to go. I will content myself here." He looked around him. "This house alone shall keep me occupied for a long time."

"I hope you don't mind the few things I changed," she said. The maid entered, and she broke away to give her instructions about his meal.

When they were alone, he settled back. She chatted pleasantly as she busied herself around the room, tidying her papers on the desk and stacking some reference materials she'd been using. She had been to the village, she told him. She clearly enjoyed it, and he found a quiet pleasure in watching her.

The air in the room, warmed by her presence, felt easy and soft on his shoulders. He was content, he realized. Had he ever known this quiet feeling before?

His eye rested on something new, a portrait hung on the far wall where a dark corner had been made cheerier by the painting. Underneath, she had added a lamp on a table and a gathering of wildflowers stuck artfully in a vase. He rose and went to get a closer look at the portrait.

"Who is this?" he asked. "He looks familiar."

With a secret smile, she sauntered to stand next to him. "Do you like it?"

"I don't recognize him."

"It really isn't anyone we know, or at least that I do. But I thought he looked like Mr. Rye."

Yes, that was it. "Ah, yes, I see the resemblance."

"So . . . *do* you like it?"

She was asking him much more, and he knew it. She wanted to know if he remembered that rainy day, if he remembered the cozy intimacy of the small room in the back of the gallery, and if he treasured it, too.

For that was why she had bought the painting and hung it.

"I do." Cocking his head to one side, he added, "It looks just the way he did when he gazed at a painting and made up a story."

"I thought so, too!" she cried with delight.

Millie arrived with a few things, and Michaela shooed her away as she laid out the soup that had been warmed for him.

"I hope you will not be adverse to my inviting my family for a visit. You said they could come. The season is drawing to a close, and Mother has hinted they'd like to come."

When had she become so efficient, so natural in this place? He felt a curious welling of emotion at this show of competence, her movements filled with assurance and comfort, as if she were completely at . . . The word *home* echoed in his head, falling softly, nesting somewhere where the briars around his heart grew thin enough to be breached.

"Whatever pleases you," he said.

Home. He hadn't had a home for a long, long time. Home.

It wasn't a house, even a pretty house with all its floors sanded and polished, fresh draperies and furnishings all in order. It was a person.

He hadn't had a person, a single other person, to call home since he'd been a child. And here she was, in his house. And Michaela *was* his home.

She handed him a plate upon which she had piled a few slices of cheese and some dried fruits, to "tide him over." He settled back, determined to enjoy the surprising delights of being fussed over.

He chose a morsel, glancing up as he chewed. He found

her eyes on him, an expression of longing so poignant on her face that he nearly choked.

She wanted as much as he.

Then, in a flash, her expression grew shadowed. He could see each and every one of her defenses come up; self-consciousness replaced the moment of revelation, and a twist of something bitter tightened in his chest.

Like sand sifting through his hand, he felt the moment pass.

He sat alone in the room later, looking at Mr. Rye. To his mind, now that he was alone with the shadows and the sounds of a silent house, Mr. Rye wasn't studying his beloved paintings. The frown of concentration had been transformed into disapproval. Mr. Rye was looking off, beyond the boundaries of his gilt frame, perplexed at the odd doings in this new home of his.

What Mr. Rye couldn't comprehend was why there was a man sitting in an old chair staring at him when he had a wife upstairs, lying in bed in this very house. Mr. Rye pondered the fool who was too afraid to take the stairs. Too afraid to take what was rightfully his because he didn't know what to do with it any longer.

He was that fool. Adrian Khoury, army major, country gentleman, war hero . . . coward. Fool.

God, perhaps he could finally forgive himself for wanting to live. After all, life was precious, was it not? Even his, as worthless as it had once seemed. He might not have agreed at one time, but some primeval instinct had urged him to hold dear the flame of life, and bring him here, to this moment.

Yes, he could forgive himself for wanting to live when he fancied himself cold inside and worth only the service he could lend. What a conceited, overwrought wreck he must have been. He had begun to believe his own legend. Khoury the brave, the invincible.

All right then. He could live with being less than the hero he wanted to be. He could even live with being weak. He was a man, not a demigod. All right then.

And, yes, he might even forgive himself for Paul Trent fighting to save him and losing his life. God's plan, Sarah had said. He was still furious about it, but perhaps he could let go of that, just a little. Life had gone on. Trent's daughter thrived; Sarah had found contentment. Perhaps he could let that go, too. All right then.

But could he forgive himself for sitting here, looking at intense old Mr. Rye when everything he wanted was just a flight of stairs away?

With a sense of resolve, he went up to bed. He kept his back to the door, the one that connected his suite to Michaela's.

But it beckoned him as if it had a voice. He turned, stared at it. He walked toward it. The room seemed to grow warmer, as if the temperature rose the closer he got to his wife, the air in tandem to his blood. He reached out his hand, saw it shake. He made a fist, drew in a breath.

One thin door, and yet it was as impenetrable as a fortress.

She wanted things from him that he'd told her he wouldn't give. Why had he been so reluctant? And did she still feel the same way?

Did he?

He opened his hand, grasped the handle firmly. Adrian Khoury was no coward. He had his fears, yes. Of hurt, of rejection, of things that plagued normal men. But he had a wife he wanted badly enough to make him tremble like this at her threshold, and he was not going to shy from taking what he wanted. He turned the knob.

It was not locked. He went into the darkened room.

Michaela was first aware of breathing. Softly in the darkness, she heard it. She came awake, opening her eyes and feeling a rush of fear because she felt a presence. Someone was in the room.

"Michaela?" Adrian said.

She sat up. "Adrian, what are you doing?"

Her eyes adjusted, distinguishing the shapes of shadows

in the dim light. Right by her bedside loomed a large, dark form.

The pounding of her heart didn't cease. "What is it? Is something wrong?"

"Yes. Something is wrong. Between us, there is something terribly wrong." He sat on the edge of the bed, twisting so that he faced her. His arm stretched across her, supporting his weight so that he effectively had her pinned.

"Are you all right?" she asked.

"No. I am not ill. I just . . ."

She tried to focus on his face, but it was cast in shadows. Was this a dream? Reaching her arms for him, she slid her hands along the crispness of his shirt. It gaped open, and the warm flesh radiated heat, tempting her touch. He was real, not a dream. She felt him and knew this. The texture of the hair feathered over his chest, the pulse of his heartbeat, the fan of breath on her cheek filled her with knowledge that this was indeed real.

"I want you. Will you send me away?"

It was hardly the declaration she would have wished, but even as her heart registered the disappointment, her hands skimmed lightly over his body.

"No. I would not send you away," she whispered. She could be bold in the dark, say the things she wouldn't dare if she could see his eyes. Her hands came to his neck, twisting in his hair and pulling him down as she sank back into the pillows. Her body thrummed, excitement filling her as she felt his breath against her mouth.

It was she who kissed him, closing the gap and taking his mouth over hers. He slipped his arm under her, supporting her as she strained against him. His groan answered the rising desire in her, and she mewled a wordless answer. His head slanted, his mouth opened hers, and their tongues met.

Her hands slipped to his waist, pulling him down to her. He obliged her summons, lying over her so that he covered her with his large, strong body. She felt the pull of the tide, the familiar swirl of rapid emotions as his hands and mouth aroused her. Sensations that coursed through each nerve left her gasping. He whipped her to the brink of pleasure, teased her as she teetered in glorious need before pushing her over the edge to tumble into the wild currents of ecstasy.

In the quiet afterward, she lay in his arms, drugged with pleasure. There were things to say, words that needed to come forth, but they would wait that night. They would wait for many nights after, so many, in fact, that they became easy to ignore. The splendor of his lovemaking made it easy to forget all else in the hours they lay together in the dark.

Only in the daytime did she wonder if such bliss were a false promise. He spoke no words of love, and neither did she.

Dorothy Standish and her twin daughters wasted no time in taking Michaela up on her invitation to visit. Within a fortnight they arrived, Dorothy writing that the timing was perfect with the season coming to a close, and they wished to leave London for a spell. She said she was looking forward to a rest after the vigors of polite society.

Michaela was excited. She had missed everyone, even Delinda. However, it was definitely a case of absence making the heart grow fonder with the latter, for once the ornately dressed twin stepped into the house, she wrinkled her nose and exclaimed, "My God, it is atrocious!"

Adrian brushed off her outburst. "You will have to excuse us. The house is under renovation."

Dorothy looked about her. She rubbed her hands together as if anticipating all the ideas she might contribute. "I can see you will be working for a long time."

"You should see the gardens. They are overgrown, of course, but show great promise. I wondered if you would lend us Albert if he is willing to travel outside of the city."

"I'll take a look," Dorothy said. She glanced about again. "Still, the place shows promise. It is very grand, if one can show off the assets buried under the gloom."

Unaccustomed to her mother's compliment—such as it was—Michaela felt a flush of pleasure. She could see she was relishing the idea of digging into the project and knew her mother well enough to anticipate a clashing of wills as Dorothy had a tendency to take control.

She was shocked when her mother viewed the strange library/parlor Michaela had cobbled together and nodded approvingly. "I can see you have the touch, Michaela. It should be interesting to see what you do with this place."

Delinda was busy gloating over the less-than-perfect home her sister was saddled with. "Good Lord," she muttered, squinting at the cherubs. "They are naked! What strange taste you have, Michaela. I would put a grand landscape here, and some Chinese vases with potted palms in them all about the place."

Lilah smiled and exchanged looks with Michaela. "Like a jungle."

"Adrian has many plans," Michaela said.

"Well, at least you will be in London for most of the year," Delinda interjected. "Good heavens, and I should expect that residence to be a tad better than this. Major Khoury will be a member of the House of Commons and there will be appearances to be kept up." Her gaze snagged something in the other room. "Good gracious, there is that awful painting."

Adrian spoke quietly. "You should know that I have decided not to run for the election. But I am still determined to work for the same social progress and governmental reforms, only closer to home."

Dorothy looked at Michaela. "I trust you will be continuing your work, as well."

Michaela was stunned. "I thought my work annoyed you, Mother."

"You always went about it wrong, that was all—all of that writing letters and going out to all those meetings when you were an unmarried lady of quality. Now that you are a married woman, you can involve yourself in these things freely."

Adrian took a seat in front of the tea tray, which had just been wheeled in by Millie. "You know, Michaela, you might wish to speak to a friend of mine, Sarah Trent. She might be interested in helping in a school for the village girls."

"Her name is Sarah Morten," Michaela corrected casually.

She smiled, pleased by the look of astonishment on her husband's face. "We met. She works in her husband's shop. She sold me the cherubs sitting on the library mantel. They were from Shepston Manor." Her eyes danced with the joke of it. "She seemed pleased that they would find their way into your home and thought you might as well. I think her husband shared the jest and sold them to me rather cheaply for the sake of seeing it just so."

He blinked and looked at the cherubs. "They add a superior touch to that corner of the room," he pronounced and grinned like a devil.

Delinda flounced down, interrupting. "I hope there is a country cotillion or something while we are here. I fear I am to be bored to tears."

Adrian regarded her, amused. "A small reception is a good idea. I should have thought of it. I am terribly lax with social duties, but Michaela can see to it."

"I had the same idea," Michaela said with excitement. "This house could use some cheer, and it would be an effective way for me to meet the neighborhood."

They were soon debating the guest list. Michaela thought of a particular friend she would like to invite, and she pulled Lilah aside. "Have you seen my good friend, the Viscount of Wickam, of late?"

"I am afraid not," Lilah said. The sadness in her voice held the answer to all of Michaela's questions.

"What?" Adrian burst in crossly. "Wicker? Who would be seeing him?"

Michaela could have kicked him had he been close enough. "Lilah enjoys his company, I believe."

"That beanpole?" He opened his mouth to make another cutting remark but was cut off when Michaela stood and said, "If you are not going to pour out, will you kindly move?"

He stood, and she came to take his place in front of the bountifully laden tray, giving him a slight shove that took his bad leg off guard and sent him stumbling backwards a step.

Once she saw he was all right, Michaela smiled at him with satisfaction. He grinned back.

Within the next few days, the plans for the party proceeded quickly. Adrian sent messengers to the other important houses in the area, but he and Michaela agreed that *all* of their local friends should be invited, so dispatches were sent into the village.

Dorothy and Michaela clashed over the plans, the arrangement of the house, the projects that had to be completed before the night of the party—all of which was business as usual between the two. What was not usual was the tone. Instead of stalking off in anger, the two frequently found themselves laughing over the silliness of their arguments. And sometimes Dorothy relented. Given this, Michaela found it wasn't so difficult to let her mother have her way occasionally.

Adrian skulked around the house, unused to the company of so many women, looking like a tiger prowling the perimeter of a herd. Michaela felt like the smallest, weakest babe who had wandered a bit too far from the others, for she could sense that it was she who was squarely in his sights.

After everyone retired one night, she sat in her room, brushing out her hair, lingering, glancing at the connecting door and wishing the knob to turn, and for Adrian to come to her.

Her heart leapt as the door opened. She turned to smile, welcoming him again and pushing aside the feelings that still nipped at the fringes of her happiness. She refused to acknowledge them, telling herself that if she had all the rest of him and not his heart, it would be all right. It would have to be.

One morning, while her mother and sisters, still accustomed to city hours, slept late, Michaela came down to breakfast dressed for travel. The gray traveling gown sported a matching short-sleeved spencer trimmed in feathers. She wore it because it reminded her of her aunt, who always managed to make the whimsical touch look like the smartest thing.

She thought she wore them rather well herself. Adrian's reaction, the way his eyes followed her advance into the room, his fork poised halfway to his open mouth, affirmed her suspicion.

"Good morning."

"Good morning," he said. He seemed not to know what to do with the eggs on his fork. She smiled, waving him back into his seat when he laid down his fork and made to rise. He said, "You look well. Is that a new dress?"

"This old thing?" she said with a coquette's smile. Aunt May had always said that, even if the dress were newly delivered from Madam Bonvant.

They chatted while she nibbled on some toast and cracked into a soft-cooked egg. He called for coffee and lingered, sipping slowly.

"Are you planning to go out?" he inquired.

"Into the village. Just some light shopping for the party. Also, I was invited to tea by some of the ladies I met at services this past Sunday. They were intrigued when I told them of my work in London with the school for girls. It seems this district is a progressive one, with some high-minded people looking to do some good."

"Ah. I have some letters to post. I'll drive you. By the by, you never told me how you made the acquaintance of my friend, Sarah."

"In the village while you were away. She recognized my name, and we began to talk."

He pursed his lips. He took up his fork again. "About what?"

She smiled, seeing his artless probing for what it was. "Don't you mean whom?"

He raised his brows.

"We did discuss you, Adrian. She told me how you were associated. She said you and her late husband were good friends."

He pursed his lips and nodded. She didn't expect him to speak, not in light of his usual reticence, and when he did, it surprised her. "He was the best man I ever knew. Incredibly loyal and possessed of a keen intelligence. He died saving my hide."

"In Quatre Bras?"

"She told you that."

"She told me what she knew."

He nodded. He picked up his buttering knife and toyed with it, sliding it between his thumb and forefinger as he turned it end over end. "We were ordered to attack by the Prince of Orange. None of us trusted him. I would have refused the order, but the other brigades were sent in, and we couldn't abandon them. The French took advantage of our disorganization, and we were quickly overcome. I got separated from the others and found myself pinned in by three French soldiers. One gashed my leg to keep me from fleeing."

She would never have imagined it would be this difficult to hear him tell the memory. It was absurd to react like this, really, for here he was, safe, but a fluttering panic filled her breast. She placed her hand over it, as if to contain her heart.

His eyes lifted to hers. "I can't account for this particular arrogance, but I had somehow thought myself immune to the kind of fear I felt in those moments I thought I would surely be killed."

"Thank God you were afraid, as anyone would be. It helped you survive."

"I was saved, rather. I was all but vanquished when my men arrived. Trent led them in. I don't know how they found me in all of that carnage. I was weakened by the loss of blood, but I fought with the fury of a demon. When it was over, two of my men had been slain. Trent was one of them."

"Paul Trent did what he felt he had to, just as you would have, I am sure."

"I thought it was wrong the way it turned out. I had joined the army because I had been hurt by Frances. I was no hero, only a lovesick cad who couldn't face his family." He snorted, the sound heavy with self-deprecation. "I didn't have anything, nothing to lose and no one to care if I did. It didn't seem fair. Trent had a family: a wife and a child on the way. He should have been the one to make it out of Quatre Bras."

She thought she should stop asking questions before he grew irritated, but it seemed all right now, and she was so curious. "How did you manage, with your leg, when you fought at Waterloo?"

He made an offhand gesture, as if the feat were nothing. "Pure vinegar, I suppose. I rode most of the time, changed my own dressings, kept it quiet. The surgeon slipped me something that helped dull the pain, just to get me through. I was Wellington's man, and I would be by his side when he faced Napoleon. That was all I cared about. It kept me alive, kept me from thinking."

"You really are a hero." She spoke softly. "Call it vinegar or what you will, to me it is true courage. It is the real stuff of legends."

Rising, she went to him. Her throat burned with all the things she wanted to say, but nothing she could think of served. In the end, she supposed silence was best.

Her fingers lightly ruffled the rough silk of his hair. She hesitated, fearing rebuff, but her fingertips throbbed, and she plunged them into the thick mass. Stepping forward, she laid her head on his, closing her eyes.

The poor man didn't even know he was wonderful.

He turned, wrapping his arms about her waist, his head on her breast. She heard a ragged sigh. She held him just so, wishing his pain away, silently pouring her love into him, imagining it could wash all the rest away.

✤ Chapter 20

They were blessed with a cool wind and clear skies on the ride into the village. Adrian chose the open brougham, and they made good time. He pointed out spots of interest he had learned about the area since moving here, and Michaela was impressed with his knowledge.

When they reached the village, he pulled the conveyance onto a side alley.

"I'll come into the Morten's shop with you," he said.

"Oh, good. I want your opinion on some things I've selected for the house."

He gave her a dark look. "I mean to visit Sarah, not browse through the shelves. Soldiers do not *shop,* Michaela."

She laughed at his pretense of disgust, belied by the way he tucked her hand under his arm as they strode into the square.

It was busy, the place teeming with people, all of whom seemed to know Adrian. True to his word, he went off—or rather was dragged off—after peeking into the Morten's shop to greet Sarah.

"He doesn't look too put out," Sarah observed, standing by Michaela as Adrian strode jauntily, cane swinging, down the road with the men who simply had to have him come and give his opinion on Joe someone-or-other's new stud horse.

Michaela folded her arms. "He says soldiers don't shop."

The women giggled and turned inside, where they set to work planning for the party. A little while later, Michaela noticed the time. "I have to meet some of the ladies for luncheon. Why don't you come with me? We are discussing the school I told you about."

Sarah agreed, and the two women packed the items Michaela had selected into crates and tidied their appearance before leaving. As they came out of the shop, Michaela spied Adrian crossing the street toward her.

"I was just coming to fetch you," he called. He was smiling, the sun warming his hair to a halo of gold.

She stopped, her heart rising, straining against the confines of her ribs, wanting to fly.

She loved him so much.

How she longed to tell him. What would he say now, when so much had been broken down between them? Would it send him fleeing if she spoke of her feelings? Was it possible he would ever welcome her love?

And could he ever love her in return?

Halfway across the road, he turned at a loud clamor coming from farther up on the street. Michaela followed his line of sight, puzzled as to what had drawn his body into tight lines and made his face go cold.

She saw nothing amiss. A well-dressed toff was driving an open phaeton rather carelessly from far down the street. A woman and her brood clamored aboard their ancient carriage, the mother shouting for the children to hurry up.

A short distance away, a man and three children were crossing the street. The threesome carried crates filled with books. One or two of the books had fallen, and a small girl, no more than four, toddled along and picked up after them. An important job, and she did it with industrious joy.

"What is it?" Sarah asked, seeing Adrian's hesitation.

"I don't know."

All at once, Adrian sprang forward. His limp hindered him more than a little, but he was efficient with his cane. He shouted something Michaela couldn't make out, drawing the attention of the pedestrians.

Michaela hurried after him, Sarah behind her. Her heart hammered. Something was terribly wrong, that was easy to see, but she still didn't comprehend what.

He was putting himself directly in the path of the fast-moving conveyance.

"Adrian!" Michaela shouted.

Sarah came up beside her and clutched her arm. "It's Shepston! He's going to ride him down."

No. That wasn't the danger. Michaela saw it all then, saw what her husband had seen. Yes, Shepston was enraged, driving like a madman toward Adrian, but that was not what had Adrian frantic.

Shepston was so eager to confront his nemesis, he didn't notice the small straggling child with her armload of books. It was to this tiny person that Adrian dashed as fast as his lagging speed would take him.

Now, as the three persons converged on the same point in time and space, Michaela screamed, shutting her eyes tightly. Sarah moaned and buried her face in her hands.

Too frightened and not knowing what had happened, Michaela opened them immediately.

Adrian stood before the carriage. The child, unharmed, scampered to her father, who, having been alerted, had flung his crate down and scooped the girl into his arms.

"Come on," Michaela said to Sarah, pulling her along with her as she raced to Adrian's side.

Having taken hold of the phaeton's ribbons just beyond the harness, Adrian was now holding the sleek vehicle captive. The driver was livid, tugging on his end, shouting for Adrian to let go.

Sarah pulled on Michaela's shoulder, holding her back as they drew close enough to hear.

"Blast you, you bloody cur. Haven't you made my life enough of a misery? Let go of my phaeton immediately."

Methodically, Adrian wound the leather strap around his

fist, shortening it with each turn of his wrist. Shepston stood on his box, waving his hands imperiously.

"Let go this instant, I say. Who the devil do you think you are? What . . . what are you doing?" He pulled counter to the inexorable drag of the reins. His face reddened with the effort, and he began to put his weight into resisting, even using two hands.

Adrian showed no such sign of strain. His face could have been carved in granite, his eyes the only animated things in his face. There was something nearly barbaric about him. Pure fury was subsumed into a quiet control that was more chilling than any outburst could possibly be.

Finally the man let go with a cry, and his hands flew up, as if he expected to be lashed with the lines that were now fully in Adrian's possession.

Michaela held her breath as she waited for what Adrian would do next. When he spoke, his words were choked, spoken in a low growl that reminded her of a mighty bear giving warning.

"When you are in crowded streets, have a care where you drive, and how." He tossed the reins. The man yelped and flailed for them, seemingly desperate to have them and be away from this madman.

Adrian pointed an accusing finger. "You almost hurt a little girl. If I hadn't intervened, she might have been injured because of your haste."

"She should get out of the street!" The driver looked down to find the ribbons, located them, and gathered them quickly. Adrian, while the man was thus engaged, leapt upon the phaeton. Michaela saw only that his great fist twisted in the man's cravat and jerked him once, hard enough to rattle what little brains the sapskull possessed. She turned away, suddenly frightened. And thrilled, she was chagrined to note.

Hurrying to the man who was cradling the little girl in his arms, she asked anxiously if she was all right.

"Yes," the man answered, close to tears. "Thank God he saw what was happening. I was worried about the books, not thinking about Sally." His voice broke, and he blanched, obviously reflecting on the possibilities.

"It's all fine, now." Her own voice wavered. "Major Khoury saw what was happening. Thank goodness."

She turned back to Shepston and Adrian, still engaged. Fisticuffs hadn't yet broken out, she was relieved to see.

The older man was beet red in the face. Spittle flew as he ranted. "I will ruin your political career. I have important friends, Khoury. They know about you. You were nearly thrown out of the army more than once. I will expose you for the liberal you are, taking all the privilege from the moneyed class. How do you think that will go, eh? You have to own land to vote, and no one with a stake in the economy is going to want a bleeding heart upsetting the way of things. Wait until they hear what you have done to me."

"That little tirade," Adrian said quietly, cutting off the man's random threats, "does nothing to endear me to you. You do not wish to anger me, Shepston. I can do you damage. I've done so in the past, and I will not hesitate now." He disentangled his hands from the man's collar and began straightening his clothing as Shepston stammered in horror.

Shepston shifted his tactics, his imperious voice breaking. He began to whine. "You reduced me to a beggar, you bastard!"

"There are sufficient monies from the fair and just proceed rate your tenants pay you."

"It is not enough!"

"Then perhaps you should think of doing something honest to gain the monies you need. The dissolution of your mansion in Belgravia, perhaps. Or the hunting lodge in Northampton." As an afterthought, he added, "That phaeton would fetch a fine price."

"That London house has been in my mother's family for . . ." Shepston's face fell. "My phaeton!" Whirling, he scrambled into the stylish carriage.

Adrian was enjoying himself, Michaela saw. He called, "I can give you more advice, if you wish. You should have a care not to get further into debt. Creditors can be cruel when they are not paid on time. You would hate prison."

Shepston's color went from vermilion to ivory in the space of a breath. But he kept his peace.

Adrian came to where Michaela stood with the man and his children. She reached for him, and he folded her hand in his.

He bore the child's father's profuse praise stoically. With a smile to Sally paired with a ruffle of her hair, he turned to Michaela. "We need to go home."

"If you gush, I swear I will leave you standing here by your-self," he said, handling the reins expertly to maneuver them through the streets.

"But you saw it all before it even happened," she gushed unabashedly.

"It comes from practice. Let us not talk about it."

"I must know, and your modesty be damned, Adrian. How is it you can order that horrid man about like that?"

He smiled. "That was rather enjoyable." He laughed, glancing over at her. He looked like a boy well-pleased with a prank.

"Explain," she ordered.

"Overcoming Shepston's hold on these parts was a partic-ular challenge. As an earl, the lands he holds are entailed and not transferable, so it is virtually impossible to evict him from the neighborhood. Besides, if what he did was immoral, even inhuman, it was not illegal."

"Yes, yes, but how did you make him afraid of you? You fairly had him in a faint."

"It is remarkably easy. One simply buys up gambling markers, promissory notes and mortgages, personal notes and loans, and any other outstanding debts. And then one simply applies a bit of pressure."

"That is blackmail."

"It is strategic use of influence," he corrected blandly. He sat back, drawing his knee up and resting the hand holding the reins upon it, smug as a fat cat.

"Adrian! It is ingenious. It had to have cost you a for-tune."

He shrugged, as if that were a minor point.

She gave him an appraising look. "Just how rich are you?"

"We," he said, squinting up ahead, "are quite well off."

"Well then. I am going to have to increase the orders for the party." She paused, giving him an evil look. "What am I saying—party? We shall make it a ball."

He groaned, if only to give her satisfaction.

Michaela moved restlessly about her room as she dressed for dinner. Her body jangled with jittering nerves plucked at every sound, every time her thoughts strayed to her plans, every time she looked at the bed. . . .

Tonight had to be perfect. She dressed carefully, her trembling fingers making her clumsy and slow. Her maid helped her into one of her favorite gowns, a creamy confection of lace and silk done up with gold cording. Then she twined Michaela's hair perfectly in an intricate piling of curls and the same cording woven in the thick tresses. A generous amount of cascading curls were left to fall over one shoulder.

She wanted to look like a gypsy tonight. Slightly wild. Slightly wanton. Adrian liked her this way.

The huge party she had planned with her mother and sisters would begin in a few hours, and she had last-minute preparations to see to before she would be ready to receive guests. It was her very first soiree, and she had worked very hard indeed to make it spectacular. Why was she so nervous? It was understandable, she supposed, as hostess. But it wasn't the arrangements racking her nerves. It was Adrian. She wanted to look her best, make the party a success—for him. Despite her initial resistance, coming to Shepston-on-Stour had turned out to be just what they needed. She loved him very much, and wished to please him, make him proud.

She had done a disgraceful job of it just after they were married. Perhaps he'd been distant, and it had been a bitter pill, but her actions only drove him farther away. It was he who had seen they needed to put their differences aside. He was so much less aloof now, here in the country. Was it really the cure?

A knock at her door made her start. Her mother stood in the hall. "I hope I am not disturbing you," she said. "I am full of energy. I am always like this before a party, but now that it is *your* party, I am inconsolable. I thought you might need help. . . ."

She came up behind her daughter, looking over her shoulder at their reflection. Touching a lock of hair, she arranged it carefully. "You look so lovely, so much like him. It comes out more and more as you grow happier and more confident."

Michaela stopped, looking steadily at her mother. "You have never spoken of my father. It surprises me that you would. I thought you hated that memory."

"Oh, I used to try to shut it out, not think of it, but how can one forget the only time in their life that they've been happy?"

That shocked Michaela. "My father made you happy?"

"Yes, of course he did. It was his gift to make a woman feel . . . well, something every woman should feel at least once in her life. Oh, Michaela, I never imagined I would have an affair. But then, I never counted on Woolrich. I fell in love with him, of course." Tucking in her chin, she studied the seam of her glove. "Then I learned I was with child and it had to end. I married Howard Standish, and you were accepted as his legitimate child. I was fortunate, and so were you, for such a good man."

"But it was not the same." She could see traces of the hurt still on her mother's face.

Dorothy shrugged. "There is no substitute for love."

Michaela flinched, lowering her eyes so that her mother wouldn't see her expression.

"Still, he gave us a good life," Dorothy went on, "and I was the best wife to him that I knew how to be."

"He didn't mind me . . . not being his?"

"You were a joy to him. More so than the twins. I suppose I used to try to even things by showing them a favor or two. That was unfair."

"I thought you didn't like me," Michaela said bluntly. "You were so impatient with me all the time."

Dorothy arched a brow teasingly. "Well, you had the Ellinsworth temper."

Michaela laughed. "Aunt May says Woolrich had no temper. I must have inherited it from you."

Dorothy shook her head, her lips twitching. "You were always impertinent."

Her mother gave her an awkward hug, and they chatted idly for a moment or two about the last-minute preparations. Another knock preceded her bedroom door being flung open to reveal Aunt May, resplendent in her feathery traveling costume.

"My darling, I am here!" She clasped a stunned Michaela to her bosom and waved her fingers at Dorothy with a wink.

Holding Michaela at arm's length, she examined her critically. "More color on the cheeks, I'd say. And a touch of lip rouge. I'll see to it after I am dressed."

"I think not," Dorothy interjected. "Too much paint will make her look tawdry. She is a natural beauty. She needs no enhancements from cosmetics."

"Ladies," Michaela said calmly and with a touch of amusement. "I do not wish to offend you, but tonight I shall not dress to please either one of you." Turning to the mirror one last time, she touched her hair, bit her lips, and gave herself an anxious check from head to toe. "I think my husband will be well satisfied. Shall we go downstairs now and check on all the preparations? Aunt May, please hurry your toilette. You have more experience than either Mother or I and will be a great help in the eleventh hour."

She led the way. Behind her, the two older women exchanged glances and satisfied smiles.

Adrian had made up his mind. He was going to have to seduce his wife. Not carnally. The bout of celibacy he'd endured was at an end. But the nightly sojourns through the door were only a tease for what burned inside of him. Nothing about making love to Michaela could be construed as unsatisfying, but there was more that he wished. He just couldn't name it.

Her guard was still in place, a wariness in her eye when she looked at him. She had told him once of her feeling for him. He was ashamed to recall how he'd responded.

He wanted her, yes, he craved her body, her touch. But it was because of all else he craved: her mind, her thoughts, her laugh, her opinions, her stubbornness, her fire.

And so he would seduce a woman as he'd never done so before. It wasn't just about the pleasure any longer. There was so much more. It was . . . God. Oh, God in heaven . . .

It was about love.

He sat down with a plop, the strength stunned out of him.

Chapter 21

The house looked completely different lit with scores of candles. In lieu of the draperies that had yet to be sewn, yards of expensive fabrics were hung. Pots with ferns and palms billowing out of them framed the rooms, and some of Morten's best antiquities were scattered on plaster pedestals painted hastily to blend with the unfinished marble floors. The gaps in the refurbishing were camouflaged by carpeting and a compilation of the best furniture from all over the house.

The extra staff teemed in smartly tailored livery unearthed in the attics and laundered for the occasion. To any casual eye, it was an impressive soiree, made more so for anyone who had an inkling of the transformation the master and mistress of the place had managed in such a short time.

Dorothy looked about, pleased. She exchanged a glance with Lady May, who nodded, understanding perfectly.

Woolrich would be so proud.

Once the guests had arrived and been greeted in the receiving line, Michaela and Adrian made their entrance into the ballroom amid a round of applause. Beaming, Michaela looked about at the people she loved. New friends and her family.

And Adrian.

He propped his cane against the wall and led her onto the dance floor.

"You do not need to, you know," she murmured. But she was flushed, pleased. Her dashing husband and she were hosting their first affair in their own home, and they were going to open the dancing as was their place.

He raised a brow. "Is the memory of our last dance so dreadful that you do not wish it repeated?"

She smiled at him, unaware that she was radiant tonight, as if all of her happiness shone out of her.

He guided her about in a sedate but respectable dance, then signaled for others to join them. As he led her off the floor, he was waylaid by some of the country gentlemen. They slapped Adrian on the back and all spoke at once.

"I heard about what you did to Shepston."

"My God, my hat's off to you, sir."

"Come, Major, give us the details!"

Disengaging herself, she allowed him his moment. He didn't seem pleased, but she had spied Lilah in the corner and wanted to speak with her.

Ever since she had arrived, Lilah had been depressed. She was usually quiet, but not so much as of late. Michaela knew very well why: Wickam.

Perhaps if the viscount was not interested, Lilah might find someone tonight to distract her. She certainly looked pretty in the soft blue gown that showed her plump figure off to great advantage. But she was moping, and no man was going to want to approach her if she continued looking like a wet towel.

With one last, longing glance over her shoulder to Adrian, she made her way to Lilah's side.

"You have got to try to have a good time, Lilah!"

"I am," she said weakly.

"You look like a lost sheep."

"I am no good at these kinds of things. Not like you. You

and the major looked so wonderful out there. I am so glad you found love, Michaela."

Bowing her head, Michaela tried to force aside the sour pang. This night was going so well, she didn't wish to dwell on the imperfections in her life. If she never had her husband's love, she would grow to know contentment with what she did have. They had mutual respect, did they not?

And companionship, yes, indeed. There was no one else whose company she enjoyed more, and Adrian made no bones about his desire to spend time with her. In fact, he had a tendency to sulk in the most adorable fashion when he felt neglected. She had camaraderie and the ability to have fun.

That was a tremendous amount with which to build a life. She was being silly to worry about a fickle emotion.

But even as she steeled her mind to this philosophy, her heart protested, twisting painfully. Some part of her argued that without knowing she was loved, she would never be whole. And Adrian would never be completely hers.

"Well," Michaela said lightly, determined to show nothing of her thoughts, "you will find the right person eventually. He could even be here tonight. One never knows."

She shook her head. "I don't think so, Michaela. You are kind to . . ."

Her voice fell off, and she seemed in shock, as if she'd been struck speechless. Her eyes were focused beyond Michaela's right shoulder. Michaela turned to find a man there, a man of great height, with blond hair and a familiar face.

"Wickam!"

He bowed, then clasped her hands. "My dear Mrs. Khoury. I am so pleased you've asked me to your home."

"Oh," Michaela said, covering her puzzlement. She hadn't invited Wickam, although she'd wanted to. But the situation with Lilah made it awkward. Adrian's jealousy made it impossible.

Wickam's sharp gaze narrowed on her. "You look surprised to see me. Your invitation said no response was required."

She had been gravely disappointed not to have Lord

Wickam on their guest list, but Adrian had been disgruntled with the proposal of inviting him, and she hadn't pressed. Her mother had given her the list of her friends, and Aunt May had sent a few names to add. No one else had had a say.

At her delay, Wickam laughed. "I know it was not a fraud, for it had the major's own seal upon it."

"Of course it did," she said, covering quickly. "I had forgotten I asked the major to personally send it to you. I am so delighted to see you." This last statement, at least, was genuine. She extended her hand, and he bowed over it. When he straightened, she slid her eyes to her sister. "I believe you are acquainted with Miss Lilah Standish."

His gaze transferred to Lilah, and there was a gleam of hope in his eye.

Michaela paused, thinking it might be a good time to make herself scarce. And, it would seem, find out if her suspicions about Wickam's invitation were correct.

"I must go see to things, but before I do, I wish you to know, my lord, that it was my other sister, Lilah's twin, who refused your flowers, not Lilah herself." She smiled blandly at Wickam's pleased surprise and Lilah's stricken look. "All right then, I'm off," she said, and excused herself to go and search for the sole owner and authorized user of the major's official seal.

Michaela's departure was met with silence.

Lilah tried to look everywhere else but at Wickam. Michaela had been so bold. Now she wanted to crawl away and hide from all that had been revealed.

But her eyes wouldn't obey. She was starved for the sight of him.

He looked at her with a strange smile on his face, appearing amazed. "You didn't toss the flowers?"

"My sister. Delinda. I suppose she was jealous."

"Why didn't you say? You put me off. I thought you didn't like me."

"I thought you were just toying with me."

"Couldn't you see how I felt? I thought I was rather clear.

I don't have time for dalliance, woman; my father is like a hound at my heels to marry. Then I finally find an incredibly lively girl, and I think to myself that if I don't move fast, some other is going to beat me out. Didn't you see that? Don't you care for me?"

She opened her mouth, closed it, anguished as she tried to find some way to say something of the burning wanting in her own heart.

Wickam cleared his throat. "Come here, where we can be a bit more private, and allow me to ask you a question." He took her to an alcove where they were sheltered from curious eyes. "Now, Miss Standish, if I were to find another spectacular bouquet of flowers and I happened to send it to your address, would you find them pleasing, do you think?"

Grateful, she sighed. "I daresay I would."

"And if this night, I asked you to dance . . . would you say yes?"

She smiled. "Yes."

He grinned, taking a step closer. "And if it were a waltz? Would you still dance with me?"

"Yes, still."

"And if I asked you a second time, even though it would raise eyebrows and cause tongues to wag, would you accept?"

"I would accept."

He moved closer. She could feel his breath on her skin as he hovered, making up for the difference in their heights by leaning in closer. "And if I asked you for a third dance and caused a scandal, would you risk it, even though everyone would say you had better marry me to save your reputation?"

"I think I would," she said softly.

"Then that is good news, indeed." He smiled. Cocking his arm at her, he pronounced, "Then we had best get started."

Michaela got diverted seven separate times before she suc- ceeded in finding Adrian. First, some neighborhood matrons wanted to give her a look-over, pulling her aside with fatuous compliments while their eyes darted over her appearance.

She was gracious and without much of an effort, charmed them. Then Aunt May noticed a problem with one of the draped fabrics sagging. Michaela fetched a few servants, and the makeshift decoration was righted. Her mother wished her to spend some time with a few of the friends she had sent for from London, and then Delinda cornered her, anxious to show off a new beau.

The round-faced young man, at the age of perhaps nine-and-twenty, was already rotund with a forehead that stretched to the middle of the top of his head, but he wasn't unattractive. He had a kind smile and nice teeth. He was obviously smitten with Delinda, who flirted outrageously back at him. Once she had bragged on the man's fortunes and pedigree, Delinda moved on, and Michaela was free.

She was truly happy for Delinda if she had at last found a match for life. Perhaps a satisfying marriage would soften the girl's hard edges.

Once she located Adrian with a group of men loudly debating the effectiveness of the House of Lords, she didn't waste any more time. Swiftly, she approached, linking her arm in his.

"Excuse me, gentlemen. May I borrow our host for a moment?"

Adrian was astonished as she led him to a private corner. Aunt May had insisted on the potted palms being arranged to provide discreet alcoves for private conversation. Mother had disapproved, but Michaela, with some preternatural foresight, had decided in favor of her aunt's wishes.

"All right, Adrian," she said as she pulled him into one of the alcoves, then spun to face him, "you are a fraud, and I want you to admit it this instant."

He gave her an arch look. "Madam, I have always considered myself the worst fraud there was. Have you only now guessed it?"

"Why then do you insist on pretending to be one thing when you are so much more?"

"Perhaps you should explain yourself," he said, folding his arms over his chest, his smile telling her he was intrigued.

"You invited Wickam here."

The smile was gone in a flash. "So?"

"You did that for Lilah."

He scowled. "She was rubbing my nerves raw with all of her moping."

"You didn't like to see her unhappy." She wagged a finger at him. "You were moved to intervene because you cared she was suffering."

He made a grousing sound and shrugged. "It seemed expedient," was all he would say.

"I cannot believe you are going to pretend that you only did this out of self-interest. My sisters and mother are leaving tomorrow, so why put yourself out when the situation would have resolved itself soon enough, especially when I know you dislike the viscount so?"

"Well, can you blame me? The man is a fool. And, as I have learned through personal experience, sometimes a fool needs to get a kick in the posterior to get him going before he watches the best part of his life pass him by. So don't look at me like I am some kind of hero. It was all very logical, not to mention self-serving. If he is enamored of Lilah, then by his marriage to her, he is eliminated as a threat for your affections."

"He isn't a threat, and you always knew that." She gazed softly at him, wishing she could read his mind. "Neither Wickam nor anyone else could take my affection from you."

The silence lay thick between them until he said in a voice quavering with emotion, "I thought perhaps you'd changed your mind. I'd hurt you so much. I wouldn't have blamed you."

"Perhaps if I could have stopped loving you, I would have. It was not very pleasant at times."

He took a step to her. She heard his cane thump on the carpet by their feet, and his hands closed warm and strong around her shoulders.

In the play of shadow and light, she could see the strain on his face. "This is not the time or place."

"No, it never is," she challenged. "We are quite private here."

He ground his jaw, apparently making a difficult decision. "Very well. What do you wish of me?"

"I want to know what you think, Adrian." She held up a finger. "No. More precisely, I would like to know what you feel."

He took a moment, then said, "Do you know what it cost me to have you by me, wanting you until I couldn't think of a single other thing, and yet not being able to reach for you?"

"I was within reach every night."

"Not just at night. In the afternoon, the evening, that bright crisp time when you wake and the day is brand-new. All of every day, that's when I need you."

She was overcome. This was more than she had expected.

He made to close the gap between them, then checked himself, turning to look at their guests. He seemed to have forgotten for a moment that their house was filled with people. "Listen," he said, keeping his voice soft, "there is much that needs to be said between us. You accused me of things, back in London. That night when you said I thought of you only as a mistress—"

She hurried to cover his words, not wanting to even think about that particular memory. "I'm sorry for that, really, Adrian. I was wrong."

"No, love. You were right. I thought to keep our marriage uncomplicated, on the level of something with which I could be comfortable and would not threaten my carefully planned life. I am not a man used to sharing emotions. I've spent my entire life closing things of that nature up inside me, and then you asked me to open it all up. I didn't know how to do that."

"I was unfair. I shouldn't have pushed. And I was so angry, I did unkind things to you, but I was only trying to get you to pay attention to me."

His chuckle was like a wave of warmth in the darkness. "Will you shut up, my love?"

She didn't know what shocked her to silence: his rude command or the endearment. He called her his love.

He let out a long breath, taking another exasperated look

at the milling people outside of their nook. "We could be overheard."

"No one is listening. The music provides ample cover, and our voices shall not carry. Besides, you never minded pulling me off into a dark place in order to get me alone before. As I recall, you were particularly fond of that maneuver. I am starting to believe you harbor nefarious intentions toward me, and the presence of a crowd brings them to a pitch."

He countered with a droll tone, "You are only now understanding the nefarious nature of my intentions? I thought your mind quicker than that." He fought his smile. "Although I seem to recall you finding the quieter moments we shared at public gatherings well worth your while."

She cast an uncertain look over her shoulder. "Perhaps you are correct about the timing of this. It *is* rude for us to disappear when I am the hostess and you the host."

"I shall keep you only for a moment longer. The thing is begun here and now, and I will see it finished. Now, wife, I am giving you an order to stay put to hear the one thing I need most to tell you. Are you going to obey or not?"

She considered insisting on the proper thing, but then, she didn't care half as much about the crowd waiting for her as hearing what Adrian wished to tell her. "Haven't I always?"

His look was incredulous. "Actually, no."

"What is it you wish so badly to say?"

"Just one thing, and it is simply said. I merely wish you to know that I am quite hopelessly in love with you."

Michaela swayed, not sure of her legs. She stammered, "You are?"

"When I look back, it was from the first, I think. Not to say I liked it very much. I am afraid you were the instigator of emotions I didn't wish to feel. But I have come to the sensible conclusion that there is no use in fighting it anymore. No soldier worth a damn would fight that fight—it is a sure defeat. Yes, I am mad for you, Michaela, completely besotted, utterly lost."

She was breathless, staring at him in wonder. All she could think of to say was, "Are you certain?"

He laughed, brushing his knuckles tenderly along her temple. "Quite. Although I don't wonder at your incredulity. I botched things terribly." He stepped closer, his voice dropping to a murmur. "But how could I run from you, when you draw me back time and time again?"

"Oh, Adrian," she murmured, and reached for him. Catching herself, she dropped her arms. He, too, recalled the teeming guests just on the other side of the palms, but he risked touching her face, gently rubbing the pad of his thumb along the line of her jaw.

"You made me see how cheaply I had sold my feelings for pride. Ah, but you have changed me. So much so that I don't recognize myself any longer. You have to be of gypsy blood, there is simply no other explanation."

She angled a look up at him. "You do not seem terribly displeased."

"How can a man be displeased when his life is so absurdly perfect?" He grinned, and her heart caught. "And you?"

"Do you need to ask?"

"I would hear your feelings." He was guarded, as if he feared a less-than-satisfactory response.

"Oh, how can you doubt it? You know you have had my heart all along."

"So that is how you bewitched me? With a faithful heart?"

"It is all I have."

"What a strong heart it is, to break through this stubborn soul." His hands, warm and pleasantly rough, cupped her face. "God, Michaela, I have to wonder how I've come to such fortune. I have fallen madly in love with a woman who loves me. She has lunatic ideas about educating the poor, and I take joy in destroying petty tyrants. We are two creatures no other could possibly understand or tolerate. We belong together. I can't imagine the future without you. I want to have children with you, grow old, see you fifty years from now in this very house with our dynasty around us."

She tilted her face up to his and murmured, "So kiss me before I expire with wanting."

"I shall not," he said, setting her away from him, "for if I do, I swear I shall not be able to stop, and after all, the palm fronds only provide so much cover. Later, love, when we close the door to our bedroom, I will kiss you senseless. And more."

She was pouting, but this last part perked her up. She gave him a kittenish smile and leaned in closer. "Do you promise?"

"Be a good wife and don't tempt me. I will only surrender too easily, and how would that look for the legend of Major Khoury? Come, if you have a care for not shocking the entire neighborhood, let us behave ourselves and get back to our guests."

She laughed gaily, taking his arm for him to lead her out. "Yes, sir, Major."

Chapter 22

The night was a spectacular success.

Adrian awoke with a start, aware of this singular, crystal-clear thought.

Not the party, although that had been a rousing time for all, lasting until the early hours. Agony for him—so much so he almost wished people were having less of a good time and would leave or retire. But how could he be so selfish when Michaela was beaming with her success, as gorgeous as a fabled princess from a fairy tale presiding over her minions? She had danced and laughed, looking happier than he had ever seen her.

He had wondered that it was he who had a part in making her so joyous. Then later, as dawn sketched pink lines in the sky, she'd settled the matter quite convincingly.

He glanced down to take in the vision of his nude wife curled into his side, sleeping peacefully. His heart did some queer machinations in his chest. He sighed, lying back again and smiling.

Why had he fought this? Because of Frances? How profoundly stupid, for she was nothing but a shallow beauty. Or maybe it was sheer pride. He had a lion's share of it, he knew. What a fool's battle he had waged.

Upon noting the time, he gently roused Michaela. "Wake up, my love."

He nestled his body against hers with languorous pleasure. He nuzzled her neck. "Come, it is well past noon. The guests will be up already."

With a gasp, Michaela sat bolt upright. "My God!"

He grinned and reached for her. She slapped his hand away. "You wretched man. You did this—keeping me up to an ungodly hour."

"You didn't complain last night. Or this morning. It is twelve past the noon hour, not so late. Relax. Most of the guests probably slept in as well. It was a wonderful party."

She grinned. "Oh, it was. I swear, I would not be surprised to hear that Wickam has already spoken to Mother for Lilah's hand. The two of them didn't seem like they wished to waste any more time. And Aunt May pronounced it a lovely affair. High praise from her. But—oh, we cannot linger. Goodness, we must get downstairs and see to the guests."

She tried to leap out of the bed. His quick hands prevented this.

"We could stay a little while, perhaps. The servants are competent. No doubt they have things well in hand."

"But everyone will surely guess why we are so late to come down. You had the look of a tiger eyeing a rabbit last night; anyone would know what you were thinking. And you danced with me five times! Now you wish to make us later than we already are. Absolutely not. It is too unseemly."

"We'll say we were up earlier and they were asleep, and so we broke the fast in our chamber. It will serve as an excuse, plausible enough to salve your modesty."

She slapped away his wandering hand and peered down at him. "Your ingeniousness frightens me. You hardly broke a sweat coming up with that."

"I'm a tactician. It's a gift. Now come here." He cupped a breast, tracing the gentle swell.

Pushing his hand away, she exclaimed, "No!"

"Why not?"

"Look at all of this light!"

He sat up and gathered a fistful of her hair gently, holding her to be kissed. "Better to see you with, my dear."

His other hand snatched the wrist upon which she rested her weight, and she fell onto his chest. His hands slipped to the place where she needed his touch. Her head fell limp on his shoulder. "Here," he instructed, riding her thigh on the outside of his hip. "Like this."

He showed her how to straddle him. She shifted eagerly, and he slipped inside.

"Now, sit back. Let me watch you."

She had no shame, no self-consciousness, as she did what he bade. She sheathed him with her body and easily learned the rhythm. Tilting her hips, she moved to make each stroke build them both toward release. When it came, it was sweet, exploding over them both in shimmering waves of delight.

What did the world matter? she thought dreamily as she lay down to catch her breath. But she was content for only a short time until conscience prodded them both to action. They rose and dressed, descending the steps together. Behind them, the connecting door between their suites stood open. They did not close it again.

𝕯 *Epilogue*

"Darling?"

"Mmmm."

"She's awake. Can you fetch her?"

"Mmm."

The bed creaked.

The squalling babe gurgled with sweet expectation as she was borne in her father's strong arms to her mother, there to nestle against the full breast awaiting her.

"There, sweetling, does that suit you? Hush now."

There was a pause.

"Thank you for fetching her. I am still so weary. I wouldn't have disturbed you but for this wretched fatigue."

"You just gave birth. Rest, and I'll take her when she's done feeding. It's too beautiful in here to sleep, anyway."

She smiled. "Go on now, or I will feel guilty at waking you."

"But I like to watch you like this, with her at your breast. It's the most incredible thing I've seen. I might take up painting just to paint your portrait with our little Gabrielle in your arms."

"You fuss so."

"And it would tell the story, too, and maybe hang in our Mr. Rye's gallery. People would stare at it and imagine the entire, fantastic tale of a feisty warrior angel in female form who found a wounded soldier and slaughtered his demons, one by one, thereby bringing him the greatest of happiness."

"You are sentimental tonight."

"It is not every day a man meets his daughter." There was a slow intake of breath, then an exhale. "I had the dream again, the one about Quatre Bras. Only it was different, as it's been of late. It used to be a nightmare, but it doesn't frighten me any longer, and I realized something tonight, just as you awakened me. I think the altered dream has come to let me know something."

"What is that?"

"I'm glad I lived."

Read an excerpt from

The Heiress of Hyde Park,

the next book in The Mayfair Brides series.

In her boudoir, Lady May Hayworth stretched like a cat. Pushing away from the small escritoire she used for her research, she put the papers she'd been reading aside and rose to give full stretch to her knotting muscles.

Looking at the tall, rangy man stretched out on the divan, she smiled. Robert's eyes were closed, his naked chest rising and falling with the deep breathing of sleep. He still wore his reading glasses, an anathema perched on the end of that chiseled nose. His features, in repose, were less severe than normal. The sharp angles of his cheekbones wore a slight flush, his sensuous mouth slack and without tension. She fought the urge to kiss him, self-indulgence quickly tamed by a rush of tenderness. She hated to wake him.

He was such a gorgeous man. His coloring was swarthy. She teased him sometimes about having Spanish blood, whereupon he would utter caressing words in that language—how exactly did a stable owner speak fluent Spanish?—as he played the Latin romancer. Half the time it reduced her to giggles—and it was not easy for a woman of her age, which was five and forty this spring—and the other half of the time it reduced her to trembling clay.

They'd been lovers for nearly a year, but while the secret liaison had yielded a comfortable and intimate relationship, there was more unsaid between them than there were truths spoken.

Robert Carsons was the owner and operator of an upscale stable here in London, a man who worked with his hands. She was the daughter of an earl. Between them lay insurmountable differences, but they had less to do with the disparity in their current social position than they did with the secrets they hid.

Strolling quietly to him, she allowed herself one small indulgence. Threading her fingers into the graying hair at his temple, taking care not to touch his skin, she smoothed back the thick hair. Cocking her head to one side, she smiled again, and whispered, "Who are you, Robert Carsons?"

She was no fool. She had always known Robert's past was steeped in fine breeding and money. He was as noble as she. It wasn't just the languages he spoke, or the cultured accent he slipped into during their quiet evenings together that gave him away. It was in his bearing, his pride, his sometime arrogance. Mother had always lectured that good breeding showed. And so it did, even with weathered skin and callused hands. But why the charade of a common stable keeper, she had no idea.

It was something they had talked about only once. It had led to a frightening quarrel that May had feared might mean the end of their relationship. Lady May, who was not without a healthy dollop of pride herself, was forced to let the matter drop once they'd reconciled, for she had been deeply shaken by the idea of losing this man she had come to love.

After all, she had her secrets as well.

So they had called a truce between them—no questions, no pasts, only the present. And it was a lovely truce, filled with passionate nights and long, philosophical debates, and silly times that left her laughing until she gasped for breath.

She started when he cocked one eye open and grinned. "Are you going to stand about all day playing with my hair?"

"You were awake the whole time!" she exclaimed. She slapped him on the shoulder, but he caught her hand and pulled her down onto his lap. Locking his hands around her waist, he held her pleasantly imprisoned.

"Are you finished with the journal?" he asked.

"It will be years before I am. So many names. My brother was a profligate and a scoundrel unmatched. Therefore, this task of finding those children he left behind after all of his numerous affairs is a daunting one."

"Well, at least Michaela is happily settled."

She bristled. "You keep bringing up the subject. I have admitted, haven't I, that I was wrong about Adrian Khoury? The two are quite happily married and the man has proven to be an asset. Now I am on to the next project."

"Who is it, a son or daughter?"

"Another daughter. Wooly was quite fond of the mother, a Judith Nash. He writes prodigiously about her in the most glowing terms. He missed her when she severed their affair, one of the few times the woman was the first to leave. Imagine, Wooly pining so. He was even over the moon on the name the mother chose for their child. Trista Josephine."

"Mmm," Robert responded, winding a tendril of her hair around his finger.

"You aren't listening at all."

"Well, it is your fault. You are distracting me. But I am listening, I promise. The woman charmed Woolrich. That's a lark." He buried his nose in the curve of her shoulder. "Daughter named Trista. A romantic name for so practical a woman to give her child."

She settled into the warmth of his chest, his arms wrapped around her and sighed. "Why do you say she is practical?"

"Because she sent Woolrich away."

"He asked her to be his mistress, but she wouldn't accept."

"No. Some women aren't like that. They have sensual natures but overdeveloped consciences. A pity. I am most grateful that you are not thusly hindered."

"With a sensual nature?"

He chuckled. "Certainly not. I meant an overdeveloped conscience."

"That is why I am doing all of this fairy-godmother nonsense, going about finding these lost lambs and bestowing upon them their inheritance, making certain they are all right and well taken care of—things my lighthearted but tragically unconcerned brother should have done."

"And you are determined to find every last one," he said.

"Indeed, I shall, but this one is proving quite stubborn. Upon the death of the mother, Trista continued at the house where she grew up as a paid companion to the fourth Lord Aylesgarth's widow for a few years, but then she all but disappeared."

He laughed again. "You love the thrill of this little hunt, the joy in the giving. And family. You feel for these children."

"Family is everything," she murmured. "And these lost nieces and nephews are all the family I have left to me."

May fleetingly wondered about him, about his family. Did they know where he was? Did they care? Perhaps they thought him dead.

Did he think of them at times, miss them?

Forbidden though it was, the curiosity that burned inside her pressed against her throat. She swallowed it back, turning her face to his for his kiss.

At times like this, when dangerous thoughts came, it was best to lose herself in the one thing that could banish all thought, all care. She gave herself over to Robert's kiss, and forgot her quest for the lost Trista Nash, if only for a while.

*There was an excellent reason why Lady May Hayworth's in-*quiries on the whereabouts of Trista Nash had gone without result. The girl, now a woman of three and twenty, no longer used that name. She went by the name of Trista Fairhaven. It wasn't a legal name, but no one ever checked these things. Just like no one knew that her status of widowhood was an equally fabricated fiction.

On this afternoon in early spring, in a bustling workroom

at the rear of a posh milliners in London's West End, she rushed about the tables strewn with netting and feathers, shouting orders to Betty.

"Goodness, child," she exclaimed as the grinning girl finally brought the correct spool of ribbon from the row along the wall. "If you do not move more quickly, I shall have to wrap you in the stuff"—she feigned a severe look as she pulled out an arm's length of bright purple gros-grain and wielded it threateningly—"and tickle you for every moment you kept me waiting."

Betty stuck out her tongue. Trista pretended to be shocked at such outrageousness.

"Betty, are you finished with your lesson?" Mrs. Hines, the milliner shop proprietress said as she propelled her large girth into the room. "I'll not have you neglecting your education."

Betty, the youngest of Mrs. Hines's two daughters, gave a pout but it was only a token one. She was a happy child. No one took her kindly, bossy, overbearing mother too seriously. However, they didn't disobey her either.

"Na, ma'am."

"Then do so right this minute, thank you. We will await your return after you've written your letters. See to it."

"Are you certain she said a nest?" Trista said doubtfully, turning the brown thatch over with a grimace. They had gotten an order for a hat by one of the richest duchesses in the city, but unfortunately the woman had only one thing in mind—to draw attention to the money she spent on her clothing. As a result, the order was so outrageous, so ostentatious, it was difficult to execute it and build the monstrous headdress without flinching.

"Indeed, indeed," Mrs. Hines replied with a flourish of her expressive hands, "and none of your artistic touches on this one. Oh, your taste is too fine; I should have Luci do it. Luci!"

"I promise to be flamboyant," Trista replied, laughing. "And to be as tacky as I know how to be."

"Then use more tulle, dear," Mrs. Hines gushed, pulling

yards of the stuff off the bolt. "And what about these cherries?"

Trista groaned. "Maybe we should have Luci do this."

"Or Betty," Mrs. Hines said with a conspiratorial wink. "She used to love to make horrid contraptions with the scraps when she was a babe. Perhaps she still has the touch, eh?" She laughed. "Ah, I know it wrecks havoc with your sensibilities to have to ruin high quality materials, but this is the burden of an artistic eye. It will stand you in good stead when you and Luci purchase the shop for you to learn to balance your own aesthetic with what the customer requires. How glad I will be on that day. I can hardly wait to wallow in the waters of Bath, and I swear I shall spare not one whit of conscience for you buried in swaths of ribbons and feathers—"

"And bird's nests," Trista said, holding up the offending object. It was affixed with a hook on the bottom in order for it to be secured to the hat whereupon the duchess had specified a plumed bird was to sit, its brightly colored tailfeathers trailing down her back. Her Grace, upon placing her order, declared it would be "spectacularly breathtaking," a description to which they all privately agreed but with rather a different meaning.

Mrs. Hines hurried away, her skirts making a loud rustle. "What is the first order of doing custom, dear Trista?" she called back.

She looked down at the gaudy mélange she'd created and squared her shoulders. "The customer's wishes must come first. I do know it well. But I do not have to like it."

Trista hoped this criminal misworking of good materials would not spoil the excellent reputation of the shop, for soon it would belong to her. It was what she'd worked for, stingily saving every farthing for Andrew's future. Her son was and always had been from his birth nearly five years ago, her utmost priority, and seeing to his security was her most cherished dream.

He would need a tutor soon, for he was to go to University—Oxford of course, for he wouldn't hear of any other since his father had been an Oxford man. He would have everything he needed to be an ordinary student. There would be no hint of scandal or any oddity to stain his growing years.

The memory of his little serious face made her smile, and then she remembered the plumed bird and the nest and sighed. Whatever it took to ensure his future, she would do it, even desecrate a perfectly good hat.

"Please the customer," Mrs. Hines whispered in her ear as she passed back towards the front of the store, giving her a pat on her shoulder. The tinkle of the bell in the showroom sent her careening through the curtain that separated the workroom from the graciously appointed outer regions with the enthusiasm with which she always greeted customers.

Working in silence for a while, Trista considered she was making good progress. She was actually pleased that she had minimized the atrocity of the plumed bird and began to have hope of not completely making a muck of it. She was so intent on this that she was startled when her cousin, Luci, joined her.

"A couple of swells just came in," she said breathlessly. "With two ladies, and I use that term loosely since the person in question is showing her bosom in broad daylight. Oh, well, it's quite a bosom. Anyway, it seems one of the women lost her hat. It was blown off and crushed under a carriage wheel. Her companion is buying her a new hat to replace it, and Dina is in a tizzy."

Dina, Mrs. Hines's eldest daughter, presided over the showroom and tended to the customers with fawning dedication. "Dina is always in a tizzy," Trista said. "Now hold that securely while I tie the ribbon."

"No, she's in a tizzy because of the man. You simply have to see him. He's fabulous."

"Hand me that thread."

"Aren't you the least bit curious?" Luci squinted at the creation growing at an alarming rate on its stand. "Are you purposefully trying to make this hideous?"

"Is it that bad? I thought I might have saved it."

"You are good, but not that good, cousin. Come here,"

Luci said, picking up the hat while jerking her head to the mirror.

"Oh, no." Trista laughed.

"It is only fair," Luci urged, and positioning Trista in front of the mirror, ceremoniously placed the complicated head-gear on her head.

"Oh, dear."

"You look like a duchess!" Luci declared.

"Of Hades, perhaps, but of any place on the surface of this earth, I hardly think so."

"Well, it is an absurd piece. Imagine if we could dismiss that ruff."

Trista turned her head, seeing the possibilities. The base of it was, as all Mrs. Hines's hats were, made of good stock. It sat snugly on Trista's soft blond hair. It even looked attractive atop the curling cloud, hiding its untidiness. She never took time to do more with her hair when working than to twist it back into a very loose knot. The undisciplined mess always managed to work loose into gentle corkscrews around her face.

What a shame about the hat, however. It could be quite grand if not for the nest and bird. The dip of the brim was slightly jaunty, curling attractively over her large gray eyes. The shape of her nose, a bit pointy, a bit pert, and her prominent chin was complimented by the impudent angle.

A shrill voice startled a cry out of both women as the curtain was jerked open. Dina stuck her head into the workroom. "Trista, where are you? Luci—oh, there you are. What the . . . ? Trista, there is a bird on your head. Oh, bother, I have no time for your silliness, get me that hat you've just completed for the Countess Dufrenay. Quickly. This gentleman is here and says he will pay thrice the price we charged the countess for it to have for his . . . er, for the lady, and then we can make another up for the countess later. They are in a terrible hurry. He is being terribly gallant about replacing it for her."

Luci gave a mock salute and ran to fetch the hat. Neither Trista nor Luci thought to tell Dina to fetch it herself. She never stepped foot in the workroom. The showroom was her domain, and she presided over it like a despot.

Glancing over her shoulder, Dina said, "Do you see him? He is simply gorgeous. Imagine, coming in off the street and expecting us to produce a hat for his companion. Yet, I must say he did it in the most charming way. Mother melted. A man like that, one simply makes allowances, doesn't one? Oh, Lord! Where is Luci with that hat?"

Through the small doorway, Trista did indeed see a man. He was very tall, with dark brown hair worn rather roughishly long and tied in a queue. An unruly forelock spilled onto a high brow, an intelligent brow. He possessed a strong nose and a sensuous mouth, below which the clean line of his jaw could be seen.

Trista took a step forward. A slow curl of excitement crooked itself around her stomach.

He looked so familiar. He reminded her of . . .

His eyes fixed on her. She felt the painful rattle of her heart in her bosom. Time stopped, her mind stopped. She was all instinct now, as alert as a deer facing a bowman in a glade.

His eyes widened, his mouth opened. Then he did something strange. As dumbfounded as she, he stared, motionless for a moment, then slowly raised a single finger as if to beckon her.

Roman. My God. Roman.

And he'd seen her.

She mewled, stumbling backward as if not trusting herself to keep from rushing forward to the summons he had given.

"My goodness, what are you doing?" Dina snapped. "Where is that Luci? Trista, please take that ridiculous contraption from your head. If our customers see you, it will frighten them off."

Bless Dina—solid, practical. Her voice cut through her befuddled haze.

"What?" Looking about, Trista was somewhat surprised to see herself here in the shop's back room. Around her were snippets of ribbon and tufts of tulle blowing like dust motes against her hem.

Mrs. Hines's shop. She was still here. For a moment . . . for a moment, she'd been back at Whitethorn.

Whipping the hat off her head, she threw it on the table.

"Be careful with that." Dina peered at her. "Why are you being so clumsy? It is not like you. Trista? Where are you going?"

"I am ill," Trista said as she ran for the back door. She almost ran into Luci, who had just emerged from the closet where they kept the completed hats out of harm's way and as dust-free as possible before they were picked up.

"I found it!" Luci exclaimed, then grunted as she quickly sidestepped to avoid her cousin, who raced by her to grab her shawl and slam through the door leading to the alley.

"Give that to me. See to Trista, she is sick," Dina said, taking the stylish hat, one of Trista's finer creations. She blew the tiniest accumulation of dust from it as she walked back toward the front of the store, muttering, "Probably seeing herself in that drafted hat that did it, Lord knows."

"I say, Aylesgarth, what's got you?"

His friend slapped him on the shoulder.

Roman Aylesgarth, the seventh Lord Aylesgarth, absorbed the blow without so much as blinking. It was nothing compared to the one he'd just been given.

He still had the finger of his one hand raised in some absent, inane gesture, as if he were making a point. He was incredulous, frozen, numb.

He could have sworn he'd just seen Trista Nash standing inside the curtained room wearing . . . a bird on her head.

"You look like you've seen a ghost." Raymond chuckled, taking a swig. Roman frowned at him, forcing himself to stop looking at the curtain which had been abruptly drawn over the apparition. A ghost?

"What is it, Roman?" Raymond asked, concern in his voice.

I've just clapped eyes on the only woman I've ever loved.

He'd not say that. Raymond would have laughed. Anyone would have. How well it was known that the cold and debauched Lord Aylesgarth did not love. He played, he lusted, he toyed, he ran in circles that made a demon wince, he didn't give a damn. If he loved anything, his reputation would have it, it was his team of perfectly matched horses, his fine, swift phaeton, aged whiskey, cured tobacco after and a pair of accommodating thighs belonging to a pretty, docile lass who understood his loathing of attachment. He was a terror, and didn't give a whit about it. Terrors did not love.

But perhaps they had, once.

"I thought I saw someone I knew once."

How paltry those words, signifying nothing of import.

"A woman, eh?" Raymond said, his humor restored. He gave Roman's back another clamp and was rewarded with a glare that left him clearing his throat. "I'll just go see if Annabelle has chosen her hat."

Roman didn't hear him. He was moving toward the curtained doorway. For some reason he was angry. If it was indeed Trista Nash back there, how dare she hide from him. He didn't know what he planned to do, but he had to find out if she was here.

"Excuse me," the shopkeeper, the patroness's daughter, said, coming to block his path, "may I help you?"

This girl's color was high. He was used to women getting flustered in his presence. It was a nuisance most of the time, the kind of thing his cronies alternately admired and rode him about.

"I wanted . . ." To go back there and search for someone. He straightened, trying to clear his head. "I thought I saw someone I knew. I . . . Does a Trista Nash work in this shop?"

The woman opened her mouth to answer, but the swoosh of the curtain being flung back startled her out of it. Another woman, dressed in a simple cotton work dress stared up at him. She had the bird on her head. Up close, he saw it was some sort of god-awful headgear. He hoped they weren't going to try to pawn that off on Annabelle. It was hideous.

"No. A Trista *Nash* does not work here." She dipped into

a shallow curtsey. "I am Luci Miller, my lord. I am sorry to
have startled you."

He narrowed his gaze on her, thinking that perhaps his
eyes had deceived him. Her hair wasn't the same, this one
being a darker blond and no wild curl to it. Her eyes were
blue, not the gray he remembered so vividly. But the build
was approximately the same, and from a distance, it might be
possible to mistake her.

The shop attendant looked at Luci, then back at him. "I
am sorry, my lord. Is there something I can get you?"

"Ally," a female voice called. He closed his eyes against
the grating voice. It belonged to Raymond's plump wife,
Marian. She had taken to calling him Ally—a shortened form
of his surname and title, Aylesgarth. He found this extremely
grating. He hadn't been fond of her upon their first meeting;
he fairly detested her right at this moment. Grudgingly, he
turned to her.

"What do you think of this one?" Turning her head this
way and that, she struck a pose. Behind her, Ray laughed. He
didn't understand his affection for the woman. She talked far
too much, and too loudly. He supposed Ray did, as well, so
perhaps they were well matched.

They were recently married and in London on their wedding trip, and he and Marian's sister, Annabelle, had met and
found a mutual attraction, enough to sustain a passably pleasant series of evenings and afternoons, a respite from the
boredom Town life had become for him.

He went over to join them, wondering what in the world
had made him think Luci Miller was Trista Nash. Was it
merely the suggestion of her hair, the pale impression of her
form? Not that he didn't think of Trista. He did so. Often.
But he wasn't prone to chasing about thinking he had seen
her.

Perhaps, he thought slyly, he had. It was impossible, and
yet he couldn't shake the feeling of excitement buzzing in his
veins, the subtle feeling of expectancy that danced along his
nerve endings, rippling along his flesh like a gentle wave of
heat. His body, he realized, felt like it was ready to run, tense

and taut. To race after a fleeting image, a memory? Or a real person?

God, he *was* bored—that had to be it or else he wouldn't be indulging in some fanciful thoughts. The day was turning out to be less than amusing. Ray was pleasant enough, but Marian plucked at his nerves and Annabelle was . . . ordinary. Disappointing. Women inevitably were these days.

He paid for the hat, and went first to hold the door. As they filed through, he looked back at the curtain and saw the woman, Luci, watching him anxiously. And the knot in his stomach gave one last, great wrench, as if something were very wrong.

He always trusted the knots in his stomach.